LOST HIGHWAYS

DARK FICTIONS FROM THE ROAD

EDITED BY D. ALEXANDER WARD

Let the world know:
#IGotMyCLPBook!

Crystal Lake Publishing
www.CrystalLakePub.com

WELCOME TO ANOTHER CRYSTAL LAKE PUBLISHING CREATION.

Thank you for supporting independent publishing and small presses. You rock, and hopefully you'll quickly realize why we've become one of the world's leading publishers of Dark and Speculative Fiction. We have some of the world's best fans for a reason, and hopefully we'll be able to add you to that list really soon. Be sure to sign up for our newsletter (http://eepurl.com/xfuKP) to receive three eBooks for free, as well as info on new releases, special offers, and so much more. To follow us behind the scenes while supporting independent publishing and our authors, be sure to follow us on Patreon (https://www.patreon.com/CLP).

You can also subscribe to Crystal Lake Classics (http://eepurl.com/dn-1Q9) where you'll receive fortnightly info on all our books, starting all the way back at the beginning, with personal notes on every release.

Welcome to Crystal Lake Publishing—Tales from the Darkest Depths.

COPYRIGHT ACKNOWLEDGEMENTS

CONTENTS

**Proudly
brought to
you by
Crystal Lake
Publishing**

For my friends and family with whom I've spent many hours in carriages of steel and rolling wheels: thank you. For the road trips and the stories, the laughter and the scares. The stolen kisses and the stolen street signs. For late night drives . . . to cold mountains and warm summer waters and spooky old houses. For making it home to plot new courses and tell the tales again.

For you, dear reader. Climb on in and get comfortable. Roll down the window for the night air if you like. The roads are legion, and we have such strange sights to see . . .

D. Alexander Ward
May, 2018

"The car aimed ahead its lowered parking lights;
under the hood purred the steady engine.
I stood in the glare of the warm exhaust turning red;
around our group I could hear the wilderness listen."

—William E. Stafford, "Traveling Through the Dark"

INTRODUCTION

BRIAN KEENE

ABOUT TWO HOURS from my home, nestled deep in the heart of Pennsylvania's mostly decimated coal belt, lies the ghost town of Centralia. When I say ghost town, I mean exactly that—an abandoned town, much like the ones that still dot America's West, but this one is nestled in the valleys and mountains of a mid-Atlantic state.

Centralia was once a thriving community, and coal mining was its lifeblood. But decades ago, one of the veins that pump that lifeblood caught fire, resulting in one of the worst mining disasters in American history. That fire has raged beneath Centralia in all the years since and will still be burning long after all of us are gone, pumping deadly gases topside and caving in the earth with smoking sinkholes that swallow houses, businesses, and occasionally people.

Visit Centralia now, and most of the houses are gone. Only three remain, along with a church. But the streets are still there, and the cemeteries. The graveyards are heartbreaking. Many of the headstones have been swallowed into the earth, and the graves themselves are warped by sinkholes as the fire changes the topography

I

beneath them. If you walk out into the forests and look down at your feet, you'll be surprised to see that you're stepping on the sidewalk—the cement and street curbs buried beneath fallen leaves and other woodland detritus. Nature is reclaiming this town, but the one area it can't retake is the lost highway running through the center of the forest. Once part of Highway 61, the state closed it down when the mine fire reached beneath it, buckling the blacktop and creating cavernous pits and craters. They built a new highway on the outskirts of town, but the old highway—the lost highway—is still there. It is covered in graffiti—some of it obscene, some of it poignant, and a few messages that are cryptic or have definite occult leanings. People flock from around the world to see it and walk this road to nowhere. But that is nothing new.

Humankind has always been fascinated with roads and trails, footpaths and highways, particularly lost ones. Ancient seafarers, explorers, and cartographers devoted their entire lives to answering that question posed by The Talking Heads, "Where does that highway go to?" If The Talking Heads had asked J.R.R. Tolkien, he would have told them that "The road goes ever on." The Highwaymen—better known as Johnny Cash, Waylon Jennings, Willie Nelson, and Kris Kristofferson, agreed, singing that "the road goes on forever."

But if the road has no ending, what is the point of traveling on it? Confucius said that roads were made for journeys, not destinations. And the English poet Richard Le Gallienne opined that roads "offer a more mystical destination." Having walked Centralia's lost highway many times, I can attest to the feeling one gets from that place. It does indeed seem almost like some supernatural journey, and one wonders what he or she will find at the end of that graffiti-covered road that terminates into nothing but deep, dark forest.

The road can lead to wondrous adventures, but it can also lead to unimaginable horrors. David Lynch knew this, with his supernatural neo-noir masterpiece Lost Highway. Bukowski and Kerouac knew it, as well. Hunter S. Thompson and Mark Twain and John Steinbeck and Stephen King have all outlined the dangers to be found out on those highways. And so have the authors of the stories in this book.

Buckle up now, dear reader. We're riding off into the darkness together, you and I. doungjai gam and Ed Kurtz will be our drivers for the first part of this trip. Others will take over along the way. They will guide us along this sinister road, this damned highway, and yes, I believe we will be lost in the shadows.

Hold tight . . .

—Brian Keene
June, 2018

Follow the Sign—François Vaillancourt

CROSSROADS OF OPPORTUNITY

DOUNGJAI GAM AND ED KURTZ

THOUGH IT TOOK Marianne the better part of a year to die, she finally got around to it on a Tuesday. By Wednesday morning, Henry was on US I-78 heading west at a steady clip of 75 MPH. He drove a baby blue Buick with the radio stuck on one station, which sometimes wasn't a station, depending on where he ended up. Country/Western in the morning, static in the afternoon, something a bit like reggae by sundown. That was after Henry passed the state line, though he wasn't entirely sure which state he'd left and which he'd entered. He didn't pay mind to much.

He just drove.

Sometime after midnight Henry's eyelids grew heavy and his stomach growled in anger. A brightly lit billboard advertised all-night breakfast at a diner on the outskirts of Effingham some miles down the road and he figured that was as good a place as any to stop for a cup of weak coffee and runny eggs. It wasn't until the billboard was out of sight that he realized he missed what exit he needed to take. There were a couple of signs that may

1

have mentioned food or gas or lodging but he noticed them in the rearview mirror as accidental afterthoughts. What lulled him out of his state of semi-slumber was the exit sign for I-57 northbound to Chicago.

Illinois, then.

But Chicago was a definite no. Far too many people, too big a city. This Effingham? He'd never heard of it. A bump in the road to a Jersey City boy. And the logo emblazoned on the water tower, the one on the east side of town when he crossed into it, after the diner he'd missed and after he realized he was in Illinois: *The Crossroads of Opportunity.* Shades of old Robert Johnson, selling his soul at the crossroads to the devil so he could play the guitar. What in hell had Marianne done it for, then? Just to live a little longer in agony, Henry reckoned. And then, once she finally died, to get back up and laugh in his face.

"Chicago would've been nice," Marianne rasped from the back seat, her voice heavy with a two-pack-a-day habit. A couple of rounds of chemo damn near destroyed what remained of her vocal cords. "I've never been to the Midwest."

You've never been outside the Tri-State area.

Henry couldn't bear to think of the thing back there, moldering under her blue wool blanket, as Marianne. As far as he could tell, the moment she went through the door, this motherfucker snuck right in from the other side. Talk about an opportunity, her death the crossroads.

He continued down I-70, which was now also I-57. 78 had ended two, three states back, he didn't know. Didn't care much, either. The key was to keep driving. The answer had to be out there.

His eyes were drawn to a light on the other side of the highway—a smallish blob on the horizon that grew larger and taller the closer he got.

"Holy shit," he muttered. It was a cross, easily a couple of hundred feet tall. He figured most people saw it as a glowing white beacon of hope in the night; to Henry it was a monstrous eyesore. He and Marianne had never been more than casual churchgoers at best—Christmas and Easter with the occasional wedding and funeral thrown in for good measure. She had flirted with the idea of converting after the diagnosis but instead became enraptured by the homeopathic lifestyle, with its essential oils and strange cocktails of ginger and turmeric and whatever snake oil was trending at the moment.

He wished that had been the end of the madness, but it was merely the beginning.

In a brief moment of desperation, Henry wondered if it was worth getting off the highway and bringing her to the cross. But what could be done—it wasn't like he could drop her off there and expect a miracle. Maybe there was a priest nearby who could perform an exorcism on whatever entity it was that had taken over her body.

He snorted at the notion. Even if he was more than half serious about bringing them both back into a religious environment, there didn't seem to be an exit to get there. He'd passed the last one at least a mile back and the road signs indicated that 57 and 70 were going to be splitting back into two separate highways in less than a few miles.

South to Memphis or west to St. Louis—neither appealed to him. But west was the way he had started this trip, and west he would continue. He moved into the right lane to continue on 70. The streetlamps on this stretch were unlit for some reason; he reckoned the situation would not improve once they were outside the city, same with the billboards.

"Stop for a pack of Winstons for me, will you, love?"

"No."

"Can't hurt me anymore."

"Shut up."

"That's not *niiiiice*," she hissed.

Henry shuddered. And then, as if mimicking him, so did the Buick.

Not now. You piece of shit, not now.

Marianne snickered. Henry shot a glance at the gas gauge, the needle at just above the halfway point. The car shuddered again, and his mind bounced around random diagnoses, though Henry knew next to nothing about cars. They were barely out of Effingham, back on a dark, empty stretch to anywhere, when the dash lights blinked off, and then on again, and finally died.

The Buick trembled violently and the steering wheel wrenched itself free from Henry's grip, spinning left and sending the car careening across two lanes. His ears filled with the loudness of the rumble strip as they hurtled onto the low ribbon of yellow grass and dirt in the median. Henry's heart pounded against his ribs and Marianne cackled the whole way.

"Shit!" Henry pounded the steering wheel. The Buick now faced eastbound, dead in the grass, dead as Marianne should have been.

"Pity," Marianne said.

A semi rocketed past, shaking the car and its occupants. Once it was gone, all was still again. Still, and pitch black. Henry's temples throbbed. Marianne was beginning to stink. Instinctively, he jabbed at the button on the armrest to his left to lower the window. It took him a second to piece together why it wasn't doing anything.

He felt like crying. His wet eyes shot up to the rearview mirror, where he saw the shape of her rising up behind him. A dark, formless shape bubbling up from the seat and the blanket, more terror than reality, for he couldn't really see much of anything at all. It was the most she'd moved since he'd thrown her back there, and this was disconcerting. The idea was that the farther they got from the source of it all, that ugly business that started this whole mess, the more likely Henry would be able to put an end to it. The stone she'd died clutching, that goddamned talisman, a thousand miles away and two and a half feet underground, but did it matter? He wondered.

"Too late," came the voice behind him, the shape trembling as it spoke. "Too late."

Henry squeezed his eyes shut and held his breath. Didn't want to see, to smell, to think. It hadn't been much of a plan to begin with, all he could think to do was drive and hope the rest came together along the way, but it hadn't. When he opened his eyes again, blinking away the sticky exhaustion and nascent tears that filmed them over, the only thing he could see clearly was the clean, white glow in the distance ahead of him.

The cross.

Talisman for a talisman, he thought. And this one was bigger. A lot bigger.

He opened the door and heaved himself out of the car. The air was cool, crisp. It felt good on his face and in

5

his lungs—each deep inhalation brought on a coughing fit but he didn't care; it was better than the smell of decay in the car that had slowly grown stronger over the course of the evening.

Inside the car, Marianne turned her head to look up at him from the back seat. Henry wasn't sure, but she seemed to be grinning at him. Fighting back the gorge rising in his gullet, he opened the back door and said, "Come on. We're going for a walk, you and me."

The outpouring of stink from the car overwhelmed him and he dry heaved a couple of times before reaching in. He grabbed her arm and quickly let go, disgusted at the feel of his fingers sinking into her cold flesh. She had dropped dozens of pounds over the course of the last year and had taken on a frighteningly skeletal form— loose skin, hair loss, sunken eyes. In those last months she didn't want anyone to see her and he did his best to dissuade even her closest friends from coming by to say goodbye. Like anyone else, she'd have preferred to go quickly, but this way it was a kind of living death before the actual end.

But not like this. Marianne really was dead now, had been for close to forty-eight hours. She'd been quiet, at least, for the first four or five hours, still and silent with her eyes closed while Henry wept beside her. He'd fallen asleep eventually, clutching her body to him as though afraid it would crumble to dust right then and there. Instead, she screamed until he jolted awake and screamed back at her. Her screams turned to laughter, his back to blubbering. One seemed to feed the other. Little had changed since.

Her hand fell upon his, cool and papery, like onion skin. Henry pulled away from her, and Marianne's hands emerged from the shadows of the Buick's backseat, silvery-white in the moonlight, and curled their fingers around the frame of the open door. She clamped down and pulled herself forward, her tight, grinning face rising quickly from the car at him. Henry staggered backward with a gasp, and he watched as she unfurled herself, spider-like, to her full height on the side of the road before him. She had been a tallish woman in life and remained so in death, though so much thinner now, her face somehow longer and limbs spotty, rubbery. Her hair, sparse before, continued to thin and drop away, leaving broad patches of bare scalp that was beginning to peel and flake.

"Christ Jesus," he muttered. He noticed her arm—the one he had grabbed moments earlier—had five new blemishes that were quickly purpling. He choked back a pained gasp.

Marianne canted her head to one side and widened her cloudy, dead eyes at him. He couldn't fathom how she could see out of them, but none of this was supposed to be possible.

"*Henreeeee*," she said, her voice lilting into something approaching a song. It made his stomach flip. "Where are we going, lover? That fucking cross? Tell me it's not the fucking cross, Henry."

"Shut up," he said.

"All this way and that's all you've come up with?"

Her shoulders raised, rolled, and sagged again. She rolled those foggy eyes, too, and worked her jaw while her tongue probed at her teeth. Whatever was in there was finally getting a shot at trying out the body, or at least Henry figured as much. The first step she took was like a newborn calf or deer, the spindly legs trembling and unsure. He noticed how long and jagged her toenails looked now, and he wondered if he shouldn't have put some shoes on her before he left Jersey. Even undertakers put shoes on the bodies they dumped in the ground. He shuddered, knowing that the Marianne he spent over a decade with would be horrified at the state of her post-mortem being.

She reached for him again and it was all he could to not recoil at her touch. She stopped just short, her fingers hovering over his forearm. They waggled ever so slightly, the fingernails grazing the hairs on his goose bump-ridden flesh. He backed away, not hiding his disgust this time.

"You're repulsed by me." Her outstretched arm fell back to her side as her grin faded.

He wasn't sure how to answer.

"Good," she said, reading his face in lieu of a response. "*Good.*"

The grin returned.

Henry's lungs deflated, and his shoulders sagged. He thought again of the enormous cross, and he silently admonished himself for having considered that for a solution. None of this was in his wheelhouse, though he shuddered to think whose wheelhouse it *was* in. All he knew was that his wife's rapid descent into the world of herbs and crystals and other assorted hokum had made him more than a little uncomfortable, but since it wasn't *his* sickness, *his* death, he resolved to keep his mouth shut and let her do whatever the hell she wanted to do. The stone, in retrospect, seemed among the least ridiculous items she'd acquired from the sundry humbug dealers she'd found online.

Five bucks, plus another three-fifty for shipping.

When first he saw it, he was reminded of the smooth, flat stones he used to search for on the shore of Lake Hopatcong when he was a kid; long, lazy summer days spent skipping them over the surface of the water as he got better at it and the stones went farther and farther. A comforting memory triggered by her comforting hocus-pocus talisman. How bad could that be?

Of course, that was before he believed in things that weren't at all possible. Black, rotted things that didn't belong in his life or this place. Things that, apparently, one could procure for fewer than ten American dollars and a healthy dose of desperation.

Things one could not outrun.

The cross loomed in the distance bright and steady, beckoning. He turned his back to it—that was a foxhole he had no desire to jump into. But to walk back that way also meant finding a place to stay for the night and maybe an all-night diner. His stomach growled. It had been hours since he had polished off the beef jerky he bought when he last got gas. He couldn't remember where that had been, just that the sun was still out at that point.

His mind wandered, and he thought of eggs, sunny side up. A mug of hot black coffee, no sugar. In the distance, a pair of eggs rose over the horizon—no, not eggs; they were headlights, blinding him as they closed in.

Beside him, Marianne fell to the ground, whacking her head against the open door on the way down.

"Marianne!" Henry rushed to her. As he bent over her, he nearly hit his head against the same door. He swore under his breath as he lifted her head and felt dampness. He pulled one hand away—it was dark but there was no mistaking what it was.

"Is everything okay here?"

He hadn't realized the vehicle was already upon them, and he hadn't heard the driver get out. But the headlights were blinding, and with one wet hand still holding Marianne's head, he shielded his eyes as a figure emerged from the glare.

"Oh, shit," the driver said.

He wore a mesh ballcap and a red hunting vest over a plaid shirt. His face was indistinct, but Henry could make out the shaggy black beard that covered a good half of it. Behind the man, a late model Chevy pickup idled, something shrill warbling from the radio inside the cab.

"She fell," Henry said.

"I got a CB," the driver said. "I'll radio for help." He moved to return to the truck.

Henry barked, "No!"

The driver stopped, slowly turned back to Henry, who rose to his feet and fidgeted with the hem of his shirt.

"I mean, I think she's exhausted, maybe. It's been a long day. A long drive."

"Is that—is that blood on you?"

Henry shot a glance down at himself, at his hands and shirt, where indeed there was something dark, wet, sticky.

"No," he said, his voice starting to crack. "No, no. Look, maybe just help me get her back into the car, huh? I don't want to trouble anyone. She's just tired, really. We're both just so goddamned tired."

He wished to hell he could see the driver's face, read his expression and maybe his thoughts. All he really wanted was for the nosy bastard to go away, but he needed to feel sure he went away comfortable enough with the situation that he didn't get anyone else involved. Though part of him considered the wisdom of making her—*it*—somebody else's problem, it wasn't going to be easy explaining any of this, especially when she was doing such a bang-up job playing dead for their guest.

No, this was Henry's problem.

"Yeah," the driver said at some length. "Yeah, okay. Sure."

He approached somewhat warily, and when he reached Marianne, he knelt down beside her. Henry crouched, too, and he didn't like what he saw in the man's face now that he was close up. The man touched her arm and squashed his eyebrows into a tight knit.

"Mister," the driver said, swallowing hard. "She doesn't look . . . "

Quickly, he retracted his hand and shot up, eyes wide and wild.

"Jesus," he said. "Jesus Christ. That lady's dead."

He edged around Marianne and cleared the Buick's open back door, and he began moving backward toward the idling truck.

"No, no," Henry pleaded. "Listen, she's a little sick, maybe, not feeling all that great, but we're just so tired, man. Come on, now. Hey, would you stop a minute, now?"

"Stay back," the man said. "Stay right there."

"Not dead," Henry said, shaking his head back and forth and advancing slowly toward the man. "You got it wrong. She's not dead. I can prove it. I can prove it to you."

As soon as he said it, he decided it wasn't true. He couldn't prove it, because she was dead. She'd died there on their bed, back in Jersey, and he knew it. One only had to look at her, to smell her, to feel the rubbery give of her cool skin, to see that. And she wasn't budging—not as long as she kept up this charade.

Yet looking at her now, still and white on the gravel and lifeless grass, her eyes sunken into her skull and dry lips receding from her teeth, all Henry could see was the same thing the frightened stranger saw.

A corpse.

His dead wife.

He said, "Oh my God."

Henry grabbed handfuls of his own hair and fought back the scream rising inside of him. *Dead*, his mind screamed back at him. *Dead dead dead dead.*

Grief welled in his chest, bleeding from his heart and spreading throughout the rest of him like the cancer that took Marianne. A grief he could not face, a grief that preferred madness to being left alone in this life.

"What have I done?" he asked, but there was no one to answer him. Marianne was dead, and the stranger was already back in the cab of his truck, holding the CB receiver to his face.

Henry fell into a stumbling gait, pinwheeling his arms as he rushed the Chevy. He was desperate to explain, to make the man see what this really was, that it was bad, but not nearly as bad as it looked. *Please please please no no no.*

" . . . a big problem here on the westbound side of 57, over," he heard the driver say.

You don't understand, please no, don't, Henry's mind babbled, but the words got stuck in his throat. It was just a mistake, not a murder. It was too much to take, but he had a grip on himself now. Why couldn't this goddamned son of a bitch just settle down and *listen?*

He reached the truck and grasped the door by the open window, and just as the startled driver dropped the receiver and recoiled from Henry in fear, the passenger side door flew open and Marianne flew into the cab like a wraith.

"Marianne!"

The driver squealed like a hog being slaughtered when her teeth sank into his neck, her jagged, gray fingernails into his face and one eye. The man's hands slapped blindly at her as he thrashed behind the wheel, but the earthly remains of Marianne didn't loosen their grasp on him. She shook and snarled, whipped her head with her teeth still clamped down on him. Blood, black as the night, burbled out of him and sprayed the windshield. Another massive 18-wheeler rumbled past on the interstate and blew its deafening horn as it swerved to avoid taking the passenger side door off the truck, but it didn't slow down.

And by the time the semi had vanished into the pitch, the driver was dead, his red throat opened and right eye ruined, his body blanketed with his own blood.

The CB crackled, then fell silent.

For the first time, Henry noticed the insects singing somewhere in the grass and brush behind him. He closed his eyes, held his breath, and listened to them.

"Henry . . . "

When again he opened his eyes, he found Marianne sitting calmly in the pickup's passenger seat, knees together and hands folded in her lap. She slowly turned her head to face him, and in the shadows the blood on her face looked like a dark beard had sprouted.

In spite of himself, Henry laughed at that.

"Now we have a truck," Marianne said. Her voice was wet and syrupy.

The task of dragging the driver out of the pickup and over to the Buick was considerably more difficult than Henry anticipated. It was the second body he'd ever moved, but substantially heavier than Marianne's. When at last he got the man into the backseat and covered him with the blanket, he was awash with sweat and his breath was ragged.

The gas gauge on the dash was close to E when he finally climbed in behind the wheel and pulled the door shut. Henry heaved a sigh, then cranked the gearshift into D. He drove below the speed limit and headed for the next exit, where there was a Shell station they'd passed several miles back. Once he was gassed up, he'd get back on the westbound side as they had been, before spinning out.

When they passed the Effingham cross again, bright in the night sky, Marianne snickered. Henry could smell the decay in her breath, the coagulating blood on her blouse.

The ocean, he thought, pushing the unpleasant odors from his mind. *I'll take her all the way to the ocean.* With this in mind, he could almost smell the salt spray, feel the sun on his neck.

"We'll go in together," Marianne said. "The water. Both of us."

"Yes," Henry agreed, slowing the truck at sight of the Shell sign ahead.

"My beloved," she rasped.

Henry smiled, knowing he was not mad, after all.

WHERE THE WILD WINDS BLOW

MATT HAYWARD

THE DYNA'S HEADLIGHT spluttered, strobing the mountain road like a bad disco. Tony gripped the handlebars and relaxed the bike to a steady twenty, unable to navigate the flickering. He rolled to a stop and kicked the stand before easing himself from the seat with a grunt. The bike purred, and he tapped the tank for good luck. If the night could get any worse, this was it.

"Baby, don't do this . . . "

He kneeled and knocked the malfunctioning light with his knuckle. It blinked once, twice . . . died.

"You givin' up on me, too? Fine."

His dry mouth tasted of stale booze and too many cigarettes. He worked up some saliva and managed to swallow as he got to his feet, the only glow now coming from the city through the matting of spruce on his right. His jeans sagged and he tightened his buckle a notch, unfazed by the past week's shed weight. Colliding with a vagrant at fifty caused all kinds of side-effects.

Tony clicked his tongue, squinting further up the mountain road and gauging the danger. Twenty-odd miles to go, the left side an abrupt plummet and the right nothing but pines. The trip home could be made. In the dark. If he was careful.

"And if I keep from seein' double long enough."

That, too, he thought. Like smacking a homeless man head-on, downing a bottle of whiskey also had its effects on the body and mind. He thought of Lisa back home, pacing the living room in her robe and chain-smoking a pack of Luckies for the sixth night in a row. He'd taken off with the Dyna for three-day stints before, sure, but not in the last decade. The fight this time, what little he could remember, ended with him getting the bottom of a bottle in the right eye socket. Now the bruised skin was still tender to the touch, but healing.

Lisa'd promised to stay sober with him, and goddamn it, if she caved then he had a fucking right to hit the town, too. Sure, he might've gone overboard with a *week*—and a fifty-worth a night in Jeff's Juke only paid back in a sore head—but the *principle* mattered. Now, at the end of this all-time low, he could return home and stitch it all back together.

Except, Wednesday night'd ended in a hit and run . . . Boy, have you fucked the puppy.

He planted his hands on his hips and scanned the road, waiting for his eyes to adjust to the gloom. The wind hissed through the trees. He could make it home . . . praying, of course, that Lisa hadn't already set fire to the place and shat in his Corvette. A seventy-thirty chance at this point. Either way, he needed to go back, if not for her then to gather his things and hit the road. Before the local rednecks slipped into gear and caught up to him for killing ol' Homeless Harry.

Unlikely, seeing as Tony'd dragged the hobo's body

to an alleyway and left him in a sleeping position. Bums died all the time, who'd waste their evening with an autopsy?

Right after, with his nerves shot, hands trembling, and with his leg screaming—the top layer of skin left somewhere on the street—Tony'd hobbled back to his bike and taken off, leaving the body behind a buzzing trash can. A three-minute ordeal tops.

"Better safe than sorry." Tony shook away his swaying vision and shuffled back to the bike, his thigh burning with each step. He'd doused the leg with whiskey the night of the crash while watching a rerun of *The Price Is Right* in a motel off the highway. So far, the wound stayed clean but he'd need proper bandages once home.

He lifted the leg across the seat and eased himself back on the Dyna. She rocked in response. Once satisfied he could see at least ten feet head, he kicked the stand off and pushed forward, keeping a stable fifteen at first. The Dyna growled, a metallic panther chewing up road.

Tony shivered in the night chill, the thought of coming home and clicking on the heater in the living-room giving his chest a flutter. He could curl up on the couch and drift off for the night, what little was left of it, deal with the inevitable argument and severe hangover after he'd caught at least a little shut-eye.

"Daddy's comin', sweetheart. Don't go just yet . . . "

As he slipped up to twenty, his confidence rose along with the speed. An urge to gun the bike—to thirty, forty, fifty—kicked in. That very urge, last time, ended with him skidding from the Juke's lot at three a.m. and smacking a vagrant from his shoes. Still, his stomach tickled with excitement. The steep drop to his left teased him to try. Or better yet, close his eyes and count to ten, see where he ended up . . . for *The Thrill.*

His knuckles whitened as his lids fought to shut but his brain refused, still having enough sense to know the consequences of wrecking the bike on the mountain. Hitching back to his and Lisa's didn't appeal, not when only the odd trucker took this route to grab breakfast at the diner in the hills or grab a beer in town before hitting the highway.

"Just get home . . . you've had your fun. Just get home."

But Lisa *had drank.* And after *promising* him to stay clean, too.

She'd *let him down.*

And you'd only be letting yourself down by getting into more trouble. You're done, Kid.

" . . . But the night ain't over yet."

Tony crept the bike to twenty-five, the speedometer jittering. Wind lifted his hair from his shoulders and the sensation curled his lips. He could go further.

The whiskey seemed to agree.

Into thirty, his heart nudged his ribs like an old high-school buddy: *That all you got, Pussy? Come on. Where's the Tony Williams the ladies gush for, eh?*

Touching fifty now, Tony surprised himself with a laugh and leaned forward, adrenaline thrumming through his veins in a good hit. He took a corner and his left hand refused to brake, the tire skidding and spitting rubble from the cliff edge. The sheer drop came into view for a split second— a chunk of dark pines separating the mountain from the town bathed in blue moonlight— and Tony had a brief impulse to leap from his seat and drop. Surely it'd last at least eleven seconds? And what a fuck load of fun that'd be! But then the bike took off again, back on course, pulling both him and his death wish away by its own accord.

He licked his lips with a chuckle and returned his stinging eyes to the road.

A fog lay ahead.

Thick as cotton, swallowing the path.

Slow swirls like beckoning fingers called Tony to gun the bike and slam right on in. Penetrate the unknown ... *for The Thrill.*

The ball of anticipation in his guts turned to a rock of fear and Tony's hand eased back the accelerator. He slowed to a stop just before the wall of white, something in the back of his brain screaming a warning. The air was warmer here, moist.

The wall of fog reached for him, curling out and dissipating, never spilling over its invisible threshold.

He glanced back the way he'd come, a good fifteen miles from town. Nocturnal creatures chittered in the thicket, but other than them, he was alone here. He could make it through the fog if he cut the crap and took it slow, eased himself along and tried not to think of the damn otherworldly warmth oozing from the stuff. He'd call round to Henry's in the morning, explain what he saw and get an answer. Henry knew plenty of trivial things, kept him king at the local pub quizzes.

"And you better have an answer for me, Henry, because this shit's givin' me the creeps."

Tony rolled the Dyna forward, and the fog enveloped him.

The sudden increase in temperature sent a shiver through him and Tony's teeth chattered. Not at all unpleasant, and that in itself was somehow . . . unpleasant. *Unnatural, more like*, he thought. *But how could it be unnatural? There ain't no factory belchin' shit out here, no one burnin' nothin' or I'd smell it, no swamps ... just woods.*

The fog eased back a touch, revealing a sliver of road before his front tire, dishing out just enough to lead him forward. The road steepened, calling Henry to give a little more power, and the Dyna roared to take on the challenge. He imagined a sudden bend, one that sneaked out of the white and caught him off guard, and imagined the unexpected plunge through the icy night air ... suddenly *The Thrill* had turned to fear, his adrenaline congealed to sickness. And what about a sneaky rock or downed tree in the path? Those would send him off into the unknown, too. Anything could if he wasn't careful.

He blinked, clearing his vision, the fog in his head competing with the fog on the road. He shouldn't have drank today. He knew better. Knew Lisa would smash his teeth in at the whiff of booze.

A scream cut through the fog, high and shrill. Tony's arm hair rose to attention. He eased on the brake and slowed to a stop, his breath visibly disrupting the thick mist before his face.

"*He's dead!*" The voice screamed. A woman. "*There's blood everywhere, Carl! Someone's killed him!*"

Tony arched an eyebrow. "Carl?"

He remembered the bartender, a burly bloke with two sleeves of tattoos and a face like a puckered arsehole. And a nametag to the right of his shirt. One that read *Carl*.

No, but I'm out of town? No way I'd hear someone finding that bum? Not out ... here ...

"*It was that bastard on the bike,*" Carl said. His voice whipped left and right like some studio effect. Tony turned his head, trying to discern the source. *"I'm tellin' ya, I was just waiting for him to slip up. Get Pat on the phone, have him come out. I'll close up inside."*

The rolling fog slipped away on the right and the sudden clearing made Tony yell. A young woman crouched over a body, her face scrunched in fear, and as Tony dismounted the bike and jogged to her, the fog reclaimed her. He reached out where he'd seen her, but his fingers clasped only on thick air, his hand slamming in an empty fist.

"Hello?" he said. "Where are you?"

No one replied.

Tony turned and backpedaled to the motorbike, his heart racing. The fog cloaked everything, licking his face, slithering into his clothes.

The bike! What if I can't find her?

Tony grunted as his stomach collided with the tank, sending the Dyna crashing to the gravel. His boots skidded in the dirt as he gripped the frame and pulled the Dyna back up. Once on the seat, his lungs burning, he wiped sweat from his forehead and grimaced as more fog slipped down his throat. The taste of rotted meat clung to the back of his mouth.

He batted his face, as if wiping the fog away could help. The ghostly figures stayed branded in his mind's eye, though, the bourbon in his stomach half-heartedly claiming responsibility for the sight. His innards roiled, a lack of food adding to his conclusion.

Tony shook the thought as he began to move, the Dyna's growl reassuring his nerves. With a nod to further steel his courage, he kept a steady eye on the road as the heavy mist dished out five-foot rolls. A bend came from nowhere and Tony balked as he whipped the handlebars right, narrowly avoiding the edge. Then a wind kicked, and the hollow gust sounded like guttural laughter. Tony's skin prickled.

"*Hey, buddy.*"

The voice came from everywhere and nowhere, from inside his head and all around, an all too familiar toothless rasp. He eased on the brake but didn't stop, the Dyna rumbling. He whipped his head left and right, but the curtain of fog kept everything hidden.

"*Spare me some change? Know I gots to get inside tonight. Lost a toe last winter. Can't lose another. Just a dollar, two if you got it.*"

"Oh, fuck this . . . "

The Dyna roared as the speedometer jittered, the wheels chewing up the gravel. Tony kept the engine gunned and fought to keep from slowing. No thrill came from the danger now, instead his stomach threatened to empty its contents and he gritted his teeth to keep steady.

"Come on, come on. End, you sonofabitch!"

The road blurred, a never-ending path of dirt, and then a figure appeared. Tony slammed the brake. The man smiled. Tony hit the dirt face first.

His breath whooshed from his lungs as pain bloomed around his nose and cheeks. Pressing his hands to the gravel, Tony pushed himself upright and gasped for air, winded. Warmth trickled down the left side of his face. He whipped around but the smoke-screen filled the road like soil collapsing back into a hole. The Dyna groaned from beside him and Tony righted the bike with a grunt, sniffling back fresh blood. Then his skin prickled as a presence came up from behind.

In his left ear, someone whispered, "Spare a dollar?"

The smell of stale whiskey attacked his nostrils and Tony leaped onto the bike with a yell. He took off as the back tire spat pebbles and smoke, fighting the urge to look back. Things just beyond the veil of white crawled and swayed all around him, shapes never quite close enough to discern. He swore he saw something slither along the ditch.

Then the fog broke.

Tony burst into a clearing, the fresh night and sudden cold making him gasp. He braked and spread his legs, the bike rocking like a bad carnival ride. A horn honked, and headlights blinded him as he veered left, back towards the guardrail, letting out a yell as chrome crushed chrome.

He landed with a thump, back screaming as air gushed from his lungs and his spine arched to breaking point. His skin burned as he clamored to his feet and watched the taillights of a hatchback disappear down the interstate. The stench of petrol sent alarm bells ringing and he spun to see puddles of brown splashing from the Dyna's tank. The petrol seeped into the forest floor and pooled across the road.

"Shit! Not tonight, not tonight . . . "

The bent handlebars sent a devastating punch to his heart and his legs almost gave up. With a sniffle, he brushed debris from his clothes, ignoring the stinging in his hands. The Dyna was dead, that much was clear, but a forest fire looked more than likely if he didn't intervene. A cigarette out the window of a passing car was all it would take.

A car honked as it sped past, and Tony waved but the driver kept moving. He gave the bastard the single-fingered salute and got another honk in response. Across the way, a warm glow from the windows of Benjamin's Breakroom beckoned, a single building in the middle of nowhere that promised safety, comfort, and a much-needed payphone. Two calls needed making: one to the police for the crash (he'd be long gone before the blue and red started flashing and could claim the bike back tomorrow. "Had to rush to the hospital, officer, treat my wounds. Alcohol? No, sir, not a drop . . . ")

The second call would be to Lisa. At this rate, he wouldn't get home for god knows how long, and her chances of leaving skyrocketed by the second. The realization that he didn't know her number forced his eyes wide and he stomped the ground, pulling at his hair.

"Fuck! Why tonight, huh? Why?"

Her mother's place. At the very least, he could show up on the doorstep bandaged and bruised and bike-less in the a.m. Worth a shot.

"Hell, it's my *only* shot."

He glanced at his wristwatch. Close to four in the morning. At this hour, the all-night diner was most likely empty, but a single red Globetrotter truck said otherwise. It rumbled in the parking lot beneath a lone, dim streetlight, the driver-side door open.

The prospect of a conversation with someone, an act so simple and normal, turned Tony's stomach. He took off, limping through the intersection like an undead ghoul. At the lot, the truck driver came into view. He sat by a tire of his vehicle, hugging his knees.

Tony fished his Luckies and Zippo free from his shirt pocket and lit a cigarette, left leg throbbing from the fall. He sucked smoke deep into his lungs, relishing the burn and the nicotine hit. The sudden silence, the cold night air, felt surreal in its normality after what he'd just been through. He worried this could be another hallucination, something shown to him by the fog just like the voices, but he pushed the thought from his mind, chalking it up to nerves. He crossed to the trucker, taking another pull from his smoke.

"I need a phone. Just trashed my bike. You got a . . . everything all right?"

The man, mid-fifties with a *John Deere* baseball cap, raised his head. His sunken eyes vibrated in their sockets, his skin ashen. His throat bobbed as he made to speak.

"I saw my kid," he said, a voice like sandpaper.

What little heat and strength Tony had left drained from his body.

The man sniffled. "I saw the rope Richie used to hang himself, swayin' off the overpass. Saw it and him and . . . Jesus, I can't stop shaking, I . . . worst night of my life, pushed in my face and I couldn't look away."

Tony's mouth dried. He tried speaking but his throat refused to open, and instead, he eased himself to the road. They sat in silence a moment, Tony unable to meet the trucker's gaze. The bike and Lisa took second place to the implications of this man's word.

A soft rain patted the pavement, then hissed all around. Tony flicked away his cigarette, the cocktail of nicotine and adrenaline in his system leaving him ill.

Finally, the man spoke. "You saw it, too, didn't you?"

Tony didn't answer.

"What'd it show you? Tell me."

Tony swallowed. He wiped dried blood from his upper lip.

"Took me over along the highway, you know. Lasted 'bout three minutes. That's how long, I think. Been sittin' here piecing it together. Just . . . couldn't see anything, man. Only white. All white."

Tony faced the trucker now, needing to see his eyes. See if he saw his own fears reflected. "It passed through the woods," he said. "Caught me on the trail."

The man nodded. "I know. I saw it slip down that way."

"What is it?"

"I have no idea. Something no one should ever see, that's all I know. But then again, I . . . "

"You what?" Tony skittered forward. "You what? What?"

"Maybe it's something I *should've* saw, after all. Things I couldn't let to the surface before, things I kept bottled . . . popped into my face, made me look. That's what I saw."

Tony thought of the vagrant, the sound of the crash that night, the lack of emotion as he'd dragged the body off-road . . .

"I do know one thing."

"What's that?" Tony asked.

"It's blowing south, past the mountain . . . and God help that town when it hits."

NOT FROM DETROIT

JOE R. LANSDALE

OUTSIDE IT WAS cold and wet and windy. The storm rattled the shack, slid like razor blades through the window, door and wall cracks, but it wasn't enough to make any difference to the couple. Sitting before the crumbling fireplace in their creaking rocking chairs, shawls across their knees, fingers entwined, they were warm.

A bucket behind them near the kitchen sink collected water dripping from a hole in the roof.

The drops had long since passed the noisy stage of sounding like steel bolts falling on tin, and were now gentle plops.

The old couple were husband and wife; had been for over fifty years. They were comfortable with one another and seldom spoke. Mostly they rocked and looked at the fire as it flickered shadows across the room.

Finally Margie spoke. "Alex," she said, "I hope I die before you."

Alex stopped rocking. "Did you say what I thought you did?"

"I said, I hope I die before you." She wouldn't look at him, just the fire. "It's selfish, I know, but I hope I do. I don't want to live on with you gone. It would be like cutting out my heart and making me walk around. Like one of them zombies."

"There are the children," he said. "If I died, they'd take you in."

"I'd just be in the way. I love them, but I don't want to do that. They got their own lives. I'd just as soon die before you. That would make things simple."

"Not simple for me," Alex said. "I don't want you to die before me. So how about that? We're both selfish, aren't we?"

She smiled. "Well, it ain't a thing to talk about before bedtime, but it's been on my mind, and I had to get it out."

"Been thinking on it too, honey. Only natural we would. We ain't spring chickens anymore."

"You're healthy as a horse, Alex Brooks. Mechanic work you did all your life kept you strong. Me, I got the bursitis and the miseries and I'm tired all the time. Got the old age bad."

Alex started rocking again. They stared into the fire. "We're going to go together, hon," he said. "I feel it. That's the way it ought to be for folks like us."

"I wonder if I'll see him coming. Death, I mean."

"What?"

"My grandma used to tell me she seen him the night her daddy died."

"You've never told me this."

"Ain't a subject I like. But Grandma said this man in a black buggy slowed down out front of their house, cracked his whip three times, and her daddy was gone in instants. And she said she'd heard her grandfather tell how he had seen Death when he was a boy. Told her it was early morning and he was up, about to start his chores, and when he went outside he seen this man dressed in black walk by the house and stop out front. He was carrying a stick over his shoulder with a checkered bundle tied to it, and he looked at the house and snapped his fingers three times. A moment later they found my grandfather's brother, who had been sick with the smallpox, dead in bed."

"Stories, hon. Stories. Don't get yourself worked up over a bunch of old tall tales. Here, I'll heat us some milk."

Alex stood, laid the shawl in the chair, went over to put milk in a pan and heat it. As he did, he turned to watch Margie's back. She was still staring into the fire, only she wasn't rocking. She was just watching the blaze and, Alex knew, thinking about dying.

After the milk they went to bed, and soon Margie was asleep, snoring like a busted chainsaw. Alex found he could not rest. It was partly due to the storm, it had picked up in intensity. But it was mostly because of what Margie had said about dying. It made him feel lonesome.

Like her, he wasn't so much afraid of dying, as he was of being left alone. She had been his heartbeat for fifty years, and without her, he would only be going through motions of life, not living.

God, he prayed silently. When we go, let us go together. He turned to look at Margie. Her face looked unlined and strangely young. He was glad she could turn off most anything with sleep. He, on the other hand, could not.

Maybe I'm just hungry.

He slid out of bed, pulled on his pants, shirt and house shoes; those silly things with the rabbit face and ears his granddaughter had bought him. He padded silently to the kitchen. It was not only the kitchen, it served as a den, living room, and dining room. The house was only three rooms and a closet, and one of the rooms was a small bathroom. It was times like this that Alex thought he could have done better by Margie. Gotten her a bigger house, for one thing. It was the same house where they had raised their kids, the babies sleeping in a crib here in the kitchen.

He sighed. No matter how hard he had worked, he seemed to stay in the same place. A poor place.

He went to the refrigerator and took out a half-gallon of milk, drank directly from the carton.

He put the carton back and watched the water drip into the bucket. It made him mad to see it. He had let the little house turn into a shack since he retired, and there was no real excuse for it. Surely, he wasn't that tired. It was a wonder Margie didn't complain more.

Well, there was nothing to do about it tonight. But he vowed that when dry weather came, he wouldn't forget about it this time. He'd get up there and fix that damn leak.

Quietly, he rummaged a pan from under the cabinet. He'd have to empty the bucket now if he didn't want it to run over before morning. He ran a little water into the pan before substituting it for the bucket so the drops wouldn't sound so loud.

He opened the front door, went out on the porch, carrying the bucket. He looked out at his mud-pie yard and his old, red wrecker, his white logo on the side of the door faded with time: Alex Brooks Wrecking and Mechanic Service.

Tonight, looking at the old warhorse, he felt sadder than ever. He missed using it the way it was meant to be used. For work. Now it was nothing more than transportation. Before he retired, his tools and hands made a living. Now nothing. Picking up a Social Security check was all that was left.

Leaning over the edge of the porch, he poured the water into the bare and empty flower bed. When he lifted his head and looked at his yard again, and beyond to Highway 59, he saw a light. Headlights, actually, looking fuzzy in the rain, like filmed-over amber eyes. They were way out there on the highway, coming from the south, winding their way toward him, moving fast.

Alex thought that whoever was driving that crate was crazy. Cruising like that on bone-dry highways with plenty of sunshine would have been dangerous, but in this weather, they were asking for a crackup.

As the car neared, he could see it was long, black and strangely shaped. He'd never seen anything like it, and he knew cars fairly well. This didn't look like something off the assembly line from Detroit. It had to be foreign.

Miraculously, the car slowed without so much as a quiver or screech of brakes and tires. In fact, Alex could not even hear its motor, just the faint whispering sound of rubber on wet cement.

The car came even of the house just as lightning flashed, and in that instant, Alex got a good look at the driver, or at least the shape of the driver outlined in the flash, and he saw that it was a man with a cigar in his mouth and a bowler hat on his head. And the head was turning toward the house.

The lightning flash died, and now there was only the dark shape of the car and the red tip of the cigar jutting at the house. Alex felt stalactites of ice dripping down from the roof of his skull, extended through his body and out of the soles of his feet.

The driver hit down on his horn; three sharp blasts that pricked at Alex's mind.

Honk. (visions of blooming roses, withering, going black)

Honk. (funerals remembered, loved ones in boxes, going down)

Honk. (worms crawling through rotten flesh)

Then came a silence louder than the horn blasts. The car picked up speed again. Alex watched as its taillights winked away in the blackness. The chill became less chill. The stalactites in his mind melted away.

But as he stood there, Margie's words of earlier that evening came at him in a rush: "Seen Death once . . . buggy slowed down out front . . . cracked his whip three times . . . man looked at the house, snapped his fingers three times . . . found dead a moment later . . . "

Alex's throat felt as if a pine knot had lodged there. The bucket slipped from his fingers, clattered on the porch and rolled into the flowerbed. He turned into the house and walked briskly toward the bedroom . . .

(Can't be, just a wives' tale)

his hands vibrating with fear,

(Just a crazy coincidence)

Margie wasn't snoring.

Alex grabbed her shoulder, shook her.

Nothing.

He rolled her on her back and screamed her name.

Nothing.

"Oh, baby. No."

He felt for her pulse.

None.

He put an ear to her chest, listening for a heartbeat (the other half of his life bongos), and there was none.

Quiet. Perfectly quiet.

"You can't..." Alex said. "You can't... we're supposed to go together... got to be that way."

And then it came to him. He had seen Death drive by, had seen him heading on down the highway.

He came to his feet, snatched his coat from the back of the chair, raced toward the front door. "You won't have her," he said aloud. "You won't."

Grabbing the wrecker keys from the nail beside the door, he leaped to the porch and dashed out into the cold and the rain.

A moment later he was heading down the highway, driving fast and crazy in pursuit of the strange car.

The wrecker was old and not built for speed, but since he kept it well-tuned and it had new tires, it ran well over the wet highway. Alex kept pushing the pedal gradually until it met the floor. Faster and faster and faster.

After an hour, he saw Death.

Not the man himself but the license plate. Personalized and clear in his headlights. It read: death/exempt.

The wrecker and the strange black car were the only ones on the road. Alex closed in on him, honked his horn. Death tootled back (not the same horn sound he had given in front of Alex's house), stuck his arm out the window and waved the wrecker around.

Alex went, and when he was alongside the car, he turned his head to look at Death. He could still not see him clearly, but he could make out the shape of his bowler, and when Death turned to look at him, he could see the glowing tip of the cigar, like a bloody bullet wound.

Alex whipped hard right into the car, and Death swerved to the right, then back onto the road. Alex rammed again. The black car's tires hit roadside gravel and Alex swung closer, preventing it from returning to the highway. He rammed yet another time, and the car went into the grass alongside the road, skidded and went sailing down an embankment and into a tree.

Alex braked carefully, backed off the road and got out of the wrecker. He reached a small pipe wrench and a big crescent wrench out from under the seat, slipped the pipe wrench into his coat pocket for insurance, then went charging down the embankment waving the crescent.

Death opened his door and stepped out. The rain had subsided and the moon was peeking through the clouds like a shy child through gossamer curtains. Its light hit Death's round pink face and made it look like a waxed pomegranate. His cigar hung from his mouth by a tobacco strand.

Glancing up the embankment, he saw an old but strong-looking black man brandishing a wrench and wearing bunny slippers, charging down at him.

Spitting out the ruined cigar, Death stepped forward, grabbed Alex's wrist and forearm, twisted. The old man went up and over, the wrench went flying from his hand. Alex came down hard on his back, the breath bursting out of him in spurts.

Death leaned over Alex. Up close, Alex could see that the pink face was slightly pocked and that some of the pinkness was due to makeup. That was rich. Death was vain about his appearance. He was wearing a black T-shirt, pants and sneakers, and of course his derby, which had neither been stirred by the wreck nor by the ju-jitsu maneuver.

"What's with you, man?" Death asked.

Alex wheezed, tried to catch his breath. "You can't . . . have . . . her."

"Who? What are you talking about?"

"Don't play . . . dumb with me." Alex raised up on one elbow, his wind returning. "You're Death and you took my Margie's soul."

Death straightened. "So you know who I am. All right. But what of it? I'm only doing my job."

"It ain't her time."

"My list says it is, and my list is never wrong."

Alex felt something hard pressing against his hip, realized what it was. The pipe wrench. Even the throw Death had put on him had not hurled it from his coat pocket. It had lodged there and the pocket had shifted beneath his hip, making his old bones hurt all the worse.

Alex made as to roll over, freed the pocket beneath him, shot his hand inside and produced the pipe wrench. He hurled it at Death, struck him just below the brim of the bowler and sent him stumbling back. This time the bowler fell off. Death's forehead was bleeding.

Before Death could collect himself, Alex was up and rushing. He used his head as a battering ram and struck Death in the stomach, knocking him to the ground. He put both knees on Death's arms, pinning them, clenched his throat with his strong, old hands.

"I ain't never hurt nobody before," Alex said. "Don't want to now. I didn't want to hit you with that wrench, but you give Margie back."

Death's eyes showed no expression at first, but

slowly a light seemed to go on behind them. He easily pulled his arms out from under Alex's knees, reached up, took hold of the old man's wrists and pulled the hands away from his throat.

"You old rascal," Death said. "You outsmarted me."

Death flopped Alex over on his side, then stood up. Grinning, he turned, stooped to recover his bowler, but he never laid a hand on it.

Alex moved like a crab, scissoring his legs, and caught Death from above and behind his knees, twisted, brought him down on his face.

Death raised up on his palms and crawled from behind Alex's legs like a snake, effortlessly. This time he grabbed the hat and put it on his head and stood up. He watched Alex carefully.

"I don't frighten you much, do I?" Death asked.

Alex noted that the wound on Death's forehead had vanished. There wasn't even a drop of blood. "No," Alex said. "You don't frighten me much. I just want my Margie back."

"All right," Death said.

Alex sat bolt upright.

"What?"

"I said, all right. For a time. Not many have outsmarted me, pinned me to the ground. I give you credit, and you've got courage. I like that. I'll give her back. For a time. Come here."

Death walked over to the car that was not from Detroit. Alex got to his feet and followed. Death took the keys out of the ignition, moved to the trunk, worked the key in the lock. It popped up with a hiss. Inside were stacks and stacks of matchboxes. Death moved his hand over them, like a careful man selecting a special vegetable at the supermarket. His fingers came to rest on a matchbox that looked to Alex no different than the others.

Death handed Alex the matchbox. "Her soul's in here, old man. You stand over her bed, open the box. Okay?"

"That's it?"

"That's it. Now get out of here before I change my mind. And remember, I'm giving her back to you. But just for a while."

Alex started away, holding the matchbox carefully. As he walked past Death's car, he saw the dents he had knocked in the side with his wrecker were popping out. He turned to look at Death, who was closing the trunk.

"Don't suppose you'll need a tow out of here?"

Death smiled thinly. "Not hardly."

✳ ✳ ✳

Alex stood over their bed; the bed where they had loved, slept, talked and dreamed. He stood there with the matchbox in his hand, his eyes on Margie's cold face. He ever so gently eased the box open. A small flash of blue light, like Peter Pan's friend Tinkerbell, rushed out of it and hit Margie's lips. She made a sharp inhaling sound and her chest rose. Her eyes came open. She turned and looked at Alex and smiled.

"My lands, Alex. What are you doing there, and half-dressed? What have you been up to . . . is that a matchbox?"

Alex tried to speak, but he found that he could not. All he could do was grin.

"Have you gone nuts?" she asked.

"Maybe a little." He sat down on the bed and took her hand. "I love you, Margie."

"And I love you . . . you been drinking?"

"No."

Then came the overwhelming sound of Death's horn. One harsh blast that shook the house, and the headbeams shone brightly through the window and the cracks lit up the shack like a cheap nightclub act.

"Who in the world?" Margie asked.

"Him. But he said . . . stay here."

Alex got his shotgun out of the closet. He went out on the porch. Death's car was pointed toward the house, and the headbeams seemed to hold Alex, like a fly in butter.

Death was standing on the bottom step, waiting.

Alex pointed the shotgun at him. "You git. You gave her back. You gave your word."

"And I kept it. But I said for a while."

"That wasn't any time at all."

"It was all I could give. My present."

"Short time like that's worse than no time at all."

"Be good about it, Alex. Let her go. I got records and they have to be kept. I'm going to take her anyway, you understand that?"

"Not tonight, you ain't." Alex pulled back the hammers on the shotgun. "Not tomorrow night neither. Not anytime soon."

"That gun won't do you any good, Alex. You know that. You can't stop Death. I can stand here and snap my fingers three times, or click my tongue, or go back to the car and honk my horn, and she's as good as mine. But I'm trying to reason with you, Alex. You're a brave man. I did you a favor because you bested me. I didn't want to just take her back without telling you. That's why I came here to talk. But she's got to go. Now."

Alex lowered the shotgun. "Can't . . . can't you take me in her place? You can do that, can't you?"

38

"I . . . I don't know. It's highly irregular."

"Yeah, you can do that. Take me. Leave Margie."

"Well, I suppose."

The screen door creaked open and Margie stood there in her housecoat. "You're forgetting, Alex, I don't want to be left alone."

"Go in the house, Margie," Alex said.

"I know who this is: I heard you talking, Mr. Death. I don't want you taking my Alex. I'm the one you came for. I ought to have the right to go."

There was a pause, no one speaking. Then Alex said, "Take both of us. You can do that, can't you? I know I'm on that list of yours, and pretty high up. Man my age couldn't have too many years left. You can take me a little before my time, can't you? Well, can't you?"

✳ ✳ ✳

Margie and Alex sat in their rocking chairs, their shawls over their knees. There was no fire in the fireplace. Behind them the bucket collected water and outside the wind whistled. They held hands. Death stood in front of them. He was holding a King Edward cigar box.

"You're sure of this?" Death asked. "You don't both have to go."

Alex looked at Margie, then back at Death. "We're sure," he said. "Do it."

Death nodded. He opened the cigar box and held it out on one palm. He used his free hand to snap his fingers.

Once. (the wind picked up, howled)

Twice. (the rain beat like drumsticks on the roof)

Three times. (lightning ripped and thunder roared)

"And in you go," Death said.

The bodies of Alex and Margie slumped and their heads fell together between the rocking chairs. Their fingers were still entwined.

Death put the box under his arm and went out to the car. The rain beat on his derby hat and the wind sawed at his bare arms and T-shirt. He didn't seem to mind.

Opening the trunk, he started to put the box inside, then hesitated.

He closed the trunk.

"Damn," he said, "if I'm not getting to be a sentimental old fool."

He opened the box. Two blue lights rose out of it, elongated, touched ground.

They took on the shape of Alex and Margie. They glowed against the night.

"Want to ride up front?" Death asked.

"That would be nice," Margie said.

"Yes, nice," Alex said.

Death opened the door and Alex and Margie slid inside. Death climbed in behind the wheel. He checked the clipboard dangling from the dash. There was a woman in a Tyler hospital, dying of brain damage. That would be his next stop.

He put the clipboard down and started the car that was not from Detroit.

"Sounds well-tuned," Alex said.

"I try to keep it that way," Death said.

They drove out of there then, and as they went, Death broke into song.

"Row, row, row your boat, gently down the stream," and Margie and Alex chimed in with, "Merrily, merrily, merrily, merrily, life is but a dream."

Off they went down the highway, the taillights fading,

the song dying, the black metal of the car melting into the fabric of night, and then there was only the whispery sound of good tires on wet cement and finally not even that. Just the blowing sound of the wind and the rain.

A LIFE THAT IS NOT MINE

KRISTI DEMEESTER

I HAVE FORGOTTEN what morning looks like.

There is a romantic, vampiric notion to such a statement. To have forgotten the sun. The pale pain of sunburn. The dazzling, bleached light of morning and the burnt sky becoming twilight.

But I am not beautiful or pale or lovely or any of the things Gothic writers put into their stories. There's a scattering of ungraded essays in the backseat of the responsible, compact car I bought third-hand at an interest rate that would make you choke. Three half empty water bottles and a pair of sneakers I'm supposed to use for jogging but still have the tags on. Crumpled bags with greasy reminders of whatever I shoveled into my mouth yesterday. And the day before. And the day before that, too.

There was only never-ending night in that first year of teaching that has somehow bled into a second and now a third year. Everyone tells me it will get better, and to just give it time, and that I'm doing noble work, but when I think back over all of those days, each one a rush of duller gray, I can think of only the road droning beneath me—so many hours wasted—and the darkness pressing in with a palpable heat.

"There are other schools, you know. You have some experience now and could apply somewhere closer to your apartment. An hour and a half one way is absolutely absurd." Every Thursday, my sister appears at my doorstep, a bottle of some cheap, red blend in hand, and we drink and eat saltine crackers spread thinly with margarine, and she pretends she doesn't know I hate my job.

"The market's bad, and there's a surplus of History teachers. All the open positions are for Chemistry or Pre-Calculus or some other bullshit I never paid attention to. And with the surplus process still happening, I can't risk being the new hire again."

Rebecca rolls her eyes, and places another cracker on her tongue, lets it linger before biting down. There is something feral in it, something that makes my stomach contract. When she came in, Rebecca reset my thermostat to seventy-seven. The room is too hot, and the drone of students and fluorescent lights and grading and lesson plans settle heavy over me, so I am drowsy and nauseated and wish Rebecca would go back home to her fiancée and chocolate Lab and plush job at the boutique marketing firm that passes out wine spritzers or Jello shots every Friday at three.

"You have to push yourself out of your comfort zone, Hanna. You don't want to end up like Mom. In her seventies before she realized she never lived her life. You don't even go anywhere on the weekends. It's just you holed up in this place with the blinds closed. Sleeping or watching television. You don't even *try* to get out," Rebecca says.

I smile instead of slapping her. She couldn't understand the exhaustion that falls heavy as lead over me every night. How I cannot seem to shrug it off.

"I should call it a night. I have kids coming for tutoring in the morning. Can't be late," I say, but I have never been late. Always too afraid, too nervous of being seen as a failure or of being watched even more carefully than I already am. Three mandatory observations a semester but usually more. Notes in my mailbox if I forget to take attendance, if I leave early, if I am not at my assigned duty station on time. Reminders that this is part of my contractual obligations, and that all infractions will be recorded on my file and considered as part of my evaluation.

Rebecca kisses me on the cheek before she goes, so light it might not even be a kiss at all, and squeezes my shoulder. "You look gray, sweetie. Seriously. Everything about you looks like it's dying. At least take a few days for yourself. Get outside. Go for a hike or something," she says, and then she is gone.

I sit at the window and wait for the moon to appear, but there are clouds, and there is still a droning in my ears that is like fever or like the sound of tires on asphalt.

The next morning my tongue tastes of salt, and I move silently through the dark contained in my apartment and then out into the dark contained within the great dome of sky where everything that crawls beneath looks like the same scrawled shadow. I drive and imagine not stopping. Driving until the car runs out of gas or until the road falls off into gravel, and then dead leaves and pine straw, and then getting out and walking until I cough my heart into my palm.

I can't listen to the radio. All of that blaring noise and

chatter that amounts to less than nothing. There is only me and the road winding before me and the occasional glare of headlights, but there is no sun.

When I pull into the parking lot, the sky has just begun to lighten, and I hurry into the building. Already, there are students outside my door. Always waiting, for extra tutoring, for make up work, to ask questions I've already answered in class or for extra credit, or to feed me bullshit excuses about why they didn't turn in their data-based responses yesterday or why they won't be able to take the reading quiz today because they were at a basketball tournament all weekend and really needed three extra days to study.

I sleepwalk through my lesson plans, pretend to watch as the students move into collaborative groups to goof off instead of finishing the assignment. They think I can't see them on their phones, or hear them talking about their sex lives or drug habits. They think so little of me. For them, I am a ghost who sometimes makes noise.

"When is this due again?" a girl with hair the color of dishwater asks, and I know I should remember her name, but I don't.

"At the end of the period. You've had almost an hour," I say, and there are a chorus of groans. I bite down on my cheeks.

"That's bullshit," a voice mumbles from the back.

Half of them don't turn in the assignment, and I spend my planning dutifully marking them and ignoring the constant pinging from my email.

At the end of the day, it seems as if the same students are there, still lingering, still asking the same questions, and their faces blend together, a nightmare blend of open, wet mouths all bleating in identical tones. By the time the students have gone, and I've marked another handful of papers and responded to three parent emails asking why their children are getting Cs when they've always been A level students, and photocopied tomorrow's assignment, I can feel the sun has set once more. The hallways are empty, the other classrooms dimmed, their windows dark mirrors that reflect my pale, bloated face as I make my way back to the car. I swipe at my eyes, and mascara flakes under my fingers.

I drive, and the road is empty. I close my eyes, see how long I can keep them closed before panicking and snapping them open only to see that I haven't drifted anywhere. I am still exactly on this road that has no sun.

Sometimes I dream that the dark is not a portion of the external world at all, but something I carry inside. I drive and squeeze the steering wheel to keep my hands from shaking. Outside of the window, there are dim forms that seem to rise and fall. I know I am only imagining these things. I feel like I remember reading about it back in college—the Psychology class I had to take—how the brain tries to find order in chaos and will trick itself into seeing images in nothing. Inside darkness, I believe there is only chaos. Not an empty expanse at all but colliding forms constantly shifting, constantly seeking something onto which it can latch and go through a metamorphosis.

There have been so many days without light. So many hours peering with bleary eyes at walls and faces and roads.

There is a message from Rebecca on the answering machine, but her voice smears, breaks apart in robotic screeching, so I delete it and don't call her back. I am not hungry, so I sit in my living room with the volume on the television muted and listen to the sounds in the building that should be there but are not. Instead, there is only a dull kind of roar you hear tucked inside of seashells. A sound meant for children and summer days with the kind of humidity that curls under your skin and lingers well past sundown. I try to follow the pattern of it, but just when I find the rise and fall, the rhythm changes like some great leviathan's breath.

I fall asleep on the couch, and at three a.m., I wake panting and shivering but unable to remember what I dreamed. The sound is still there. Something in the walls, like a forsaken God howling behind plaster.

I make a pot of coffee and wait until it's time to go. I am grateful to leave that sound behind me, to fall into another kind of roaring that I understand. The road and the sound of the tires against it. There's some comfort in that.

There are at least two or three kids missing from each of my classes. Some kind of flu going around. Administration emails about it—offer extra help sessions, be mindful of scheduling make up assignments—and the remaining kids are quiet, sniffling in their seats, and staring back at me with pink, glassy eyes while I force myself through a PowerPoint. Eventually, I give up and put on a movie. I try to grade, but the glare reflecting from the papers gives me a headache. Instead, I watch my students' faces and wonder when it was that they all started to look alike— hair pulled forward, so it covers their eyes and faces, the skin sallow and seeming to droop downward. Maybe it's whatever's going around.

The girl with the dishwater hair appears at my desk, and I gasp. I didn't see her get up. "Bathroom," she says.

"You need to go?" I ask, prompting her to ask me, to show me the minimum respect anyone would show any other fucking person, but she blinks back at me. There is crust in the corners of her mouth.

"I'm sick," she says, and I write her the pass and hand it to her with the tips of my fingers. She doesn't come back, and I don't email the nurse to ask.

At the end of the day, I spray all the desks with disinfectant and wipe down my pens, my markers, the keyboard on my computer. I douse my hands in sanitizer, rub it up and over my arms, and then over my mouth and chin.

I don't see the paper until I have finished and am packing my bag to leave. Folded into a tight square, it sits perched on the edge of my desk. It is the kind of thing that is meant to be seen, and I glance about the room even though I have been alone for hours now. It's just something I missed. This is what I tell myself even as my heart rabbits in the cage of my chest, and I hold the paper away from my body and unfold it quickly as if whatever is contained inside could unstitch the world.

The paper is blank. I turn it over and over, but there are no words scrawled there, and I toss it into the trash, my throat suddenly aching. I worry that maybe I've caught whatever bug is going around, and swallow again and again, each time a lingering reminder that there may be something festering inside of me. I cough, and it is weak, and I tell myself I'll take some cough syrup. There are only three more days until the weekend. Three more days. I repeat this over and over to myself until it means less than nothing. I glance once more at the paper in the trash, and then grab my bag. There is an irrational fear damp and heavy in my mouth, and I hurry out the door without looking back at that blank sheet of paper that should have words but doesn't.

I drive home in the dark and wonder what it would be like to have sunlight refracting back through all this glass and metal. There is a part of me that shudders, but I shrug it away. I am tired, and it is only nerves and anxiety jerking at my body like some absurd puppet.

On my fingers, I can feel only the emptiness of that paper, and I cough, but it is dry and unsatisfactory.

Tomorrow, Rebecca will come to the apartment, and I will cook her dinner and listen to her tell me about all the things wrong with my life, but tonight, I delete the message the moment I hear the high-pitched whine of her voice. There must be something wrong with the answering machine because at the end of the message, there is a long screeching that extends downward into a kind of howl before cutting off. This weekend, maybe I'll venture out. Buy a new one. But I am so tired. The thought of doing anything other than this learned routine exhausts me.

I try not to drink liquor during the week, but tonight, I dig out the bottle of gin hiding in the same cabinet where I keep the mixing bowls I don't use and pour three fingers over ice. I do not turn on the television, and before I have finished the glass, that roaring sound from the previous night is back. I smile and lift my gin in a mock toast, but there is nothing that responds, and so I drain the glass and wait for the night to become another version of night.

There are fewer students in class the next day. While my back is turned, I can hear them whispering to each other—that same sound as the roar in my apartment—but when I turn to face them, they are still, their faces impassive and mouths damp and slightly open as if they have forgotten who they are, and I want to slap their faces, and clamp their jaws shut, and then run from the building, but there is the paycheck and the rent and the insurance and all of those adult responsibilities you learn about without ever truly understanding how little all of those things add up to.

I ask questions, but no one answers even though I wait and wait. There is none of the awkwardness, none of the shuffling of bottoms in seats and darting eyes until one student dares to lift a hand just to ease the tension.

These are not children before me. I tell myself this and shiver and remember that it's likely they are sick, likely their parents have forced them to come to school even if they have coughs that rattle deep in their chest or are more tired than usual.

Their eyes are too bright—glittering as if with fever—and I open my mouth to keep on with the lesson but then trail off. There's no point. Instead, I turn off the lights.

"Put your heads down. Quiet," I say, hoping administration would understand if they venture past my room and peek through the window. The students comply. One by one, they lean over their desks, and soon enough, the room is filled with the sound of their slow breathing, and it is somehow like being trapped in an echo chamber. When the bell finally rings, the sound is muffled, and the students peel themselves away from the desks and trundle out.

There are no students in my last period. I wait and wait and then check the hallway, but all the other doors are closed, and I walk past a few of the classrooms and look in to see a handful of faces I don't recognize seated calmly at desks or standing at the front, their mouths curving over silent instructions. Substitutes more than likely. Whatever's going around is hitting the teachers now.

I cannot see if there are students in those closed off rooms, and so I return to my own classroom and think of contacting administration, letting them know that all my students are sick, but what could they do? I check my email to see if there's something there, some indication of what to do if we should be in a room with no students, but there's nothing.

There are papers to be graded, always a stack of something to do, but I know that it is daylight, and there are no students to teach, just this empty room, and so before I can tell myself I shouldn't, I grab my bag, my keys, and lock the door behind me. I keep my eyes down so that there is no opportunity if someone sees me in the hallway to ask what I'm doing. I hurry. Suddenly, there is a desperate need to see that there is still sun, to come through the doors and know that there is still a different kind of life that exists outside of my own.

The hallways divide and divide again, but soon enough, I am in the main corridor, and it is empty, and I am panting. There will be no one to stop me leaving, no one to keep me from the sun, and I reach for the doors, my hands trembling, and I could almost cry out with this deep need. I bite down on that animal-like noise and push through the doors.

Outside, the sky is the color of charcoal.

I shrink backward, the door easing shut as I go, and squeeze my eyes closed. "No," I whisper, but I know what I've seen. That whatever exists behind that door is the terrible thing that has been opening itself up for all this time. I rest my fingers against the door and swallow down the bitterness flooding my mouth. I do not want to go forward. I cannot go back. I could scream, but it would not bring back the sun.

I open the door and fling myself out into the night, my keys sweating in my palm. My car is still in faculty parking, but everything is quiet. I ease the door open, afraid to make any sound. I drive, take the turns too quickly, and I do scream then. Again, and again, but there is only the road and the dark and me moving through some awful thing, and my throat goes raw, but I cannot stop myself.

I can hear the roar from the apartment before I'm even to my door, and I don't want to go in, don't want to finally discover whatever it is that's making that same sound as tires along an endless road, but there's nowhere else to go. Inside, there's another message from Rebecca, and her voice isn't hers anymore but something like that roaring, and I pick up the phone and dial her number.

"Hanna," she says, and I sob. She is there, and I am not alone, and the thought of it is too much.

"There's something wrong here. Everyone is sick, and there should be sun, but there isn't, and it feels like there's a road that I can't get off. A road where there's no sun, and that everything I think I've been doing isn't real," I say, and the panic is slick on my tongue.

"Hanna," Rebecca says again. "Hanna, Hanna, Hanna." The voice is flat and without emotion, and I picture a recording on the other end, my name endlessly looping, and I drop the phone, scratching at my palms as if I could remove the stain of that alien creature speaking my name.

A LIFE THAT IS NOT MINE

Underneath the roaring, there's another layer that is somehow worse than the first—a delicate scratching as of small limbs scrabbling along a hard surface. The sound of some many-legged insect working its way out of a cocoon or from a nest where it has slept and woken up hungry.

I close every door in the apartment, and I do not look into the darkness contained within the rooms, afraid that I will see the shadows bend and shift into the slack faces of my students or reflect back many eyes that no longer blink but watch and wait. I go back out into the hallway and move up and down between the other apartments, pressing my ear to each door, but there are no other sounds other than the roaring.

I tell myself I will knock, that there will be someone who comes to one of the doors, and smiles and tells me that everything is fine, everything is wonderful, and there is no darkness here, there is no road that eats up everything that once was, but the first door I come to opens when I push my knuckles against it.

Inside the apartment, there are blank walls and empty floors—no indication there has ever been a human occupant. Here, there is only the dark pushing outward in small bursts of putrid air, and I back away. It's only one empty apartment. They can't all be like this. I've seen other people. The edges of their coats as they unlock their doors and scurry inside. I've heard their noises—the dull static of a television or low murmur of conversation. I have not been alone this entire time. Rebecca has come here. She would have noticed if there were no other people and commented on how weird it was to be the only occupant of an entire complex. She would have said it was like a haunting.

On my left and right, the doors trail off in receding parallel lines, and in the periphery of my vision, they all seem to open at once, several pale hands all reaching outward only to vanish just as quickly. One by one, I follow the doors, peek inside those great, blank spaces, until my breath is ragged in my throat and my cheeks damp with tears. I'm not sure when it is I started crying.

I find my way back to my apartment. The phone is still there, and I pick it up, but there is no dial tone, only that worming sound I've been hearing for days, and I throw the phone onto the carpet. It doesn't break. Nothing can be so easy.

My purse and keys are where I left them on the kitchen counter, and I fumble for them and am out the door again. My feet are bare, and they slap against the concrete stairs as I make my way down. I do not trust the elevator, cannot imagine being trapped in that metal box while the roaring gets louder and louder as I wait for this world to collapse in on itself and finally reveal whatever creature has come awake. Because surely this is what has happened. Surely, I have stumbled into the long, cold dark I have found on the road.

There are other cars in the parking lot—twisted bits of metal that look like great, humped beasts—but they are empty, and there is no light other than a dim streetlamp that seems made more of shadow than anything else.

But the car cranks easily, and there is nothing to stop me, no looming monstrosity or invisible barrier, as I pull out of the parking lot.

There is only one road now, no option to turn left instead of right. It is the same road I have traveled, the same one I have known, the one with endless banality and no sun. I have sculpted these same, repeated moments with my hands. I should not be surprised that they have found me again, that they are mimicking my memory to construct the endlessness of this road.

I drive, and there is no end to the trees, their branches heavy and arching over the road, and there is the roaring, and I could laugh instead of cry. The trees have begun to move. Their shadows bend and jerk, dipping toward the earth as if in honor of my passing.

If the school is at the end of this road, I am certain I will find it emptied. Or, if there is anyone left, that they will be faceless bodies propped up in desks. Pale imitations of the students they are trying to become until eventually, their mouths form into gaping holes that make that same roaring sound as the road.

I could press my foot to the floor, accelerate and then jerk the car off the road and into the trees, but I am afraid they would make space for me, afraid they would not let it be so easy as all of that. Death is not anything to vanish into. Not here. Not now.

The roaring is a screaming now. The sky tearing itself asunder, but there is no light beyond the darkness, and I lift my voice up in chorus and laugh. High and clear.

I take my hands off the wheel. The car does not drift but stays steady on the road, and I think of Rebecca, of her carefully constructed life and my jealousy, and how even now, I would wrap my hands about her throat if it meant I could have all of the things she has or *had*. There's no way to be certain this darkness hasn't swallowed her up, too. But I don't think it has. It is meant only for me.

Perhaps the car will run out of gas, and I will begin walking until the breath comes gasping out of me, my body failing and dropping under this black sky. Perhaps there will be only this movement without any true destination. I do not know which is worse, and I cannot be certain I didn't wish for this. Standing in front of the mirror before another day of classes and students and boredom and wishing for an end to this existence, I somehow opened a door that will not be closed. I think of those pale hands, those fingers curling around wooden frames, reaching. I think of the shadowed forms of the trees and how they look like those fingers.

When I reach the end of this road, I will look for something sharp. I hope that I will find it.

The Mag-Bat—Wes Freed

MR. HUGSY

ROBERT FORD

"DID YOU PAY this time?"

Andy watched his father in the mirror as the car turned back onto the road. Daddy looked sleepy. His whiskers were thick on his face.

"*Yeahhhh*, I paid this time."

"Mommy says stealing is bad."

"Andy, I *know*, all right? But sometimes to get ahead, you gotta do *bad* things to make *good*. That's *grown up* life. Stealin's bad but spending your life behind the damned 8-ball is worse."

"8-ball?"

"Yeah, the 8-ball. Bustin' your ass workin' for the man."

"Ass is a bad word."

"*Butt,* then." Daddy rolled his window down a little and spit. "Don't worry, though. You and me? We ain't *never* working for the man again. Partners in crime, you hear? Daddy and you, buddy."

"Okay."

"Try to get some sleep. There's a blanket beside you and I got you some of that beef jerky you like for when you wake up."

Andy stretched his legs and kicked his feet together, watching his light-up sneakers come to life. He leaned his head back and turned toward the sunset. It had been a long, *long* time since Andy had seen Daddy and he said they were going on a surprise trip. *Boys only.*

The desert blurred by. The sky was smeared with reds and oranges, and reminded him of finger painting with Mommy. Andy was excited about the trip, but he missed her. He was a little sad he hadn't been able to give her a goodbye hug and kiss. Daddy said it was okay though, that he could hug and kiss her twice as much when they got back from their trip.

Usually, Mommy wasn't very good at keeping secrets, but this must be a *really* special trip because she hadn't said a word about it. Not one single word.

✴✴✴

Dixon Keller was a man given to sly glances and nods.

In the first grade, Dixon planned a heist on a classmate named Susan Silhan. His partner in crime was Preston, a kid with red hair and freckles who lived five houses down the block from him. Preston liked to let Elmer's Glue dry on his fingers and nibble at it all afternoon.

During lunchtime, Dixon told Preston to slow down when he got close to where Susan sat in the cafeteria—slow down, and *accidentally* trip and spill his carton of chocolate milk.

Preston nailed the performance and all heads turned toward the carton, burping the milk onto the gleaming tile floor. When everyone's attention was on the spill, Dixon ducked beneath the table. He unzipped her backpack and took the two boxes of Crayola 64 packs from Susan's backpack. Snooty bitch had been bragging all week about them and the built-in sharpeners, and Dixon had heard enough. After paying Preston fifty cents and a new carton of chocolate milk, Dixon had two almost brand new boxes of crayons for himself.

For a full month afterward, he smiled to himself every time he used the sharpener.

That childhood score started Dixon down a path he could not bring himself to veer from. Didn't much *want* to, either. Fixed card games. Collecting payments for bookies. The horse track. Insurance scams. The short con. The long con. Grifts.

Name almost anything that lived in the gray area of life and Dixon had been involved. And every shady deal, every back alley exchange of cash and greased palms, began with half-assed plans. Those plans, for Dixon Keller, all started with a sly glance and a nod.

It had been almost a year since he'd seen the wrong side of prison bars for the last score that had gone in the shitter. Two weeks before he was going to get released, Dixon Keller sat up on his prison cot in the middle of the night. He thought of Andy. Right after Andy turned four, Dixon pulled a score that went bad and he ended up back on the inside.

But that was before he saw Andy's dancing shadows trick.

Granted, he had only been around his son a total of two and a half years, and even *that* time hadn't been consecutive. He was there for Andy's birth, went behind bars about six months after, and came back when Andy was almost three. That time was good. He was there almost a full two years. Oh, Dixon had *tried.* He had tried best he could to lean toward the straight and narrow. He enjoyed being a father. He and Loretta were making an effort to get along. He got hired down at Walder Hardware. It was a shitty job, but it was a paycheck.

It was a *normal* life.

But the thing about a normal life was that it was . . . *So. Fucking. Boring.*

Every night, Dixon put Andy to bed. Some nights he read a book and some nights he sang, and if Andy had been especially good that day, Dixon would do both. It was on one of those nights Dixon found himself singing the Eagles' *Hotel California*.

Andy had closed his eyes, but Dixon knew from experience he had to keep singing for at least another thirty seconds or else Andy would wake up like an alarm had gone off.

From the corner of his eye, Dixon saw a flutter of movement on Andy's bedroom wall. Like most kids, Andy had a dim nightlight plugged in, and it cast fuzzy silhouettes across the canvas of his room.

But these, Dixon saw, were shadows on the wall behind the top of his dresser, below the SpongeBob poster. Two of them, moving and swaying and seeming to dance with each other as he continued to sing.

Dixon stopped singing and the shadows stopped moving. Their heads shifted and looked at him. Andy turned over in his bed and let out a relaxed sigh. Dixon watched the shadows fade into the light blue paint of Andy's wall.

The night Dixon sat up in prison, stark awake, it all became clear. *So* many things became clear. The dancing shadows. His Granny. And *going over.*

His father couldn't do it, but Dixon's Granny could.

She was the one who called it *going over*, as in going over to the other side.

His father had told Dixon about the things Granny could do, but even as a kid, he thought it was bullshit. Daddy said Granny could heal people of the cancers—had seen it himself when he was young. She washed her hands in cold creek water and ran them over the sick person. Granny would squeeze her eyes shut and the person would get feverish and start to shake. Granny would pick a spot on the person's body and start tapping her fingertips in a light rhythm on their skin. Not long after, the flesh would start to bulge and move, and something would start to crawl out of the person's body. Odd little creatures the size of newborn kittens pulled themselves free as they clenched something gray and spindly in their mouth, like a dried root. They would march up to Granny, their bodies slick and wet, and drop what they had fetched right into her open hand. Granny would throw the twisted thing in a jar of alcohol and the little creatures would fade away into nothing. Granny had gone over and brought them back to do her work for her. Their deed was done. They went back. Sick person healed.

She asked for donations but never outright charged for healing folks. All her life she lived in a small shack without any running water or electricity, while the townspeople she cured stayed in fine homes with lights and indoor plumbing.

What a fuckin' waste. Woman didn't know how to get ahead. Didn't realize the edge on life she had. But Dixon Keller knew. Oh, he knew too well how to use a gift like that. He glanced in the mirror at Andy, the boy's head angled down toward the driver's side window, eyes fluttering behind his lids.

Ohhhh Andy, son of mine, there are so many great things in store for us.

Dixon shook a cigarette from a half-empty pack, lit it, and rolled the window down another few inches. *Can't expose the kid to second hand smoke. Have to start thinking* healthy. *Time to quit the smokes and heavy drinking.* What use was there in getting rich if he died from lung cancer or an enlarged liver?

Dixon took a long drag from the cigarette and blew it through the open window. He'd quit. He *would*. Once they got to where they were going, he'd quit the damned cigarettes. And the booze? Well . . .

Dixon reached for the cold Coors in the middle console. He twisted the top off and took a long swig. *I'll try to quit the goddamned booze, too. No smoking. No drinking. As soon as we get where we're going.*

They were about a half hour from Prescott when Dixon twisted the cap off his third Coors. At the sound of the fresh beer, his kidneys decided he had to pull over and take a piss.

Andy murmured in his sleep, but Dixon couldn't make out the words. Long day for the little guy, but it was going to get better. A *lot* better.

Dixon killed the engine, but left the headlights on, pinched his cigarette between his lips, and got out. *Goddamned beautiful out here with the moon shining over everything.* If it weren't so damned far away from life, he'd consider living here permanently.

Dixon let the piss fly and tilted his head back with relief. *Christ Almighty*, the sky was so clear you could almost see the letters on the satellites. *Goddamned beautiful.* Maybe he and Andy would buy a second home out here just to get away from it all.

He was squeezing his ass cheeks together and streaming his last bit of piss when he heard the huffing, snorting sound in the darkness ahead of him. There was a black shadow in the distance, just beyond the reach of the headlights, about fifty yards out in the desert. It snorted again, and Dixon heard the heavy thumping noise of stomping. The dark figure broke into a run. It wasn't graceful and light. It was fucking *thunder*. Whatever it was, it was *hauling ass* toward the car like a runaway freight train.

The shape broke the reach of the car's headlights and for a moment, Dixon stood there like an idiot, holding his dick in the open air, mouth open enough to let his cigarette fall in a shower of firefly sparks down the front of his body.

The thing was bigger than a mini-van, and gray in the Chevelle's headlights. The speed of it. The *goddamn speed.* Thick trunks of legs blurred among the flying dirt. But what held Dixon's focus was the head of the thing. Ash-colored skin, wrinkled with deep grooves surrounding pothole nostrils and angry obsidian eyes. Planted firmly in the center of its face were two horns, one longer and slightly curved, the other shorter and wide, like an inverted shark's tooth. And along the ridge of its spine were two rows of protruding fins, long as Dixon's legs. A thick tail swung side-to-side, yard-long spikes coming out of it at odd angles.

Dixon stumbled from the edge of the road. "Andy!" He screamed, ignoring his pants as he hobbled to get inside the car. The sounds of thunder were closing in.

The boy's murmuring was getting louder. Andy was thrashing his head and his hair was pasted to his forehead with sweat. Dixon scrambled over the driver's seat and slapped his son across the face. "ANDY!"

He opened his eyes and stared at Dixon, confused, his face pinched up. "*Owwwww . . . *" Tears rimmed his eyes and Andy rubbed his cheek.

The quiet in the middle of the desert was the loudest thing Dixon had ever heard.

"Are we there?"

Dixon slumped in the driver's seat, pants down to his thighs, and wished he had a shot of Jack Daniels. "Not yet, buddy."

He stared into the reach of the Chevelle's headlights. He could still see the trampled plants and wide tracks in the dirt. *Jesus Christ.*

Dixon turned to look at his son. "Andy, what happened just now? What happened while you were sleeping?"

"I was dreaming."

"About what?"

Andy reached into his lap and held up his toy Stegosaurus. "Dinosaurs. And Rhinos, too. Did you know their name means horn nose?"

"No, I . . . " Dixon looked at the rubber toy in Andy's hands. "But you can do more than just dream, can't you, Andy? Things other kids . . . other *people* can't." He reached out and patted his son's leg. "Special things?"

Andy put the toy back in his lap and stared at it. "Mommy doesn't like me to."

"Yeah, well Loretta doesn't know what the fu—" He cleared his throat, stopping himself. "I hate to say it, but Mommy's a little . . . *jealous*, okay? She loves you, but . . . I mean, *she* can't do it. That's why you're so special. It's okay around me, though. It's a *good* thing. A *gift*. I'll never be jealous, buddy. I *want* you to use that gift."

"Sometimes . . . " Andy stared at his lap. "Sometimes bad things come through."

"Bad things?"

"Like Mr. Hugsy."

"Who's Mr. Hugsy?"

Andy's face scrunched up. "I have bad dreams about him sometimes. He scares Mommy, too. She gets mad at me and I get in trouble. Mommy says bad boys need correcting."

"That sounds like some shit your mother would say."

"I don't want to talk about Mr. Hugsy anymore." Andy yawned and leaned his head back. "Will you sing to me, Daddy?"

Dixon ran through his mental catalog of songs and decided on Johnny Cash's *Ring of Fire*. He started singing and the silent black desert wrapped around the two of them.

Dixon heard the pace of Andy's breathing change as he slipped back into sleep. He turned, his gaze falling on the rubber Stegosaurus toy in Andy's lap. Dixon picked it up and looked at the ridge of plastic fins on its back. *Dinosaurs and rhinos. Son of a bitch.* He shook his head and tossed it out the window.

"Fucking Animal Planet," he whispered. "You need to watch more cartoons, kid. *Bugs Bunny* never killed anyone." Dixon pulled up his jeans and buckled them. He started the car, threw it in drive, and punched the gas. The driver's door slammed shut on its own.

The next town was about ten miles out. Dixon would gas up again and after that, they were in the home stretch. He tilted the last of his warm beer and felt an odd lump swirling in the liquid. It was both soft and brittle, and Dixon felt a rapid vibration against the roof of his mouth and then a white-hot sting against the back of his tongue.

Dixon bit down and swallowed reflexively. The fluttering tangle of a wasp's body slid down his throat among the mouthful of Coors. The pain was an atom bomb and Dixon's stomach flipped as he realized what had happened. As his tongue slid across his teeth, road flares of pain ignited. He slung the beer bottle out the window, shattering it on the asphalt.

"Fuuuuucckkkkkk meeeeeeeeeee!" Dixon spat the words through a grimace and opened his mouth like an overheated dog as hot spit flooded over his tongue. Heat flushed through his body. He figured he had fifteen, *maybe* twenty minutes before his throat closed up. Dixon pushed the Chevelle's speedometer up to 90.

He'd been in and out of prison. He'd been caught up in the Mexican mafia as a drug mule for a while. He'd been on the wrong end of a gun barrel more times than he could count.

But for the first time in his life, Dixon Keller was truly worried he might die.

***

The blue-white tower lights of a gas station announced *Papi's Gas-n-Go* and Dixon slid into the gravel lot. He killed the engine and grabbed the keys as he jumped from the Chevelle, not bothering to close the door behind him.

His head was on *fire* for fucksake. Snot ran from his nose through the stubble on his chin. His tongue felt foreign, like a piece of sunbaked rubber. He could feel scalding pressure in his face and his eyes were starting to swell shut.

A bell jingled on the door as Dixon ran inside and walked straight to the cashier. The skinny teenage Mexican boy sat on a stool behind the counter, his eyes bloodshot and heavy-lidded. He gave a nod and his eyes went wide as they took in Dixon's condition.

I must look like the goddamn Elephant Man.

"You have EpiPens?" Dixon's voice had turned to sludge. It sounded wet and reedy passing over his vocal chords.

The kid blinked at him. He shook his head slightly.

"Fucking EpiPens! *Do. You. Have. Them?*"

The kid shook his head again but found his voice. "Habla español?"

Snot trickled down Dixon's chin and he could feel it hanging in rivulets like dog slobber. "You've gotta be . . . No, I don't abla fucking *espanyolll*!" He looked behind the counter. Cigarettes. Cigars. Chewing tobacco. Handwritten signs in Spanish hanging above the products. He motioned with his hand and made a buzzing sound.

Cashier boy looked at him like he was a stalk of cauliflower.

Dixon slammed the palm of his hand down on the counter. "Fucking . . . *MEDICO!* Emergencia. Allergi . . . *FUCK!*"

He wiped the snot slobber off his chin with his soaked sleeve, only succeeding in pulling away glistening threads. Dixon turned to go through the aisles to find the section of Tylenol, Band-Aids, and no-doze pills for truckers.

Donuts and pies. Bread. Coffee. Ketchup, mustard

and mayonnaise. One aisle over, Dixon saw the recognizable bottle of black-green Nyquil. He stumbled around the corner, almost knocking over a spin rack of sunglasses, and stopped at the medical section. Sweat dripped down his spine as Dixon scanned the shelves through squinted eyes. Sinus meds. Extra-Strength migraine pills. Hemorrhoid cream.

"Fuck. Fuck. *FUUUUCK!*" Dixon's voice was nothing but a croak and his breathing had turned to an outright wheeze. His stomach cramped up and he doubled over. Dixon turned from the shelves to the section of hanging packages. Bandages big and small. Icy Hot. Aspercreme.

The bell of the door jingled, and heavy footsteps run into the store. Dixon heard the recognizable metallic sound of a pistol being cocked.

"*Heyyyyy* there, spunky! Give me all the fucking money and you won't die a virgin."

Dixon dropped to a crouch and peeked around the aisle. A man in a gray ski mask was pointing a .38 revolver at the kid behind the counter. English speaking or not, the teen understood the language of a gun and looked ready to shit his pants. He popped the register and started handing over the cash.

Another stomach cramp hit Dixon like a spike in his gut and he sputtered with pain. He reached out to grab a rack to steady himself and knocked several boxes from the shelf.

The man with the gun turned. "Two for one special tonight." He kept the pistol trained on the cashier but took a few steps closer and Dixon looked up at him. "What the *fuck* happened to you, circus freak?" He glanced back at the cashier, then back to Dixon. "Nevermind. Don't really give a shit. Just hand me your wallet."

Dixon felt the world spin and he fell onto his side. The dirty floor was cool against his face and he stared, through the slits of his eyes, at the line of dust along the bottom of the shelving unit.

He was going to die in a shitty convenience store in the armpit of Arizona from a bee sting. *Fucksake.*

The bell on the door jingled and the man spun, aiming the pistol at the entrance.

Dixon turned his head to watch Andy walk down the aisle toward him. He was rubbing sleep from his eyes. He stopped and looked up at the man with the gun, then down at Dixon.

"Daddy?"

"Well *shiiiiiiit!* A family reunion! Lemme guess . . . " He waved the .38 at Andy and chuckled. "Got your looks from your momma?" The man's eyes were hard behind the ski mask. "Get over here, boy. Sit down beside your daddy. He was just about to give me his money."

It was like breathing through a straw. Dixon struggled to pull in a breath and noticed black spots at the corner of what little sight he had left. He reached out and held Andy's arm as the boy sat down. "Mr. Hugsy." The words were barely a whisper.

Andy's face scrunched up and he shook his head. "No, Daddy! I don't want to!"

"Do it . . . " Dixon could hardly swallow, and another stomach cramp racked his body.

Tears rolled down Andy's cheeks and then he squeezed his eyes shut tightly.

"Just give me your wallet and you can get back to whatever this—"

The overhead fluorescents crackled and went dark. The piss-yellow emergency lights came on. Dixon heard some kind of movement at the cash register and the .38 roared in the tight quarters. There was the thick sound of wet meat falling to the floor and Dixon saw the blurry inkblot splatter of blood against the wall of tobacco.

"*Haaaad* to fuckin' go and do something *stupid*, didn't ya?" He turned and knelt down to Dixon, patting his pockets down.

Andy opened his eyes. "I'm sorry Mister, but you're a bad man."

In the space behind Andy, Dixon watched the air begin to swirl, like mercury pooling together. It grew in size and thickness, towering above Andy until it reached the drop ceiling. It grew in density as Dixon watched it take the size of two refrigerators stacked one on top of the other.

Broad shoulders supported a taffy stretched head crested with a black derby hat. A face as smooth and white as fine china—void of wrinkles and eyebrows—held lidless eyes, a sharp triangle of a nose, and thin lips the color of raw liver. It stretched arms that reached over and beyond the tops of the aisles, and it trembled for a moment as it looked down. Cue ball eyes swiveled in their sockets and it opened its skewed gash of a mouth. Rows of teeth—thick as framing nails—lined the cavern, and they glistened in the yellow emergency light. It trembled again, and a rope of spit spilled out over its chin.

"Christ Almig—"

It moved like black silk, launching over Andy and cutting off Ski-mask's words. The man didn't even have time to scream. Dixon heard a violent thrashing and sloppy liquid sounds, cloth tearing, and the unmistakable noise of flesh being torn open. Blood didn't fall in gentle drops, it *splashed* onto the linoleum around Dixon's face, close enough he could feel the spatter on his skin and smell the copper.

Andy never moved, never even *flinched,* even as a pile of intestines fell to the floor with a wet mop *squelching* sound. Ski-mask's body followed, and Dixon could make out a hollowed rib cage, bones gleaming like bloody fork tines.

The air in front of him darkened and Dixon saw a bone white Silly Putty face lean close to his own. A sound like wind over road gravel whispered from the gaping mouth and Dixon could see the rows of spike teeth, now dark red and caked with bits of pink tissue. He closed his eyes and the world faded into oblivion.

✳✳✳

"How did you know how to do that?" Dixon glanced in the rearview mirror at Andy. The boy was staring out the window. "Andy?"

"I watched Mrs. Holicutt at daycare do it. My friend Billy Scavone got stung one day when we were playing soccer. His neck and face swelled up like a balloon and Mrs. Holicutt came running outside to help him. Travis said Billy's eyes looked like a Chinese person, but Billy's my friend and that wasn't nice." Andy turned from the window and looked at Dixon in the mirror. "Travis had an *accident* later that day on his bike and broke his arm."

"Where the hell did you even find the pen?"

"There was a First-Aid kit by the sodas. Nurse Holicutt told us about things like that."

Dixon shook his head. His throat wasn't completely normal, but when he breathed, it no longer felt like he was pulling air through a cocktail straw. Hell, even his eyes were starting to become unglued.

"You done good, kid." Dixon took a drink of the bottled water he'd stolen. He tossed a bag of beef jerky into the back seat. "Got you some more beef jerky. Or some chips if you want those instead. And water."

Dixon spun the cap on his own water and set the bottle down. "Andy, the other thing that happened . . . "

"I don't want to talk about that." He turned to stare out at the dark desert again.

"Damn it, Andy, it's something we—"

"That's a bad word."

"*Ahhhh* shit, I—"

"That, too."

"*Fucking hell!*"

"You say a lot of bad words."

"It's just how grownups talk, okay?"

"Mommy doesn't say bad words."

Dixon gritted his teeth. "Well that's 'cause after Mommy got off the smack and found God, she got a big stick up her—"

"Did you steal that money, Daddy?"

Dixon bit his lip and jerked the car to the side of the road, skidding to a stop. He threw it in park, took a deep breath, and turned around in the seat. "Steal . . . did I *steallll* the money? Look, they weren't going to be using it. We *need* this money, Andy."

"And the gun?"

Dixon glanced over at the passenger side. Blood spattered cash was crumpled on the seat and the silver revolver rested on top. "I took the pistol, too. So what? Sometimes, you do what you need to do."

"Even the snacks?"

"Yes, Andy, even the snacks. I stole the snacks and the money and took the gun. Yesterday, I stole gas twice and ... " He ran his hand over his head. Son or not, Dixon could feel his blood getting hot. "Are we fuckin' done with confession time now? Can we get back on the road?" Dixon took another deep breath, forcing himself to calm down. It was like having a mini Pope as a co-pilot, though Dixon thought even the Pope was a little more relaxed on the fucking rules.

"Stealing is bad." Andy put the bag of beef jerky down on the seat beside him as if it was dirty. "I miss Mommy."

"I know."

"I'm sorry, Daddy."

"It's okay."

"No, Daddy. I'm sorry. But you're a bad, bad man."

Dixon saw a flutter of movement on the passenger side of the car—swirls of liquid onyx taking shape. A canyon of jagged teeth appeared in the middle of a misshapen dough-white face. The smile grew wider and Dixon turned away to look in the rearview mirror.

Andy's eyes were squeezed tightly shut.

SWAMP DOG

LISA KRÖGER

THERE ARE TWO ways to get to The Yellow Store.

One is by turning down Vic Taylor Road, off Louisiana Highway 90. The road isn't paved. It's rocky and often turns to mud in the rainy season. People don't turn down Vic Taylor unless they are lost, in need of direction.

The other is by boat, by way of Pearl River.

Most people take a boat. Most people who come to The Yellow Store are looking for it.

It's why I came.

✳✳✳

You are not who you used to be.

This has become my mantra—I've become the kind of woman with a mantra. And I repeat those eight words from when I wake up to when I go to sleep, if I sleep. Hell, I probably repeat those words in my sleep too, though I have no one to tell me if I do or not.

I am repeating those words under my breath as I take the night's trash bag out to the green dumpster at the other end of the parking lot. I have to unlock a chain link fence to get to it, an act that I've learned to do with one hand.

The bag is heavy with bottles, and the dumpster is ripe with three-day-old trash, fryer oil baked in the Gulf Coast summer sun. But there is something beneath it, lingering. A soured sweetness. It's what interests me.

I climb to the top of the dumpster and push my body over. My legs are stronger than they once were. The running has done its job. I'm leaner.

You made me meaner.

My arms are still weak. My shoulders will never be stronger than this, no matter how many planks, burpees, push-ups I do. The right one screams as I push my full weight on it to get into the stinking box. I sink into a mound of trash bags. Something wiggles next to my left leg. I reach down without even looking and pull up a small raccoon.

I was expecting a rat and nearly fall backwards.

The thing hisses at me, and I toss it outside. It lands with a thump and a crack, but I hear the damn thing skittering away, its long toes scratching at the dirt.

I paw my way through the debris, not finding what I'm looking for.

✢ ✢ ✢

I ride my blue bicycle, with a brown basket tied to the front, home, the night quiet. The night dark. I'm looking for dead things, dead animals.

Or more precisely, I'm looking for the thing that may have killed them.

Morning comes soon. And I ride back to The Yellow Store.

A bicycle is not as fast as a car, and it's rather impractical in this heat. But no one can hide in the back seat. And I can quickly veer into the dark pine woods if someone follows me home. I can come up quietly too. No sound of an engine turning on to startle anyone into watching.

I need to be invisible, or close to it.

At The Yellow Store, I work the register, for what it is. The boaters stop for gas. I take their money when they want chicken on a stick or corn nuggets.

It's easy.

My name tag says Lucy.

It's not my name. I think they know that. The man who hired me didn't ask too many questions. I get paid in cash. He gives me hours when I need them, doesn't question when I'm not here. Most around here are like that.

He's nice—he leaves me alone.

Every day, I watch the door open, the tin-can wind chimes blow together, metal against metal. The men who come here are all the same. Quiet. Steel-jawed. White tee shirt turned yellow from sweat and brackish water. They walk past the dusty fake feathers, hanging on a spider-webbed plastic dreamcatcher. They don't look at the painted sea shells. They don't look at me. I've worked hard to keep it that way.

I think of you when the big ones come in. The ones who have already had too much to drink. The ones who think they are funny and laugh too loud when they talk to their friends. They usually only notice me when they throw the bag of Zapp's potato chips on the counter in front of me. Lick their lips. Lean in. Look at my chest, even though I've bound it in bandages. Flat as a pancake.

I said I wasn't who I once was.

You wouldn't know me anymore.

My hair is brown too. Cut to my ears. It looks thin,

stringy. I didn't realize I was losing so much at the top. It's stress, most likely. My poor diet. Leftovers that have been sitting under the heater lamps all day. The ones that were going to be thrown away. The grease has left me skinny. But with a flabby paunch of a belly.

Mr. Woodson, I've let myself go, and I laugh every time I think about what you would say about me now.

✻✻✻

I haven't stayed in any place as long as this one. Not since I left your house. But I'm close. I can feel it. I can't let my guard down. Not now. Not when I've almost found it.

The night is for hunters.

I stop my bike at a familiar grease spot on the road. This time a beaver. Usually it's a coon. Still, I let the bicycle drop, and I walk over to the dead animal. It looks whole, save for a velvet strip of deep red oozing from the underside. A car. Probably didn't even know it nicked the animal.

They never know how deeply they hurt you.

You never knew how deeply you hurt me.

A shadow moves through the trees. I pause, watching. The sun will be up soon and I have to wait. Tomorrow.

✻✻✻

I cycle through the early-morning air. Even this early, it's still sticky hot out. My tee shirt is sweat-slicked to my skin, chaffing under my arms. The skin rubs red-raw with each pump of my legs. Up, down. Scratch, red. I'll be bleeding by the time I get home.

The blood always makes me think—not of you, Mr. Woodson, you'll be disappointed to know—but of me, of who I was. Mrs. Ada Woodson.

A list of adjectives. Petite, blonde. Housewife. Perfect.

I know what everyone else saw when they looked at me. A beautiful wife. A happy wife. I know what they saw because I carefully crafted my mask every day. My mask of makeup to hide the bruises, the dark circles under my eyes from tear-stained nights. The long sleeves, even in the heat of summer. They thought it was modesty. They spoke about me, their comments like a Greek chorus.

"There's a woman who knows how to dress."

"Classy but covered up."

"Proof you don't have to show off your body to be beautiful."

They saw a pinnacle of Southern Christian virtue when they looked at me. Do you realize what a feat that was? I was covering up your mess on my body all the while making them think I was something to be envied.

It was my power. But it wasn't enough.

They saw the mask, but I saw the truth.

At home, I felt the pain in my side as I peeled off the clothes. I winced when I passed the brush through my hair. You always did prefer the back of the head, the places where the black and blue wouldn't show.

But what did you see?

A wife? A partner? A prize? A possession? A punching bag?

Whatever I was to you, I know you aren't finished with me yet.

I know this to be true because you always came back to finish what you started. When you pushed me so hard that I stumbled backward into our cheap Walmart bookshelf, and books rained down on me, you grabbed me by hair to pull me back up again.

When you hit the back of my head so hard with the flat of your palm, so hard that I saw stars and went to my knees, you kicked my ribs. You continued to kick my ribs until we both heard a crack. And you kicked one last time, sending blinding white pain.

You tackled me to the ground. You hit my head until I blacked out and you were still hitting me when I woke. That time, my shoulder tore and my scapula bone winged out like an angel sprouting wings.

You told my friends that I had a stomach flu. I got excited texts asking if I might be pregnant.

I had become too good at the mask.

No more.

***

The next night, I close shop and cycle to the spot where I saw the shadow man. The air is different. Thicker. It smells of mildewed earth and animal, pungent and wild.

I wait as the moon rises. It's full tonight, the pine woods lit up as if under a disco ball, fragmented light scattered around the sandy dirt of the forest floor. I walk until the land gets marshy, wet and soft beneath my feet. Bayou land.

I walk carefully, watching for knotty logs that may be gators in disguise.

I see none. They are gone from here. They know a bigger hunter is on the stalk.

I pull a pocket knife, the one with the engraved, pearl-inlaid handle, the one I took from you the night I left. For protection, I thought. But also, to keep us connected.

Because now I'm not through with you.

I run the blade across my left palm. It hurts worse

than I thought it would. I whimper and bite into my lip, but I get it done anyway. I watch as the deep red blood pushes up from the stinging flap of skin. My palm aches. I turn it over, let the blood hit the dirt beneath. I hold it out and let the scent of it drift through the sultry air.

Soon, I hear the crunching of feet, of twigs snapping. It is here.

✷✷✷

The man who hired me at The Yellow Store told me that there was a *rougarou* here. Killed his dog, he said. Not a gator neither, he'd assured me. Gator would've dragged the body away to the water. A rougarou, though. It devours from the inside out, leaving the tell-tale claw marks.

He'd taken pictures of the mutilated half-animal that was once his dog. He'd shown me.

Now the thing—the rougarou—was standing before me. A beast-man walking on two muscular legs. It could've just been a fur-covered man were it not for the massive shoulders, twice the size of a man's, making its upper body hunched over, as if the thing were just about to drop and gallop ahead on all fours. It had the thick neck of a man, but its head was smaller, narrowing to a point at its long dog-snout.

The thing stank to high heaven.

It looked at me and took a step back. I'd heard these things preferred to hunt smaller game. They didn't often take humans. And when they did, they didn't leave any behind. If they don't devour human prey completely, then a new rougarou is born.

The exchange of blood.

I held out my blood-soaked hand, and the thing

stopped, turning its head to the side, as if it were considering my offering.

I waved it, hoping the scent would entice. When it didn't move, I squeezed my left hand into a fist, trying to get more blood to spill.

The thing looked at me and turned, with almost a sigh. As it took a step away, panic filled me. This was my chance, and I couldn't let it slip through my fingers. Not now.

"Wait!" The word was a scream in my head, but it emerged from my mouth as a dry and hoarse whisper.

The thing turned to me, looked over its shoulder.

I swiped my bloody hand across my neck, spreading as much of the sticky liquid from my wound as I could.

"Please," I said. "Please."

The thing looked at me for a moment, and I thought I saw understanding in its eyes. It pounced, the full force of it knocking me back.

The world went black.

✳✳✳

There are two ways to get to The Yellow Store.

I'm hoping that you, Mr. Woodson, will take the road. It's harder to find. But I'll smell you coming. I'll be ready.

NO EXIT

ORRIN GREY

THE LANDSCAPE OF western Kansas lends itself well to conspiracy theories and apocalyptic visions. The plains, vast and windswept, bending imperceptibly to the horizon. The small towns, unmoored from the highway, like ships cast adrift on a fathomless sea of grain, with silos and brick church steeples their only masts.

I saw a lot of it as my parents drove me back and forth after the divorce—my mom moved to Kansas City, my dad to a little town north of Boulder. "The kind of place where you can still get your teeth knocked out by a cowboy, if you put your mind to it," he liked to say. They split custody, so I spent a lot of time in the passenger seat of one car or another, driving those long, blank miles that stretched between the relative civilization of Topeka and Denver.

I spent the school year with my mom, my dad driving into town for the occasional weekend, when we would stay in a hotel and eat ice cream and waffles for just about every meal. During the summer or on holiday breaks, he would pick me up and take me west, stopping at gas stations along the way to buy slushies—"Don't tell your mom," with a conspiratorial wink in my direction—or at the dinosaur museum in Fort Hays. When mom was driving me back, it was never anything but my forehead pressed against the cool window glass, watching the alternating signs condemning abortion, promising eternal damnation, or advertising sex shops.

When I was a little girl, we had lived in one of those tiny towns that we passed along I-70, with their football fields pressed tight up against the highway. I could remember a house and a yard, a tire swing hanging from the branches of a tree, the golden sunlight and skin-flaying wind that came with life out in the western plains. I could remember my older sister Danielle, only barely. She was a blur of brown hair and freckles, as tall as my mom, with a barking laugh that seemed to echo.

I was six years old when she died, and my parents divorced within seven months. Years later, I would look up the divorce rates for couples who have lost a child and find that it was much lower than I had been led to believe by counselors and self-help books. Only about sixteen percent, and most of them said that there were problems in the marriage long before the child died. Were there problems in my parents' marriage? I never asked and they never told me.

Of course, Danielle didn't just die, either. That would have been one thing. This was something much worse.

***

While snake handlers and the like tend to stay down in Oklahoma and farther south, western Kansas has been home to more than its fair share of fire-and-brimstone revivals, to preachers spewing admonitions about the end of days, not to mention less prosaic cults. The people who planned the bombings of abortion clinics in Wichita in 1993 got their start here, and so did Edward Murray and his "dynamo-electric messiah," and the Increase Brothers, who claimed that the Garden of Eden had, in fact, been located just a few miles outside of the little town of Lebanon, Kansas.

And, of course, most infamously, Damien Hesher and the Spiritus Aetum Sperarum, which Hesher claimed translated to the Breath of the Spheres, though that's probably a little loose. The Spiritus would have been a nothing cult, a footnote in the history of the region's odd beliefs, had it not been for one afternoon in 1987, when Hesher and a bunch of his cronies kidnapped a bus full of seven high school kids and their coach as it was on its way back from a debate championship in Manhattan, Kansas. One of those kids was Danielle.

Hesher and his followers forced her and the others into a beat-up RV, leaving the bus driver where he sat on the shoulder of I-70, with the added gift of a sucking chest wound from a double-barrel shotgun. Then they drove to a little rest stop west of Topeka, situated on a limestone outcropping where I-70 split, its top crowned with spidery scrub trees.

That rest stop was where my sister died, and we drove past it every time my parents ferried me back and forth from Kansas City to Colorado. By that time, though, the turnoff leading to it had been stoppered with blue wooden sawhorses and concrete blocks that had previously been highway dividers; the brown sign that once said "Rest Stop" plastered over with other official signage, white with black letters spelling out two simple words: NO EXIT.

✳✳✳

Maybe it would have been enough if Hesher and his followers had just killed the handful of kids they took from that bus. Certainly, it would have made the national news, maybe even gotten a few books written about it. But it probably wouldn't have closed down the rest stop forever. It took something special for that.

The kids weren't just killed. They were torn apart. Limbs and guts and heads and whatever else strewn all over the place, like something from a Halloween haunted house. They say that the blood soaked into the parking area and wouldn't ever come clean.

At least one of the kids threw themselves from the limestone cliff and smashed on the rocks below rather than face whatever reckoning was taking place at that rest stop. The coach managed to crawl some twenty yards from the parked RV where the slaughter began, albeit leaving parts of his legs behind as he did.

The crime scene photos were all dark and blurry. They reminded me of photos of bigfoot or cattle mutilations; nothing in them identifiable except by its vague shape. The RV parked in the lot of the rest stop, and on its door, painted in what looked like blood, an image of a circle being pierced by a line from above.

Not all the bodies were ever even accounted for, and there was a period of time when the police entertained the idea that some of the kids had managed to escape, that they might just show up, bloodstained and in shock, standing by the side of the highway. A time when Danielle was simply "missing" instead of "presumed dead."

It's impossible not to wonder how the story would have gone differently if Hesher and his crew had survived to stand trial, but when authorities arrived they found Hesher and all of his followers dead inside the RV, symbols carved into their skin, their throats cut.

"Murder/suicide" was the official conclusion, though I found a coroner's report that had been excised from the public record—performed, according to the official account, by a junior medical examiner who had been too shaken by the grisly scene to render an accurate verdict—that said Hesher and his people had died sometime *before* most of the other victims.

Even leaving that report aside, it was difficult to square up the crime scene with the murders themselves. Though obvious acts of cannibalism had been performed on the victims, no human remains were found in the digestive tracts of either Hesher or his followers. For a while, the authorities sought other accomplices who had fled the scene rather than participate in the cult's mass suicide, eventually chalking the partially-devoured state of the bodies up to the depredations of scavengers.

My parents never talked about what happened—not with reporters, and not with me. If they ever talked about it between themselves—as I know they must have—I never overheard it. I would wonder later if they were trying to protect me by never speaking of it. The Satanic Panic was still going strong when the murders were committed, and there was a media frenzy surrounding the slaughter for months, with local and national news stations trotting out stories of animal sacrifices, kidnappings that predated the murders, and, of course, other, more salacious stuff. A few years later, *Unsolved Mysteries* even ran a segment and called my parents, who refused to comment or appear on the show.

Being in the crosshairs of that kind of hyperbolic

attention would be hard enough on grieving parents, let alone a confused kid. Maybe by the time public interest in the murders faded, my parents had decided that it was easier to ignore what had happened than it was to face it, leaving me alone to take the opposite route.

The proximity of the murders was what kept me at KU when I went to college, even though my dad could have gotten me reduced tuition at CU Boulder, where he was teaching by then. From KU, I could go around to those local stations that were still extant and go through their archives for any old footage about the murders. I probably read every newspaper article ever printed on the subject; police reports, autopsies, anything that I could get my hands on.

When my parents divorced, my mom switched my name and hers back to her maiden name, and though she changed hers again when she married a man named Dale years later, I kept the old one, so there was nothing left to tie me to Danielle in most peoples' eyes. I could check out books about the murders from the library, request newspaper stories on microfiche, ask around at news stations, and nobody would think I was anything but a morbid kid with a curiosity about a grisly local crime that had taken on the proportions of urban myth.

Most of the time, anyone who reported on the killings was content to conjecture wildly about Hesher's motives and the beliefs and practices of the Spiritus Aetum Sperarum. Hardly anyone bothered to read the admittedly nigh-unreadable book that Hesher had written and self-published, under the unhelpful title *Wizard's Ashes*.

The book cover was simple, dominated by a drawing of a red circle being pierced by a line from above, done in a style like calligraphy. That was on the original edition. After the murders, it was picked back up by a small press called Hex Books and reissued under a new title—*The Breath of the Spheres: Secrets of the Spiritus Aetum Sperarum*—which attempted to market it as a "true" book of dark spirituality, in order to cash in on the notoriety generated by Hesher's crimes. That book's cover featured a blurry and distorted photo of Hesher himself, as he had been found by police when they raided the RV: A cow skull on his head that had been denuded of its horns and carved out inside so that it covered his face like a mask.

That was the version I read, complete with typographical errors and pages that didn't always line up correctly with the margins. It contained a brief, and completely fictitious, biographical sketch of Damien Hesher in the "About the Author" portion at the back of the book. In reality, Damien Hesher had been born in Topeka, and had lived his entire life in Kansas. Starting out as Jeremy Miller, he had legally changed his name when he turned twenty-one, the same time he started the Spiritus Aetum Sperarum. All that I learned from other sources. From his book, I learned that the place where my sister was murdered hadn't been chosen randomly.

While Hesher's book didn't lay out the specifics of the killing spree, it was full of distressing hints. Hesher was clearly obsessed with the rest stop, which he referred to in the book not only by number but by latitude and longitude. He called it a "thin place," and said that it was somewhere that "communion" was possible, if the proper sacrifice was on hand.

According to Hesher, it wasn't the first time that blood had been spilled on that very ground. In the book he told a story about a family called the Millers—no accident, perhaps, that they shared his own born surname—who had diverged from the Oregon trail and found themselves on that same limestone outcropping where the rest stop would eventually be built.

By Hesher's account, their wagon wheel broke on that spot and they didn't have another one to replace it. What led them from that predicament to what came next is unclear, but he wrote that they took the broken wheel and laid it on the ground, and from there they drew lines, extending the spokes of the wheel outward and outward, decorating them with orbs, sometimes drawn in the dirt, sometimes represented by the smoothest rocks they could find in the surrounding cliffs and gullies. Then, they sat down among the lines and spheres, and they ate themselves. Not the desperate, no-other-choice cannibalism of the Donner party. Intentional, premeditated anthropophagy.

The *why* of it was tougher to pin down than the what. Hesher's writing was rambling, inconsistent, littered with typos and odd grammatical choices, the voice constantly changing, as though the book had been written by diverse hands. What was clear was that Hesher believed that the earth was filled with what he sometimes called "abysses" and other times "spheres."

"Not hollow," he wrote, "as an egg might be hollow, but carved out, digged full of holes, as a cork, or a nest." There was no heaven or hell, according to Hesher. No higher power, and no lower one, but in these holes there were *entities* who could do things, and sometimes they would whisper to those of us who lived above, as they had to the Millers, as they did to him.

These were what he was planning to "commune" with when he killed my sister and her classmates. "Eternity is a cruel thing," he wrote, "but long lastingness is within our grasp, if we are willing to sacrifice much. Being a man is a thing that we can easily cast off, if we are willing to reach past our own bodies to what lies beneath.

"What scuttles in the shadows when the light of the sun is turned off? Why would we dream that we have seen but the tip of its great limb? It is in the shadow of the world, and it is in the shadow of our hearts. If we open ourselves up to the breath of the abyss, we will hear it whisper our name."

***

Given my preoccupation with the circumstances of Danielle's death, I don't know why it took me so long to go to the crime scene. By the time I did I had graduated from college, taking a job as a file clerk at a Kansas City law firm, pushing wheeled carts down long aisles in the dim basement of a tall building. My dad had been in and out of the hospital with colon cancer, and I had driven my old Passat out to Boulder easily more than a dozen times to visit him, passing by the rest stop and the NO EXIT sign each time I did.

I think maybe I put off visiting it because I knew that there wouldn't be anything left after that. Danielle was gone, Hesher and his people were in the ground. I had read everything I could find, watched everything there was to watch. My parents never spoke about it, and I never got up the nerve to ask. The rest stop would be the last place I could go to feel closer to Danielle, to make her something more than a fading memory.

"Legend tripping" is what they call it, I guess, and I could tell before I saw much else that I wasn't the first to make the journey. I moved the blue painted sawhorses but parked my Passat next to the chunks of concrete, hiking the rest of the way up to the top of the limestone hill, topped with a line of scrub trees that circled it like a crown.

From the highway, the restroom building and the rotted remains of the picnic shelters didn't look much different from their brethren at other, less-neglected stops. Up close, though, I could see that they had been visited by graffiti in all its varied forms, from pentagrams and inverted crosses to swastikas, declarations of love, and crude drawings of male and female genitalia.

Some aspiring graffiti artist had even done their homework. A red circle pierced by a line was spray-painted onto the sidewalk directly in front of the restrooms, in the spot where you would stand to look at the map behind the plexiglass—if such a map were still present, instead of an empty box with webs in the corners and the dried-up bodies of dead spiders collecting at the bottom.

In the light of the setting sun, I could see stains on the overgrown parking lot, though whether they were made by oil or blood it was impossible to tell. Some of the picnic shelters were missing their roofs, others their picnic tables. All of them had suffered more from the years of neglect than the restrooms had, the wood splintering and breaking apart while the tan brick of the restroom building simply faded.

The door marked "WOMEN" was oddly difficult to open—like there was something behind it, holding it shut, but not anything substantial. Shining my flashlight into the dark on the other side, I saw why.

The restroom had probably never been very tidy or welcoming. It was the same as the ones in every other rest stop I had ever visited; concrete floors, windows set high in the walls to let in what little light could force its way past the dust-coated plexiglass, a trio of metal stalls and boxy troughs for sinks. I knew such rest stop bathrooms well from my many pilgrimages along I-70 and was familiar with them as homes for dead leaves, dead bugs, cobwebs, and dust. But this one was positively *festooned* with spider webs.

It was as if the decorator for an old Gothic horror film had gone to town but had never been told to stop. The webs filled the room with such proliferation as to make no sense. No insect could ever penetrate them deeply enough for any but the ones nearest the door to catch any prey, and yet they filled every space, the strands sometimes the monofilament thickness that I was used to in spider's webs, other times reaching a ropy girth that called to mind alien slime or the webs of mutant spiders from the movies.

These were what had made forcing the door open feel like fighting my way past marshmallow fluff, and as I flashed my light across the sticky strands, I thought I saw something writhing in their depths. Something much too big to be an insect, and too malformed to be human. It let out a mewling sound, and I stumbled back, the door swinging shut behind me.

Or had I gone through a door, after all? The light on the other side seemed changed in some subtle way, the setting sun painting the sky with the radiation glow of a post-apocalyptic future. That wasn't all that had changed, either. There was an RV in the parking lot that hadn't been there before. One that looked all-too familiar, down to the circle being pierced by the line daubed onto the door in something too dark to be paint.

All around me, it seemed that the trees were moving closer whenever I wasn't looking. I imagined them turning upside-down, their branches becoming spidery legs on which they crept nearer, only to plant themselves again, head down in the dirt, whenever my eyes swept across them. For all that I told myself it was a panic response, a trick of the mind, there was no denying that when I looked again what had been thirty paces from the picnic shelters became twenty, twenty became ten.

With the trees closing in, I don't know why I thought the RV was a safer place to be, but I found myself standing in front of its door nevertheless.

On the other side I could hear sounds. Voices whispering, and something else. The sound of a dozen blades sawing flesh. The door had a handle, the kind that turns downward, a line piercing a circle into the earth, and I turned it and the door opened outward, and from inside came the reptile house smell of pennies and fresh soil.

Inside was Damien Hesher. On his head he wore that same cow skull, its teeth and horns missing, transforming it into something else, the helmet of a cyclops, the head of an insect. On his hands he wore claws made from the bones of small animals; the same claws he had used, according to the coroner's report, to tear out his own throat, though I saw now that those claws were unstained by blood.

His neck was still a bloody, ragged wound, though something now moved inside it, working open and closed. "Eternity is a cruel thing," are the only words he said to me, the sounds coming not from where his mouth should have been, but from the ragged hole in his neck. Then *they* came for him.

The floor of the RV opened like a series of trap doors held tight by webbing, the seams invisible until triggered. Black limbs rose up from the floor, scuttling bodies like the ones I had imagined attached to the spidery trees. They embraced Damien Hesher, taking him back with them to wherever it was he now resided.

The hand that he reached out toward me was not threatening but supplicating. Beneath those claws of bone, the pad of his hand was pink and soft. I felt sorry for him, this man who had thought he could peer into a dark well and not be frightened by what he saw. I stumbled back, as more of the dark shapes came surging up from the glowing trap doors, and felt a hand fall on my shoulder.

She stood behind me, still as tall as my mom. She wore the same jeans and hoodie that she had worn when she disappeared, but the hand that touched me wasn't anything I recognized, and in the dark shadows of that hood her eyes seemed to glitter, and a seam split her face, running up her neck, up her chin. Her smile was the same, though, and she said my name as my arms went around her and I pressed my face into her shoulder, realizing only as I did so that I had gotten to be just as tall as her, over the years.

When I could no longer feel her arms around me, I opened my eyes, and found myself standing in the parking lot of the rest stop, my shoes on the asphalt. The RV was gone. The sun had set completely, and the night sky was filled with stars, the stunted trees having retreated to their usual distance, though I had the feeling it was only a temporary armistice, not a permanent peace.

When I got back to my Passat and sat down in the driver's seat, I felt something crinkle in my back pocket. Pulling it out, I found a faded polaroid of me and Danielle. I was sitting in front of her on the brass bed I had when I was little, and she was braiding my hair and smiling, her face suddenly clarified in the blur of my memory.

Looking up, I thought I saw her watching me from the tree line, those black eyes sparkling, but when I shut off the dome light there was nothing there. Just the fading hint of a door closing in the rocky cliffside, maybe, nothing more.

THE LONG WHITE LINE

MICHAEL BAILEY

"That saying, about how you always kill the thing you love, well, it works both ways."—Chuck Palahniuk

"THEY ALWAYS HUG the line," Tracie said, pointing to whatever black creature had died on the side of the road, and then we smelled it. Tracie drove, steered with her knees for a moment and tapped a snort of coke from a small glass vial to the underside of her pinky nail. She took in the drug, wiped her nose with her fingertips. Sniffed. She offered me the vial. I shook my head no and watched her slip it into her black jeans. "The long white line," she said, batting her hands against the steering wheel. The radio was off, but she had some song in her head.

I'd had too much to drink and avoided recreational drugs.

"Don't you wanna know why?" Tracie said, watching me and not the road.

We'd had sex in the car, under a streetlamp. I was thinking about that, about the bra on the floorboard, her torn underwear on the middle console. She'd used me, I knew, had finished and climbed off before I could and slid naked into her jeans, started the car and drove.

"Don't I wanna know what?

"Why they always hug the line?"

Cars hit them, I told her, all the damn time: chipmunks, squirrels, skunks, raccoons, deer; cars hit them as they tried crossing from one side to the other, the impact forcing them forward and to the side of the road. It was an odd conversation to have after what we'd done. We were late, a few hours past when I told my dad I'd be home, and he'd be passed out on the couch, I knew, but I'd never been out so late on a school night, and we were discussing roadkill. We should have been talking about us, about our plans after we graduated.

"Kids?"

"Huh?"

"You think kids ever get hit?"

Sometimes, I told her, or so I guessed. There was always debris on the side of the road, like old shoes—always one and never two—and clothes, toys, a helmet, a crumpled bike, or a stroller, broken glass and bumpers and hubcaps and ash from flares and red taillight remnants from past accidents. Kids probably got hit now and again.

"Why, have you ever seen a kid on the side of the road? Dead, I mean."

"I don't know," she said, tapping the wheel. "Maybe."

"What do you mean, maybe?"

"It may have been a doll."

"You didn't stop to check?"

"My mom was driving, and I think it was a doll. She said it was a doll."

I let that sink in and adjusted in my seat. It was almost morning and we were going seventy, at *least*, and I expected at any second for something to jump out in front of us from either side of the road, an animal with reflective eyes, a damn person even, a child ...

"Dead things are always hugging the white line," Tracie said. "What mom hit was already in the road. Sounded plastic. I remember looking back. Looked like a doll, like one of those old ones in white frilly dresses with ceramic faces, you know?"

Jesus, I thought, and let her talk, let the drugs talk. Her eyes were shifty.

"Worst I ever hit was a squirrel," she said. "I remember the sound."

I'd hit a deer once, or the deer had hit me, but I didn't tell her that. Put a nice dent into my front right fender and broke the headlight on that side, but the deer had lived—at least for a while—and had sprung off into the night. I still remember the adrenaline rush I felt when pulling over, the blood and hunk of pelt on the grill. There were two: a doe and a buck, jumping either into or out of my way that night, and I'd hit the doe.

"Sometimes you see squirrels in the middle of the road, or chipmunks," Tracie said, "but the bigger things, they always hug the white line."

I couldn't help but think about the coke she'd snorted. The first time I saw her with any, she'd been straddling the toilet at her parents' house. They were out on one of those parent date night things and Tracie wasn't supposed to have anyone over, especially boys, so of course she invited me over so we could fool around. I'd knocked on the door, no one answered, and it was unlocked so I went inside. I found her in the bathroom snorting a credit card cut line from the back of the tank. *Want some?* she'd said, holding out a rolled dollar bill, but I shook my head *no* because I'd never done drugs, had never *seen* any before meeting Tracie. I'd only drank.

"My older sister," she said, no longer tapping, the song in her head over, "she told me once, a long time ago when I was still in kindergarten or maybe preschool, that animals came to the road for warmth, mostly at night, because the sun beat down on its black surface all day and at night the heat drew them to the roads, and that that's why so many animals were drawn there. Everything in this world dies alone. It makes sense. If I were an animal and about to die, I'd come to the roads. I'd be drawn to the warmth."

I imagined a single-file procession of animals, their cold and dying bodies wanting something more before passing on to the great beyond . . . vultures waiting on fence posts.

"You'd hug the long white line?"

"I would."

And it sounds cliché as all get out, but that's when we hit something, or something hit us, something large—a deer, a dog, a coyote, a person—smashing into the front bumper and tumbling over the hood, caving in and spiderwebbing the windshield. A cacophony of noise, as if someone were pummeling the car from front to back with giant fists and then it was over.

I'd been looking at Tracie and she'd been looking at me, the car apparently pulling ever so slowly to the side of the road, the tires grating over the rumble strips. The noise had pulled our attention back to the road and we were riding that white line for who knows how long, the car half on the asphalt and half in the gravel and Tracie braked, and the car skidded, fishtailed, jumped back onto the road, but she'd kept going. We'd slowed to fifty or sixty but kept going.

Jesus, I thought and looked over my shoulder. The road behind us was red-illuminated-black, like the world looks when closing your eyes against the sun.

The shape of something on the side of the road shrank with distance.

"Stop," I said. "Stop the *car*, Tracie!"

She nodded in agreement, these little short, rapid nods, and her shaky hands pulled the steering wheel clockwise until we were on the shoulder.

"What was that?" she asked. "What was that, what was—?"

"I don't know just stop the car," I said, like one giant word.

When we stopped, she let go of the wheel and looked to her trembling hands, which opened and closed and opened and closed. She reached for a pack of Marlboro Lights in the center console, removed a cigarette and tried to light it with a Bic; she flicked the sparkwheel three or four times before giving up and throwing all of it to the floor.

I unbuckled and opened my door, but just sat there, the car chiming.

We stared at each other.

She was high as fuck, her pupils dilated, her nose red and sniffling.

Tracie reached into her pocket and pulled out the vial and I thought she was going to take another hit, and I probably would have let her, but she squeezed the vial in her fist and threw it out the driver's side window as hard as she could. She pulled another cigarette from the pack on the floor and was able to light it this time, held it out to me, and for some reason I took a long drag, although I'd never smoked before, the smoke tasting like I felt.

What hit us had smashed her radiator; steam rose like an apparition from the hood.

Splatters of red filled the broken windshield, but not a lot.

"My parents are going to kill me," Tracie said.

The thing behind us had crawled closer. OBJECTS IN THE MIRROR ARE CLOSER THAN THEY APPEAR the side mirror read, but the thing in the road was definitely closer, with something like an arm now stretched out in front of it. A black moving shape in the dark, irradiated by taillights.

"It's still alive," I said, coughing.

Tracie turned around, said, "What is it?" and we both stared.

She got out first, and then I followed.

It was crawling toward us; not an animal, but a person.

"Oh my god!" she said, cupping her mouth.

I tried calling for help, but my cell phone didn't have signal this far out from town and Tracie's phone was dead and she didn't have a charger. We were stuck in a bad situation.

Whoever we'd hit, we'd hit him or her going who knows how fast—*sixty-five, seventy, had we slowed to fifty?*

He or she wasn't crawling toward us, we soon realized, but convulsing into spasms, his or her arm twitching against the road, and as we drew closer, we discovered the body was so mangled it was impossible to discern male from female. Its face smashed into the road, arms hugging the white line, his or her clothes mostly black, like Tracie's, but seeping, the body like a ragdoll, the fingers on the most outstretched hand clenching and unclenching until finally still. The body was small, like us, perhaps a fellow student at our high school.

I threw up right there, onto the asphalt.

Tracie didn't say anything, just kept looking at the body and saying *Oh my god* over and over again, like a mantra.

The road was dead. We hadn't passed a single car in either direction all night. We waited for what seemed hours, neither of us knowing what to do. No one ever came to our rescue, and we were about a half-hour drive to either of our homes, much too far to walk.

She found the vial of coke she'd thrown out of the car, unbroken, and after hesitating she bent down and picked it up, gave me a guilty look, and slipped it into her jeans.

"We need to do something," she said.

"I *know* we need to do something," I said, "but *what*?"

The mutual idea was to move the body away from the road, so we each grabbed a leg and pulled, the body hesitant against the road, arms dangling behind like streamers. The non-mutual idea was to keep going, deep into the woods, and so we kept going, pulling the body over pine needles and fallen branches and rocks until we were under a canopy of darkness. And we conspired to keep between us what had happened, to restart the car if it could restart and to let the engine overheat as we rolled into town. *We'd hit a deer*, we'd say, and of course everyone would believe us, because it happened all the time on this particular stretch of road.

We were far into the woods, using what little light my cell phone offered to lead us through the dark, and covering the body with branches when Tracie screamed. She'd accidentally touched the person's hand, tripped over a rock while backpedaling, and fell onto her ass.

"She has the same ring as me," Tracie said.

"Everyone has mood rings," I said, and in the dark her mood looked black.

Neither of us recognized the hand, although the fingers were delicate and for the first time I realized the nails were manicured. We'd hit a teenage girl.

"I need to get out of here," Tracie said, her words convincing enough to follow. "I need to get out of here, get me out of here!"

Something snapped in the woods and it was enough to get us moving.

I led us back the way I thought we came, through bushes and tall grass, but Tracie's car wasn't waiting for us at the road, no headlights or taillights in either direction.

"Where's my car?" she asked, but I didn't know.

No blood on the road.

"We must have walked farther out than I thought."

"So which way?" she said, but I didn't know that, either.

We walked what seemed north for a quarter mile or so, and then turned back. It was a dark and winding road, but there's no way we could have missed the car; every damn turn seemed the same, especially at night. We walked back for what seemed another quarter mile, but everything looked so familiar, and so we kept on walking.

"Where the hell's the car?" Tracie said, nearly frantic, her words like static.

Suddenly there were headlights around the next corner.

Tracie stuck out her thumb, and then thought aloud, "Oh shit, what do we tell them? What do we tell them?"

"We tell them our car broke down and ask for a ride,"

I said, and it wasn't a lie, but what if they'd seen Tracie's car? What if they'd already seen the accident or the blood or the big red smear? "What if it's a cop?" I said instead, and this was enough for Tracie's arm to fall to her side. She looked to me and I looked to her and neither of us knew what we were going to do.

It was a long stretch of road and the car came fast and as it approached I wondered if it were slowing as it edged onto the shoulder to give us a ride—it seemed to slow, anyway—as rumble strips created a raucous noise beneath the tires before they hit gravel.

"Tracie!" I screamed, and we both found each other staring at growing headlights, eyes wide, and I sprang like a deer to the ditch and tried pulling Tracie with me but our fingers failed to intertwine and the car struck her, Tracie bent in half by the bumper before rolling over the hood and smashing against the windshield, her body flung what seemed a hundred feet away and flopped over the car and smashed against the asphalt, tumbling and tumbling and finally still. And then *not* so still, the mass in the road reaching out, quivering.

The car finally stopped on the side of the road, taillights glowing like the eyes of a beast, and then the eyes blinked to a softer red, the driver inside taking her foot off the brakes. It was Tracie's car, or so I thought at first. I ran up the stretch of road.

The body in the road wore mostly black—the same body in the road as the one we'd hit, a silver mood ring on one hand with whatever mood it portrayed now black under the moonlight, and the other hand clenched around what I knew would be a small glass vial.

Up ahead, the car was indeed Tracie's, and I found myself stepping away from the road and watching another version of Tracie and another version of me assess the situation, both smoking, like the front end of the car. *It's still alive*, the other me was saying to the other Tracie, who turned around and was then asking, *What is it?*

I ran into the woods, then, until my lungs caught fire and a dagger pierced my side and I collapsed. There were other versions of us out there, and all I could do was run. I sat on a log for what seemed hours but was probably only minutes, and then I heard a rustling. I stood behind the trunk of a pine tree and hid there, knowing what made the noise.

I watched the other version of me and the other version of Tracie pull Tracie's mangled body into the woods. They covered her body in pine needles and branches under the light of a cell phone screen until the other version of Tracie screamed.

"She has the same ring as me."

"Everyone has mood rings."

"I need to get out of here," the other version of Tracie said, her words convincing the other me to follow. "I need to get out of here, get me out of here!"

I stepped back and snapped a branch, and this got them moving.

The night seemed to stretch indefinitely, and when I finally made my way back to the road, the white line kept on going as far as I could see in either direction. I walked all night, the moon never moving in front of me, its light masking the world in grayscale, and the white line I followed went on and on and on. I'd had too much to drink, I knew, the road a blur.

An engine and the sound of gravel under tires turned me around and I found myself squinting into headlights.

I went around to the passenger door and inside was Tracie, high as fuck, her nose red, and her eyes black discs.

"Need a ride?" she said, and I said I did and hopped inside.

We drove forever that night, had sex in the car, under a streetlamp, and I found myself thinking about the bra on the floorboard, her torn underwear on the middle console. She'd used me, I knew, had finished and climbed off before I could and slid naked into her jeans, and then she drove, and we talked about dead things and dolls.

I shook my head no when she offered me the vial of coke. I'd only drank.

"The long white line," she said, batting her hands against the steering wheel. The radio was off, but she had some song in her head. The song was in my head, too, so I played along.

What you do you want to do when we graduate? I wanted to ask.

Some Day, Soon—Luke Spooner

JIM'S MEATS

KELLI OWEN

JANET REACHED OVER and gripped his knee, shaking it as she spoke. "Brad. *Brad?*" She didn't look away from the dark Michigan highway as her tone grew an edge of both urgency and annoyance. She'd been trying to wake him for several minutes and was starting to panic, her anxiety apparent as her volume suddenly matched her tone. "Brad!"

He bolted upright in the passenger seat and shot both hands to the dash in a reflexively defensive move, as if they were about to crash. When they didn't, he looked around at the black night and then to Janet's face, illuminated by the dim green of dash lights. "What the hell is wrong?"

She swallowed hard enough for him to hear but didn't look toward him, "I was wondering how much farther you can go after the Low Fuel light comes on . . . " Her voice trailed off, the panic on her face did not.

"Oh no. No no, baby. Don't say—" He leaned toward her to look at the gauges on the dash, stopping when the seatbelt tightened against him. "Ah shit, hon." He scanned the lonely stretch of empty highway and found nothing. No lights in the distance. No soft glow of a town at the horizon.

"Where the hell are we?"

"Lower Michigan. The last town I went through was a while ago. There were gas stations back there, but I didn't realize we were that low. If I had . . . " She swallowed again and gave him a sheepish glance. "I'm sorry."

"Well, there's got to be something out here. And there's gas left after the light comes on." Brad popped open the glove box and pushed around a stack of outdated registrations and insurance card printouts. "Don't we have a manual?"

Janet shrugged. "I don't remember one."

"Well damn." He sighed and leaned back in his seat. His head against the side window, he willed something to appear on the horizon.

Janet pushed the INFO button on the dash and cycled past the coolant temperature and oil life before arriving at the average mileage: twenty-two.

"We gotta have about twenty miles, right?" She worked through the math out loud. "Average gallon worth? Well, fifteen miles now, because the light came on before I woke you."

"Probably . . . Let's see what the closest option is." Brad retrieved his phone from the center console and pushed the button to bring it to life. "Shit. No signal. Not even roaming or data." He opened the Road Ninja app anyway, hoping it had loaded their entire route. It scanned for a moment before boldly announcing No Signal. He sighed, the heat of disappointment beginning to fester toward anger in his mind.

Janet squinted and leaned forward. "There!" Janet smiled. "It's all good. Sorry I panicked you. See? There's something coming up. What's the sign say?"

They read the road sign in silence and kept driving without discussing it. The sign had been green rather than blue. Instead of promising food and gas or lodging, it instead told them it was forty-eight miles to the next town.

They didn't have forty-eight miles worth of gas.

Brad looked around. "How can it be so black out here? No nothing. I mean, the stars look great, but my God, don't people *live* in this state?"

"Welcome to the great Midwest—all trees and fields and farms and crap. Worst case scenario, we go until we're out, then we walk until we find a gas station or a house. There's got to be *something.*"

"Walk? Out here?" Brad stared at her as if she'd suggested he light himself on fire. "They'll capture me and make me a pet!"

"Oh Christ, please. This isn't *Deliverance*, it's Michigan." Janet laughed uncomfortably at his snark, knowing it was anxiety and not serious, but worried herself about walking in the pitch black of the dark highway.

"Hey!" Brad yelled, and she snapped out of her thought. "Slow down. There's something. An exit? Exits are for a reason, right? Crossroads. Small towns. Might not have signs for travelers but they have to have amenities for residents, right?"

Janet squinted at the dark strip of road splitting off from the highway. The sign didn't claim a mile marker number, it simply read: EXIT. She exhaled heavily, puffing her cheeks out like a chipmunk, and turned the wheel. The off ramp rose slowly for several hundred feet before coming to a stop at an intersecting gravel road. They looked left and saw nothing but darkness. To the right, the same. Below the faded stop sign a long piece of weathered board, which may have once been white, was tied to the post with wire. Homemade stenciling declared JIM'S MEATS, with an arrow pointing toward the dark road on the right. Scrawled underneath someone had added "and gas."

Janet shook her head, eyes wide and mouth open.

"Oh hell no." Brad once again opened his phone. He huffed as he held his phone up against the roof of the car.

"Seriously?" Janet's gaze moved from the handwritten sign to Brad's hand above his head. "You understand the signals come from towers and satellites thousands of miles above us, but yeah, raising it sixteen inches will *absolutely* help you get a signal."

He pulled his hand down and turned off the phone. "I do not need your snarky logic right now." He pointed down the road indicated by the arrow, "Wanna check that out?"

"Nope." She crossed the intersecting road and returned to the highway. "Even the locals need to have better options than that, right?"

"There's got to be something . . ." Brad tried to sound hopeful but heard his own doubts hang in the stale recycled air of the SUV's interior.

Three more miles of nothing and the darkness started to feel oppressive, as if fate were hugging them tight against their will. Panic had become a backseat driver. The hot invisible breath of personified fear blew on their necks, its fingers tracing their nerves in a jittery caress. Their own breath became an alternating dance of jumping panicked staccato, and forcibly controlled breaths designed to calm the mind and outward appearance.

It didn't work.

"I'm sorry." Janet offered, as she listened to his breathing become agitated.

"Well, I'm not saying it's your fault, but—."

"Wait, you're going to actually throw blame around right now? How about, *why weren't you driving?* We were an hour past time to switch, but *you* couldn't be bothered to wake up."

Ignoring her attempt to make it his fault, he continued. "How do you drive for hours and hours and *not* watch the gas gauge? Who does that?"

"I do, okay! Apparently, I do. And we can't change that right now. So how about you be a little less of a dick about it."

He could see the moisture in her eyes as tears of rage, fear and guilt built up and threatened to spill.

"I'm not . . . " He stopped, pursed his lips for a moment and reworded his thoughts. "I *said* I wasn't blaming you."

"But you are . . . "

They swallowed arguments and excuses alike. Unspoken tension filled the Explorer as silence became yet another passenger. She kept an eye on the gauges as they traveled. He studied the road ahead. As the trip odometer ticked off another mile and Janet mentally noted it marked the seventeenth mile, Brad screamed and made her jump.

"There!"

"What? Where?" Janet looked around and saw the faint outline of a large square sign. The town signs were small. The bigger ones were reserved for lodging, food, and *gas.* She smiled as she saw this one said the most important thing: GAS. She slowed as she steered the SUV onto the off ramp. At the stop sign, another marker informed them GAS was two miles to the left and she inhaled with trepidation.

The red Low Fuel light flashed in a cry for attention, as if they could forget they'd been staring at it for almost twenty miles. And to really grind the point home, a triple beep repeated itself several times as a warning. Brad pointed down the road, "We don't have a choice."

She turned the blinker on and sat for a few beats before easing the car into the turn. "Two miles though?"

"Sure. Not all towns are built on the highway, right?"

"I suppose." Janet sighed.

Two miles felt like twenty by the time they saw the first signs of life—a small forgotten single-story home. They didn't voice their worries, but each presumed the other must be thinking the same thing. Ghost town? Outdated sign? And now they were two miles off the highway in the middle of nowhere. They'd have to walk back there before they could even begin to hitchhike or find help.

Before either could voice their concerns, a bright white two-story home loomed out of the darkness. Then another. And another. And they found themselves in a full-fledged neighborhood.

"Oh, thank God."

Janet slowed the SUV and crept along the road until she found a side street and stopped. In front of them the road continued with a smattering of homes, to the right it appeared to be a plotted neighborhood.

"Maybe go down there and see?"

Janet turned without a word.

The street was lined with simple homes, all of which seemed to be of similar design, with trees of all sizes speckling the boulevards and dark yards. There seemed to be no porch lights turned on, no interior glow of lamps or televisions as proof of life, and no streetlights to shoo away the shadows of the neighborhood.

Janet glanced at the clock on the dash, "The whole town goes to sleep by 9pm?"

Other than the lack of life and light, the small town seemed clean and well kept. *Preserved*. Brad squinted in the dim light, his gaze flitting from home to home. There were no cars on the road and he guessed they must be in garages or carports behind the houses. One lone house sported a swing set, tilted with age and neglect, marring the otherwise picturesque village.

After another block they came to a T-intersection. A brick building on the right declared POST AND GROCERY above the door. The dead-end in front of them housed a gravel lot with a small garage and gas station.

Hope.

Janet and Brad sighed in relief and smiled at each other.

The building had an office on the left marked by a full picture window, and a single raised garage door on the right. In front of the building was a small, simple gas pump with two handles. The flickering yellow light above it was hidden until you were close enough to see its meager, sickly glow. Its reach wasn't much, but it was enough to see the pump was modern, digital. Brad smiled, even if the place was closed, it might still take their credit card for gas.

Janet pulled into the parking lot and circled around toward the pump. The SUV sputtered as if to announce their arrival and lurched the final few yards.

"Is this place even open?" Janet looked around.

"Hopefully it doesn't matter." Brad held up his VISA card as he opened the car door.

Brad stepped out and examined the darkness. With the headlights off, the small town was swallowed by the starry night. The flickering bulb above him barely illuminated the SUV and pump. And the slight promise of light from somewhere in the back of the garage felt more like a forgotten flashlight than anything else in the pitch black the night had become. He walked around the Explorer and inspected the pump. It was digital. It was apparently working. And it did indeed take credit cards—*at some point*. Unfortunately, the credit card slot was covered with a strip of duct tape on which someone had used marker to write PAY INSIDE. Brad felt his shoulders slump.

He turned toward the little building in time to see a man emerge from the darkness of the garage.

"Evening," Brad called out to the man, who immediately reacted as if he'd been bit—flinching and shaking his head before putting a finger to his lips.

As he got closer, Brad watched the man wipe his hands on a rag and tuck the soiled cloth into his pocket. The man looked around the intersection and town itself as he briskly approached Brad. His dark pants and uniform style mechanic shirt were as filthy as his hands had been, the nametag on his shirt identifying him as FRANK.

He held a hand out to Brad, "Name's Everett, but most just call me Rett. Let's get you inside with that card. I got a machine on the counter."

Brad squinted an unspoken question as he looked between the man's face and his nametag. *Borrowed shirt?*

"Come on now." He looked at Janet through the car

116

window, "We should get you two back on the road." Rett turned and headed toward the office, leaving Brad no choice but to follow.

Setting his credit card down on the counter for the man, Brad looked around the tiny office. Snack sized bags of outdated chips and pretzels hung from a metal rack next to a small refrigerator. A paper taped to the front of the grease stained refrigerator stated fifty cents a can. He opened it, saw several flavors of some off-brand soda, and grabbed one each of the orange and cola options. Setting the sodas down, he spotted another snack option and had to stop himself from snickering. In a basket next to the register, a handful of handmade labels were stapled to bags declaring JIM'S MEATS: Local Game.

Rett punched buttons on the register and swiped the card.

Brad wasn't opposed to jerky, liked it actually. He picked a bag from the basket out of curiosity, "Local game?"

"Sure. Deer, moose, turkey, whatever's in season. You wouldn't like it." Rett handed the card back and took the jerky from Brad, tossing it into the basket. "I charged you for twenty. That'll get you up to Saginaw and you can fill up there. Now let's hurry up and get you back on the road."

Rett walked out from behind the counter, his movements were as rushed as his words. He held the door open for Brad, "Don't forget your sodas there."

Janet met them halfway to the SUV. "Is there a bathroom inside?"

Rett sounded annoyed, "No. It's 'round back. Hurry up though." His tone almost shooed her on like a stalling child.

Janet walked around to the back of the building, tightening her muscles and holding it in the best she could. The urge had struck out of nowhere when she stood to stretch and now she prayed to get there in time. She rounded the back corner of the building and night swallowed the paltry light from the flickering gas pump. Her eyes adjusted and she saw a small overgrown lot separating the garage property from the backyards of several homes. The silhouettes of trees and—

Those aren't trees.

She squinted—allowing the shapes to become only slightly more focused—and she realized there were several people standing there. She couldn't gauge their sex or age in the dark, but spaced several car lengths apart she counted four. No, six.

Seven.

They were coming closer. Coming from the houses.

The hair on the back of her neck reminded Janet that in fight or flight, she'd never been one to fight. She forgot about her bladder and turned around, heading back out front without a second thought. She walked fast enough to feel rushed without seeming to run. She tried to remain calm and not presume anything, but broke into a jog the last few feet.

"That was quick." Brad was standing by the pump with Rett.

"Changed my mind. People back there . . . they freaked me out."

"People?" Rett looked toward the building as if he could see through it. "How many?"

"A handful."

"Shit. Not quick enough." He spun and looked toward the pump, he'd only just begun pumping. He pulled the handle and stepped back, "Get in the car and get out of here. Go for the highway. I'll try and bring you gas there. Otherwise wait there for someone. But *stay on that highway.*"

Janet jumped in the passenger seat.

Brad furrowed his brow at the man, "What? Why? We haven't even—"

"Boy, I ain't joking around. Get a move on!"

Brad fumbled with the door and got into the car, the driver's seat was up too far from Janet driving and he rammed his knees into the bottom of the dash. With his left hand he reached down and flicked the release to send the seat back a couple inches, his right hand turned the key to start the car.

The gas gauge needle didn't move above EMPTY. *Fumes at best,* he thought. *Maybe enough to get back to the highway.*

He held a hand up to wave at the attendant but pulled it back when he saw his face. Fear shown through the grease and dirt, widening his eyes and making the whites appear jaundice in the yellow light of the pump lamp.

Brad put the SUV in drive and pulled forward. As he steered left to get out of the lot, his headlights washed across a dozen faces blocking their way and he hit the brakes.

"What the—?" He let the question hang in the air.

"Drive *through* them." Janet sounded unreasonably panicked.

"Jesus, Janet, that's murder."

"Look at them. *Look!*" She flicked her hand forward, overtly motioning toward the crowd. "Do they *look* like they want to invite us to a picnic?"

Brad considered the group in front of them. Each one

dressed in dark clothes, their blank expressions neither welcoming nor menacing. They made no noise, took no action. They simply stood and stared at the SUV.

Taking in the broader details as he scanned the crowd, Brad realized they were standing in the road—*not* on the lawns—and revved the engine as an idea formed. He let off the brake and drove for the corner, hoping to shoot through the break in their line and escape across the lawns. As he approached, they moved as one—each taking several steps to the side—and closed the gap. Brad slammed on the brakes and stared at their disturbingly emotionless faces in his headlights. The crash of breaking glass combined with Janet's scream broke his momentary trance.

Glancing over, Brad saw something had been thrown at the backseat window, shattering it. He could feel the cool night air. He heard absolutely no sounds other than the engine of the SUV and Janet's staccato breaths. He threw the Explorer into reverse and hit the gas.

He felt the thump before he heard it.

His rearview mirror showed more people surrounding them from behind.

He checked his options—a dozen townsfolk in front of them, another handful behind, and the gas station garage to the right. The only opening was the road to their left, but the pump stood between them and it.

As if to rub in their limited options, the Explorer's engine chugged and coughed, reminding them of their lack of fuel.

Brad watched in the rearview mirror as the man he'd knocked over stood up and took his place back in the line of residents. A shiver ran up Brad's spine.

"What shoes are you wearing?" Brad asked without

looking at Janet, as he kept darting his eyes between the crowd in front of them and those in his rearview mirror.

"What?"

He could feel her staring at him.

"Can you run?" His words were punctuated with an unspoken seriousness, but his volume was low, his tone calm.

Janet's eyes got bigger as she turned in her seat. In her sideways position, she looked from the group in front to those behind and then to Brad.

"How? Which way?"

"Back there . . . " Brad jutted his chin toward the garage. "What was back there?"

"Houses. And a handful of people just standing in the dark."

"You think they're still back there? Or did they come out here and become part of this mess? Do you recognize any of them?"

Janet shook her head, "I don't know. I couldn't see much. It's dark back there. Really damn dark."

"Then we go *that* way." He glanced to his left, indicating the road on the other side of the pump. "Crawl into the backseat. If we both open the doors and run at the same time, maybe—"

"To where?"

"Rett said get to the highway. It's back that way."

She pointed beyond the POST AND GROCERY, "Technically—as the crow flies—it's *that* way, but who knows what's in those fields and yards." She acquiesced with a nod he didn't see. "Okay. We run. Okay."

He knew repetition was her way of convincing herself she could do this. He needed *her* to be ready. "*You* say when."

"Okay . . . " Her voice trailed as she climbed over the seat. "Oh, there's glass back here."

"You cut yourself?" He heard the bits of glass clink in protest of her movement.

"Nah, I avoided it." She took a deep breath as she reached for the door handle. "Don't you leave me, okay? Don't . . . don't outrun me . . . "

"I won't." He looked at her in the rearview mirror. "But don't look back. Don't slow down. You run straight down that street until we get to the main road that leads out to the highway. Okay?" He didn't wait for her to agree. "How far is that? A couple blocks, right? Maybe three."

She squinted and tried to see down the dark road. "I think . . . yeah, three sounds right."

The Explorer's engine sputtered and coughed its way to a full stop.

"Oh God . . . " Janet took a deep breath and exhaled loudly. "Okay. Okay, let's do this . . . on three?"

"One." Brad started the count as he grabbed the door handle.

"Two." Janet pulled the handle on her door slowly, quietly, to release the latch.

"Three." They spoke simultaneously and pushed, their doors swinging open in a fluid movement that ended with each of them free from the vehicle.

Janet slipped between the pump and garbage can, while Brad ran around front of the pump.

"*Kill* him." The elderly female voice exuded power and leadership. "*Grab* her."

Brad heard Janet gasp as she took off. They ran across the parking lot but dared not look back to find the voice demanding their doom. Reaching the pavement of the small street, they picked up speed, running straight down the road. Straight into the darkness.

Brad kept Janet in his peripheral vision—either right next to him or slightly behind, but never out of sight. "Faster!" He spurred her forward.

"I'm trying!"

Brad heard the panic catch in her breath. He glanced back in time to see her eyes widen in fear a moment before he felt the slam from his left that knocked him down to the pavement. Janet shrieked but kept running, adrenaline more in charge than her desire to stop. He saw her run thirty feet farther before coming to a halt and turning back toward him.

Whoever had knocked Brad down had run past him and crossed the street. Brad scanned the lawn, searching for his assailant. With his attention diverted, he didn't see the second one come from behind and deliver a swift kick to his torso before darting back into the shadows.

Janet's scream pierced the quiet street as pain shot through his ribs.

He reflexively curled up to protect himself and frantically looked around for his attackers. Three figures ran from the shadows to become a flurry of feet and fists. Something solid in one of their hands caught the back of his head and Brad went down. Darkness greeted him before his face bounced off the pavement.

Janet's open mouth was poised for another scream but she held it when she saw Brad fall. She turned to run. She had to get out. Find help.

Survive.

In front of her, several silhouettes slowly walked toward her, fanning out and flanking her as they approached. She turned to the right and ran between two houses only to come to another street filled with people, as if they'd been waiting for her. She turned back the way she'd come and darted through the yard to make her way back to the street.

She came out next to Brad's unmoving body. His attackers had gone back to the shadows, perhaps to join in the hunt for her. Janet bent down, eyes warm with the threat of tears. Even in the dark street she could see the pool of blood under his head. She felt panic rise in her throat, tasting very much like bile. She put a hand to her mouth and looked around.

The light of the gas station called her like a beacon. *The attendant didn't chase us.*

She ran for the small building, hoping to at least hide long enough to collect her thoughts and form a plan. Janet skidded to a halt in front of the open garage door when Rett appeared at the edge of the light shaking his head.

"No no no. I said *run.*"

"They killed Brad!" The reality of her own words cracked her voice and gave her heart a pause.

"Girlie, *RUN.*" Rett's words were emphasized without volume—all the tone he needed was written on his face. "There are *worse things* than dead. Get to the highway."

He pointed at the same area of open field and backyards *she* had mentioned to Brad before they left the SUV—*as the crow flies.* She couldn't see well enough in the dark. She didn't know the area. She didn't believe she could make it through the—

"Run!"

Rett's command broke through her thoughts and her feet followed his directive. A small pickup truck came from her right. Its headlights washed across the landscape and cemented her decision for her, as she saw the uneven ground and large rocks in the field behind the small post office. She turned up the street she and Brad had initially taken to the gas station. The one they'd both tried to leave by.

The one where his body lay crumpled.

The truck turned to follow, the headlights illuminating the road ahead as it gained on her. She moved toward the side of the road, not wanting to be an easy target in the center. She passed Brad's body without pause. The headlights fell behind, as she seemed to outrun them. Janet risked a backward glance and saw the truck had stopped by Brad's body. The possibilities were outnumbered by her imagination and she gasped as she turned back to the road in front of her. She sprinted with everything she had.

Her leg muscles burned. Her side hurt, and she remembered her full bladder. Her mouth and throat felt dry from harsh breaths. Her heart beat in rhythm with her pounding feet. She got to the main road and swung left. One more block of houses and she'd be out of the town. Then it was a couple miles to the highway.

Okay, she thought. *Okay, I can do this.*

Janet didn't see the truck coming from her left, from the yard between the last two houses. With its headlights off, there was only a blur of motion before she was bumped off her feet to land in an unconscious heap in the ditch.

***

Janet opened her eyes to lost time. It was still dark out. She remembered being hit, but the pain was subdued by her inability to move and confusion at the loud rumble surrounding her. It took only a moment for her to realize she was tied in the back of a pickup truck, tape of some sort across her mouth. The sound had been the grinding of gears as the truck came to a bumpy halt. Her eyes widened as she realized Brad's body was lying next to her.

The driver's door opened behind her and she kicked frantically at Brad's shoulder, nudging him as an unseen man spoke behind her.

"I'm getting real sick of cleaning up your messes. Why you think I moved away?"

A mumbled reply was answered with, "Well don't bring me *that one* if she don't make it."

Janet couldn't twist enough in her bindings to see who was talking, but she could hear the irritation in the deep voice.

Boots crunched on gravel as they walked past her, and she watched the silhouette of a man open the back of the truck. She pulled her feet back, curling up defensively. Hands reached in and grabbed Brad's ankles. She thought she heard Brad groan in protest as he was pulled from the truck bed in one swift motion. His body landed on the ground with a sick thump followed by silence. Janet felt the heat of her bladder releasing as she waited for the arms to come back for her.

They didn't.

Instead, the man slammed the tailgate shut and hit the side of the truck twice to indicate he was done.

Wait . . . Why wasn't I taken with Brad? What are they going to do to Brad?

Janet's confusion turned to fear as she recounted the things she'd heard: kill him, *grab* her.

My God, why?

What are they going to do with me?

The truck lurched into gear, moving forward again as the night air chilled the wet skin between her thighs. She watched as Brad's body was dragged into the shadows.

Hot tears of selfish dread ran freely. She wondered what could be worse than Brad's fate—worse than dead—as the truck bounced down the road away from the handwritten sign for Local Game.

BACK SEAT

BRACKEN MACLEOD

THE COLD MADE her feet hurt. She was wearing the same sneakers she'd had since before the beginning of the school year, even though her feet had grown and her toes were pushing up against the ends. They were thin canvas and the flat soles were slippery on the black ice coating the road, but they were what she had. To combat the cold, she doubled up on socks even though that made the shoes feel even smaller and crunched up her toes more. Layering her socks worked at first, but the cold still crept in like needles slowly being pushed through the canvas and into the layers of cotton underneath.

There was snow on the ground on the side of the road, but it wasn't deep, not like the year before. She didn't have to slog through it like then. This was that dry, powdery kind that you couldn't make a snowman or even a ball out of—it just sifted through your fingers like weightless sand when you tried to shape it. It was the kind of snow that fell when it was so cold the condensation from her dad's breath froze tiny icicles in his mustache and beard. When that happened, she used to laugh and try to pick the little pieces of ice out of his

128

facial hair. He'd smile and bat her hands away, telling her to keep her paws off his beard diamonds. But the novelty of it wore off after the second week of record low temperatures, and neither of them acknowledged the tiny icicles anymore. They were headed into the second *month* of frigid temps now. That's what they said on the radio. Record lows not felt in New England in a century. At nine years old, a century was a mythical length of time. Like "once upon a time" and "happily ever after." One hundred years only existed in stories. Though plenty of things in New England were much older, she'd never met a *person* who'd lived a hundred years. She knew she wouldn't be around in a century to tell anyone how numb her toes were. Cold wasn't supposed to last like that.

They walked along the side of the road toward the next house. She didn't want to leave tracks, but the ice on the road was too slippery to walk on. She'd fallen a couple of times when they first got out of the car and her dad told her it was okay for them to walk in the snow on the shoulder. That was tricky because it was dark and there were no street lights out here to illuminate something in the shallow snow that might trip them. Just a faint, unsettling glow from the reflection of the moon behind the clouds. Hidden roots or not, if anyone came driving along, neither of them wanted to be *in* the road.

The snow crunched softly beneath her feet. Her dad's footfalls were louder, though he did his best to stay quiet—he couldn't help his size. He walked in front of her and she tried to step in his footsteps. Though the snow wasn't deep, it still got in over the tops of her shoes and froze her ankles along with her stinging toes. Walking in his tracks kept that from happening as much, though it still did.

She made a game of it, pretending she was a ghost stalking him, walking in his tracks so when he looked behind him, he couldn't see where she'd been. She'd stand in his footsteps and he'd see right through her and shiver at the thought that something was following him. What could it be? The spirit of a tragically lost girl he once knew? She thought it might be fun to be a ghost. Then, she could sneak into some of these houses—pass right through the doors and walls—and sleep in an empty room all by herself. Instead of in a car.

The shelters in the city wouldn't take them. A single man with a child was bad enough, but they definitely wouldn't take in a single man with a *girl*. Men and women were kept apart for safety reasons, they said. Her dad argued that she was his daughter, and they said it was policy. She couldn't stay in the men's area and he couldn't go in the women's. We're sorry, they told them. So, they had to sleep in the car. Her dad turned on the engine every couple of hours to run the heater. The sound of it turning over woke her up every time, but she pretended to sleep through the noise. She knew he wanted her to get good sleep so she could be alert in school. But then every few nights, they had to go for "The Walk."

She moved quietly behind him, pretending to be a spirit until they reached a driveway and he turned to remind her with a raised finger to be extra quiet. She didn't need reminding. She knew.

Stepping around her dad, she glanced at the mailbox, as if it mattered whose address this was. Most people bought those brass-colored metal numbers to stick on the side of their mailboxes, but this one had been carefully hand-painted. It was hard to read in the dark, but up close she could see. The person who'd done it hadn't painted the street name, just the numbers five and seven. That was enough. She remembered they were on Summer Street. That had made her smile at first. It was nothing like summer out that night, but it was nice to think about warm weather. She was ready for some.

Her father leaned down and whispered in her ear. She wanted to pull back her stocking cap to hear him better, but her ears were as cold as her feet. They hurt in the biting wind, so she leaned closer and turned her head, but left the hat in place.

"You know the drill. Don't forget the cup holders."

She nodded. She never forgot, though when she came back without anything in hand, he worried that she wasn't looking hard enough. She tried to find what he wanted everywhere she could think of. Sometimes, she even checked under the floor mats in the footwells.

She crept up the driveway. It was clear of snow, though there was some salt spread out. She tried not to crunch when she stepped, but couldn't help it. She was small, and the noise was slight. Still, it sounded loud to her. At this time of night, every house on the street was dark; everyone was asleep. She knew how tiny little sounds outside of the car made her wake up all night long. She tried to move as silently as a ghost.

She hesitated beside the car and looked back at her dad. He'd melted into the shadows of the trees beside the driveway. The shadow he'd become nodded at her and she turned back to the passenger door and pulled up on the handle, gritting her teeth, waiting for the electronic chirp that would tell her to let go and run for the shadows. The door clicked faintly and popped out an inch. No alarm. She lifted and pulled hard and it swung open. And *that's* why they were in the town they were, instead of Manchester or Concord. No one out here locked their doors.

She jumped inside and pulled the door shut to extinguish the dome light overhead. It was still cold with the door closed, but the breeze couldn't get in anymore. She wished she had the keys so she could start the engine and let it idle for a little bit and heat up—take some of the chill out of her feet and hands. That was as sure a way of getting caught as leaving the dome light on or just standing out on the front step and ringing the doorbell. No. She had to wait. The drive back to Manchester would be warm. She'd snuggle up under her blanket and get some sleep when they were through. And tomorrow was Saturday. No school. She could sleep in. Though she never did.

She opened the center console, knowing she probably wouldn't find any quarters in the coin slots, but still hopeful for something. No one out here locked their doors, but they didn't need meter money either. Free street parking in small towns meant no one kept quarters in their cars. The best she ever seemed to find was what someone got handed back in change from the Drive-Thru window along with their Whopper and Coke. That ended up in the cup holders most often, as her dad reminded her. But she checked everywhere. Her mouth watered at the thought of a hamburger. She loved Whoppers so much! They were better than a Big Mac or those dry, square burgers from the other place with the girl on the sign.

She gasped when she saw the roll of quarters wrapped in one of those paper bank sleeves in the console. Ten dollars! Whoever drove this car must go into a city a lot. Maybe even Boston if he needed that much change. She'd never found a whole roll of change before and her heart started to beat fast with excitement. Dad would be so happy. Maybe he'd even let them quit early tonight. They could be out for hours on any other night before she found as much. She tried to imagine what his face would look like when she showed him. How the crinkles at the corners of his eyes would deepen and that one eyebrow would arch up the way it did. She loved that eyebrow. It only went up when he really smiled. It was how she could tell when he was faking.

Still, there was more looking to do before she could go back to him with her treasure.

She stuffed the coin roll in her pocket, closed the console, and started feeling around in the cup holders. Nothing. As if she hadn't found enough. She popped open the jockey box and felt around inside. Once, she'd found a checkbook and had taken it back to her dad. He'd gotten excited at first, and then his face fell and he told her they couldn't keep it. He didn't say why, he just said he couldn't write bad checks. She didn't know what made them bad. If they were filled out they were good, right? Still, he'd thrown the checkbook in the garbage and told her to focus on cash and anything they might be able to pawn.

Once, she found a toy. Nothing big. Just was a tiny fashion doll of a blue skinned girl with bright pink hair. It had little removable bracelets and a belt that she was careful not to lose and the blue girl was beautiful even though she had little fangs. She knew it was a Monster High figure, though she didn't know the character's name. She'd hidden that find from her dad. She didn't want him to accuse her of having bad toys and throw that

133

in the garbage too. When he found it in their car a week later, he'd asked where she got such a thing and she lied to him and said that her friend at school, Holly, had given it to her. She was ashamed to lie to him, but it wasn't a bad toy; it was a good toy and she wanted to keep it. The kid she took it from had a big house and her parents drove a big SUV and she didn't even care enough about the figure not to leave it on floor in the back seat like an empty wrapper. She loved that monster girl better than that other kid had.

There was a book in the jockey box. Who kept books in a place like that? she wondered. It was some grown up book with a pair of bare feet on the cover. She thought for a minute about taking that too and giving it to her dad. She didn't know whether he liked books, but maybe it was like the figure. Something he could love better than whoever had left it in a car. Sometimes, they went to the library and she sat and read while he looked at his e-mail on the public computers. He never checked anything out. He never had time to read, he said. This book though, stuffed in with the car papers like it wasn't anything important, could be his and he could read it and not worry about it being due or late fees or anything. He could take all year to finish it if he wanted. And he could love it like she loved her blue girl.

It was probably a bad book. Like a bad check. He'd throw it away and then no one would have it. She put the paperback novel with its one-word title back and closed the jockey box.

Her dad would be getting impatient soon. He didn't like her to take too long. She had to hurry. She checked the floors under the mats and stuffed her fingers deep in the cracks in the seats, but she knew the quarter roll was all she was going to find. It was enough. Still, she turned to crawl into the back seat and look for other treasures.

The boy sitting there stared at her from the shadows.

A shout she couldn't control escaped her lips. She clapped her hands to her mouth. She lurched away from the boy, hitting her back against the gear shift and then the dashboard. Another cry escaped her lips at the sudden insult of the little knobs that jutted out of the dash jabbing into her back between her shoulder blades. If she'd been in the driver's seat, she would've honked the horn and they'd be caught. She arched her back and her foot slipped. She fell face-first into the passenger seat, dragging her cheek down the cold leather. The quarter roll in her jacket pocket pulled heavily, like a weight, but didn't fall out.

She whimpered at the pain of her neck craning back against the upright seatback as she pushed up. The side of her right leg hurt where it scraped against the plastic of the center divider. She wanted to cry and call out for her dad, but she had to keep herself together. At least until they got back to their own car. She sniffled and gritted her teeth and got up on her knees.

Peeking over the back of the seat in the dark, it looked like a doll. Pale and still and small. And for a single second, an unwelcome thought about how much she'd love to have a baby doll intruded in her mind. But this wasn't a toy. It was a boy. He sat in his car seat, the harness over his shoulders holding him upright, head tilted to the side on a thin neck. His skin wasn't like a piece of plastic painted to look like a real kid; it was pale in the moonlight and looked unreal. His eyes were open, but they were dull and unfocused. Not like sharp plastic eyes that looked alert and had bright irises. His eyes weren't any of those things.

He had on mittens and a snowsuit with little built-in booties. She didn't want to know what his tiny fingers and toes looked like. She didn't want to know anything. Tears blurred her eyes as she struggled not to scream. But . . . the boy. The tears in her eyes made him waver in the dark, and it looked like he might be wriggling against the straps of the car seat, trying to get free, trying to reach for her and close his tiny little fingers around her throat and squeeze. Once, she'd seen a part of an old movie about dead people coming back to life and they were a horrible blue color that made her laugh because it was so fake-looking and how could anyone be scared by a blue person? And then they bit people and the crazy extra-red blood squirted out and she got scared. Even though that was fake-looking too—like a living cartoon—it was terrifying. Because it was blood, and nobody lost that much blood and stayed alive.

In the diffuse moonlight, this boy was blue like that. The thought of him biting her and crazy bright blood spurting out of her body onto his round baby face made her breath hitch and she pushed away from the seat back.

The boy didn't move. He didn't look up or cry or even breathe. He sat there in the dark and looked somewhere, a million miles away—maybe in a whole different world. Looking at her from the ghost world.

She pulled off one of her gloves and leaned forward to touch his cheek with the tip of a shaking finger. She didn't know why she wanted to touch him, but she did. The boy terrified her, but she *needed* to touch him.

Needed to know he was real and not a ghost. It felt like he needed her to touch him.

He was so cold.

The car moved, and she heard laughter and loud talking. She tumbled into the back seat as the car took a corner too fast and she heard a woman say, "Take it easy, Louis." The driver replied, "I'm fine. It's fine," and he gassed the engine. The baby in the seat next to her sat there, his head dropping with heavy sleepiness until his eyes closed and he slumped down. The grownups in the front seat kept talking and it sounded like when her own Dad and Mom had wine and their words got mushy. She could smell wine and bad breath like when her own mom would kiss her goodnight. They turned another corner and the car stopped too fast and the woman snapped at the man and he repeated, "It's fine. I'm fine." She said, "Go open the door and I'll carry the baby in," and he replied, "Let him sleep for a minute." He pawed at her chest through her coat and she shoved at his hands and said, "Your hands are cold," but he insisted and started kissing her neck and she moaned and let him put his hands back inside her coat. They kissed and then got out of the car, laughing and she heard the woman say, "I should get the baby," and he said, "He'll be fine for ten minutes." "Ooh, I get *ten* minutes, huh?" She fumbled at the man's pants and he unlocked the door to the house and they nearly fell inside. They kept laughing and then the door slammed. And the baby woke up and began to sniffle and then started to cry. She tried to comfort him, saying, "Shh," and "It's okay; they'll be out in a minute." But they didn't come out. Not in a minute, or in ten, or in an hour. They stayed inside, and she knew they fell asleep like Mom and Dad used to sometimes after too much wine and she saw the baby's breath in the car and he started to cry harder and harder and she got more worried and tried to get out of the car, but she couldn't move. She was frozen. It was cold. So cold. And the baby cried more, until it started to lose its voice and then his head began to bob again like he was tired and he sobbed and looked at her with glassy, accusing eyes she didn't want looking at her. She wanted to look away and be anywhere but in this car, but she couldn't get out. The baby boy looked at her and his lips were turning blue and then his head bobbed down and he stopped crying.

Everything was quiet for a long time while she watched the little puffs of breath from his mouth grow smaller and less frequent, until they stopped altogether.

Then she blinked and was back in the front seat reaching out to touch the blue boy's cold cheek. She drew her arm back like her hand had been burned and fell against the dash again. She started to cry harder, unable to control the hitching sobs that were building in her chest and her throat. She let them out and it was wrong because they could get caught but there was nothing she could do to stop it. She was only nine, after all. So, she cried.

The door to the car swung open and the dome light lit up the night and she screamed and stiffened, waiting to hear the angry shouts of the owners of the car, demanding to know in that way angry grown-ups did *what the fuck* she was doing. Instead, the dark blur in the door was her dad, and she lurched toward him, wrapping her arms around his neck.

"Daddy, daddy! There's a boy back there! He's in the back seat and he's blue and—"

He shushed her a little too sharply. Angrily. She

repeated herself, trying hard to keep her voice down. "There's a boy in the back seat. A baby."

He shushed her again, softer, and held her tightly, pulling her out of the car and turning away. "It can't be," he said. "I'm sure it's just a doll."

All she could manage was "no" and "no" and "no" again. She said it and he replied with "Shh, it'll be all right," and "calm down," as if she could. Not after what the blue boy had shown her.

Her dad looked at the house at the end of the driveway. Her crying was noisy and they had to be quiet ... like ghosts. *Ghosts don't cry*, she told herself and tried to stop sobbing. But they do cry. They were sad and lonely. That's why they were ghosts on Earth instead of souls up in Heaven.

But being a ghost meant being dead.

Like the boy in the back seat of the car.

He's dead.

He froze *to death, because his parents left him in the back of the car and they went inside and fell asleep.* She'd seen them do it. The blue boy had shown her. He showed her the things she didn't want to see. The man's hands on the woman's chest and her hands in his pants, each other touching their private places, and then laughing and going inside while their baby froze to death in the back of a car. Now he was a ghost and he was sad, and he gave her a little piece of his death and now she was a ghost, too, like him. Except not a dead one. He killed her inside. It felt like she'd never be happy again.

She tried to calm down, but her heartbeat and her breathing were beyond her control. Instead, she put a hand over her mouth, so at least she wasn't sobbing out loud. Snot slipped out of her nose and she felt ashamed for being a baby, but she couldn't help it. She wiped it away with the back of her glove and sniffed hard. The sound was loud and she gritted her teeth when her dad flinched at the noise of it in his ear.

Her dad whispered, "Are you sure?" She nodded. He set her down on her feet and dragged his hand down his mustache and beard the way he did, smoothing it down. It was the way he moved when he was feeling troubled. Even when he said he wasn't, if he did that, she knew he was. And that worried her. If the grownups were afraid, what hope was there for a kid?

"You go stand over there in the trees, okay? Go wait for me over there where it's dark and I'll be right over."

"Don't leave, Daddy."

"I'm not leaving. But I gotta have a look, okay?"

She drew in a long wet sniffle and pleaded quietly with him. "I'll be good, I promise. I won't shout or cry or anything, I swear. Just don't go. Don't touch him!" Her heart thundered in her little body. She didn't want him to get in the car with the blue baby. She didn't want him to be frozen with the sadness like she had been. If he did then they'd both be ghosts and nothing would ever be right again. She had been so wrong. The blue boy gave her what she'd wished for and it felt so bad.

It's a dream. I'm in the car and I'm dreaming we're out for The Walk. We're sleeping and the boy is blue because I found that stupid blue girl toy in the back seat of a car and I'm having a nightmare about her and that movie and none of this is real, it's all a nightmare. I have to wake up!

A chill breeze rustled through the trees and it hurt her face and made her eyes tear up more and convinced her she wasn't asleep and dreaming. The wet lines the tears had traced down her cheeks stung, and she wiped at them with the glove she hadn't wiped her nose with. "Can we just go? Look, I found money." She reached in her pocket and pulled out the roll of quarters. She held it out to her dad, trying to press it into his hand. "I'll stop crying and be good if we go. I promise."

Her dad got that look, the one when he was worried. She knew it because his eyebrows came together and his eyes looked bigger somehow and his lips got so thin and tight they disappeared in the hair on his face. He looked like that a lot, so she knew it very well. He looked like that now. She knew *all* his looks.

"You *are* good, honey. You're the best. And I'm not leaving. I just want you to go stand over there and wait for me so I can have a look."

"I'll stay with you. Right up next to you. I can be brave." She wasn't sure if that last part was a lie, but she wanted it to be true, so she meant it even if she couldn't actually do it. *That* wasn't a lie, was it?

"Oh, honey. You don't need to look again, okay? Let me be brave for both of us." He put his hands on her shoulders and gently turned her toward the tree line at the edge of the property. "Go wait for me over there. Don't move. Just wait and be brave over there. I'll be right over."

"Promise you won't touch him." It wasn't a question. "Don't touch him. Promise."

He blinked. "I promise," he said, and nudged her away. She did as he told her and walked toward the darkness in the trees, wanting instead to hold on to her father and hold him back. She hadn't wanted to touch the blue boy. But then, she had. Something moved her arm like she was in a dream and what she wanted to do and what she actually did were two separate things. Before

141

she realized what was happening, she'd reached out, and there was no way what she *wanted* was going to stop what happened next. Just like now that her dad had sent her away, and all she wanted was to make him come with her instead, leave the car and the boy in it alone. What if he made her dad do it even if *he* didn't want to? She wanted to plead with him to just leave. She could show him the roll of quarters again and say "breakfast is on me," the way grownups did on TV, and he would smile and kiss her forehead and they could go out for an eggamuffin and stare into each other's eyes because it was the weekend and she didn't have to go to school and they could go window shopping at the mall the way they liked to do and look at all the things they'd buy if they had the money to buy anything and she'd promise to get him a big leather chair he could put in his own room of the big house they owned in her dream and she would sit in his lap while he read her books all her own and not borrowed from the library or anywhere else and fall asleep and he'd carry her to her room where she'd lie in a warm bed with cozy Monster High sheets and on a shelf nearby would be a whole collection of beautiful dolls that would be her friends because she would buy all of them so they'd never be lonely or sad ever again. Except for the blue one. She didn't want the blue one any more.

Except, that was only a dream.

Her feet crunched in the snow in the dark of the trees. She turned and waited. It was cold, standing still. Her breath billowed out in front of her face and hung there for a half-second before blowing away.

She watched her dad open the rear passenger door and he gasped and said, "No," loud enough for her to hear, even though he'd never made a sound before on any of the nights they went walking on the road. She looked at the house. No lights went on. No one emerged with a shotgun or phone in hand already dialing 9-1-1. There was nothing. Like the night had swallowed everything up, leaving them all alone.

Don't touch him. Don't touch him. Don'ttouchhim!

He leaned into the car. She watched his broad back convulse once. Twice. Was he crying? She'd never seen her dad actually cry. He'd look like he might feel bad for a second and then he swallowed it up. She knew he swallowed it up for her. That's why she tried to be brave, so he wouldn't have to eat so much sadness.

Her dad backed out of the car and closed the door. He turned and walked toward the house. She said, "Daddy." He held up a finger to shush her and climbed the front steps. The door was unlocked. He walked inside.

The girl wanted to run after him. This was the worst thing to do. They'd be caught. And if they were caught, people would take her away from him, because it was mommies that raised girls, not daddies. She knew they'd send her to live with someone else and then she'd be a real ghost—sad *and* alone all the time. She stayed put. Her feet were numb and felt frozen to the ground, and she was too afraid to follow him into the house. She tried to picture the people inside, blue like the little boy. As if they were all dead and this was the end of the world like that movie and she and her dad were the only non-blue people left alive. They weren't though. She knew they were pink and warm and asleep.

After a few short minutes, her dad walked out of the house. To her it had felt like forever, the way time feels to a child. Long and uncrossable, like an ocean. Or a hundred years. He came walking out, wiping at his eyes and joined her in the dark. "Time to go," he said. She wanted to ask why he had to go inside. What he'd seen. But she didn't say anything. Instead, she grabbed his hand and they walked up the driveway to the road.

In the distance, she heard a siren wind up.

They turned back the way they'd come, in the direction of their car. The weight in her pocket made her remember and she pulled her hand away and dug out the roll of quarters and held it out to him. "Here, Daddy." She wanted to see him smile. Ten dollars was a lot. It would make him smile.

A tear rolled down his cheek. He didn't bother to wipe it away. He said, "That's yours. Maybe you want to buy a new toy. A new monster doll."

"No. It's for breakfast."

He shook his head. "Huh-uh. That's yours, sweetie. We'll go find something you can buy with it this afternoon." He paused. The siren was getting louder and she wanted to run. But he stood there. He crouched and more tears dripped down his face. "I'm so sorry, baby. I'll never make you do that again."

"It's okay. I understand."

"No. It isn't."

"How will we eat if I don't go look in the cars?"

He shook his head. "I don't know. We'll find a way. But you don't ever have to do that again. Not ever."

Her dad picked her up like he did when she was six and carried her the rest of the way back to the car, walking slowly so he wouldn't fall on the ice. She held on to the roll of quarters.

When they got over the hill and were on their way

down the other side, she saw the flashing blue and red lights appear behind them. The sirens were loud now and lots of lights were coming on in the houses along the road. People were looking out their windows.

They reached the car and he tried to put her down so they could get in, but she didn't want to let go of him. With her chest pressed to his, she felt her dad's heartbeat. She held him tighter and never ever wanted down. But she had to get down to get in the car. "Can I sit in the front?" she asked. He nodded.

"We'll both sleep in the front tonight," he said.

"Did you touch him?"

He shook his head.

"Are we going to be okay?"

He nodded. "We're going to be fine, hon. Everything'll be okay." She let go and climbed in ahead of him, dragging her blanket out of the backseat up front with her. He climbed in behind her, started the engine, and turned the heater on full. Cold air blasted out, but soon it'd be warm.

For a while, anyway.

THE HEART STOPS AT THE END OF LAUREL LANE

JESS LANDRY

EVEN WITH HER back pressed against the trees, the growl of the truck's engine reverberates through Beth's chest. Its headlights cut in and out of the treeline as it slowly creeps along the highway, its tires rolling over the loose gravel of the road's shoulder. Beth squeezes harder against the bark, her boots sliding on the icy forest floor.

She brings the canvas bag in her frostbitten hands closer to her chest, keeping her breath locked in her lungs, fearing that the condensation escaping her lips will get her caught.

The growl passes, the dark truck speeding off down the road, for now. It will pass again; it's been following her for hours.

But she will not let it find her.

Beth continues on as the night grows quiet once more, cradling the canvas bag. She sticks to where the trees meet the road, the highway's mile markers always in her sight.

✳ ✳ ✳

When Linda opened her eyes, she expected two things: the TV on some shitty daytime talk show and a pounding headache brought on by last night's bourbon bender.

She sat up in bed as quickly as a thirty-something-year-old woman with a bad back could. Sure enough, Dr. Phil rattled on to some I-do-what-I-want teenager with a serious drug problem and a forty-year-old boyfriend, while the pressure in her head mounted.

"You're breaking your mother's heart." The doctor said in his Southern drawl just as Linda pressed the OFF button.

Linda rubbed her eyes, trying to alleviate the self-inflicted throbbing. The sun pierced the cheap plastic blinds that had come with the rental house, a few slats in one corner bent out of shape. Birds chirped in the distance like it was the best day ever and not some cold-ass day in northern Minnesota, and like the past week hadn't even happened. *The world keeps spinning while we stand still*, Linda thought, pulling a bottle of ibuprofen from her nightstand.

She slowly got up, stretching and yawning, and dug through a pile of to-do laundry, pulling out her housecoat.

The house was still as Linda shuffled down the hallway, running a hand through her tangled brown hair, her slippers sticking to the hardwood floors. She stopped at Beth's room and readied to knock but stopped herself short. Instead, she listened, listened for movement—a breath, a laugh, a sob—from the other side, but none came. *Just go in, she needs you*, nagged the mom-voice inside her, the one she'd tried to silence during Beth's formative years when Linda convinced herself that being a "friend-mom" was a much better strategy to raising a child than being a "mom-mom." Stepping back from the door, Linda decided to let Beth sleep a bit longer. It was the least she could do.

Linda groaned as she stepped into the kitchen: the worst part of any party was the next day clean up. Crusty paper plates and still-full red Solo cups spilled from two large garbage bags, the room stinking of stale pickles and day-old cream cheese sandwiches. Dirty mugs gathered by the sink, each with different levels of old coffee sitting in them. The sink itself had dishes piled high—fancy platters and chip bowls left with their dips and finger foods to solidify overnight—though, in all fairness, the well-to-doers hadn't had much time to gather their things when the party had come to an abrupt end. The wide-eyed stares came flooding back to Linda as she stood in the mess, those glances that the guests had exchanged as Beth had ran inside the house, something clutched in her hand. She'd talked to Linda, hadn't she? Linda could recall Beth's pale face, her brown eyes that seemed to glow red, her mouth moving, but no sound followed. Linda had sat on the couch, half-tanked in her Sunday best, rising whispers and hushed gasps cutting through the silence that followed Beth to her room, slamming the door behind her. Then, Linda had poured herself another bourbon.

Tucked away in a corner of the kitchen sat Linda's coffee maker, a little white-stained-brown one that she'd had for years. She grabbed the pot, dumped in some water, and let old faithful do the rest. The clock on the machine flashed 10:22 am. The stench of sour food and fresh coffee made her stomach churn, so she shuffled over to the front door to grab some air and get the paper.

Linda shivered in the November wind, wrapping her housecoat tighter around her body. She looked on her doorstep—no paper. Sighing, she took a step out, the cold stinging at her exposed skin. The newspaper kid only bothered to lob it from the gravel road about 50 feet away. Kid had a shit arm—he could barely get it past the ditch that ran along the property.

Linda squinted, her vision nothing like it used to be, looking out onto the snow-filled landscape. It was just her and Beth out here on the outskirts of Warroad, Minnesota, with nothing but the trees to keep them company. She thought the solitude would've kept them both out of trouble. So much for that.

They'd moved from Minneapolis three years earlier. Beth, only fourteen then, had already spiraled out of control: she was failing all her classes (when she actually showed up), she would sneak out in the middle of the night and be gone for days, she'd even gotten physical with Linda after an argument about Beth's boyfriend of the week. Had Linda been a better parent—a better *person*—she would've gotten them the hell out of Dodge at the first sign of trouble. And she should've known better, having lived through her own rebellious teen years, but it was only when Linda came home to their shitty two-bedroom apartment in North Minneapolis one night to find Beth passed out on the bathroom floor, a dirty needle dangling from her arm, that she decided it was time to get away from it all. The next day, Linda packed up her '89 Passat and shoved a screaming Beth into the back seat. She drove them as far north as they could get without becoming Canadian.

Linda came to the ditch and, sure enough, two blue-bagged papers sat at the point where the land curved downwards. She snatched both bags from the snow and ran inside.

Her coffee ready, she took a seat at the table, nearly tripping over the phone cord—she'd unplugged it two days earlier, tired of the incessant ringing. She sipped her coffee, the warm liquid instantly bringing new life to her frozen bones and quieting her pounding head.

She untied the first bag and removed the paper—it was already four days old. Sighing, she shoved the paper back in the bag and threw it at the garbage pile. It hit some paper plates, knocking them onto the floor. She took another sip of her coffee and went for the second bag. It was already untied, and the paper was damp, the snow having found its way inside. She managed to unfold it and found the front page had been ripped clean off.

Her inner-mom nagged her to call the *Warroad Chronicle* offices and complain about the god-awful service, but she couldn't be bothered. It's not like it was the *Washington Post*. No, the *Chronicle* was more of a *National Enquirer* meets small town America gossip mill than an actual paper. If you wanted to read about the library's three (three!) new books, or how Farmer John befriended a pizza-loving sasquatch after he caught it rummaging through his trash, the *Chronicle* had you covered. As ridiculous as it was, it always brought out a chuckle or two from Linda—this was small-town living at its best: new books and a hungry bigfoot. Wasn't this the American dream: a simple, uncomplicated life? A small town where everyone claimed to like you, even when you heard their whispers as you walked past them with your daughter, all of them passing judgement on who you used to be and who they assumed you still were?

Even so, these people, they showed up without you asking them, they came to your house with every dainty under the sun, every eye shedding a small tear.

"I'm so sorry," they had all said yesterday afternoon, sympathetic hands on her, on Beth. And though Linda couldn't say it, so was she.

***

Linda tidied the kitchen the best she could, filling another garbage bag full of day-old food left on the counter. Just after noon, she finally decided to plug the phone back in, get dressed, and wake Beth.

"Sweetie?" Linda asked, knocking at her daughter's door. "Are you hungry? I can make you a grilled cheese."

Linda had never been one to barge in—she understood that a teenager needed her space—but something in her gut felt off. The feeling had been growing stronger over the past week, but she had shrugged it off given the circumstances, assuming that it would've passed by now. Instead, it was at its strongest.

"Fuck it." Linda said, opening the door.

The phone rang as she stepped into an empty room.

***

Tiny snowflakes glide down from the sky, the glint of the moonlight caught in their crystals. Beth kneels behind a large tree, eyes and ears on the road—the coast is clear. Still clutching the canvas bag in one arm, she pulls out a small flashlight and a folded paper from her back pocket, reading it as quickly as she can. She looks to the dark highway and smiles.

Putting the light and paper away, Beth steps out from the woods and onto the icy black asphalt, the truck nowhere in sight. It's just her and the snowflakes, the moon and the road. She crosses the snowed-over highway, her footprints and the truck's tread marks the only signs of life.

She grips the canvas bag a little closer and makes her way down the road at mile marker 156.

Linda jammed the key into the Passat's ignition. The engine turned over once ("Come on."), twice ("Come on!"), three times ("Piece of shit."), before it coughed to life. She sat in it for a moment, rubbing her cold hands together and letting the engine warm, trying to push the uneasy feeling out of her body. Beth was gone, and there was only one place she could be. There were no boys in the picture, no friends that had come around, she was alone. Alone with Linda.

Her fingers still cold and the engine barely warmed up, Linda told herself everything was fine. Still, she put the car into drive and stepped on it.

Twenty minutes later, she passed the bend on Lake Street, coming to a stop outside Solace Gardens' wrought iron gates. The place was deserted, only two vehicles sat in the parking lot.

She felt it now, sitting in her shitty VW, that feeling in her gut spreading outwards, digging its claws into her veins, rolling through her blood. Something *wasn't* right. She had to find Beth.

Pushing through the dread, she took her foot off the brake and drove through the cemetery gates.

***

The winding gravel road is overgrown with frozen prairie grass and ice-filled potholes, but Beth is careful to mind her footing. The forest huddles around her, dense like a Terracotta army watching her from the shadows. All the while, the canvas bag feels lighter, like she could walk with it a thousand miles more. And she would. She would.

The road feels like it winds forever. After every turn lies another and another, until finally it straightens, the trees still dense.

How long had she been walking? Eight hours? Nine? After the sun went down, she lost track of everything, even the feeling in her toes.

She stops, releasing one hand from the canvas bag. She pulls out the paper again, her fingers stiff, a frown spreading on her face. There's no mention of where to go, just that she needs to be on this road.

She looks up to the moon, a lighthouse over a still sea. Clouds threaten to mask it, heavy clouds bringing with them a wave of big, full flakes that float by like dandelion fluffs.

She watches them fall around her, but then something catches her eye, something hidden off to the side, past the road, past the shoulder, in a tangle of branches and vines.

Placing the paper back into her pocket, she clutches the bag once more and lifts her feet through the prairie grass, the snow up to her knees.

There, obscured by the trees whose branches seem to shift as she steps closer, is a piece of wood, too smooth and clean-cut to be here by accident. She brushes the tangle with a free hand, stepping through it like a curtain at a psychic's salon. Beyond it is a path, as clear as the highway she's been walking on. Warm air surrounds her, the feeling returning to her fingers and toes.

She reaches out to the foliage that surrounds the wooden sign, and sees the letters written on it, drawn with a loving hand.

Laurel Lane.

As she lets the brush drape behind her, the roar of an engine sounds off down the road.

✳ ✳ ✳

Linda parked next to the police cruiser, the sun already starting its descent in the late November afternoon. She gathered herself and exited the car, making her way up the small hill to the black slab of polished granite that glimmered in the fading sun. It was etched with three simple things: a name, a birth date, and a death date. She'd stared at that final date yesterday, her eyes boring a hole into the stone, her hands clutching Beth's quivering shoulders all while trying to keep her own body from shaking.

There'd been moments in her life when the thought of packing up and leaving it all behind—Beth included— had crossed her mind. She'd told herself over and over that those thoughts were normal, that every parent had them. But watching Beth's face yesterday as she'd stepped away from Linda to drop a single rose on the oak lid, to see the light forever gone from her eyes, to feel her twitch under Linda's hands as clumps of the cold dirt thudded against the coffin, it was then that Linda knew that she and her daughter were bound to tragedy. And no matter how far she went—with or without Beth— they were both doomed.

Linda approached the headstone from behind, the

black granite rising from the earth like an obelisk. When she rounded the tombstone, she held her breath, expecting to see Beth, the small girl that she was at seventeen, curled up on the dirt, cold, broken.

But there was no Beth.

Only an open grave and an empty casket.

✳✳✳

The trees hang high above like a cathedral ceiling, arched and stoic, completely blocking out the moon and the sky. Yet even without the light, Beth can see the path with perfect clarity, as though the road itself is its own moon. The more she walks, the lighter each step feels. The crunch of the stones under her boots echo all around her like she's stepped into a vacant hall.

There's a break in the trees up ahead, at the end of the path. And there, dead centre, sits a well. It rests in the middle of a clearing, the trees thick around it any which way she looks, so thick that a body couldn't pass through them. Fluffy snowflakes hover around her, floating neither up nor down, just stuck in place, twirling like a pendant on a string. She looks to the sky, still bright, but the moon is gone.

Beth comes to the edge of the well, its rough stones faded and chipped away. She kneels at its base, by a groove in the snow that fits the canvas bag perfectly. She places it there, softly, and rests a hand on it.

After a moment, she takes a deep breath and approaches the well. She peers over the side into the black mass, no bottom in sight, no sounds coming up. "Hello?" she calls out, her voice coarse and gravelled, small and broken. No echo sounds back.

Her hands touch the cold stone, she closes her eyes.

The slightest vibrations run through her finger tips, and for a fleeting second, she feels it in her chest, imagining the well's power surging through her. She brings her legs over the edge and sits, the vibrations growing stronger, a sound rising under them.

The roar of an engine.

***

Linda ran to the funeral home, each step like quicksand trying to pull her down. In the lobby, where only yesterday she'd greeted all the mourners as Beth wept alone in the bathroom, stood Nancy, the funeral director, and Officer Daniels, a young cop that Linda had seen around town.

"Christ, we've been trying to reach you!" Nancy said, running to Linda and grabbing hold of her. "Your line's been busy all morning."

"Where's Beth?" Linda screamed, her eyes darting between both women. "Where's April?"

"April's body . . . " Nancy started, looking back to Daniels.

"Ms. Jeanson," Officer Daniels took over, her tone soft. "When was the last time you spoke to your daughter?"

Linda stepped back, the air around her heavy. "You're not saying what I think you're saying."

Nancy looked to the ground, while Daniels kept her eyes on Linda. "Ms. Jeanson, we have reason to believe that Beth—"

Linda took off out the doors without letting Daniels finish, hands grasping her pockets for her keys. She got into her car and shoved them into the ignition. The engine turned once. Twice. Three times. Nothing. She tried again. And again. And again, until the car coughed no more, only clicked.

"Fuck!" Linda screamed into her steering wheel. "Fuck fuck fuck fuck fuck!"

She gripped the wheel, her head falling against the cold leather.

This is all your fault.

Everything poured out then: if she hadn't moved them to this fucking town in the first place, this never would have happened. Beth would've never wound up pregnant at seventeen; Linda would've never cursed her daughter out that night she told her the news, all the hate that she'd built up inside for being a reckless teenager herself spilling onto her poor daughter; April would've never been born, a sweet, wide-eyed girl that'd made Linda's heart melt the moment she first saw her; and April would've never died, Beth's sleep-deprived body rolling on top of her. Beth waking hours later, a tiny blue arm sticking out from under her.

Nancy knocked at the car window. Linda rolled it down, wiping the tears from her face. "My car's dead," she said, her voice cracking.

"Here," Nancy said, opening the door and pulling Linda out. "Take my keys."

Linda paused. "Are you sure?" She looked back to the funeral home. "What about Daniels?"

"Go find Beth." Nancy smiled, pushing her along.

Linda hugged Nancy as she climbed into the vehicle, the engine roaring to life.

Now what?

She looked down to the floor, a few bunched up McDonald's wrappers and empty Pepsi cans lining the mat. On the passenger's seat was yesterday's paper, the front page still intact: the church bake sale, the terrible weather they'd been having, and an *Enquirer-*

esque piece on something called the Resurrection Gash.

Linda tried to pull her eyes away, but that same feeling that roiled through her body told her to keep reading. So, she did.

And when she was done, she threw the truck into reverse and went to find mile marker 156.

***

"Beth!" Linda screams as she jumps from the truck, the *Chronicle* falling from her lap. "Stop, please!"

The truck's headlights strike Beth, her pale face awash in the white glow.

Beth remains seated on the well's edge. She looks down into the Gash, the black pit looking back at her.

"Beth, this isn't real. Whatever you think is going to happen, believe me, it won't."

Linda moves closer, steadying her pace. Beth's eyes meet her mother's, then move to the small canvas bag, still under a thin blanket of snow. Linda's eyes follow. At the sight of the bag, she stops.

"Please, sweetheart," Linda pleads. "You've already lost your daughter. I can't lose mine, too."

Tears run down Beth's face, a sob escaping her lips. Her eyes stay on the bag, small and motionless. She squeezes her fingers harder against the cold stone. It vibrates back.

"Sorry, Mom. Sorry."

Linda throws herself forward just as Beth pushes off the ledge.

Beth's scarf tickles the edges of Linda's fingers as they desperately try to grasp onto something—*anything*—but when Linda pulls her arms back, her hands are empty.

Linda screams, the rage flying from her body out into the snowy night. The screams burn a hole inside her, tearing at her flesh, ripping through her bones. She cries out harder, louder, into the hole, into the night, as though all her fury will somehow bring Beth back up. As though it will somehow reverse time.

Under the glow of the headlights, Linda falls to her knees. Fluffy snowflakes drift downwards, coming to rest on the truck, on her shivering body, on the little canvas bag.

A quick movement catches Linda's eye. She turns her head and looks to the empty forest, its branches still and rigid. The force of the truck's still-running engine reverberates against the cold bricks of the well, a rumble that rises in her chest.

Another movement, lower this time. Her eyes find the canvas bag. The night is frozen, nothing moves. She holds her breath. More snowflakes gently float down, resting on the bag.

She stares for minutes, minutes that feel like days.

More screams want to escape her throat, more tears want to pour from her eyes, but there's nothing left inside her. Nothing but horror and pain and love and loss all rolled into one, a jagged, disfigured mass occupying the cavity where her heart once beat.

She wills herself to look away, from the bag, from the well, from everything.

Look away and forget you were ever here.

But she can't. She won't.

Then, the bag twitches.

TITAN, TYGER

JONATHAN JANZ

WHEN THE BEAMER broke down, Peter Zink was stranded somewhere along County Road 1200 without a cell phone. Since Greta had become more vigilant in her sleuthing, Peter had grown more paranoid. He'd read somewhere that phones could be tracked, and he had no desire to arm her with more information than she already had. He'd told himself to pick up one of those cheapie phones, the kind you bought minutes for and used only in emergencies, but life was busy, and the prospect of an emergency like this had seemed so remote that he hadn't followed through on purchasing the cheap-ass phone.

Now look at him. Peter pocketed his hands in his cashmere coat, sighed, and performed a slow revolution. No houses in sight, no cars. He inclined his face, surveyed the black velvet sky. Empty. Not even a plane up there, a slow-moving red light reminding him that no, he wasn't entirely alone in this rustic wasteland.

Peter shook his head, checked his Rolex. It was half past two in the morning.

It's what you get for cheating, Tiger, the voice in his head mocked.

Scowling, Peter set off at a sullen stroll, his coat scant protection from the early March wind, his suede loafers ill-suited for the crumbly macadam road. He supposed he could return to Janice's, but things had ended badly, and she needed time to cool off. There'd been an uneasy moment when he believed she'd actually follow through on her threat, would actually call the police, and that was why it had been necessary for him to end that talk pronto.

No, Janice's was out of the question.

Peter strolled on, a vague recollection flitting through his mind about the way they numbered country roads. 1200 meant he was twelve miles from the county's center, or at least that's what he thought he'd heard. If that was the case, this was going to be a hell of a cruddy night.

His eyes had adjusted to the darkness, but he could discern no glow from where he believed town to be. God, that far away? Peter kicked a stone the size of a golf ball and watched it skitter into the weedy shoulder. He stopped and grinned ruefully. He hadn't remembered to lock his car!

Peter turned, extracted the key from his pocket, and thumbed the Lock button. As the familiar chirp sounded from the Beamer and the twin headlight blinks told him the car was indeed secure, Peter glimpsed something that made the grin on his face wither.

There was a truck parked beside the Beamer. A giant white truck.

Peter swallowed, screwed up his eyes. Yes, he was certain of the truck's presence, but to remove all doubt, he depressed the Lock button again, and in the pallid flicker of his headlamps, he made out the sleek white length of the pick-up truck. A newer model. He could see it gleam in the meager illumination filtering through the late-winter clouds.

Peter started toward his car. The fact that the truck was a newer model and, from the looks of it, polished to a pearlescent gleam, should have reassured him. But something about the way it idled in the road, its engine so noiseless Peter had to strain to pick it up, sent a ripple of unease down his back. It occurred to him he'd left his Browning at home in the nightstand. He ordinarily only carried the gun when there was business in Chicago or some other big city crawling with thugs, but now he realized how foolish he'd been. What if the driver of this truck—a Nissan Titan, he now saw—planned to rob him? Peter was in decent shape. He walked the treadmills at the country club fitness center, but at fifty-two years old and without much muscle, he knew the chances were slim he'd be able to overcome the Titan's driver in a fight.

Ten feet from the truck's gleaming grill, Peter halted, a new worry assailing him. What if there were multiple occupants inside the pick-up truck? What if this was a gang of rowdy teenagers out hunting for a cheap thrill? *Hey, look at the rich white guy! Let's see how loud he can scream!*

Peter reached into his pocket, his fingers probing for the keys. Maybe if he unlocked the Beamer, raced around to the passenger's side door, lunged inside, and locked himself in he could just wait these thrill-seeking bastards out. Maybe he could—

The Titan's interior lit up. A sole figure stared back at him.

It was a man. Peter could see that clearly. But unless he was deceived, the driver was smallish, almost feminine, with his narrow, bony shoulders, and his celery-stalk neck. Peter peered at the driver's face: brown hair matted down and tufted a little behind the ears, as if he'd been wearing a ball cap.

Well, of course he's been wearing a ball cap, the voice in Peter's head declared. Have you ever seen someone in a full-sized pick-up truck who *didn't* wear ball caps?

It emboldened Peter, started him forward. He owned several caps of his own, often wore them while driving his boat.

He reached the passenger's side of the Titan, watched the window descend. An odd aroma wafted out at him. Cinnamon, maybe. Some sort of cheap air freshener.

Peter leaned an arm on the window aperture and nodded. "Don't suppose you'd give a guy a lift home, would you?"

The driver swiveled his head, and Peter had to strain to maintain his smile. Creepy, the way the driver had turned. But not as creepy as the mindless grin. *Alfred E. Newman*, Peter thought. The mascot for the old *Mad* magazines. No, this young man wasn't as cartoonish as Alfred E. Newman, but there was something of the cartoon character's mischief in his grin, too much of Newman's jeering mockery. God, Peter thought. Like a ventriloquist's dummy sprung to life.

Peter glanced at the road to escape the guy's disconcerting grin. "Maybe I'll walk. The night air—"

"It's no trouble," the driver said.

Peter glanced at him sidelong.

"Come ride with me," the driver said.

The message was innocuous, Peter knew, but something about the driver's choice of words . . .

"Wanna see my hands?" the driver asked, and actually showed his palms as though to prove he wasn't a threat.

The goofiness of the gesture released some of Peter's tension. Chuckling, he glanced down at his loafers, dusty already from the road.

"Alright," Peter said, opening the Titan's door. "A ride would be nice."

"Depends on the chauffeur," the driver said as Peter settled in. This close, the guy looked even younger than Peter had first estimated. Barely drinking age.

The door thudded shut. "Well, I certainly appreciate it," Peter said.

The driver switched off the interior light and twisted on the headlights. "I had a feeling you would."

"It's frigid out tonight," Peter said. "Mind if I roll up the window?"

The driver shifted the truck into gear, and they began to roll forward. "Do what you want. Cold doesn't affect me."

That's because you're tougher than I am, I suppose. Peter suppressed a smile and kept his opinions to himself. This kid had saved his ass, after all. He'd have been hiking until dawn without the intervention.

Peter introduced himself. When the kid didn't answer, Peter said, "Are you going to tell me your name, or should I just call you my guardian angel?"

The kid's smile went away. "Oh, I wouldn't do that."

Peter studied the kid's profile. Despite the disappearance of the goofy grin, the kid looked more like a ventriloquist's doll than ever. *Okay*, Peter thought. *Be a weirdo. God knows the world's full of them.*

"Merry," the kid said at length.

Peter raised his eyebrows. "Excuse me?"

"My name's Merry."

"Like Mary, mother of—"

"Like the hobbit," the kid said.

Peter grinned. "As in, Merry Christmas?"

"Yes," the kid said, his lips drawing downward at the corners. "Like Merry Christmas."

***

"So, is this where we share our life stories?" Peter asked. He nestled into the leather seat, smoothed his coat over his legs. "I don't really know much about hitchhiker's etiquette."

The kid's easy grin returned, though his eyes remained on the road. "Surprising. I figured you knew everything about everything."

Peter narrowed his eyes and let them linger on the kid's profile. Definitely a bit of a smartass, a trait Peter could not abide. His son, fourteen, was more than a bit of a smartass, and Peter planned to nip that behavior in the bud—

"Pronto," Merry said.

Peter blinked. "What did you say?"

An infinitesimal shake of the head. "Nothing, tiger."

Peter reached up and adjusted the collar of his coat. "Well, Merry. Tell me about yourself."

"Your imagination couldn't handle it."

Definitely a smartass. "This truck, for starters." Peter spread his arms. "This is a nice truck. It can't be more than a few years old." Peter leaned sideways and tried to see the odometer. "How many miles are on it?"

Merry didn't answer.

Peter pushed up higher on his seat, but other than

the bluish glow of the speedometer, the dashboard appeared dark.

"You ought to get that fixed," Peter said, settling back. "You get pulled over ... "

"What were you doing tonight?" Merry asked.

Peter stiffened.

"It's awful late," Merry continued. "What were you doing out so late at night?"

Peter glowered out the passenger's window. "Business."

Merry guffawed. Peter jolted in his seat. Merry slapped the steering wheel, brayed his donkey's bray. "'Business,'" Merry said. "He's a businessman doing his business." Merry wiped an eye.

Peter glared at the kid, made no attempt at hiding his asperity. Had Merry been drinking? He certainly acted like it. Or perhaps he was merely a simpleton, amused by his own dull-witted jokes. At any rate, it was a nuisance. The sooner he got home, the better.

Peter nodded ahead. "Up here at the stop sign, take a right. That'll send us through Shadeland."

But Merry rolled right through the stop sign and kept going straight.

Peter turned in his seat. "You missed—"

"You don't wanna go through town, tiger. Business like yours, it's best to keep things quiet."

Peter realized his mouth was hanging open, and closed it, fast. *Time to take control of this situation*, the voice in his head declared. *Show the little cretin who's in charge.* Peter placed his hands on his legs and let his fingers dig in. His father's voice invariably brought on a sweltering heat in the base of his neck, but that was because the voice reminded him of what he was failing to do. Dammit, he thought. Life was a series of confrontations. In his business dealings, in his personal life. And now with this goddamned kid.

So be it. Peter Zink had worked too hard and was too fucking important to allow this yokel to dictate the terms of their deal, even if the kid was doing him a favor.

"Listen," Peter began, letting the steel permeate his voice, "I see a security light up there on the left. Pull in there, turn around, and—"

"She knows."

Peter stopped and stared at Merry. "What are you talking about?"

"Greta," Merry said. "She knows all about your cheating."

A freezing tide washed over him. "Stop the car."

"Under your back bumper, there's one of them hidden GPS thingies. She attached it back in July."

Peter stared at Merry, appalled. Back in *July*? Jesus Christ, that was more than seven *months* ago. But how . . .

Peter gave himself no time to think. He seized Merry's shoulder and squeezed. "Tell me who you are. How do you know these things?" God, the kid's shoulder had almost no meat on it. Just knobs of bone. "Did Greta pay you to follow me? That's it, isn't it? You were stationed outside Janice's house, waiting for me." He released Merry's shoulder, punched himself in the thigh. "Of course! That's how you showed up in the middle of the damned night. I can't believe I fell for this."

Merry had said something while Peter was speaking, but Peter couldn't make it out. "I didn't hear you," Peter said.

"Never met her," Merry repeated.

"Who?" Peter asked. "Greta? Janice?"

"Sarah, Carolyn, Ashley, Michelle." Merry chuckled. "How 'bout that escort you hired when you were in Denver?"

Peter's thoughts pinwheeled. There was no conceivable way. He'd *flown* to Denver, not driven. Greta couldn't have known about the "escort," as Merry referred to her, the stunning blonde with the gravity-defying breasts.

They passed the farmhouse with its dreary security light and were swallowed up again by the stygian darkness.

Peter licked his lips. "Clearly . . . clearly Greta paid you handsomely. I won't deny anything you've said."

Merry's lips curved, the ventriloquist's dummy resurfacing. "Poor Janice, motionless on her kitchen floor."

Motionless? Peter thought. *Jesus Christ.* He hadn't hit her *that* hard. Surely she wasn't . . .

"Merry?" he asked.

"Hm."

"Whatever Greta is paying you, I'll double it."

When Merry only laughed softly, Peter pressed on. "I'll triple it. I'll . . . what do you want me to do?"

"It's simple," Merry said. "When we get back to your mansion—"

"It's not a mansion."

"And Janice doesn't *have* a house," Merry said. "She's got a trailer."

"What's your point?"

"You go inside," Merry continued, "and you grab the keys to that black Hummer you keep in the extra garage. The detached one with the guest house above it?"

Everything, Peter thought. *He knows everything.*

"Take that gas-guzzling abomination over to Janice's *trailer* and go inside."

But Peter was shaking his head. "I can't take the Hummer. The engine . . . it'll wake the kids."

"Stop acting like you give a shit about your kids."

Peter's mouth fell open. "How dare you?

Merry's easy grin widened.

"No, really," Peter went on. "How dare you impugn my parenting?"

"'Impugn my parenting!'" Merry repeated, slapping the wheel. He wiped an eye. "Golly, that's a good one. 'Impugn my parenting.'"

A switch flipped inside Peter's head. Maybe it was having his words thrown back at him. Maybe it was the fact that he was still, no matter how much he'd hated the man in life, his father's son. Whatever the case . . .

"You're guilty of unlawful incarceration," Peter began.

Merry was nodding. "And you'll sic the police on me, and they'll lock me up—"

"You're goddamned right."

"—and throw away the key. Just like when I snipped Daddy."

"Let me out of this truck!" Peter shouted. He pounded on the dashboard, kicked the underside of the glove box. "Let me out right now!"

"I let you out, you'll end up in jail."

Peter's breath caught. His lips began to quiver as the images strobed through his mind: Handcuffs, bars, beatings. Even worse, he saw his family without him, Greta marrying some boy toy, some oily-chested masseuse at an all-inclusive resort who didn't need pills to make his dick stand up, who'd live large on Peter's savings, while Peter's kids drove expensive cars too fast and cursed their jailbird father the same way Peter cursed his own father, the Great Peter Zink Senior, who sure as hell belonged in jail, who scammed everybody he knew, who cheated on his wife unapologetically, who smacked his wife around when the whim arose, who taught Peter everything there was to know about getting what you want.

"I said pull over," Peter said, but the fog had settled over him, a steel-hued panic that deprived him of reason, that reduced him to a caged animal.

When Merry only continued to drive, Peter lost his composure, thrashed in his seat, thumped the window with a fist, kicked at the base of the glove box, and that was when the glove box door flipped open and the glossy black revolver tumbled out.

Peter's eyes shot wide. Merry hadn't reacted, but Peter knew he would. Before this deranged idiot grabbed for the gun, Peter lunged for it, got ahold of it, and without thinking he jammed the revolver against Merry's temple, hard enough to shove him against the driver's side door. The car slued to the left.

"Pull over!" Peter commanded.

Merry eyed him askance. "Unless you want us to end up in a ditch—"

"*Stop the fucking car!*" Peter snarled.

"You might wanna think about this."

Peter thumbed off the safety.

"There's things you don't understand," Merry said. "You won't get another chance."

Peter squeezed the trigger.

Merry's head twitched and a gout of red syrup splashed the driver's side window. Lolling sideways, Merry's slack arms hauled the Titan across the gravel road, straight toward the shoulder, and the Titan tremored as it jounced over the shallow ditch and took out a fence post, the attached wires twanging loudly enough to make Peter's ears ring, and then Peter was wrestling the wheel, the Titan thumping over a lumpy bean field, gradually circling back, nearing the road, then lurching as it bounced over the shallow ditch once more. His whole body numb, Peter crowded Merry's legs aside, finally located the brake pedal, stepped on it indelicately, and the Titan skidded sideways, two tires actually leaving the road, before slamming back down and shivering to a stop.

The engine light was on, its orange eye blinking. The Titan had stalled.

Peter sat there, the Titan sideways in the road, the sound of trickling liquid just audible above the dinging of the engine light.

Gasoline, Peter thought. *My God, the gas line's ruptured.*

Then he grew aware of Merry's body against his, of the pattering sound. Peter looked down, thought, *Blood. That's what's trickling. Merry's blood.*

Murderer, he thought.

Self-defense! the voice in his mind responded, but its protest was feeble, the denial of a child with a chocolate-smeared face who claims he never went near the Halloween candy stash.

The reality of his situation flooded over him. Gasping, he shoved away from Merry's corpse and scrambled toward the passenger's seat. There was a subtle ticking from somewhere in the engine. Other than that, the night was utterly silent.

Peter swallowed, glanced about, saw they were alone

on the dusty road, but for how long there was no way to tell. That was the problem with people around here, always in each other's business. If someone happened down this country road now, the driver would stop, ask Peter if he needed help. And in Peter's current state, slathered with sweat and no doubt looking guilty as hell, there'd be no hiding his crime.

What could he say anyway, should someone arrive? *Naw, you go on. I prefer to sit here in the middle of the road beside a gore-streaked corpse in a truck I don't own.*

A fit of hysterical laughter threatened to rise up, and he bit back on it.

Okay, he thought. *One thing at a time. See if the truck will start.*

Keeping his eyes studiously averted from the body, he reached out and keyed the ignition.

The Titan gave a slow, drunken chugging and devolved into a rapid tick.

Fuck!

He was precariously close to hyperventilating, so he closed his eyes, heaved a deep breath. *There's no choice*, he told himself. *Either remain calm or go to jail.*

Or, the hectoring voice added, *you could suck on the barrel of that gun. It'd be preferable to facing a trial—*

No!

—public ruin—

Stop it.

—seeing your kids' faces when Daddy gets sent away—

Peter sobbed.

—of Greta's contemptuous gaze when she learns of your serial infidelity—

Christ.

—and when you're charged with two murders.

Peter froze, his eyes opening. My God, he'd almost forgotten about Janice. Was it possible she really was dead?

It wasn't possible. He'd barely hit her!

Impulsively, he reached out, twisted the key, and cried out in relief when the engine rumbled to life. *Yes. Yes yes yes yes yes.*

He glanced at Merry. Still lolling, still dead.

He couldn't drive with a corpse practically in his lap. *The truck bed.*

Yes, Peter thought. But he didn't relish the prospect of opening Merry's door from inside the Titan and watching Merry spill out into the road. Peter opened his own door and hurried around to the driver's side. No sign of other cars yet.

He opened the driver's door and still almost missed catching Merry when the dead body slumped sideways. Peter caught the body under the armpits, his back twinging at the sudden load, and managed to backpedal until the corpse's boots smacked the gravel. Knowing the job wouldn't be made easier by delaying, Peter dragged Merry's body toward the bed of the Titan, but there, a new problem presented itself. Merry was a little guy, but Peter figured he still weighed one-sixty or so. The treadmill hadn't prepared Peter for hefting that much dead weight into the bed of a pickup truck.

The tailgate!

Yes, Peter thought, his spirits surging. He towed Merry's body around to the rear of the Titan, released the tailgate, and took a moment to catch his breath. He surveyed the road to make sure there weren't any cars coming—there weren't—and resumed his grip on Merry's armpits. His back groaning, Peter hauled

Merry's body higher, higher, and then, miraculously, Merry was facedown on the tailgate, his legs poking over the edge. Wincing, Peter leaned against the Titan, but only for a moment. He had to finish this.

He had to return to Janice's.

It was a vague notion, but a scenario of sorts had begun to form in his mind. If he could plant evidence that Merry had been at Janice's, he might be able to build a story around it. He shoved Merry's legs into the truck bed, slammed the gate shut. He hustled around the Titan and climbed behind the wheel. The Titan's engine was rumbling softly, so he shifted into gear and began the job of turning around. It took him a good twenty seconds— the Titan was massive and the road was narrow—but he finally managed to head back the way he'd come.

As he drove, he worked out the details:

There'd be no denying he'd been at Janice's. The affair would come out. He wished he could avoid it, but his fingerprints and DNA were everywhere. God, he hadn't even used a condom, instead trusting Janice's birth control.

Forget it, he told himself. *Figure it out.*

He'd admit to sleeping with Janice: *I'm not proud of it, but yes, I was unfaithful to my wife.* A corner of his mouth twitched. It could just be the sort of bullshit contrition that would render him more sympathetic to the police. Or a jury.

He'd slept with his mistress and left. His car broke down. He hoofed it back to Janice's trailer, and there he saw . . .

. . . the Titan.

That's right, he told himself. *It was parked outside Janice's trailer.*

And from within . . .

. . . from within he heard the sounds of a struggle. He rushed to the porch, pounded on the door, but by that time, the sounds had ceased. He opened the trailer door, went in, and saw . . .

Janice's body.

Yes, he thought, now at the stop sign. He glanced both ways, judged it safe, and continued on, the image of Janice's prone body floating in his mind's eye. When he'd left her before, she'd been weeping, prostrate, her pitiful display somehow satisfying in the basest region of his soul. To her he'd been godlike, all-powerful, and even though he'd been wrong to strike her, he knew she'd never tell the authorities about it, knew she was too frightened of him, too worshipful to risk his wrath.

So yes, he'd tell the officers who'd show up shortly after he called from Janice's landline, *we had an affair, and when I returned and saw her body lying there, when I beheld the lunatic who'd struck her the fatal blow, the gun in his hand and a maniacal grin on his face, it broke my heart.*

Perfect, he thought. *You have nothing to hide, after all. You've done nothing wrong.*

He'd tell the police Merry had marched him to the Titan at gunpoint. They'd climbed inside. Merry had driven him out to the country for God knew what reason, but Peter had overpowered Merry, had wrested the gun from his grip and shot the man in self-defense. Then he'd motored back to Janice's in the slim hope she'd still be alive.

He bit his bottom lip. It was outlandish, but the truth was outlandish too. One story was as believable as the other. If he played it right, he thought he could sell them on the fake story.

Stop thinking of it as fake, he told himself. *It's the truth. Merry killed Janice. You merely saved yourself from dying too.*

Better still, he reminded himself, Janice might not be dead. He only had Merry's word as proof, and maybe Merry had been lying. And if Janice weren't dead, Peter believed he could get her to forgive him. She might even help him. They could wipe down the Titan, drive it fifty miles away from here, and she could give him a ride back to her trailer. My God, if that were possible, the truth about his affair wouldn't even have to be made public. Life could go on as it had been.

Nodding, Peter depressed the accelerator. Five more minutes and he'd arrive at Janice's trailer.

Lord, he hoped she was still alive.

***

She wasn't.

She was just as he'd left her, only now there was a lake of blood surrounding her head, the dingy beige linoleum stained a deep crimson. He swayed in the entryway of her trailer and tried to sort it out. Yes, he'd belted her in the face, but at worse he figured he'd bruised her. When he'd stormed out, she hadn't even been bleeding, at least not that he could see. She'd been facedown, her shoulders had been racked with sobs, and she'd been undoubtedly, indisputably alive.

How in God's name had she died?

Maybe, he thought, closing the door swiftly behind him, Merry really had entered the trailer after Peter, really had murdered Janice to frame Peter.

Peter took a steadying breath. He had to learn the truth.

Before he could lose his nerve, he scurried over to where Janice lay, and taking care to keep his loafers clear of the blood spill, he grasped a hank of Janice's brown hair and lifted.

He gagged.

Janice's eyes were gone. The hollowed-out cavities gaped at him in messy accusation.

He scrambled away, his loafers skimming the blood pool and leaving scarlet scuff marks in his wake. His shoulder blades connected with a free-standing cabinet, its contents rattling around inside. He clapped a hand to his mouth and stared at Janice. Mercifully, her hair had tumbled over her gory eye sockets.

The implications began to swirl. Merry *had* killed Janice! He'd killed her and led Peter to believe it had been Peter who'd committed murder.

He drew a hand over his mouth and struggled to process this. He hadn't killed Janice, and when he'd shot Merry, he'd been executing Janice's killer.

But how to escape unscathed?

Peter closed his eyes, and now, shut of the sight of Janice's corpse, a new plan began to crystalize.

Tell the truth.

Well, he amended, *the truth with a single fact omitted*.

He'd never struck Janice. No, he'd never laid a finger on her, and tragically, after he'd left her trailer, she'd been murdered by a psychopath. After executing Janice and ritualistically removing her eyes, Merry had picked up Peter, whose car had broken down. From that point forward, he'd just tailor the story to make himself the victim.

Peter opened his eyes. It was insane, but it just might work.

True, there would be a hellstorm of legal hassles. Yes, it would cost him his marriage, and his law firm would no doubt let him go.

But his kids might forgive him. He wasn't the first husband to cheat, after all. And he would have plenty of money to build a new house. And he'd be free of Greta's incessant carping.

All he had to do was pick up the phone and call the police.

Peter got slowly to his feet. His knees felt creaky, and the clammy fear sweat coating his flesh had begun to stink. No matter. He'd been through a traumatic event. The more shaken up he acted, the better.

Taking care to avoid Janice's corpse, he made his way through the kitchen, past the single bathroom, and into her bedroom, where a phone sat atop her nightstand.

He was reaching for it when a voice said, "You got your souvenirs."

Peter shrieked. He stumbled backward, his feet tangling, and hit the cheap paneling headfirst. There was a crunching sound, and his vision grayed. A moment later the world stopped carouseling and he was able to make out the figure sitting on the edge of Janice's bed.

It was Merry.

"Hey, tiger," the young man said.

❖ ❖ ❖

Peter licked his lips and stared at Merry's form in the semidarkness. He couldn't be sure, but the side of Merry's head appeared to glisten. "You're . . . you're dead."

"I *been* dead. Long before I met you. I been drivin' around for weeks, waiting on the tug."

178

"Tug?"

"The pull that tells me where to go."

Peter's thoughts churned. "You're telling me you we were . . . *pulled* in my direction? After I hit Janice?"

The jeering grin resurfaced. "First smart thing you've said tonight."

Peter stared at Merry, the fine patina of sweat on his neck like an icy drizzle. "Is that what this is? Like a second chance kind of thing?"

Merry eyed him. "Come on, tiger. Use that rich boy education your papa bought you."

Peter clenched his jaw. "I see. I'm supposed to believe I'm the bad guy. Because I had the audacity to make money?"

Merry chuckled, his fingers touching something that bulged in his hip pocket. "This might come as a shock, tiger, but not everything's about you."

Peter fell silent.

"I'm talking," Merry went on, "about why *I'm* here. Why I'm doing this night in and night out. Roamin' the countryside. Goin' where I'm called to go."

Peter sat there trembling.

"I had an English teacher," Merry continued. "She was okay at first. But the more you had her, the more you realized she had it in for you."

Peter began to ask a question, but Merry was already waving him off. "Not me personally. I mean kids in general."

Peter waited, knowing he could do nothing to brook the flow of words.

"She had us pick a poem, one from what she called the Romantic Era. I skimmed a bunch of stuff, but none of it made sense. Till I stumbled upon a poem by a guy named William Blake." He glanced at Peter. "Ever hear of him?"

Peter hadn't.

"I picked this poem," Merry said. "Was called 'The Tyger.' I memorized it just like we were told to, and even if I didn't understand it, I still suspected it meant something."

"Look, Merry," Peter began, but Merry's eyes had taken on a glaze. Staring at the paneling above Peter, he started to recite:

> "Tyger, Tyger, burning bright,
> In the forests of the night;
> What immortal hand or eye
> Could frame thy fearful symmetry?"

Peter shook his head. He was aware of his gaping mouth, the drool stringing from his bottom lip, but the words Merry had uttered kept reverberating in his brain, condemning him, teasing him, and when he was able to speak, his question surprised him. "Who are you?"

Merry slouched on the bedside, elbows on knees, fingers drooping limply, head down, the side of his head a glistening goulash of blood and curly hair. Staring at the ruin of Merry's temple, a thought began to tickle at Peter's subconscious. Not a clear thought, but persistent.

"*Say something*," Peter hissed. "Tell me what the hell you are. Whatever's going to happen to me, why don't you get it over with?"

Merry shook his head wearily. "You don't get it."

Peter wanted to scramble to his feet, to seize Merry by his flannel shirt and shake him until he started making sense. But he couldn't. The sight of the gunshot wound, so real and undeniably *fatal* rendered Peter powerless.

Peter asked the question, though he dreaded the answer. "Are you really dead?"

"Only guys like you can see me," Merry answered. "I'm here because of what I did."

Like a rat darting from beneath a dumpster, the thought for which he'd been groping finally scurried into the light. "You said 'when I snipped Daddy.' Earlier, in the truck. You said—"

"*I know what I said*," Merry snapped, and when the eyes met Peter's, they were tinged with a red glow. "How was I supposed to know?"

"Merry, I—"

"*Don't Merry me!*" he shrieked and launched himself off the bed. Bent at the waist, he shoved his face in Peter's, shouted at him, his breath like carrion meat. "I shouldn't've done it, I know that, but he was always on me, always tellin' me I wasn't no man. When I'd come home from drinkin' and found him passed out, even more shitfaced than I was, I told myself he deserved it, he got what was comin' to him."

Peter shook his head slowly. This capering little fool was insane. The bullet had somehow grazed Merry, had somehow spared him. It was the only explanation.

Merry crouched before Peter, eye to eye now. The carrion breath was withering. "I drove off in his truck, thinking I'd leave town. Then I—" Merry broke off, and tears shimmered in his eyes. "I ran into someone. On the road."

This isn't happening, Peter told himself. *This is madness.*

"He took me for a drive, and when we were a good

ways from town, he gave me the same choice I gave you."
Merry's chest hitched. His teeth bared, he grasped
Peter's shoulders and spoke directly into his face. "*And I
been drivin' ever since!*"

Peter swallowed. "What are you telling me?"

Merry grinned a terrible grin. "Shit, you still don't
get it? Head on back to that fancy car of yours, you'll
see." Merry's fingers went to the hip pocket of his jeans
again.

Peter gaped up at him. "You mean I'm free to leave?"

Merry bellowed laughter. When he got control of
himself, he fixed Peter with a look so haunted, Peter
could scarcely stand it. "That's the hell of it," Merry said.
"We're always free. Free to do good, free to fuck up. Free
to ruin our lives and other lives, just as pretty as we
please. My daddy, he was a stone-cold sonofabitch. Got
what was comin', he did . . . no doubt about it. But what I
done to him . . . uh-uh. I reckon I had it comin' too."

Peter got up. "You won't follow me?"

Merry squinted. "Why would I? You made your
decision. Once you decided you weren't going back, you
reserved your ride."

"My ride?"

Merry chuckled. "A special kind of hell. You'd be
surprised at how many people hurt others and just leave
'em like roadkill. What we do is give assholes like you the
choice to go back, to make things right." A shrug. "Or
righter. But once you shot me, you made your choice.
Now you carry your keepsake just like I carry mine."

Peter patted the pockets of his coat. "Where's the
gun? I swear I . . . "

Merry only watched him, a disdainful grin twisting
his lips. Merry again touched his hip pocket, the fingers

stroking whatever lay within. Peter began stepping toward the door.

"Go on," Merry urged. "Head back to your car. It'll start now."

Giving himself no time to lose his nerve, Peter hastened toward the bedroom door, jogged down the short hall, kept to the right side of the trailer to avoid Janice's body—still motionless, the head still surrounded by a penumbra of congealing blood—and then he was out the door and sprinting across the front yard. He didn't even spare the Titan a sideways glance.

It was—he checked his Rolex—well after three in the morning. He had no idea what he'd do now but getting away from Merry was his first priority. Madness emanated from that bleeding, cryptic hilljack. The farther he got from Merry, the better.

Though a stitch had started in his side and his feet were blistering from the friction between his loafers and his heels, he reached the BMW in ten minutes. Before getting in, he peered through a window into the backseat, certain Merry was lurking there in the murk. Although it was difficult to tell for sure, the backseat appeared to be empty. Still . . . the terror of having Merry speak to him in Janice's bedroom when he'd been absolutely certain that Merry was dead was fresh enough that Peter paused at each window of the car to peer inside. When his inspection revealed nothing except his briefcase and a cardboard McDonald's Big Mac container, he climbed inside, engaged the door locks, and sat there for a moment to allow his throbbing heartbeat to calm.

Headlights appeared behind him. *Oh hell*, Peter thought. *Not the Titan. Not Merry.*

He knew he should be trying the ignition, should attempt to drive away, but the sight of the swelling headlights had petrified him. He could only watch the vehicle draw nearer.

It wasn't the Titan. Was just a compact car; he could tell that by how near the road the headlights were.

A new fear assailed him. What if the car clipped his BMW?

In dread, Peter watched the car approach. It drew nearer, nearer, definitely heading toward a collision with Peter's rear bumper. Then, as it reached him and Peter closed his eyes to prepare for the impact, he experienced the oddest sensation. Like a gust of cool air blowing through his body.

When he opened his eyes again, the car—a silver Toyota Corolla—was motoring away.

My God, he thought. He could almost swear that the car had passed right through him. Through his BMW, as well.

He exhaled shuddering breath. After thirty seconds or so, he removed the key from his coat pocket and inserted it in the ignition.

It'll start now, Merry had promised.

With nerveless fingers, Peter twisted the key.

The car started immediately.

A lifting sensation, a quickening of hope. Peter actually felt a smile threaten.

He reached out, took hold of the gearshift.

He stopped. His smile faded.

For some reason, the sight of the glove box made his stomach muscles tighten. He had no reason to open the glove box, but some unseen force lifted his hand, made it drift to the handle. Peter pulled on it, and the glove box door dropped open, and then he was sucking in air, jerking away his hand as if scalded by boiling water. He crowded into the door, afraid of what lay outside the car, but more terrified of what the orange glove box light illuminated.

A handgun. He didn't know what model, but he knew it wasn't his. His gun was at home in the nightstand. This one looked very much like the gun with which he'd shot Merry.

Hand trembling, he reached over, pushed the glove box shut. Seething bile rose in his throat. He thought he might vomit.

Peter reached out and depressed the door locks again. But something told him this was a pointless measure. What was the poem Merry had recited? Peter despised poetry, but for some reason he had no trouble remembering this one.

Tyger, Tyger, burning bright, he thought.

He became aware of a pressure in his hip pocket.

In the forests of the night.

Peter swallowed, raised his hips so he could slide his fingers inside the pocket.

What immortal hand or eye.

And felt something cold and squishy within.

Two somethings.

Could frame thy fearful symmetry?

A scream rose to his lips even before he grasped the pair of moist souvenirs and removed them from his pocket. As he gazed down upon the severed ocular nerves, the light brown irises—*Janice's* light brown irises—he realized what had lain within Merry's hip pocket, the eternal reminder of what Merry had done to his father. The drunken castration.

185

For a long time, Peter sat there screaming.

Then, he returned Janice's eyes to his pocket and began to drive. There was a peculiar sort of peace that came from knowing that Greta, his children, his business associates could no longer see him.

Peter drove. He had no idea where to go, but he knew when the time came there'd be a tug.

Witness—Tyler Jenkins

YOUR POUND OF FLESH

NICK KOLAKOWSKI

JILL CAFFERTY THOUGHT of herself as a smart woman with good instincts. Certainly not the type to pick up hitchhikers on dark roads. So why did she pull over for the rail-thin girl with stringy blonde hair?

Later, in the brutal light of day, Jill would blame it on the divorce, combined with the two beers and a shot she downed at the Will O' Wisp ("Home of the Flaming Cocktail!") before climbing behind the wheel. Leaving her husband had been easy, especially after he cracked her cheekbone—it was the aftermath that was proving difficult. Over the past year, as the balance in her bank account dipped toward zero and her credit-card bills bumped against her limit, she had found herself caring less and less about her worthless little life. Now, roaring down I-84 in an alcohol haze, nothing but black fields on either side, she pressed her foot a little harder than usual on the gas, and let the wheel drift ever-so-slightly in her hands. Testing. Would a crash at this speed kill her?

Probably not, she thought. That was the bitch of it: they built cars so well these days, even a collision with the concrete pillar of a highway overpass was no guarantee of instant death. Knowing her luck, the impact would probably just cripple her, and then she would have giant medical bills on top of everything else.

Something wispy and white flashed on the highway shoulder: a blonde girl, young but worn, maybe a hundred-ten pounds at most. In the glare of headlights Jill could see the narrow ravines of ribs through the girl's torn t-shirt. The girl's bony arm extended, the thumb jutting high.

Jill hit the brake. Reality became distant, a movie that she could settle back and watch. It was a weird feeling, different than the liquor buzz, but not an unpleasant one. She came to a stop on the shoulder maybe a hundred yards beyond the girl, flicking on her hazard lights as she did so.

In the theater of her skull, Jill the Filmgoer asked: *Why are you doing this?*

Before some other part of her could answer, the girl was at the passenger window, the headlights' glow casting her eye-sockets in deep shadow. She looked like all kinds of trouble, and yet Jill's hand zipped down the window a few inches. *I demand an explanation*, Jill the Filmgoer yelled at her traitorous body, in vain.

"Hey," Jill said.

"Hey," the girl replied, almost too soft to hear over the night wind rustling the endless grass.

"Need a ride?"

The girl smiled slightly, her crooked front teeth poking beneath her lip. "That's why I'm out here."

Don't you do something this stupid, Jill the Filmgoer yelped, even as the girl climbed in, and the car accelerated back onto the road. The girl settled into the passenger seat with her arms folded tightly over her chest; she had no bag, no wallet shoved in the pocket of her threadbare denim shorts.

"What's your name?" Jill asked.

"Sarah," the girl said.

"Where you headed, Sarah?"

"West, as far as you're going."

"I can drop you off in Boise. That okay?"

I must have had a stroke, Jill the Filmgoer murmured. *Or someone put something in my beer.* The speedometer crept toward eighty, her old car creaking in protest. Cops were rare on this stretch of highway: great if you were a leadfoot like her, bad if something happened to you.

"Yeah, sure, whatever," Sarah said, shrugging.

"You hungry? We can stop somewhere, get some food."

Sarah patted her pockets. "I don't have anything. Money, I mean."

"That's okay, I think I can cover us." *Barely.*

"No, it's okay."

"You won't owe me or anything. I don't . . . "

"Seriously, it's okay."

Jill's sweaty palms made for a slick wheel. "Kind of dangerous, being out there."

Sarah stretched out an arm, revealing a vicious bruise on her elbow. "Not as dangerous as staying at home."

"Got friends you can crash with?"

"That's where I'm headed."

A white pickup passed on the left, its lights and engine filling the world. Jill noted its panels smeared with drying mud, the empty rifle-rack bolted to the rear window, the fading bumper sticker that announced: 'KEEP HONKING: I'M RELOADING.' As it pulled away, she glimpsed the driver in profile, illuminated for an instant by her headlights: a stubbled jaw, a cheek etched with a curlicue scar, the eyes hidden beneath a fading red baseball cap.

"Honk your horn," Sarah said.

"Why?"

"Because that guy's a jerk."

"No. It's . . . rude."

"Whatever." Smirking Sarah flicked the truck off. The driver accelerated, his brake-lights disappearing beyond the next bend.

When Jill turned her head again, the girl was gone.

✳ ✳ ✳

At three in the morning, Jill stopped for an early breakfast at an all-night diner a few blocks from her house, hoping that she had enough credit on her cards to cover it. It was an old-school place, heavy on the neon and chrome, and it served the best pancakes and finger steaks in the valley. Her arms shook like tuning forks as she parked the car in the diner's lot.

Jill was the only customer. The waitress served her coffee and took her order. The television above the counter showed the news. It was easy to tune out the litany of bombings and preachers-turned-politicians—until she caught a familiar flash of white out of the corner of her eye. It was the girl again, onscreen, staring at her above a single line of massive, crisp letters that blared the word: 'MURDER.'

The coffee cup dropped from Jill's numb hands. The waitress advanced on her with a towel, her murmurs of comfort drowned out by the blood roaring in Jill's ears. The newscaster reappeared, mouthing the words "corpse," and "no witnesses," and "ditch."

The girl's photo flashed up again: a high-school

portrait, taken against a light blue background. She wore a gray sweatshirt two sizes too large, with tape over the holes in the sleeves. Jill remembered doing that as a youngster, when her mother had no money for new shirts or skirts; the other kids always laughed at her, especially when she tried using a marker to color the tape to match the clothes.

The newscaster said, "Sarah Zupan, twenty-four years old."

Through cold lips, Jill asked the waitress if she could box up the breakfast. She made it to the parking lot before her stomach hit the eject button, so hard she doubled over and dumped her Styrofoam carton of pancakes right in her own mess. The carton opened on the way down, soaking eight bucks' worth of perfectly good food in bile.

Leaning against her car, wiping her mouth, Jill cast a furtive glance at the diner. The waitress wasn't watching, and that was good: she didn't need a witness to this misery.

Jill unlocked her car and climbed in, thinking: Just this once, thank God I'm alone.

The shadow in the front passenger seat said: "I'm sorry."

Jill screamed through a raw throat.

Sarah raised her hands, palms out. "It's okay," she said. "You're kind. You were the first person to stop."

There was no Jill the Filmgoer this time, no sense that she was a prisoner in her own body. Her fingers clawed for the door-handle, and when the door slammed open she fell onto the pavement, scrambling away from the car as fast as she could.

"I'm not going to hurt you," Sarah called after her. "Actually, I need your help."

Jill stopped and spun around. "Sarah Zupan?"

"Yes."

"You're . . . "

Sarah smiled. "Dead?"

"I mean, you don't look dead."

Sarah leaned forward and drummed a short beat on the dashboard. "I'm real, okay? Maybe not alive, but real."

Jill stood on quaking knees. Nausea roiled her belly again, and she bent over. Maybe I've had a psychotic break, she thought. I've finally snapped. Gone off the deep end. Totally bonkers.

"It's okay," Sarah said. "Deep breaths. So, you saw the news?"

Swallowing down bile, Jill straightened up and nodded.

"That's good. So I don't have to explain a whole lot." Sarah patted the driver's seat. "I know who killed me. He's still driving the highway once, twice a week. I can't do anything about it, but maybe you can."

Jill took a step toward the car, wiping her mouth. "Sure, anything. Give me his name. I'll call the police."

Sarah patted the seat harder. "If only it was that simple, Jill. You call the police, then what? 'Hey, Mister Detective, that dead girl told me who killed her.'" She laughed softly. Autumn leaves rustling the pavement. "I bet they just hang up on you. How many crank calls you think they get a week?"

"A lot?"

"A lot is right. And the guy who did me in, I bet he was careful. He called himself 'Tom,' but I doubt that was his real name."

"But you know what he looks like."

"That's right. And that's where you come in. We're going to find him."

Jill braced herself against the door. "And then what? Get evidence? I'm not a cop."

Sarah's face was a black hole, her eyes twin pinpricks of white light. "I don't know. We'll figure that out when we find him. Not a great plan, but it's the best I got, okay? Besides, what else you have going on?"

Jill rubbed her ring finger, with its lighter band of skin. "I have a lot going on."

"Like what?"

She shrugged. "My dog."

Sarah slid across the seats, slipping from the car smooth as smoke, so fast that Jill retreated a startled step. "This guy did me with a knife," Sarah said, poking at her neck. "He takes I-84 every Thursday night. Stops at that big truck stop a couple miles from here, you know the one, even got the showers and stuff for truckers?"

"I know it," Jill said. "Their gas station sells wine in boxes. Pretty good wine, actually." *You should go home,* she thought, *and curl up with the dog until this whole rotten night fades from memory.*

But you can't, said Jill the Filmgoer, sitting in her theater. *Because whatever this is, it's bigger than you. This is your role, like it or not.*

"Okay, I'll help you find him." The words sounded weird and stupid, and yet she already felt a little stronger, more sure of herself. "But no guarantees beyond that. I'm not . . . Wonder Woman or anything."

"Oh, that's a start." Sarah returned to the car, curling on the passenger seat like a street cat. "A real start."

✳ ✳ ✳

YOUR POUND OF FLESH

The detective, James Peabody, was a big man with sloping shoulders and scruff on his chin thick enough to likely violate some police department regulation. Later, somebody told Jill that he had moved to Idaho after a bad experience with some missing kids in Cleveland. He had the hard, bright eyes of a crusader—the sort of man who will beat you with a phone book because he believes you're guilty.

In the windowless "interview room" that stank of piss, Peabody took a seat across from her and opened a manila folder on the table. He flicked the photos from the folder like playing cards, a full deck of evidence photos: a soiled blanket, a gaping neck wound with a white ruler beside it, a bit of silver jewelry spotted with blood.

"How long were you married?" Peabody asked, consulting a piece of paper.

"Five years," Jill said, trying to ignore her stomach rumbling.

"Why'd you get divorced?"

"He beat me."

"Sorry to hear that. You have my sympathies."

Somehow Jill doubted that; she thought the man was trying to build a rapport with her, like they did on the cop shows. "Why does that matter?"

"Just want to know your mental state," Peabody said. "People go through a major life event, like a divorce, it creates triggers. It isn't their fault. We're just wired in some pretty weird ways."

"I'm not strange," Jill said. "I know what I saw."

"The dead girl, as you said." Peabody pursed his lips.

"That's right. I can't explain it. All I can do is tell the truth."

"She made you do this?" Peabody tapped one of the

photos between them, but Jill refused to look at the gore, the split bone, what was left of the eye. Instead she focused on her clenched fists, the nails clotted with dried blood.

✳✳✳

For once, Jill drove the speed limit. The truck stop was busy at this strange hour, the dinosaur rumble of trucks echoing off concrete. She parked in a space close to the brightly lit restaurant that served as the stop's central hub. "What now?" Jill asked.

"You find the guy," Sarah said, leaning back in her seat. "I'll wait here. Let me know when you see him."

"You're not coming with me?"

"I try to go inside, I'll disappear. That's how this ghost thing works, okay?"

"I don't even know what this guy's supposed to look like."

"We saw him before. Big truck, red cap, scar."

Jill white-knuckled the wheel. "Really?"

"That's why I wanted to honk. Just to taunt him a little."

"But he could have noticed."

Sarah shrugged. "What's he going to do? I'm already dead. He gutted me like a chicken."

"Hey, I'm still alive." Jill leaned close. "And yes, my life is in the toilet right now, I'm broke, my dog's had these weird orange poos lately, this car has too many miles on it, but it's my life, okay? It's the only one I've got."

"Great speech." Sarah shrank in her seat, and for a horrible moment Jill could imagine her cowering at home, hands raised to block whatever lamp or pan some horrible relative threw at her. "Can you please go inside and see if he's there?"

"Remember what I asked before? What do we do when I find him?"

"I still don't know. Kill him?"

Jill swallowed hard. "I'm not going to do that. Could *you* do that?"

Sarah looked away. "I don't know."

Jill opened her door, the car's warm air leaking away like blood from a wound. "At least I can go in and see," she said, and stepped into the night, leaving the ghost alone.

Yes—but if you see him coming, you run, Jill the Filmgoer offered. Trotting across the parking lot, Jill found herself feeling good for the first time in ages. Her stomach had settled, and the last of her alcohol buzz fended off the first stirrings of the inevitable hangover. So what if this whole situation was insane? It was an adventure, a thrill cleaner than anything she could find in a bottle.

She spied the white pickup at the gas pumps adjoining the restaurant, and the man in the red cap paying for fuel with a credit card. He was surprisingly small, dressed in a dirty white t-shirt and a pair of faded jeans. Strong-looking, his muscles like cord wrapped around bone.

Something was wrong with his pump's credit-card reader. The man—Jill dubbed him the Killer—cursed loudly enough to hear across fifty feet of parking lot and smacked the device with his palm before heading inside the gas station that adjoined the restaurant.

Take a peek inside his truck, Jill the Filmgoer advised. *It's the safest way to confirm. No muss, no fuss.*

Jill pulled out her phone, a flip model that had come free with her cellular plan. The camera was ancient but (she hoped) useable in low light.

I had a gold necklace with a little dolphin, said Sarah, sitting next to Jill the Filmgoer. How had the ghost gotten in her head? Probably another supernatural power, like disappearing from cars moving at a high rate of speed. *Serial killers take trophies. And when they do, sometimes they keep them close.*

Jill crept forward: forty feet, thirty, ten. A hatchback at the adjoining pumps blocked anyone inside the station from a full view of the truck. The hatchback's driver sat behind the wheel, headphones on, head down as she stared into the glowing light of a phone.

Reaching the passenger door of the pickup, Jill paused to wipe her hands on her jeans. Her heart thundered in her throat. She took a deep breath, gripped the handle, and pulled.

The Killer had left it unlocked. Jill glanced at the front windows of the station. Behind the counter, the clerk struggled to keep his eyes open as he flipped through a magazine. If the Killer was using the bathroom, or shopping for snacks, that would buy her two or three minutes.

The inside of the pickup was smeared with dirt. A pair of fuzzy dice dangled from the rearview mirror, and a jumbo-size fast-food cup jutted from the central drink holder like a rocket on its launchpad. There was a light blue blanket in the passenger seat, which she lifted by the edge. A spray of black stains on the underside, tacky to the touch.

Could be old ketchup, Jill the Filmgoer suggested. *Could be anything.*

Yeah, right.

She snapped a few photos of the stains, with no flash, before setting the blanket back down. Peeked through the windshield at the station: all clear. Do the glove-box next.

The glove-box, unlocked, unhinged its jaw to reveal a rat's nest of papers: registration, old Chinese restaurant menus, a few crumpled parking tickets, receipts. She poked at the mess with her finger, and something metal tinkled. Shoving the papers aside revealed a clear plastic bag stuffed with jewelry: a gold necklace with a small dolphin, a few bracelets of chunky stones, a pair of pearl earrings.

It's really him! Jill the Filmgoer shrieked.

Told you, Sarah said.

Jill snapped a few photos from different angles, hoping the faint light was good enough, before pushing the bag aside to see if anything more lay beneath. Her fingers touched bumpy plastic, cold metal: a knife, curved like a raptor's talon, sharp enough to zip your throat wide open.

I barely felt it when it cut me, Sarah said. *Even when he went deep.*

Jill's reflection distorted in the steel as she balanced it on her finger. Too late, she realized she was leaving fingerprints on the handle. Shit!

Before she could return the knife to its home, a heavy hand slammed on her shoulder.

✳✳✳

When Detective Peabody slipped the next photograph from his file, Jill's heart spasmed for a few beats.

The man in the photo was unmistakably the Killer: same red baseball cap, same scar carving up a rounded, surprisingly pleasant face. He had a big smile for the camera, and an arm draped across the thin shoulders of the woman beside him on a picnic bench.

Jill took deep breaths until her heart found its normal

rhythm, then tapped on the woman in the photo. "That's Sarah," she said. "This guy, he killed her."

Peabody's left eyebrow twitched. "Who?"

"Sarah," Jill said, tapping harder. "She was murdered. It's been all over the news. I didn't know that she knew the guy."

Peabody lost his poker face, his brow scrunching in confusion. "Who? What murder?"

✱ ✱ ✱

Jill Cafferty, who cried whenever she saw dead birds in the road, who hid in the basement whenever her husband began to make that hissing sound that indicated he was in one of his violent moods, would have never recognized the creature of pure instinct who spun and buried the knife in the man's soft throat. The curved blade punched through the thin skin over the jugular, and blood jetted in a hot spray that coated her face, hands, arms. It splashed in her eyes, stinging, blinding, and she pulled out the knife and slammed it home again, through softness, and again, glancing off bone, and again, into something tough that snagged the steel.

She blinked, and her vision returned, blurry but clear enough to see the Killer flailing across the concrete between the pumps, his neck and face jetting red like a clogged fountain. Gushing, he fell to his knees, and then onto his face.

Jill stumbled out of the truck, almost slipping on the blood. People were running from the gas station, drawn by the Killer's messy demise. The hatchback's driver had her phone raised, filming Jill as she bent over and vomited for the second time that night.

Sarah was nowhere in sight.

YOUR POUND OF FLESH

Holding the photo of the Killer and Sarah, Peabody asked: "Who is this couple?" His voice was loud, ringing off the walls, burrowing into Jill's head. "Who do you think this woman is?"

"Sarah," Jill said, and her vision wavered, like it did when the Killer's blood splashed her face.

"There is no Sarah," Peabody said. "This is a photo of you and your ex-husband."

"No." Jill shook her head.

"I understand if you killed him," Peabody said. "Guy who beat on you like he did? I read the reports. If I were in your shoes, I'd have taken a knife to him, too."

She shook her head so hard, something in her neck popped. "No."

After a long pause, Peabody began slipping photos back into his folder. "If that's how you're going to play it," he said, voice thick with disappointment, "I guess we're going to need to get the shrink in here."

"I know what I saw," Jill said, quieter than she intended. That couldn't have been her ex-husband. Maybe a man who looked a lot like him, and who drove the same kind of truck, but not him.

"We'll see," Peabody said, and left the room. His body had blocked the one-way mirror along the far wall, and now she could see Sarah staring at her in the glass, sitting in her seat, her shirt crusted with dried blood, smiling despite the tears streaming down her face.

REQUITAL

RICHARD THOMAS

Open your eyes, Graysen.

The shack is filling with a heat that rises up from the desert, a weight on my chest slowly spreading to my limbs, as a flicker of this journey unfurls in black and white photos, one horrible image after another. My breath is shallow, hard to summon up from the depths, and then I'm sitting upright on the cot, the thin blankets green and itchy, coughing up blood into my open hands. Sand sifts in through the open frame, the actual wooden door painted red, splintered into sections, and scattered over the front yard. Emaciated, and nude, I squint, looking out the opening into the pale sunlight, unwilling to turn toward the corners of the empty hut, the shadows filled with memories.

And the girl.

Always the girl.

She smiles in the darkness, blonde hair pulled back into pigtails, red ribbons holding the braids tight. Today it's a light blue dress, ringed with daisies at the waist and collar, her black patent leather shoes buckled, shimmering somehow, the dainty little socks as white as bone. Her hands are behind her back, a grin holding her face intact, and I know what she's hiding. I don't want to see it again, but soon enough she'll show me. Yesterday it was a mad dash into the desert where I collapsed in the blazing sun, dust filling my mouth, my skin turned to parchment.

Today?

The car.

I close my eyes, and I'm flying down the highway, the wind in my hair, the windows open, the beat-up Nova purring across the desolate landscape, the girl and house no longer in the rear-view mirror. Jeans and a white t-shirt, scuffed boots, my hands grip the wheel as I push the accelerator down, lunging forward. The blacktop spirals forward like a slick of oil, and I chase it—anything to be out of that room, away from her. I click the radio on. Static, up and down the dial, as flashes of faded billboards and dying cactus fill my periphery vision.

I look in the side mirror, and there's nothing back there, a smile as blood fills the cracks between my teeth, my gut clenching suddenly in knots. Under my fingernails, there is so much dirt and grime; I can never seem to get it out. Eyes to the horizon, I cough again, a mist of red spraying the windshield, wiping my mouth as I sneer.

Dammit.

I never smoked a cigarette in my life.

Eyes to the side mirror, the rear-view mirror, and the world framed in the windshield shimmers like I'm underwater.

It feels good to be moving.

For a moment, I can almost forget why I'm here.

This particular black and white photo comes in several different versions—the grandmother in Alsip growing old and feeble, finally made obsolete; the neighbor hurt on the job, unable to work, abandoned by insurance and company alike; the sister and her addiction, garnering no sympathy, an inability to empathize. But closing my eyes won't help.

I want to be hungry, I want to pull over and order a cheeseburger and fries, a large coke, a diner filled with shiny, happy people. I want to say hello to Mabel or Alice and have her smile and put her hand on a cocked hip, call me Hon or Shug, a bell dinging in the window, the counter filled with cowboys, and truck drivers, and that one haggard salesman with his tie loosened, dingy white shirt unbuttoned.

I want it so bad that it aches.

Instead, I get one more photo—and it's Jim from accounting, and his wife. Jennifer? Julie? There are doctors and beeping lights, the cold tile holding wheels that squeak, as machines are pushed around, a flurry of footsteps filling the cold, sterile air. There was a child, I was told, but whether it was a boy or a girl, I can't tell you. I should know those details. If I was anything resembling a human being.

I take a breath, the road unfurling, and yet, the desert stays on my right, the horizon forever looming, the mountains to the left quiet in their dismissal.

On that particular day, something was due. It's not important what it was—report, numbers, article, paper, results, opinion, facts. I grip the steering wheel harder, knuckles white, pushing the car down the never-ending highway, that diner always just out of reach.

A sharp pain in my ribs causes me to let go of the wheel, gently massaging the spot, knowing it won't do me any good. A cough rattles into my fist, and I rub the red on my shirt.

REQUITAL

Here we go.

What did I say? I can't remember.

I yelled at my secretary, it's coming back now, the desk, the glass windows in the office spilling the city for miles in every direction. My back was to her, as I screamed, face red with rage, fists clenched at my sides. Tan, standing tall, the suit custom-made, the tie special-order, the ring on my left finger platinum, the watch shimmering gold.

Never sick a day in my life.

She pleaded with me.

Stockholders, I said. I can't count on him.

Her lips pursed.

You don't understand, I argued.

Rubbing my temples, I never looked at her once.

Make it happen.

Not long after that, she was a ghost too. Marlie. Or Mary. Dammit. What was her name?

The road turns to the right, as the Chevy hugs the dotted yellow line, and I cough again, slow with my hand, spattering the dashboard, and it's the mirrors again, the road behind me empty, the back seat slowly filling with shadows.

No, not yet.

This one, it hurts less, it's almost bearable.

And then it shifts, the pain, my hands curling into claws, as my mouth opens in a silent gasp.

This is how it goes, I know.

I can't hold the wheel, so I ease off the gas, the car drifting to the right, trying to bat at the controls, to keep this ton of steel from veering off the shoulder and into the desert, but this will fail too, I know, and then we hit something.

Rock, hole, curb, turtle—who the fuck knows.

Doesn't matter.

I'd like to say there was disorientation and then darkness, but not here, not now. That would be a gift.

Out of reflex I stamp my right foot toward the brake, but it's too late. And then we roll. I push my foot against the floor to try and brace myself as glass shatters, shards imbedded in my face and neck, my eyes closed tight. The car dents and shudders, my right leg snapping at the ankle, something pushing into my chest, the steering wheel fracturing my ribs, and then it stops.

I'm briefly granted a respite, the darkness finally slipping in, and for a moment, I forget it all. But not for long. It's the pain that brings me back.

The sun fades while I bleed, as I labor for breath, in and out, a stabbing pain when I try to inhale, my hands throbbing, a dull panic all the way to the bone, a whimper escaping my split lips.

When I open my eyes, in the last remnants of daylight, as I count the pulsing horrors that riddle my body, and a dozen voices scream out in suffering.

I hear footsteps in the dirt, and gravel, and glance to the open window.

It won't be the cancer that gets me. Maybe not even the accident. And certainly not old age. I see four legs saunter up to the car—gray fur, and paws with sharp black nails. I hear a panting that I had thought was in my head, my own struggling for breath, but no, it's something else. The heavy breathing turns to a low growl, and then the four legs turn to eight and then sixteen.

So, this is how it happens, I laugh.

Points for originality.

And amidst the musky smell of mangy fur and sour urine, I see her black patent leather shoes. The shiny buckle. And the dainty white socks.

And then I smell the gasoline.

When I turn to the window they're gone.

Out of the frying pan, and into the fire.

There is a spark, and I start screaming.

❊❊❊

Open your eyes, Graysen.

The shack is filling with a heat that rises up from the desert, and I run my fingers over my body searching for the new marks—gently touching my ribs, covering my eyes and feeling my face for cuts, mottled flesh, rotating my ankle in slow, little circles.

There is the cot upon which I lie, the same itchy, green blankets and the door frame open to the elements, sand slipping in, a single red scorpion ambling over the threshold. As always, I am naked, and alone. My lips are cracked, mouth dry, so I sit up and contemplate water. There is a well outside, I think. There used to be, anyway.

I know, I say to the critter as it skitters toward me. It's not your fault, it's merely in your nature. It heads between my bare feet and under the cot, to a tiny hole in the back of the room, where it disappears.

Water.

I turn to the corner first, take a deep breath, and nod at the girl.

Today she is in a pair of denim overalls, her feet bare, with a pink t-shirt under the straps, ruffles at the edge of the sleeves, and a silver necklace that looks like a daisy.

Always the daisies.

Her hair is loose today, down past her shoulders, and she smiles a little, eyes on me the entire time, taking a single step toward me. Her hands are still behind her back, but I don't need to see. I've been shown already, so many times.

But I'd like to mark our progress.

She'd like to see me suffer.

Before I can find my way to the well outside, my throat clutching, forcing down a swallow, a tarantula the size of my fist meanders through the door, and I back up a bit, uneasy with the way its legs move, undulating over the faded wood floor, skimming the dust, the hair on its legs making my skin crawl. It looks so meaty—the idea of my bare foot squashing it sends a shimmer across my flesh, as my stomach rolls, my top lip pulled back in a snarl.

It follows the path of the scorpion, but this time I pull my feet up, letting it move past me, under the cot, and into the hole in the wall, which seems to have expanded.

Eyes to the girl, but she's gone now.

I'm not surprised. So much work to do.

I stand up, licking my lips again, my swollen tongue gently prodding the cuts and sores that line my mouth, trying to find any moisture at all. The photos spiral into the air, one after another, back to my childhood, fanned out like a hand of cards, as the memories come rushing back. I want to open my eyes, to push the images away, but open or closed, it doesn't matter, as these visions force their way into my mind. The magnifying glass and the ants; the pet hamster set on a record player as it spins around and around; the egg found in a henhouse and squashed, it's pale flesh wrapped around that singular bulbous blue eye; the cat buried up to its neck, so trusting in its innocence as the riding mower started up; the family dog wolfing down the steak while I waited for the poison to take effect.

And then I hear a woman scream.

The flash of red stands in the doorway—the desert fox still, as if stuffed—black beady eyes on me, ears turning this way and that. It barks once, and looks around, as if wondering where it is. It opens its jaws wide again, and then screams into the room.

It is unholy.

And then it's gone.

When the rattlesnake slithers into the room I know there won't be any water for me today, and I can hardly swallow. It's getting difficult to breathe, the snake's tail shaking like a baby's rattle, winding its way across the sandy floor, and then darting under the cot and through the hole.

Too easy, I know.

I close my eyes for a second, and when I do there is a cavalcade of clicking insects, scurrying through the door in a wave of tiny bodies. Centipedes in red and brown, beetles with their iridescent shells, a flurry of wasps and bees filling the air with a dull buzz. I cover my eyes and cower in the corner, but they only dance about the room and then disappear.

And then they get larger, the creatures of the desert, progressing up the food chain. A pack of dogs, sniffing and yipping, fill the room in a clutch of mania—coyotes and jackals and wolves circling each other, snapping and tearing out mouthfuls of fur, their eyes wide in a seething mass of hunger and anxiety, as I push back against the wall. They weave in and out, like some biting, dying ocean of gnashing teeth, and yet they hardly seem to notice me at all.

What I'd give for a single glass of water.

What I'd give to not be torn limb from limb.

In their sudden absence the soft, red glow of the sun descending fills the empty door frame, and a shadow lurches past, a head of horns leaping, and landing, and then leaping again. It passes by, never entering. As I hear the dull thud of its movement push on down the road, it screeches as if caught in a trap, and then suddenly it goes quiet.

When the darkness fills the opening again, it is much larger, blocking out the light bit by bit until there is no sunlight left to give. And yet, it still is not in sight. A smell wafts into the room, something thick and meaty, and I gag in the growing night. Whether on two legs or four, hooved or clawed, the thick odor of rotting flesh and fetid liquid spills across the room, filling my mouth with a bitter, itching sensation. It is the smell of burning carapace, the sickly-sweet copper of blood crescendoing across a flat surface, the foul rot of diseased flesh slipping from the bone.

I hold my hand to my mouth and close my eyes, trying to remember the shine of her buckle, the gentle fabric of the pristine sock, as my flesh is painted crimson, skinned alive—flayed for the desert to feed on in primal hunger.

***

Open your eyes, Graysen.

The shack is filling with a heat that rises up from the desert, and I do not open my eyes this time. I sob in my solitude, understanding so many things now.

And yet, there is more.

I have not been enlightened just yet.

There are depths to be plumbed, dark sparks that were pushed so far down that I thought they'd never see the light of day again.

The girl is here, but I refuse to look at her, whatever romper or summer dress she might be wearing today. Her innocence is a skin she wraps around her like a snake, ready to shift and molt at a moment's notice.

I can see her anyway, and this time she holds her hands out, something in them, reminding me why we're here.

I don't want to see it.

I won't open my eyes.

You will, she says.

When the perfume drifts to me, it is as if I have awoken in a field of flowers—a basic pleasure that was taken from me such a long time ago.

It takes me back to my youth.

The citrus is a sharp note in the dry, acrid desert— the orange and plum making my mouth water. The jasmine and rose are a lightness that washes over me, so I inhale deeply, the tension finally unclenching. The patchouli and sandalwood conjure up slick flesh and burning incense, the images spiraling back.

No, please.

My first love.

I try to sit up, to open my eyes, and yet, there is only the darkness. And then I feel her touch.

It is such a simple mercy.

Her hands run over my scarred, withering flesh and she whispers in my ear, unintelligible words, a cacophony of gentle incoherence. Her eager mouth and gentle tongue press up against my neck, and my heart beats a rabbit-kick in a ribcage crisscrossed with scars.

What, speak up, say it again?

She pushes me back down, her lips brushing my mouth, my eyelids, my cheeks, and then she bites, drawing blood. Pushing me down harder, my head strikes the wood of the cot frame, her mouth at my neck where the whispers turn to threats.

My eyes are open now, and yet, I cannot see.

Her fingernails run down my arms, beads of crimson rising to the top of my leathery flesh, and I am so weak now, so vulnerable.

No, I say.

If only it was that simple, she replies.

The photos appear now, in black and white—flashes of skin across so many years, in the back seats of cars, in dingy apartments where beer cans litter the floor, and then later, on glorious sheets made of Egyptian cotton, the thread count in the thousands, instrumental music in the background, candles burning in the muted darkness.

Not yet, she said.

The others, the same. An echo into the void.

Not tonight

Wait.

Please.

And the notes change now, to something musky, my stench rising to the surface—the salty tang of panic, my sour mouth gasping fear and confusion layered over shock.

Her hands are so strong, in the dark, and I am vulnerable to her base defilement, flipping me over, her strength growing, as the air grows foul. There is something else with us now, whatever love becomes when it is betrayed, the jasmine wilting, the fruit decaying in a liquid covered by buzzing flies, and she takes from me now, what I took from her then.

I plead for her to stop, asking for forgiveness.

But it does me no good.

✳✳✳

Open your eyes, Graysen.

The shack is filling with a heat that rises up from the desert and the girl holds out her hands, the scroll unfurling, to the floor and out across the empty room, the scripture filled with so very many transgressions.

THAT PILGRIMS' HANDS DO TOUCH

DAMIEN ANGELICA WALTERS

I WAS NINE when the first god took residence in the roadside shrine. There were no pronouncements, no fanfare, no displays of divine power. She was just there, sitting cross-legged in the shrine as though she'd always existed in that space.

Impossible, of course. The shrines themselves were an art installation constructed of scrap metal and cheap wood and put in place the summer before. Twelve of them, spanning a ten-mile stretch of highway in Maryland. Emulating the Shinto shrines found in Japan, they were empty on purpose. No figurines of Jizo, the protector of travelers. No stones, no empty sake barrels, no paper streamers.

The artist was as surprised as anyone that a deity had shown up. She said, "I didn't know anyone was listening. I didn't know anyone was paying attention."

A few weeks after the first god's arrival, eleven more followed suit. By that time, the artist was forgotten.

That was nine years ago, but it felt like decades.

Sometimes it also felt like yesterday. On the morning of my eighteenth birthday, it felt a little of both.

My father was slouched on the sofa in the living room watching a movie filled with villains and explosions, never mind the early hour. A mug, contents curling steam into the air, sat on the coffee table next to a plate with a half-eaten bagel smothered in cream cheese. I lingered in the doorway, shifting the weight of the backpack slung over my shoulder, holding an old photograph of Mom and me, both of us wearing wide, nearly identical smiles, in my hand, waiting to see if he'd say something or maybe waiting to see if I would, but he didn't and neither did I. It didn't surprise me; over the last eight years we'd done our loudest speaking in silence.

He knew where I was going, even though I hadn't mentioned the pilgrimage in years. Not that I thought he would be, but he wasn't happy about it either. Unlike me, masking emotions wasn't a skill he possessed. "Good luck, Cate. Be careful," I imagined him saying, but those words belonged to a different Dad, one whose wife was still by his side.

As I tucked the photo in my pocket, my fingertips brushed the edge of the Zippo lighter I carried. It had belonged to Mom, yet another thing she'd left behind. I'd filled the reservoir before I packed my bag. She'd had one cigarette a day, going out onto the back porch after dinner, turning the Zippo over and over in her hand as she exhaled long plumes of smoke. I'd always wondered what she thought of while she stood there, if the Zippo held a story she'd share with me one day. Not that I gave a shit about it now, but maybe she'd share it when I found her. *If* I found her.

As I drove away from the suburban chaos, heading

toward the interstate, I didn't look back. What was the point? I probably wouldn't ever return. I clenched and unclenched my fingers on the steering wheel, the traffic around me there but not at the same time. Part of me didn't believe I was actually making this trip. I'd planned it a long time ago, before I was old enough to drive. I'd sit with a map, nose nearly touching the surface, finger tracing the highway lines. I chose routes, discarded them for others, tossing it all away and starting from scratch after the ten-mile stretch of highway was closed off and traffic rerouted, once it became clear the gods were here to stay and the pilgrimage wasn't going to cease. Early on, Dad told me to knock it off, to let it—*her*—go. Later, he didn't even bother.

Seven hours and three states, the words a litany in my head. But even if I needed to go to the other side of the country, I would've made the trip. When I pulled into the parking lot of an old rest stop, I smiled. All around me, lines of pilgrims' cars coated in grime, time, and abandonment, some with flat tires, others with keys in the ignitions. My used Camry had seen better days, but even so, it looked out of place, the windows too clear, the paint too bright. I didn't need to lock it—no one would bother it here—but old habits. The sharp chirp from the key fob echoed into the trees surrounding the lot, and I darted nervous glances in every direction, dreading a shout that didn't come.

I hoisted my backpack, adjusting the straps so the weight rested against the center of my back and took a deep breath, trying to quell the shake in my fingers. Wayward strands of ivy covered the small building housing the bathrooms, and long arms of the same extended across the parking lot. The air tasted heavy and still. Apocalyptic. I fished the Zippo from my pocket and flicked the wheel with my thumbnail. Ready or not, here I come.

With a soft exhalation, I headed into the trees, stepping over roots and branches and wincing every time a twig cracked beneath my heels. A squirrel ran across my path, stopped in the middle with its head cocked toward me, then took off with a scatter of dead leaves. A yellow-winged butterfly darted around my face. Clouds alternately obscured then revealed the spring sun, taking away then returning the early evening warmth and shrouding the trees in disconcerting shadows.

I heard the pilgrimage before I saw it. A low susurration, similar to the ocean from a distance, growing louder by degrees. The trees ended abruptly, and I staggered to a halt. I thought I was prepared. I'd seen videos on television and YouTube. I'd seen hundreds of pictures and spent way too many hours on websites solely devoted to the pilgrimage. But even the videos didn't capture the feel of this sea of bodies, about a dozen across with neither beginning nor end anywhere in sight, moving in one long, slow wave down one side of the highway and back on the other.

In no small way, it reminded me of a zombie horde from television or the movies, that mindless forward locomotion. I curled my toes inside my sneakers. All those whispers, all those exhalations, all that fervent devotion. And somewhere in it all, my mom. Panic coiled on my tongue.

I didn't have to be here. What did it matter that I didn't have a mom to talk to when things were tough, that I had to do my own laundry when I was ten, that I learned about my period from other girls at school, most of whom knew barely more than I did? It could have been worse.

A man swung his head in my direction and the heat in his eyes sent me back several steps. I gripped the straps of my backpack until the edges dug into my skin. I dropped my hands to my sides, wiped the sweat from my palms on my jeans. I didn't have to do this.

I narrowed my eyes. Bullshit. She didn't give me a choice.

There was no pushing, there were no elbows in my ribs or abdomen, no sharp glances. Without words, the pilgrims made a space for me and it was as if I'd always been a part of the ouroboros. My pace slowed to match everyone else's. I'd dreaded the reek of unwashed bodies, of rotting teeth. Dirty faces, tattered clothes and slack mouths. Instead, everyone had clean cheeks, some pinkened by the sun, and clothing well-worn but obviously cared for. Here and there, I breathed in hints of patchouli, of laundry detergent, of contentment and purpose. Whispered prayers filled the air with a soft syllabic hum, footsteps acting as punctuation.

I wasn't the only person with a backpack, but most carried nothing, their arms swinging gently with each step or linked together with the person next to them. There was a camp along the highway, with food, water, tents, sleeping bags, and medical care donated by many different organizations. These weren't the forgotten homeless. Anyone was welcome, and no one ever needed permission to stop walking, to rest. No one was in charge, except maybe the gods. And even that was suspect.

The pilgrimage was its own organism, started by a

small band of people now called the Firsts and grown on the asphalt until it turned the lanes impassible by any car, no matter how long and hard the driver pressed the horn. Over the years, the number of people who joined had lessened, and a few of the elderly had passed away— all peacefully in their sleep, it was noted time and again—but only a handful of people left of their own accord. Several underage participants were removed by authorities in the beginning, but once the pilgrims' numbers grew, even before the serpent swallowed its tail, that became all but impossible.

Moving with the crowd, I understood why. I felt as anonymous as the pilgrim beside me, as though I'd shed my identity simply by joining the masses. Easy enough to walk and sleep and eat and walk, to forget there was an outside world. I pinched my cheek between my teeth. Most of these people had left their lives behind. Their friends, their families, their daughters. They'd left behind empty places at the dinner table and houses full of hurt. Had they bothered to say goodbye or had they snuck out in the middle of the night when everyone else was asleep?

I tucked a hand in my back pocket, my fingers tracing first the edge of the photograph, then the Zippo. I'd find her, no matter how many hours or days or weeks I had to spend walking and pretending I was devout.

The whispers ceased and even the footsteps quieted as we approached the end of the highway. The sun emerged from another dance with the clouds to shine down onto the first shrine, gilding the metal frame and giving the wood an amber sheen. The first shrine, the first god.

Every photo, every video, of the gods was slightly

blurred, suggesting they were constantly moving too fast for a lens to catch. There were sketches and paintings, but they were all slightly . . . off, distorted as though gods resisted being recreated in pen, ink, or charcoal. It didn't stop people from selling medallions or even T-shirts, nor did it stop people from buying them.

A grey-haired woman stepped free from the crowd and knelt near the shrine, or as near as she could get. The ground was littered with twig figures, bent into triangles and tied with vines. They brought to mind the Maiden, the Mother, and Crone, but if *this* god was indeed *that* god, she never confirmed nor denied.

The shrine was also triangular-shaped and at the roof's peak, another triangle the offerings emulated, both crafted from metal, curiously rust-free. The front of the shrine was open, the back and sides simple wood darkened almost black with varnish. A tree trunk served as the base the shrine was fixed upon, whether there first or put into place by the artist, I wasn't sure.

The god herself took up most of the shrine's interior. She was seated with folded legs, her chin resting on her chest. I slowed down, a stone in the river of people flowing around me. I stepped free, and the grey-haired woman shot me a look—not unkind, but mindful—so I knelt, too, peeking up at the god. She was small, which I expected, and appeared to be asleep. Her face was a wizened apple, her body a gourd, her limbs tucked in such a way to make them nearly invisible. Her hair, the color of storm clouds in winter, twisted in a long intricate braid cascading over one shoulder. A linen tunic appeared to be her only garment.

All the accounts I'd read said looking at the gods directly gave you the sensation of insects creeping on their skin, not unpleasant, but strange. They described a feeling inside, an expansive, awe-filled opening of sorts that brought unexpected tears, but I felt nothing. Nothing that explained anything. Nothing that made me want to abandon my life and take up the pursuit of walking this pilgrimage. I closed my eyes, emptied all my thoughts, and looked at the god again. This time, she was looking back, her eyes blue and penetrating.

I dropped my head and shrugged my shoulders forward, trying to make myself as unobtrusive as possible. Could she tell the real reason I'd joined the pilgrimage? Would she let anyone else know? With a hard swallow, I darted back into the sea of people, pushing my way to the center. Once there, I couldn't see the god through the crowd. Good. It meant she couldn't see me either.

When she was well behind us, I moved closer to an older gentleman who had the look of a long-time pilgrim—weathered face, purposeful steps, soft shoulders, rapt, yet introspective eyes. But mostly, no audible prayer. The newer the pilgrim, the more they prayed, as though they had to prove their devotion and their place in the pilgrimage.

My shoes scuffed on the asphalt and I leaned a little closer to the man. "Are you one of the Firsts?" I asked, pushing a touch of the vacuous in my voice.

He scoffed, but the corner of his mouth lifted. "No, I'm not, just old."

"I'm sorry, I didn't mean—"

"It's fine. You're not the first to ask and you won't be the last. Anyone over the age of fifty here has been asked the same. The Firsts," he said, lifting a hand, "are wherever they want to be. Sometimes here, walking with us, sometimes at the camp, sometimes tending to the shrines, but they're always here with us." He patted the center of his chest and smiled.

I nodded, but my guts twisted. If they were here, there, and everywhere, how was I going to find them? They were the only people I definitely knew who'd been here before my mom joined, their faces graven in my memory due to all the press. Seven of them, all older, all devoted. If they'd snapped at a reporter or uttered a curse, if they'd acted anything other than serene and perfectly happy, maybe no one else would've joined the pilgrimage at all. Maybe my mom wouldn't have walked out on us. My fingers tiptoed to the edge of the photograph and tugged it free.

The man glanced over, as I'd expected he would.

"My mom and I," I said, holding out the picture. "A long time ago."

"You look a lot like her."

"Yeah, I guess I do. We have the same hair."

"Same smile, same eyes, too."

I nodded. No recognition on his face whatsoever, unfortunately, and I returned the photo. It was a long shot anyway. Eventually we drew near to the second shrine, and the man left the group with a small wave to me as he went. I watched him kneel but made sure not to look too closely at either shrine or god. A brief glance gave me the impression of something vaguely elephantine tucked deep in an ornately carved structure.

I scanned the faces near me and those further away, looking closely at anyone with grey hair and lined faces. It would've been easier to sit on the side of the road and watch everyone as they passed, but no way that wouldn't have made people suspicious.

Twilight descended and still, I walked and looked, sometimes dropping my pace to fall back into a new group of people. Dusk tumbled into full dark as we passed other shrines, and I avoided looking in their direction although lots of people stopped to pray or think or whatever they chose to do while others rose from bent knees and rejoined the rest of us.

A while after we passed the eleventh shrine, the pilgrimage curved back around, but before people continued on, they bent a knee facing away. A youngish guy with dreadlocks left the procession and disappeared into the trees. Two seconds later, another person did the same. I tugged the sleeve of the pilgrim nearest to me, a woman with a peaceful expression on her face and a skirt the color of a summer sky.

"Did they move the twelfth shrine?"

Her brow furrowed. "No, why would they do that?"

"But we didn't pass it."

"We can't because of the road."

I shook my head. "I'm sorry? I'm new, I don't understand."

"Part of the road washed out after the big storm a couple months ago, so we can't pass it this way. If you want to go, there's a path through the woods, but I don't recommend you go at night. Not if you're new. It'll be fixed this summer, that's what the Firsts say," she said and moved along before I could ask anything more.

I lost track of time, caught up in the endless lifting and dropping of my feet. When my legs started to ache, I slowed my pace, pausing now and again to rub my shins or flex my toes and ankles.

"You're allowed to stop, you know," a woman to my right whispered as she passed. "We're pilgrims, not martyrs."

My face burned with heat, but I didn't stop, not until a stone found its way into my shoe and dug into my heel. I limped to the side of the road and plopped down, undoing the laces of my sneaker. I threw the pebble—way too small for so much pain—behind me and put my head in my hands. The pilgrimage went on and on, their feet whisking on the road. I felt as tiny as the stone yet even more insignificant.

The weight of the day and the long drive settled on my shoulders. I should go to the camp and find a place to sleep, if they'd let me, and if not, I'd come back. Everything I'd read said new pilgrims were welcome at the camp, but I'd find out if that were true soon enough.

A couple people pointed me in the right direction and signs large enough to find with my flashlight pointed the way through the woods. The clearing seemingly came out of nowhere. One minute I was dodging branches, the next, I stood on the edge of the camp, although camp, with its mental pictures of quaint two-person tents and stone circles for roasting marshmallows over a fire, was definitely the wrong word. I'd been to the Renaissance Faire last summer and the sprawl ahead reminded me of that, even in size. There were plenty of fires, dotting the expanse with golden light, and there were also tents, but not the small triangular sort. These, of canvas and metal and wood, gave the impressions of permanence with wide pathways, illuminated by solar lamps, in between the structures. Thick stands of trees bordered each side, giving the whole place a feeling of isolation. And the noise . . .

Here, the respectful quiet of the pilgrimage was replaced with the sounds of life, of many lives. People walked and talked and laughed. I smelled roasting meat and saw kids running around, despite the late hour. Little kids. What the hell were their parents thinking, having them here? How could they be so dumb? I almost retreated back into the woods, but someone came up behind me.

"If you're new, go to the right. That big tent, all the way over there?" the person said, pointing. "They'll help you out."

After a brief hesitation, I followed her instructions and everything I'd read proved correct. I was given a warm meal, a cot in a small but private tent, a bag of toiletries, and basic instructions on how the camp functioned. And like that, I was a part of it all. No questions about my reasons for being here or my devotion or anything else. Not exactly smart, in my opinion, but way easier for me.

In spite of being so tired my eyelids closed as soon as I was horizontal, I had trouble sleeping with so many bodies, so much movement, around me. I was up and back at the pilgrimage before the sun finished rising. The day passed slowly. Walking, the endless walking—I stuck to the middle of the pilgrimage so the people on either side of me blocked the gods from my sight. I searched for the Firsts, I searched for my mom, seeking her face in every woman about her age, wondering how changed she'd be now. Hair grey? Lined face? Would she be thinner? Heavier?

I pulled out the photo now and again and always with the same result. Comments on how I resembled her and nothing more. When I got hungry, I went back to camp and ate at a long table with a bunch of other people. A cheeseburger from the grill, potato chips, an apple. I set the photo near my plate and after a few minutes, it was passed around while people commented on our appearances. No recognition though, at least not that I could tell.

I didn't want to go back to the pilgrimage—my feet already hurt—but I did anyway. More walking, more sharing the photo, more nothing. After, it was dinner at the same table. Different people, but they might as well have been the same ones. I spent another restless night and, in the morning, I stared up at the dull grey canvas of my tent. The cot wasn't particularly comfortable and the air outside was already thick with voices and laughter, but I didn't want to get up. My third day here and I couldn't stand it already. Even just the thought of walking made my jaw clench.

I rolled onto my side, the cot creaking the entire time. A human-shaped shadow moved across the side of the tent. Moved, then grew larger as whoever it belonged to stepped closer to my tent. Then it moved even closer. I held my breath, and the shadow withdrew.

I clambered from the cot, spilling the blanket and pillow onto the floor of the tent and rushed through the entrance flaps, grateful that I'd slept in sweatpants and a T-shirt. A narrow pathway ran behind my tent, extending the length of the camp. I checked right and left and saw plenty of people but no one rushing away or looking back at me. No one familiar. No Mom.

I stormed back in my tent, grabbed shoes and socks, and wandered to the back of the camp. The whole place was setup in a well-planned grid pattern, the pathways packed firm. The Firsts were responsible; when people had begun arriving in droves, they refused to allow it to turn chaotic.

As I walked, I wondered if the Firsts were even still

here. Maybe they'd left—or died—and it was some big secret kept from the newbies. I scoffed, drawing a quick glance from a man with a shaved head tending to a pot suspended over an open flame. When I reached the end of the path, I took the one running perpendicular but turned onto the next that ran parallel to the first. I checked and double-checked the faces of everyone I saw and when a tent had its flaps open, I glanced in, although I was as careful as I could be not to make it look like I was looking.

Maybe I'd only imagined the shadow. Maybe Mom wasn't even here. Maybe the note she'd left behind was a lie. But that also meant that the way she'd acted, the way she'd changed into practically another person—watching everything on TV and reading every article she could find about the gods, praying to them, trying to get Dad and I to do the same—until that night was a lie, too, and I didn't think so.

I raked my fingers through my hair, pulling it away from my face as a commotion began to my right. I turned to see a group of elderly men and women walking the path and people emerging from tents or moving closer to greet them. *The Firsts.* Seven people with wrinkles, white hair, and slightly stooped shoulders. Seven people with serene countenances I recognized from the net, the TV. Seven, all present and accounted for. So much for hidden deaths and big secrets.

A tall man walked ahead, another behind, scanning the camp and everyone who approached. The four women and three men they guarded took hands that were extended, not to shake but to cup it briefly between theirs, speaking in a voice too low to discern and continued on the path. Heading toward me, so I forced my spine straight and my face neutral. They drew even closer and I dropped my gaze as I held out a hand. The one that took mine was delicately boned, her skin warm and slightly dry.

"The gods thank you," she said.

I nodded, glancing up. Her blue eyes widened, and her grip tightened on my hand momentarily before it released. She blinked twice and smiled, patting my shoulder before continuing on, fluffy popcorn hair bouncing atop her head. My fingers twitched, yearning to grab the photograph, to demand to know where she was, but I had to be smart about it. Didn't want to get kicked out for being a fraud.

When I tipped my chin back up, they'd already moved on. Standing with my hands on my hips, I stared at their backs. She recognized my face. I knew she did. I was such a chicken shit. I should've pulled out the photo.

It wasn't that hard to keep track of the Firsts' progress; with everyone coming up to them, they were slow. I kept to a safe distance, safe enough so no one would really notice me, especially their guards. At least I hoped not. When they neared the food and kitchen end of camp, they stepped off the path into the trees there. I counted to ten, peeked around to make sure no one was paying any attention, and followed. A narrow path twisted its way around and I got about twenty paces in when a man—not one of the two who'd been walking with them in the camp—emerged from behind a large grouping of trees. He wore a loose fitting tunic, faded jeans, and an easy smile, but there was no doubt as to his role.

"Can I help you?" he asked.

"I saw them in the camp," I said, clasping my hands in front of me. "I was hoping to talk to them."

"This is a private area, not for pilgrims."

"But I—"

"Let me take you back to the camp."

"No, that's okay, I know the way," I said, already walking back, my mouth acrid. "But thank you."

I moved fast, but his footfalls followed. I tensed, preparing for a grab of my arm or being told to stop but neither happened. When I reached the tents, I turned to see him standing a few feet in the trees. I smiled and waved. He nodded.

While the camp never fully quieted, there were lulls, especially after midnight. A few stragglers from the pilgrimage would return, but for the most part, those that walked all night didn't return until after sunrise. A little before three in the morning, dressed in dark clothes, I crept from my tent. I kept my steps soft, walking on the edges of the pathways, sticking to the shadows as best as I could. At the treeline, I walked a little past the narrow path until the full moon illuminated a space between two trees I fit through with ease. I was lucky, the canopy was thick but not so thick that it blocked every speck of light. Keeping parallel to the path, I moved deeper into the woods.

A vine snagged on my pants and stifling a curse, I bent to untangle it. Footsteps approached, soft and quiet. I crouched, making myself as small as possible. The footsteps drew nearer, and the arc of a flashlight came dangerously close. My muscles tensed, but before I was found, the steps and light receded.

After tugging the vine free, I shrugged off my sweater, shivering in my tank top, and pulled the Zippo from my pocket. Twigs and dead leaves made a neat little nest underneath the bundled cotton, but I crawled away, molasses slow, until I came across a felled tree. During the day, it wouldn't hide anyone except a small kid, but at night it would work.

One flick of the Zippo and flames began to eat the sweater. I returned to the tree and waited, barely breathing. When the shouting and running started, I took off. I was closer to the Firsts' camp than I'd thought. It was small, with their tents arranged in a loose semicircle around a firepit. Not a guard in sight, although a couple of tents that probably belonged to them sat off to the side. The Firsts were emerging from theirs, shrugging on robes and wiping sleep from their eyes. As soon as I saw the woman who'd recognized my face, I tucked deeper into the trees. When the chaos was over, I returned to my tent and slept like a milk-drunk baby.

Breakfast was cold cereal and toast. The picture stayed in my pocket; I kept my head down and my voice to myself. Nothing seemed different in the camp. No guards trolling around, no strange looks from or directed to anyone. I loaded my backpack with bottles of water, a couple bananas, and a bag of trail mix, and headed for the pilgrimage, but when I drew close enough to hear the whisper of steps I turned and smacked my way through the trees.

It was a long, miserable trek to get to the woods behind the Firsts' camp, but as hoped, I didn't run into anyone else along the way. As a little kid, I loved climbing trees, the taller, the better; turned out I was still pretty good at it. The guards weren't armed, nor did they patrol the camp, but they checked out a noise in the trees more than once. No way to know if this was normal or because of the fire I set, but they didn't seem overly worried.

The Firsts spent the day going in and out of their

tents, eating food brought to them by people from the main camp, and occasionally visiting a small wooden building set a ways back in the woods. After dinner, they all left together with guards in tow, and I guessed they were going to shake hands with pilgrims and all that bullshit.

I shimmied down from the tree and went to check out the building. It held a small toilet on one side and on the other, a sink, and a shower, the latter two hooked up to what looked like rain barrels outside. While I didn't love the idea of staking out a toilet, it was better than walking a million miles every day. So, I climbed another tree, ate my trail mix, watched, and waited. It only took a couple of hours for the Firsts to return, and the woman with the fluffy hair was the third visitor to the bathroom.

I waited for her just outside the door. She emerged, shaking her wet hands dry, her eyes widening when she saw me.

"Please," I said, my voice soft. Unthreatening. I held out the photograph. "I'm looking for my mom. I know she's here, but I can't find her. Can you help me?" Tears burned in my eyes. The perfect touch.

She looked over my shoulder and I knew she was debating whether to call for help so I grabbed her arm. Not hard enough to hurt, but firm. "Please, I miss her so much."

She sighed and patted my hand. "Valerie always spoke of you fondly. Cate, isn't it?"

I nodded. It took everything I had to keep my face serene.

"I thought it was you. You look just like her. But you should go, honey. This place isn't for you. And people are starting to talk. You showing the picture around to everyone, then trying to get to our camp . . . "

"You don't understand. I just want to see her. Just once, that's all."

"I do understand. I know it's hard. You're not the first person to come looking for someone."

The kindness in her eyes made my grip tighten, my fingers digging into her papery skin, and she winced. She'd have bruises, and I was okay with that. "I'm sorry, please, I've missed her so much, I feel like if I just see her, if I talk to her, everything will be okay and I'll be okay and then I can—" My voice choked into sobs.

"Sheila?" a man said from not too far away. "Are you okay?"

"I'm fine," she called out. "Be there in a minute."

"You need to go," she mouthed.

"Please, just tell me where she is."

Twigs cracked under someone's feet, and I let Sheila go.

She leaned close to me and whispered in my ear, "You'll find your answers at the twelfth shrine, but think carefully before you go."

Before she slipped away, she gave me a look of pity. I crossed my arms under my breasts and watched her go. Her cryptic words lingered in the air. Truth or bullshit?

I wiped beneath my eyes and flicked my tears away. I had no idea how to get to the twelfth shrine from here, so I went back through the woods. Once the sun began to set, I turned toward the pilgrimage and joined at the edge of the line, trying to keep some distance. The footsteps, the breath, the quiet prayers, it all felt ominous now. I had a bad feeling I was being lured to the twelfth shrine on purpose. They were probably going to throw me out.

I sighed. So be it.

And then what? I shoved my hands in my pockets. But I came here not knowing the *And then what?* Not knowing and not caring. So I kept walking under a darkening sky until I reached the very end, past the eleventh shrine. My flashlight found the path through the trees and while it wasn't as well-trod, nor was it a straight route, it was relatively easy to follow. It traveled a fair distance away from the road, because of the washout, I assumed, then arced back around. The trees broke ahead, and I saw the corner of the shrine, an ornately carved piece of wood, repurposed from an old cuckoo clock. Clicking off my light, I squatted beside a tree. The minutes passed slowly, but I stayed where I was. If it was a lure, they were probably hiding as well, waiting for me to emerge.

When my ankles ached from the squat, I stood, bracing myself against the tree until the hurt ebbed and, holding the still-off flashlight in my hand, I walked out of the trees and scanned the shadows. Nothing and no one. I shivered and turned on the flashlight.

"Cate?"

I whirled around, the flashlight cutting crazed lines in the air as I did. No one was there except the god in her shrine, a small pile of offerings on the ground below like totems to the victim of an accident.

I took a step closer and then another. And there, in the shrine, not a god, but my mother. Too small, too misshapen, but her face, an older version of my own, was undeniable. My legs went rubbery and I put my hands on my knees to keep from falling. When I could breathe again, I rose and stepped even closer. I never imagined something like this. It had to be a mirage or a trick, whether of my mind or designed by the Firsts.

But it wasn't.

The twelfth god had multiple limbs and a spheroid body. Somehow, my mother had been altered to match her shape. Condensed, broken, changed. Arms and legs bifurcated into many with joints bending the wrong way. Torso stretched wide, crushed down. It shouldn't have been possible, but it was. And worse still, she appeared to have grown into the shrine itself, her pale flesh seamlessly joining the wood and iron. An experiment that went wrong? Or something designed to hold her there?

She was monstrous. An abomination. And she didn't look much like my mom anymore. That made things easier.

"The gods had to leave," she said, smiling sadly. Her voice was thick and rusty, as though speech took far more effort now. "What were we supposed to do? All those people, all that hope . . . "

"You weren't supposed to be here in the first place," I said, the words barbed. "How could you? How could you just leave like that? In the middle of the night like a coward? You didn't even say goodbye."

"I knew you wouldn't understand."

"Understand? How could I ever understand? And how could you let them do this to you?"

She lifted one arm, the resulting movement reminding me of a child's rubbery toy, and my gut clenched. "The god picked me to take her place," she said.

"You could've said no."

"You don't say no to a god," she said with a sigh carrying a faint whiff of decay and brackish water.

"*You* should've. You should've come home."

"I couldn't." She leaned forward with a crackle of bones unaccustomed to movement and a creak of wood.

"Bullshit. You chose not to. And for what? To be a stupid fake god sitting here while people, while the world, thinks you're real? While people pray to you?" I kicked the pile of offerings, sending the eight-limbed figures scattering in all directions.

"Cate, sweetheart, I never meant to hurt you." She held out a different arm, a different hand, palm up. Two other arms crossed over her abdomen, the way a pregnant woman would. If that pregnant woman had vipers for arms.

Hideous. *Obscene.*

"Dad thought I came here to find you and bring you home." I dropped my backpack to the ground and rummaged in my pocket for the Zippo. "You recognize this, don't you? I've carried it every day. I *waited* every day for you to come back. Every. Single. Day. I waited and hoped, but you chose all this over me, over your own daughter."

"They were gods, Cate. Can't you understand that?"

"I hate you," I said, the words soft as a feather pillow. I sparked the flame and held it to the canvas material of my backpack until it caught, then I nudged it with my foot until it was beneath her shrine.

The flames began to lick at the wooden support post. Her serpentine arms, now wearing bracelets and armbands of smoke, writhed in a tangle of fear and panic. She screamed, but it was high and thin, and I backed away from the heat. I didn't care if anyone heard. It was too late to save her. It had been too late for a long time.

"You were already a god to me, Mom," I said, but the growing roar of the fire swallowed the words whole.

OUTRUNNING THE END

CULLEN BUNN

A BLACK HIGHWAY, *stretching into darkness.*

Headlights. Distant pinpoints at first, growing larger—brighter—as they draw close.

In the oncoming cars—faces. Drivers and passengers. They fade into view as the glow of headlights fill the passing cars. Just quick glimpses, their faces frozen in a single fleeting second.

Dour-faced. Smiling. Laughing. Weeping.

Screaming.

And then gone.

Why do they scream? Is it because something chases them? It can't be. The Blight hasn't spread this far yet. No. They scream because they can see what lies before them.

The rear view, reflecting the red flare of tail lights, fading into nothing.

Somewhere back there . . . in the darkness . . . in the heart of the spreading Blight . . . the dead man follows.

***

Tires hiss over wet pavement as Brandon steers the car into the parking lot. A light mist dances in the air, churning, coating the windshield in a blurry mess. The light of the convenience store sign—GAS & GOODIES, it proclaims—is muted by the wet, murky haze. He pulls to a stop next to the gas pumps. For a minute or two, he sits behind the wheel, staring at the bright store front. He's been behind the wheel so long, anything else feels unnatural. But he pries his fingers from the wheel, shrugs his way out of the car, opens the gas tank, and takes the nozzle from the pump.

The nozzle's handle is warm and fleshy in Brandon's hand. He feels a steady throbbing, some sort of thick fluid pulsing sluggishly through inhuman veins. He quickly shoves the nozzle into the tank. He can't be sure, but he thinks he hears a satisfied grunting. He starts the flow of gasoline, sets it, and then steps away. He rubs his fingers against his palm as he watches the shuddering nozzle, then gazes into the distance, back the way he came.

The Blight is close.

The digital gas pump meter flashes, counting the gallons. Brandon hurries across the lot toward the store. There is only one other car here, a beaten Ford Festiva with the windows down. The interior is covered in a watery residue. But it's not his problem. As Brandon enters the store, an electronic bell chimes. From behind the counter, the clerk—the owner of the Festiva most likely—looks up from his phone and nods in Brandon's direction.

"Slow night," the clerk says, and returns to texting or sexting or whatever the Hell he is doing. Brandon did not bring his cell phone with him on this journey. It felt like a distraction. It felt unnecessary.

Brandon moves toward the back of the store.

And he curses under his breath.

All he wants is a soda, something with some kick,

something with enough caffeine to keep his eyes open a while longer, but the refrigerated cabinet is full of wet, squirming things, slapping and slithering against the glass, leaving viscous slug-trails of blood and ooze.

The pattern is hypnotic.

It draws him in, urges him to open the door and let them roll out in a glistening sheet across the tiled floor.

The pattern-eels want him to sleep.

They serve the dead man who hunts him.

The bell rings again. Brandon's heart skips a beat. He crouches a little, hiding behind bags of tortilla chips, watching. Has the dead man caught up with him already? It seems impossible, especially after he's done so much to shake him—taking back roads, backtracking, driving night and day without resting—but he couldn't be sure. These days, the roads seemed to twist and squirm and contract, not all that different from the pattern-eels.

For all he knows, he is chasing the dead man now, not the other way around.

Another customer enters. He's young, just barely out of his teenage years, wearing slouchy jeans, a tight tank top, and a flat-billed cap pulled low over his eyes.

"Slow night," the clerk says, an autopilot greeting.

Making a bee-line for the restroom, the new arrival moves quickly, but to sleep-deprived eyes, it looks like he's moving in slow motion, too.

Coffee, Brandon decides. Coffee will do. He's never liked the stuff, but tonight's not about enjoyment. It's about staying awake. It's about driving for his life.

It's about outrunning the end of the world.

The coffee is black and thick. Brandon imagines it has been sitting in the glass pot all day. He fills one large Styrofoam cup with the steaming liquid, then a second.

As he walks to the front of the store, he slurps one of the coffees down, savoring the searing heat, the bitterness, the rush. He's emptied the cup by the time he reaches the counter.

There, he finds a cardboard display of energy shots, and he selects three—no, four—of them. Next to the cash register is a rack of plastic single-dose pouches of migraine meds and no-doze tablets. He grabs a handful of each, pushing them across the counter, along with the empty cup, the untouched coffee, and the energy shots.

"Long trip ahead of you?"

The clerk slides the items across the counter, scanning each one, making a show of examining the energy shots, as if he'd never seen them before.

"Long trip?" The clerk asks again.

"That's right," Brandon says.

"Hey, you know," the clerk says, "if you're dead behind the wheel, you can always just park in the lot, get a couple of hours of sleep before setting out again. I won't give you trouble about it. My manager would. He's a dick. But he doesn't clock in again for several hours. Might be a bit safer for you if you get some rest."

"I appreciate that, but I'll be fine. Only a few more hours ahead of me."

This is a lie, but the truth was none of the kid's business.

The clerk nods absently, scanning the last item, tossing it in a plastic bag. "Where ya headed?"

Brandon hesitates.

How a man faces death—or flees from it—is a private matter.

"Home," he says. "I've been traveling for work."

This, too, is a lie.

Or is it?

His brow furrows as he tries to remember—

The truth.

Yes, the truth.

But what does that even mean?

Truth is subject to interpretation, filtered through your own perception.

But what if your barn is shot so full of holes that all the chickens just slip out to hunt pattern-eels in the dead of night?

Barn?

Chickens?

Not that. Your *brain*, not your barn. What if your *brain* is so rotted and full of holes that all your thoughts—true or otherwise—escape you . . . what do you do then?

Brandon lies to the clerk because he knows the young man will not understand the truth. He is on the run, fleeing something vicious and unforgiving, trying to shake a relentless dead man on lonely stretches of blacktop weaving through the fields and hills and forests, past truck stops and secluded strip clubs and oh-so-many cruel and mocking mile markers.

And even if he could understand the truth, the clerk will be gone soon.

The surroundings already displayed signs—symptoms—of the encroaching Blight.

"Traveling for work, huh?" The clerk shakes his head and sucks his teeth. "That's rough. Well, I can't even imagine being away from my Kendra for that long. Working this counter, there ain't much special about it, but at least I get to see her when I get home."

Brandon eyes the total on the cash register, hands

some crumpled bills to the kid, and scoops up his purchases. He doesn't wait for change before turning away. "Tell Kendra I said hello."

The clerk cocks his head, his brow furrowed.

"What's that?" he says. "Who's Kendra?"

"Sorry, I thought you said—" Brandon catches himself. He must remember that the Blight is close now, tendrils flowing in around him, waiting to envelop him completely. "Never mind."

He shuffles out the door and across the lot. In a parking spot near the front door, a fourteen-foot centipede waits. Its chitinous hide glistens wetly from the misty drizzle. It has a saddle on its segmented back and handlebars sticking out of the back of its head. It must belong to the other traveler, the kid who is visiting the store's facilities. Brandon gives the creature plenty of space as he moves toward his car. He tears the no-doze packet open, popping the pills, chasing them with a five-hour energy shot, chasing that with a swig of coffee. He yanks the nozzle out of the tank, returns it to the pump, then slides back behind the wheel.

From the window of the store, the clerk watches him.

Who the fuck was Kendra? Where did that name come from? He digs deep, trying to remember where he might have heard the name. Maybe it was someone he had known in college, in high school. Maybe he worked with her at some point. She might have been one of the many faceless co-workers who rotated in and out of one of the many forgettable jobs he'd held over the years.

That's how the Blights works.

Sometimes, it called up long forgotten names or faces. Sounds. Bits of church hymns you might've sang when you were four. Sudden, sharp smells and tastes.

Your mouth might water at the thought of a ribeye you ate 30 years ago. Goosebumps might rise on your skin as you recall in vivid detail a drunken one-night stand that you barely remembered the day after it occurred.

Even as he speeds out of the parking lot, the muscles of Brandon's neck and shoulders tighten. The sudden burst of energy from the coffee and the no-doze and the energy shot is already draining away. He is already . . . *dead* . . . behind the wheel. He shifts in his seat, hoping the movement will keep him awake long enough for him to put some distance between himself and the expanding borders of the Blight.

The desire for sleep pulls at him.

If he sleeps, though, he might meet the same fate as the world around him.

If he sleeps, he might wake up different.

✳✳✳

Pale, emaciated figures running alongside the car, keeping pace at 80 miles an hour.

They look sickly, but they move fast. They glide along the road, moving in a unified herd. They know the terrain so well they don't need to watch where they're going. Instead, they look toward the car.

Their faces are blank. They have been wiped away. Erased.

One of the faceless white things breaks away from the others, turns sharply, darts out into the highway.

The car swerves.

The brakes catch on slick pavement.

The car jerks to a stop.

Headlights wash over pale skin, making it glow.

And then the errant creature comes apart, like a puff

of smoke, vanishing, as if it was never there in the first place.

The others have stopped, and they stand alongside the road, as still and as straight as signposts, waiting, watching without eyes.

When the car starts to move again, so do they.

They are pilot fish swimming in the wake of a shark, eating scraps.

✥ ✥ ✥

Another hundred miles, and Brandon's eyes betray him. He glimpses movement in his peripheral vision. He slams on the brakes for no reason at all, and he spills what's left of his coffee all over his lap. It's gone cold. He tries to blink the hallucinations away, but when he closes his eyes, they resist opening once more.

And he can't sleep, no matter how much he wants to, not even for a second.

Somewhere out there, the dead man stalks him. He never relents, never gives up. And when Brandon sleeps, that's when he moves most quickly.

The dead man created the Blight Engine—a great, grinding mass of gears and pistons, with towering smokestacks. Instead of smoke, the pipes billow horror and insanity, an endless deific cloud of it slowly spreading across the sky, mutating anything it touched. Brandon saw it in a nightmare the last time he slept, the night before he rushed out to his car, left everything and everyone behind, and . . .

. . . just . . .

. . . started . . .

. . . driving.

He left his wife and son at home.

No, not a son. He's remembering wrong. He always wanted a son, but he has daughters.

How many?

Just the one, and her name is—

Kimmy?

He crept out in the dead of night, jumped into the car, and drove.

He had no destination in mind. He only wanted to avoid getting swept up in the Blight for as long as possible. He had not told his wife and son—his *daughter*—about his plan because he knew they would try to stop him. The infection . . . the entropic influence . . . had already seeped into their flesh.

Knowingly or not, his family served the dead man now.

And the dead man hated Brandon almost as much as he hated the world.

✢✢✢

And, lo, the dead man so hated the world that he deemed to destroy it.

He started small, so no one would notice, so no one would rally against him.

Methodical.

Patient.

But now, he pushed his machine to the limits, filling the world with strange terrors.

All because one man had discovered him.

✢✢✢

Red and blue lights flash in the rearview. Brandon looks up, squints at the glare. A state trooper's cruiser rides his bumper.

Brandon pulls to the side of the road, and the trooper's car pulls up behind him. He leans to the side, watching in the side view mirror as the trooper gets out of his car and dons a hat covered in plastic. The trooper moves alongside Brandon's car slowly. Brandon rolls his window down.

"Evening," the trooper says, leaning in. It's night, but the trooper wears mirrored shades. He puts a hand on the side of the car to assert dominance, as if to say, "This vehicle belongs to me until I say otherwise."

"Good evening," Brandon says.

"License and registration?"

Brandon fishes his ID from his wallet. The registration is in the glove box. As he gathers the paperwork, he considers grabbing the other object he keeps in the box. The thought plays in his mind only for a second before he dismisses it.

The trooper looks at the license, his face impassive.

"You're a long way from home," he says. "Where are you headed?"

Brandon looks into the distance. He doesn't even know what highway he's on. He tries to remember the last road sign he saw, tries to remember what city or town lies ahead.

The trooper doesn't wait for an answer. "You were weaving quite a bit back there. That's why I pulled you over. Have you been on the road for a while?"

Brandon nods.

"Thought so." The trooper hands the license and paperwork back to Brandon. "Look, driving exhausted is dangerous. You should get some sleep."

The trooper turns his head, his gaze following the painted lines on the pavement. Behind the shades,

Brandon sees tiny pattern-eels wriggling in the man's eye sockets.

"There's a motel a few miles down the road. If you follow me, I'll lead you to it. You should check in for the night. Wherever you're headed, you'll get there safe after some rest."

"That's a good idea," Brandon says. "I was hoping I'd run across a place to crash—uh, a place to sleep—soon."

The trooper nods curtly, drums his fingers against the side of the car, and saunters back to his cruiser.

Brandon grips the steering wheel, blinks . . .

. . . and the trooper is gone.

Brandon turns in his seat, looks out the back window. There is no sign of the cruiser. Could he have fallen asleep while the trooper drove past? If that was the case, why wouldn't the trooper stop and backtrack when he saw Brandon wasn't following?

He puts the car into drive, eases off the brake, and drives on.

In ten minutes, he finds the police cruiser. It is parked in the middle of the highway, crossing two lanes. The lights on top flash steadily, pulses of red and blue coloring the surroundings, and the doors are open. There is no sign of the trooper. The cruiser sits at the back of a long line of empty, unmoving vehicles, hundreds of cars and trucks and massive centipedes, blocking both sides of the highway. It looks as if a mass evacuation had been taking place, and when the road became impassable, the drivers abandoned their transport and continued on foot.

Brandon sits there, unable to decide what to do next. Should he leave the safety of the car? It isn't like he will be going anywhere. The other cars that choke the road are empty, engines dead, doors hanging open. They've been abandoned by their drivers. There is no way around them. Even the shoulders of the highway are blocked by driverless vehicles.

Sluggishness threatens to overtake him once more, and Brandon shakes his head, forces himself awake. He chugs the rest of his energy shots, one right after another. If he stays here . . . if he just sits in his car doing nothing . . . he will surely fall asleep. If he falls asleep, the Blight will overtake him.

He will wake up different.

So different, it won't be like waking up at all.

He opens the glove box. From within, he takes a folding pocket knife. For years, the knife had rested unused in a cluttered drawer in his kitchen. Almost as an afterthought, he had grabbed it before leaving on this trip. He had left his wife behind. He had left his daughter. But he hadn't left the blade. The knife isn't for protection against some outside threat. It isn't made to hold up in a struggle.

He keeps the knife so that, when the time came, he might kill himself.

Shoving the knife in his pocket, he exits the car. He knows he will never see the car again, but he doesn't bother looking back. By the time he has taken ten steps, he has almost forgotten what the car looks like.

He walks.

Soon, he sees other people walking along, winding through the maze of bumper-to-bumper vehicles as far as the eye can see. There are men and women, children and the elderly. Some are dressed in business attire. Others are dressed in pajamas, as if they woke from sleep and hurriedly fled down the road. Brandon hurries to catch up with them.

"Hey!" he calls. "Wait!"

No one acknowledges him. They move forward, their eyes fixed on the blackness of the horizon.

"Are you running from him, too?" he asks, hoping to find someone who can share the burden of his fear.

Silent, they keep walking.

Not just walking—marching. Their legs move in unison. Their feet beat a staccato on the pavement. Brandon feels a moment of terror as he realizes that he has fallen in line with their progression. He must concentrate to break free from the herd.

The towering sign of a roadside motel rises out of the darkness. This must be the place the state trooper had tried to lure him to.

THE SLUMBER INN
AMERICAN-OWNED
WEEKLY RATES AVAILABLE

And below that, in bright neon:

NO VACANCY.

Of course, no rooms are available. More than four dozen people walk alongside Brandon now, all of them fleeing the end. They do not talk. They do not look at one another. They trudge along somberly, heads down slightly, mechanically putting step after step between them and the dead man's influence.

And their faces are vanishing.

The skin of their eyelids grows together, sealing shut. Their noses recede, leaving small nostril holes in the flesh, and soon those too pucker closed. Their lips wither, their atrophic mouths nothing but a thin line that will disappear altogether soon. A dull glow shines beneath their skin.

Every step makes the other travelers less and less who they once were.

Brandon touches his own face and breathes a sigh of relief when he finds his features still intact.

But the people around him—if they could be called people at all anymore—continue to change. With every step, they become more glow than flesh. Soon, they will come apart, like mist, and cease to exist altogether.

Brandon's heart sinks. He thought he was ahead of the Blight. He thought if he kept moving, he might avoid it. Now he knows that is not the case.

The disappearing travelers lumber forward—and entropy embraces them.

The Blight, Brandon realizes, is not behind him. It is all around him, closing in. He stands in the eye of a storm. The eye, though, like the eyes of the other travelers is sealing shut. The influence of the Blight rushes in all around him, filling the world like water filling a gaping hole, and soon it will drown him.

The light of the motel sign flickers. Where once the words NO VACANCY had glared through the mist, now it reads VACANCY.

Brandon breaks away from the other travelers. He pushes past them, pushes through their ghost-like countenance. He approaches the motel. Dozens of cars and trucks are lined up alongside the two-story structure. Inside each, something slithers and oozes against the windows. Pattern-eels fill the vehicles completely. Brandon hopes that the passengers were able to escape the vehicles before they were suffocated by the slimy creatures.

He steps into the motel office. No night manager greets. He taps the ringer of a little metal bell on the counter a few times, but no one appears. "Hello?" he calls, but no one answers.

Music plays softly from little speakers on the counter.

A popular song.

He's heard it on the radio many times.

The shrieks of mutilated infants and the bleating cry of sacrificial goats.

A ledger sits on the counter. On the ledger is a key on a plastic, trapezoid-shaped keychain labeled with the number 1E. At first, Brandon thinks another guest must have left the key there as they checked out, but as he looks more closely, he sees his own name had already been written in the book.

His own name—in his own handwriting—written next to the denotation for room 1E.

Brandon scoops up the key and hurries out, heading to his room.

1E looks like any other cheap motel room. Heavy, dark curtains were drawn across a large window, a gap that cannot be closed letting the harsh glare of the street lamps into the room. The bed is made neatly, cheap, stiff blankets smoothed over the mattress. Bad flea market art—featuring a sinking ship and women and children drowning in a sea of blood—on the walls. A small TV on a dresser before the bed. A connected bathroom. The cloying stink of carpet cleaner and Lysol heavy in the air.

He realizes that he hasn't visited a restroom in a long time.

Now, it hardly matters.

His pants are damp and stinking.

He has pissed himself, and more than once.

On the table next to the bed is a telephone. He picks it up, starts punching numbers randomly, and holds the receiver to his ear as he hears a ringing from a cross the line.

"Hello?" A voice answers. A woman's voice. Worried and worn thin. "Hello?"

"I shouldn't have called," he says. "I can't be sure if it's you I'm talking to, or if you're just a ghost."

"Brandon? Brandon, is that you? Are you all right? Where are you?"

"This is the end, I think."

"Brandon, I've been so worried about you." The woman speaks a name, but it comes across as an electronic screeching, like the connection of a fax machine. "—has been so worried. We want you to come home . . . or at least tell us where you are so we can come and get you."

Through the gap in the curtain, Brandon sees a shadow pass, someone moving slowly down the walkway that runs along the front of the motel.

Someone is coming.

"Are you there?" the woman says. "Hello—"

"Unzip me," he says, "and I am full of squirming, festering things."

"I'm sorry," the woman says, "but what does that—"

"I have to go. I have company."

Brandon hangs up.

Did he make the call or had the phone been ringing when he walked into the room?

He watches the door.

Someone knocks.

Brandon doesn't answer. He holds his breath.

He digs the knife from his pocket.

The knocking intensifies.

Brandon unfolds the knife, grips the blade tightly.

He crosses the room. The steady knocking rattles the door in the frame. He holds the knife in one hand, keeping it flat against his thigh. With his other hand, he grips the doorknob. He doesn't bother looking out the peephole. He knows who he will see. He opens the door.

The dead man stands across the threshold from him.

Behind him, the world ends. The misting rain has stopped. Now, the world heaves and bucks and undulates, coming undone, substance and form bleeding into nothingness like paint breaking apart in water. It is no longer night, no longer dark. Instead, a borealis of bloody light roils through the sky. Faceless, ghostly figures tumble through the air, rising, raptured from this world, but unable to see or hear what is happening. Pattern-eels swim in the spaces between substance and oblivion, devouring the featureless travelers, snapping at them as they tumble upwards. Some of the eels are thousands of feet long, and they tear through the curtain of reality, burrowing through existence, leaving a shit trail of writhing memories in their wake.

Names, sensations, phantom-like faces—wash over him in waves.

His wife. His daughter.

His house.

His boss and co-workers.

His doctor, stone-faced as he delivers his diagnosis.

Before he can grasp hold of any one memory, they all roll away.

The dead man acknowledges none of this.

He has murdered the world with as little care as he might give crushing an ant under his thumb.

Looking into the eyes of the dead man, Brandon feels himself smile madly.

The dead man mimics the expression.

"You found me," Brandon says.

The dead man speaks at the same time, saying the same things.

"I wasn't looking for you," both men say.

And, "You were never lost."

Brandon can't be sure if he is looking into the face of a world-destroying monster . . . looking into the eyes of the awful creature he had been fleeing from . . . or if he is peering into a mirror.

✳✳✳

The doctor's office is cold, quiet, sparse.

Morgue-like.

"This is a lot to take in," he says. "I'm sure you have questions."

"This can't be happening."

"I would encourage you to seek out a second opinion, of course." He is the harbinger of the Blight, the servant of the dead man. "I can offer some referrals if you like."

"I'm too young. This only happens to old people. Old people, hobbling around with their walkers, shuffling through nursing homes, drool running down their chins, eyes wide and confused, unsure where they are, unsure who they are. And now . . . Now, I'm going to be one of them."

Early onset—that's what the doctor calls it.

His face is a mask of practiced non-emotion.

"When you're ready, we should start discussing a course of treatment to slow the advancement of—"

✳✳✳

Moving suddenly, Brandon lashes out with the knife, the dull blade ripping a ragged tear through the dead man's throat.

The reflection shatters. The dead man's eyes widen, and his mouth falls agape. His head lolls back, and the gash in his neck suppurates, blood gushing out, spilling down his chest. He clutches one hand feebly to the wound. He reaches out, a pleading gesture, toward Brandon.

Brandon strikes with the knife again, slicing across the fingers of his mirror image.

The dead man steps back, shaking his stinging fingers. His digits are loose now, hanging by tatty shreds of flesh, flapping loosely. Brandon slams the motel room door closed.

Brandon can't catch his breath. He spins in place, looking around the room. Questions form on his lips. But there is no one to ask. The bloody knife falls from his fingers, thumps to the carpet. His heart races.

What has he done?

Through the gap in the curtain, he sees the red, undulating glow of the Blight fade.

He moves to the window and pulls the curtain aside.

The world is back to normal. The sky is dark and clear. The cars in the parking lot are empty. Nothing moves within. In the distance, cars cruise along the highway.

Brandon coughs out a laugh.

His legs give out from under him and he drops to a sitting position on the edge of the bed. His shoulders sag.

The world—he's saved the world.

The world . . . with his wife Margaret and his

daughter Kimmy . . . with his job at the insurance company . . . with the receptionist, Kendra, who brought in cookies every Wednesday . . . with his doctor, who had been so wrong about the diagnosis.

It was all clear—lucid, now.

He looks at the phone.

He needs to call his family, to apologize for scaring, to promise he'll be home soon.

He's succeeded.

He's won.

He outran the corruption and the madness.

The Blight.

The end.

His fingers tremble as he picks up the phone. He dials the area code, the first three digits, the fourth. But he hesitates.

The next number—what is it?

From outside, he hears the awful, scraping grind of machinery.

He finishes dialing.

"We're sorry, but the number you have dialed is not a working—"

Through the gap in the curtain, red light spills into the room. Serpentine shadows move in the glow.

He drops the telephone's handset.

Frantically, he looks around

The knife—where did he drop it?

Someone knocks at the door.

Never Walk Alone—François Vaillancourt

MOTEL NINE

CHRISTOPHER BUEHLMAN

OF THE MANY chain motels he has come to know in his time on the road, he likes Motel Nne the best. He likes the one in Ames, Iowa for the tomato-red carpet that blazes like a challenge to the snow so often lurking outside the pale of artificial heat. He likes the one in Berea, Kentucky, for the false-medieval roof beams and garden *trompe l'oeil* that betray its origins as a Knight's Inn. The one in Weeki Wachee, Florida boasts a mermaid statue in the lobby, and a vending machine that only offers peanut M&Ms; he can't say why that charms him considering he prefers plain M&Ms, but it does. Something to do with a certain level of dedication, perhaps. Another thing about this chain is that the price is right. Money isn't a particular problem for him, but it makes no sense to spend it on nothing. He isn't entertaining sexual partners. He isn't hosting clients. He just needs to get from here to there, from now to then, and get what sleep he's able to. Also, and most importantly, whether the chain is calling itself Motel Nine, Motel Six, or the less common Motel 66, all of them always welcome pets. Even cats. The man travels with a brownish-black cat that some would still call a kitten.

The animal seems infatuated with, and perhaps even loyal to, everyone who meets it, which can be a source of bother to the man, whose preferences decline toward solitude. Even the most conscientious people briefly consider stealing the cat because they sense it is actually *their* cat, mistakenly placed with the thin, balding young man who seems to hover more around it than it around him. Taking the cat wouldn't be theft, it would be correcting a wrong. Nobody does, though.

"What's his name?" a clearly covetous woman in Hope, Arkansas asks the man as he sits outside his room in the humid morning air. When she turns her eye away from the tabby, she finds herself looking at the man's bald spot, wondering what flaw others first perceive in her. How could she know that every person instantly wonders the same thing when they see his scalp shining at the crown of his head, ringed by mouse-brown hair it looks like a strong showerhead might wash off? This woman is really staring at the bald spot. "Her name is Hattie," the man says, smiling despite his desire to cover his head then bodily push the woman off to her own open doorway.

In Independence, Missouri, the cat is Harry. In Xenia, Ohio, he calls the cat Toast for the benefit of a one-legged man enjoying the bike trail with the aid of a good prosthesis. "She looks a little like toast," the cyclist says. "He does," the man replies, taking another bite of his cheese sandwich and brushing crumbs off the bench. Anyone who presumes to know the feline's sex is always contradicted, unless the questioner is a child.

The small, balding man indulges children.

Now there is the matter of his car. He drives a 1979 Mercury Cougar with two huge doors and no modern circuitry that might be affected by the conditions of his particular sort of travel. The cat alternates between sunning itself on the beach-like dashboard, curling up in a ball on the passenger seat, or peering out the window. Other drivers who see the cat looking at them frequently remark upon it to their passengers, noting its steady gaze or its sharp ears or the golden color of its eyes, which varies between molten steel and a just-risen moon.

At this moment, the diurnal moon hangs pale and chalky like its own ghost above a McDonalds Play Place in Mineola, Texas as the man asks a five-year-old girl, "Do you know that this town was named for two little sisters, Minnie and Olla?" She just stares. "Did you know that you are not the only *you* that God made?" he says, before her mother, who had been planning to call her lover on the cell phone, and who would have been engrossed for nearly an hour while her daughter grew dangerously bored, leads her by the hand away from the slide. The woman demands a manager. The manager cranes to see who the child-approacher may be, but the man is already gone. When the other version of him pulls up, the one without the cat, the one with a little less hair, the little girl and her mother are also already gone.

He eats in McDonalds from time to time, though he prefers Wendy's. If he takes an exit in just the right way, he can hit Wendy's in the early nineties, when they still offer the baked potato bar. You can just keep topping that baked potato for about three dollars, filling the skin with salad, cheese, chili, whatever you fancy. There isn't a better deal on the highway. He can also take an exit in just such a way as to go back to when he isn't so hungry, but eating gives him something to do.

The man likes the highway. He likes the juniper smell of the air freshener hanging from the mirror and the way his own eyes look in reflection when he checks them, thinking:

Yes, these are the eyes of a man doing the right thing. I am not a good man but nonetheless I am doing the right thing.

Nobody can find him here, call him, send him a bill, or a summons, or even a postcard from any place real or imagined. His solitude is a small price to pay for making himself benign. It is a small price to pay for seeing inside creation, just a little, just at the margins. He embraces the knowledge that he will spend the rest of his strange days alone, except for the cat and, of course, the radio.

He enjoys National Public Radio, enjoys hearing an older or younger Garrison Keillor talking about Lake Woebegone. It's hard to get NPR in the sticks, though. He hates it when All Things Considered, with its endless variations of this or that world event—President Hart, President Clinton, President Bush bombs Serbia—blurs back into the static it came from, or worse, gets overwhelmed by the inevitable country station or fire-and-brimstone radio preacher. The preachers irritate him with their twanging-tin-can self-righteousness and mind-numbing repetition. It isn't that the hell-sellers are all that wrong about justice and redemption, it's just that they seem to see themselves above it. They underestimate their own capacity to harm by spreading the germs of pride and blindness.

The cat seems indifferent to the long hours in the car, as they hurry to meet some conjunction or kill time until another one presents itself, but it always perks up for their nightly stops at Motel Nine, where the man turns it loose to comb the brush of the Nowherevilles for small, peeping things to tear open under the children's-aspirin-orange or sulphur-white lamps. Coyotes approach the cat outside Prescott, Arizona, hoping to add to the collection of collars and nametags they've harvested from adventurous pets, but the way the cat moves towards them with its shoulders low makes them yip away into the cooling desert air and darkness beneath the deaf stars. While this happens, the man is sitting outside his room on the motel's other side, watching Mars glimmer pale red like a king among courtiers, wondering if there are other versions of it, too, where life continued, and earth shines pale and dead in their night sky.

When the man confronts his other selves, he rarely needs to speak. This is because he enjoys the element of surprise. It is also because in most of his incarnations he is a frail thing, barely possessing the dark courage needed to transgress. In Victor, New York, he stares at himself in the parking lot of a farmer's market and gas station until *that* him, who was peeking into the back of a station wagon, glances around and goes white. The frightened one scrambles toward his own car, this time a Honda with pewter-grey duct tape ringed in layers around the right headlight and drives away. The man stays near the station wagon until the father comes out with a paper sack of apples and opens the door, giving the man a hard look. The man turns away.

Most of the other versions of himself are corrected by that one fleeting glimpse of their own doppelgänger, in whose appearance at a moment of temptation they divine the wretched course their lives will take if they progress beyond their current stage of illness. Many will be arrested for passive consumption of media, some will be suicides. But they don't do *That*.

The Hard Cases are of course the worst. The cat lets him know when they've got one, growling a low warning as they approach the conjunction, causing the man to wipe his sweaty upper lip and say, "Oh God. Oh God. Okay. God." The hard cases won't be scared, so there's no point trying. They tend to be thinner, though the one in Zion, Illinois is packed in ropy muscle and covered in blurry-looking tats. The man finds himself sitting outside Motel Nine, smoking a small, noisome cigar. Tobacco is not a common vice among his iterations, but sitting outside motel rooms in the early evening is. He has to work himself up to approaching the Hard Case, taking a beta-blocker to keep his hands from shaking; he knows it won't have time to kick in, but knowing that its calming, flattening magic is on the way helps him open the door, swing his leather shoe out to scuff on the asphalt.

I am not a brave man but I am doing the right thing.

He walks towards the motel.

"Shit, you my brother?" the stronger, slightly older him says.

"Actually, yes."

"Well, have a seat, brother. You want a beer?'

The man sits. He's trying to think of what to say. He knows it's dangerous to say anything because his natural tendency is to try to please, to ingratiate, and that's not what he's here for. Besides, he immediately likes this one, likes the crow's feet around his eyes, how much more self-possessed he seems than the man himself has ever been. He immediately feels the prick of guilt for indulging even that venal spark of envy.

"So, I guess it's bound to happen. All the people in the world, one of em's bound to look like you. I mean, just fucking like you. In the joint, lots of fuckers say there's somebody looks just like them, you know what I mean? But here you are. My alibi. Maybe *you* robbed that Lebanese place."

He pops a beer open.

"Nah, that was me. I remember it."

He passes the beer to the man.

"Here, skinny brother, wet your whistle."

He drinks, his hand shaking a little.

"You okay?"

"Yeah. Sure. Just thinking."

"What about?"

He's thinking that if he says just the right words he can make tonight come out better, do the work gently. He's thinking maybe there's been a mistake—this guy doesn't feel like one. So, he goes straight for the button.

"Kids."

The man seems to draw in a little. His eyes narrow.

"What about 'em?"

Shit. He is one. He's like me. And he's already done That. *He'll keep doing it.*

Back in the Mercury, behind him, in the parking lot where broken glass twinkles under the streetlamp, the cat growls. He can't hear it but he can feel it. The gooseflesh ripples on the back of his neck.

"You're starting to freak me out a little," the tattooed man says.

The man vocalizes something meant to sound like 'sorry,' but it doesn't. The stronger one stands up. Afraid, the small one stands up, too, puts his hand in his coat pocket.

"What you got there anyway?" The stronger one's voice is friendly, seductive even. Hypnotic. He moves very close, unafraid of the man.

"Thought it was a little warm for a coat. You mind if I look?"

The beer is foreign and bready on his other self's breath, as it was on their father's breath. The tattooed man keeps eye contact, slips his hand over the smaller man's hand in his coat pocket, feels the small revolver gripped in the white, sweating fingers. The bigger man's hand is irresistible. He pulls it out of the pocket, uses his other hand to strip it away.

"Come inside," he says, backing into his dank room, pulling the man with him by the collar. The man notices the red carpet that for some reason makes him think of the sands of Mars.

The man hears his car's huge door open. Then close.

"Sit down," tattooed him says, gesturing at the bed. He obeys. The larger man shuts the motel door, looms over him, keeping the gun close to his own body where it won't be easy to grab. Not that he'd have the guts to grab it.

"Suppose you tell me who the fuck you are and what you want."

"Okay. Okay. God. I'm ... "

"Quit shaking, you pussy, and talk."

He points the gun at him.

"Okay. You won't like it."

"I already don't like it."

"Okay."

"Stop saying okay."

"Yeah. Well, it's like this. I'm you. But not you. And we're both bad. Just made wrong, you know? And I was given a choice to clean it up. Or get cleaned up. And I'm not always sure I chose right, but here I am. Scooting around in odd corners, cleaning up the mess that is me. *Us.*"

He tries a smile but knows it doesn't look like a smile. The cat is in the room now, behind the tattooed one, dark as an oil slick against that red, red carpet. Maybe it slipped under the door like a newspaper. Maybe it came in through the light socket. He's not sure, because he'd seen it do both.

The tattooed man is bothered by what he said, but lets his shame turn to anger.

"Suppose I clean *you* up? How would you like that?"

"Well. That is the best thing to do with a bar of soap."

The tattooed man knits his brow together and looks at the bar of soap which is now in his hand instead of the gun he had stripped. While he does that, his smaller self pulls the actual gun out of his coat pocket and points it at the man standing over him, squeezes the trigger three times with three harsh bangs. The light-framed gun leaps painfully in his hand. A picture falls off the wall behind the big man and he crumples like a cut-string puppet, falling so his leg is twisted behind him.

"The FUCK!" the tattooed man says, bewildered by pain and also by the impossibility of what just happened. He jerks his head but can't stand because one bullet wrecked his spine. Another lanced his heart and one lung. The third blew his keys and change out of his pocket. "The fuck," he says, weaker, but it turns into a bloody cough. He throws his arm up twice, and twice it falls back in his wet, dark lap. The smaller man fishes in

10

the dying one's pocket, pulls out his wallet, takes the seventy dollars out. He tosses the wallet down on the other man's ruined chest, almost says 'sorry.' Despite himself, he stares at the dying man's features, so like his own, thinks in a flash about his own nose, his ears, his eyes burned in the retort of a crematorium or embalmed in a casket. Feels nothing about that except the oddness of it.

The cat nips his ankle and he comes back to himself.

Through the ringing in his ears the man hears someone yelling in the next room and, for a moment, he is worried.

Fuck, he thinks. *I shot someone through the wall!*

The cat faces the door, growling as if to say *hurry*. The man springs up and opens the door for it, for himself, and they run. A guy from another room runs after him, yelling "Stop! You stop!" but when the man points the revolver at him, he turns around ducking under his arms as if caught in a sudden rain. The man re-pockets the gun and swings the Mercury's door open. The cat bounds in, and he starts the motor.

Did he shoot someone in the neighboring room, or were they just scared?

The radio is playing a song he doesn't know. He wheels the big car out of the parking lot, drives fast, but not crazy, drives 173 to the interstate as he hears sirens, sees the far-off blue ghost-lights in the distance. He takes the ramp in such a way that the sirens stop altogether, and he's near blinded by light.

It's daytime now. Morning. Where? South of Atlanta, he thinks, because there are so many lanes and they drive fast here. They drive like if they hit you, you will die and they will live because they are from there and strong and you are from somewhere else and weak. He thinks he knows what kind of thread they're in, checks the radio. The music playing, which is different in every cluster, confirms his guess.

He merges with trucks and hits seventy, seventy-five, eighty, still breathing hard.

"Did we shoot someone? In the next room?"

The cat purrs. He knows that isn't an answer. Knows there won't be one. Knows that they'll just keep working. Collateral damage is acceptable.

To whom?

He sees the blue and red sign advertising I-75 south.

"You want to stop?" he says. "We haven't for a while."

The cat ignores him.

"You do, don't you?"

He bends to grab for a battered Rand McNally Atlas, one of six different versions he's got on the passenger side floor, folds the big pages of Georgia in his lap. He swerves a little and a truck blatts its horn at him. He adjusts, bends his head to the page again, looks for blue ink dots he inked in himself. Finds one not too far away.

Half an hour later, the small man with the bald spot pulls into a park in Hampton, Georgia. A green, shady park with lots of trees and a sweet breeze flowing among the limbs and branches of those trees. He carries the cat in his arms from the car to the playground area and sets it on a swing.

Pushes it, gently, then a little less so.

The cat loves it.

It swings pretty high.

Leans into each push like a small child would.

DEW UPON THE WING
RACHEL AUTUMN DEERING

Stage One—Denial and Isolation

I WATCHED MY wife walk away, carrying everything that was ever important to her in an overnight bag. She looked good. I couldn't remember the last time she had put so much effort into her appearance—her hair, seemingly weightless, falling around her once-kind face in dark curls and spilling over pale, freckled shoulders. Shoulders that had recently taken to bear some secret burden I was never meant to know. I could have pried the details from her, and that's just what it would have been, prying, but I didn't bother. She hated being questioned about even the smallest thing. I wanted to reach out and touch her, but I stopped myself, recalling the last time I tried to show her any kind of tenderness and how she shrank away from me without realizing what she had done. Her withdrawal was so subconscious, so natural to her. The rejection hurt, but I didn't mention it. She pulled the front door closed as she stepped beyond the threshold and the smell of honey and vanilla sweetened the air she left behind.

"Ma has cancer," I whispered to the abandoned space. "Stage four."

DEW UPON THE WING

I heard the car start and back out of the driveway. She always tapped the horn twice when she left for work in the mornings—her way of telling me to have a good day and that she loved me. Not this time. All I could hear was my heart beating an unnatural rhythm in my sinuses, teased by her fading scent.

She was gone but the house was still full of her. The bright orange curtains which had somehow made the sun even more blinding still hung in the windows. Throw pillows adorned with the curved silhouettes of wine glasses and quotes about love were still clustered on a sofa that was too large for our living room. The color yellow. It was everywhere. They were all things I would have hated on my own, but I had grown to cherish them because they were what she wanted. They were her. She was orange and yellow and curves and love. She was sunshine and life, and she was too big for my heart.

I decided I would burn the house before I got on the road.

***

I have always preferred the solitude of a late night drive, so I lit out when it felt like all the eyes in the world but mine had shut. On the lonely highway, I can watch the yellow slashes that divide the lanes whipping by and I am absorbed by the hypnotic magic of something so consistent. I step on the gas, demanding more speed, and the engine growls, seeming eager to oblige. The steering wheel responds to the slightest touch, never questioning my direction. For a while, I am one with the road and the car is nothing more than an extension of my will.

Ma used to like to guilt me about making these long trips after dark, back when I was still welcome to come see her, but I wasn't about to hang around and wait for sunrise with the ghost of Karen haunting every corner of Traverse City. Not like daylight would matter anyway. I wasn't getting any sleep tonight. I passed the green metal sign that marked the edge of the city limits and I watched in the rearview mirror as the lights of the town faded and the buildings shrank down to nothing more than a speck in the murk.

Dark clouds crowded the moon and fat drops of summer rain swarmed the air, making a mess of the world beyond my windshield. The storm might be able to save the house from the fire, if it kept pouring like it was. And if I had actually been able to start the fire. Standing on the front porch, I was paralyzed by the idea of so much change. I imagined the flames climbing the steps and swallowing the bed Karen and I had shared, erasing us. The thought of it made me retch and I felt the acid sting of disappointment rise up from my stomach. I knew I couldn't do it. The house was stronger than me. We had fed it with the power of all our many years of memories together and it dominated me. I looked down and saw a message spelled out on either side of my foot—We come Home. I lifted my sneaker and saw the L beneath it. I decided I would burn the house later, if I got around to it.

I left my heart folded into thirds on the kitchen table, next to an uneaten plate of food that was meant to be my last supper. It said everything I wanted to say to Karen before she left. The words that might have saved us if they hadn't been caught just beneath the hard, stinging lump in my throat. She might find it, if she ever came back. I went to the garage and dug out an old wooden sign that read 'Gone Fishing' and nailed it to the front door. It felt permanent and I thought of the crucifixion of Jesus and finally let myself cry. Betrayal hurt, even when you could see it coming.

Stage Two—Anger
The Gentleman was waiting for me in a nowhere town off route 23, somewhere south of Flint. It was coming up on 2:00 AM and the lullaby of road noise had me drifting over the lines. *Wake up, sissy.* The motherly direction swirled in my head, clear as a bell. *You might ought to stop somewhere for a minute and get yourself a cup of coffee.* I did as I was told.

I eased off the road and into a gravel lot with a well-lit filling station advertising twenty-four hour service. My car crawled up next to pump four and I cut the engine. He was there, the Gentleman I mean, under a neon Marlboro sign, leaning against the icebox in his too-tight jeans, scuffed boots, Allman Brothers t-shirt, and aviator sunglasses. I watched him in my periphery as I slid the nozzle into the fuel tank and began to pump. He swiped at some dirt under his fingernails with a pocket knife and wiped the blade across his jeans before snapping it closed. He slipped the knife into his front pocket and checked his work.

I finished topping up the tank and started across the parking lot for the station. The Gentleman didn't speak as I approached, just nodded and cleared his throat. The night air was chill, and the dew had started to fall, and I could see that beads of it had settled on his clothes, glowing with reflected neon light. I wondered how long he must have been standing there.

I took my time pouring a cup of coffee and made small talk with the clerk at the checkout. *How's your night going* and *See a lot of weirdos working this late in the middle of nowhere*? I hoped she might mention the Gentleman outside and assure me that he was some harmless local or a co-worker on a break. She didn't speak a word of him. I hoped too that the chatter would fill enough time that he might be gone when I came out of the store. He wasn't. He was still leaning there against the ice chest, like he belonged nowhere else.

I did my best to ignore him as I passed, but I could feel his eyes on me, dissecting me. He knew he had my attention.

"In a hurry?" His voice was bourbon and ginger beer, pouring from the near-lipless slit of his mouth. Obscenely casual. I knew it was a stranger's voice, or it should have been, but I couldn't swear it was so. It seemed somehow more familiar than my own. I turned and gave him a look as if to say *you're wasting your time.* He slid the aviators down the ridge of his nose and I could see that his eyes weren't much more pronounced than his mouth. They were drawn thin and dark and too close together, sitting just above his aquiline beak. They seemed to catch the light of some ember that wasn't apparently there, and it reflected out at me from the deep sockets set beneath his heavy brow.

"I'm not into men, so you can lay off it," I said in a flat tone. The last thing I wanted was to stir any excitement between us that he might mistake as interest.

"Me either. Can't say I blame you." He laughed. I didn't.

I'd heard that line, or some variation of it, a million times. It was his way of continuing to flirt, trying to somehow relate to me, even after I had shot him in the balls. *You have to admire the tenacity*, my aunt June always told me. She was an old school dyke with a sense of humor about that sort of thing. Everyone said I took after her more than I did my own parents, and they blamed her for making me gay, but I was never able to break out of my hard-ass ways when it came to men like she had.

"What do you want? A couple of bucks? A ride someplace? A blowjob? What can I do for you, man?"

"I just wanted to know if you were in a hurry. That's it." He repositioned his sunglasses and crossed his arms. "You like to read into things, don't you? Your girlfriend must have some patience."

I was biting my nails. A nervous habit I had developed as a kid to keep my mouth busy when I wanted to say something mean. I couldn't help it. Karen wasn't here to defend herself and I could let fly every horrible thing I had ever wanted to say about her —things I wanted to believe and would want other people to believe—and nobody could speak a word to the contrary, but somehow it didn't feel right. "Yeah. She used to." I removed the bleeding fingertip from my mouth and spat a nail into the dusty gravel at my feet.

"Past tense, huh?" he said. "Makes sense."

"What the hell—" My throat was dry, and I choked on what remained of my protest.

"You look like shit." He pointed a finger in my face. "The bags under your eyes. Them all bloodshot. You been crying. Miserable. If that's how she makes you feel, you might just be better off without her, that's all I'm saying."

A slow ringing began to build in my ears, as if every part of me wanted to drown out the Gentleman's truths. "Get fucked," I said, defeated. I hadn't considered just how much and how hard I had been crying since I left the house, but if it was obvious enough for a stranger to point out in low-light, Christ I must have looked a horror and a half to the checkout clerk, painted by the fluorescent glow inside the store.

"You're in some mood, huh? And hey, I been trying to get fucked all night," he said. "The only pussy I've met out here was a couple of stray cats and a sad-sack lesbian. Them cats wasn't yours, was they?"

"I don't have time for this shit." I turned and started for my car.

"Hey, listen, I'm sorry. I'm just trying to lighten the mood, huh? You look like you could use a laugh."

"Motherfucker. No." I stopped but did not turn to face him. "My wife left me today and my goddamn mother is dying of cancer while I'm here, standing in some bumfuck parking lot, letting . . . whoever the fuck you are . . . chat me up. I don't need a laugh, I need to leave."

"I'm the Gentleman," he said, sounding like he actually meant it.

"The Gentle—seriously, man, go fuck yourself." I reached my car and threw open the driver side door, turning to give him one final look. One last glare at this cocky prick of a man who was now far too privy to the dirty details of my bullshit life.

"If you could get her back, would you? I could help with that sort of thing, you know?"

I slammed the car door and cranked the engine.

"Think about it," he shouted and waved goodbye.

The '68 Charger roared to life and I mashed the gas pedal to the floor a few times, sending the tach needle into the red and making more than a little racket. I pulled the console shifter into drive and stomped the gas, cutting the wheel and spinning up a cloud of gravel dust, hoping to choke some of the smugness out of the Gentleman and put a little grit in his smile.

Stage Three—Bargaining

I crossed over into Ohio with the Gentleman's question burrowing deeper into my brain. *If you could get her back, would you?* I wasn't sure. If Karen did come back, she could just as easily leave me again. Would it even be worth it? To feel that helpless ache splitting my heart into pieces as I watched her leave a second time. Could I put myself through that kind of pain, or would I finally lose my shit for good?

Then again, there was a chance she wouldn't leave. If I had been more present in our relationship, she might not have abandoned what we had in the first place. If I had listened more closely to her stories—all of them, not just some. If I had responded with some kind of genuine interest instead of a distracted grunt. If I could have taken my head out of my work long enough to give her just a few minutes of my time, I might not be in this shit situation. Ma would still be sick, sure, but Karen would be here next to me. I'd still be moping down the road to Kentucky to watch my ma die, but I wouldn't be doing it alone. I'd have a hand to hold onto. I'd have something to keep me grounded, some way to connect myself to the real world and let me know there was a life to come back to when the sadness had passed.

Would I get her back if I could? Yeah, probably I would. I would fight for Karen if I knew I stood a chance of making the sort of future together we had dreamed up during our courting days. I could make her happy, I was confident enough about that. I had for many years.

All I needed to do was be less of an asshole. Make my heart a big enough place for her to live.

I puffed up my cheeks and let out an annoyed gust of breath. I don't even know why I would entertain the notion. Karen wasn't coming back. She was too proud for that. Still, the thought gnawed at me like a dog on a rawhide. What had once been my ma's voice swimming through my head with sweet Southern doses of practical advice was now replaced with the Gentleman's hypothetical nonsense. *I could help with that sort of thing, you know?* Like hell he could.

For more miles than I cared to count, the only luster that broke through the inky gloom of the pre-dawn was my headlights. There were no street lamps overhead and no real glow of the moon or stars to speak of on this particular stretch of road. The thick canvas of oak and birch climbed high on either side of me and choked out heaven. A little way ahead, the asphalt raised slightly to a set of railroad tracks. Any other time I had driven this road, the thought of touching the brakes wouldn't have entered my mind, preferring instead to sail over the ridge at full speed and catch a little air. Now, though— and for the first time I could recall—the shafts of light from my high beams clashed with the flashing red crossing lights that warned of a coming train, accompanied by a knell that split the usual still of the hour.

The train was a cyclops with one giant beacon that shone, dim and ghostly, through the morning mist. It moaned and shrieked, slowing as it approached, belching plumes of smoke. I thought it looked like a thing out of time but had little opportunity to dwell on the peculiarity of it. The engine passed, a distorted head with too many teeth, long and black and riveted, arranged into an unnatural smile. A few railcars followed after it, each one passing a little slower than the one before, until the metal behemoth let loose a final scream and stood still before me. There, in an open box car, with his legs dangling from the side was the Gentleman. He grinned out at me, much the same way the engine had, and I wanted to vomit.

"Did you think on it?" he called out.

I couldn't speak a word. I sat frozen with confusion and swallowed hard.

"What's that you say? I can't hear you. Roll down your window."

I opened my door and swung my legs out and stood to my feet before I realized what I was doing. I didn't feel in control of myself. "I'm dreaming," I blurted.

"You have some shit-ass dreams, then," the Gentleman said. "Do you want my help or not?"

"No."

"You're a shit-ass liar, too."

"I don't."

"Then how come your eyes are saying you do?" He hopped from the boxcar and walked toward me.

"Stop," I said.

"Stop what?" he put his hands into the air, showing his empty palms, doing his best to appear harmless.

"What do you want?"

"Not much at all," he said. "I need to deliver a message and I need you to help me deliver it."

"I don't have time to help you. I told you, my mother is dying, and I need to get to her. Now. Right now."

"Well, now that's convenient because that's just exactly where I need you to go."

"What?"

"Your ma a church-going woman?" he asked, stopping just short of my car, resting his hands on the hood and leaning into the question. He gave me a look like he had something to sell. Something he knew I'd want to buy.

"The goingest you ever seen. What's that got to do with anything?" I asked, shaking my head.

"That's about what I figured. I need to talk to her."

"Yeah? Good luck with that. She's old-fashioned, man," I said. "She's not going to talk to a strange dude. Especially not some hippie-looking motherfucker like you."

"I didn't say she had to talk to me. I'll do the talking. All she has to do is listen. One sentence. Five seconds. Then I'm gone, and you'll get another shot at that girl you're missing. You have my word."

"What sentence? What do you want to say to her? And why my ma? She ain't nothing to nobody."

"Can't say," he said. "Now listen, you don't stand to lose a thing here, but you sure as shit have something to gain. I'm not gonna lay a finger on your ma, and hell, she's knocking at death's door anyway. What can I do that'll make it any worse, huh?"

"I don't know, man. This is weird. How the fuck did you even get here? How did . . . that train?"

"I know this all seems weird. Trust me, I understand, but that's just how some things are. You're wasting my time and your time and you're sure as shit wasting what's left of your ma's time. You're sweating these details—shit that don't even matter," he said. "And you wouldn't believe me even if I did give you all the answers, so can we move on and help each other out or should I hop this train and let you be on your way?"

"Is this some kind of fetish thing you've got?"

"Okay. I read you loud and clear. Good luck with your shit," he said, turning back toward the train.

"No. Wait."

Stage Four—Depression
She hardly looked like the woman who had raised me and my brothers, this pale and fragile thing, but there she was laying in my ma's bed, wearing my ma's clothes, and mumbling something low and somber in my ma's voice. I didn't know what to say to her, so I knelt on the floor next to the bed and held her hand, watching her eyelids flutter and her lips quiver. I hadn't talked to her or anyone else in the family in years—had no clue she was even sick—and now here I was, feeling her slip away for the last time. They had stopped calling when gay marriage became legal and I ruined the sanctity of the whole thing by opting in. They had even liked Karen before that, but something about us making things official just set them off. *My friend*, they always called her, but after the wedding they just couldn't see themselves calling her my wife, so they decided to call us nothing at all. I hated myself for crying over that.

I remember the last time she called. She asked me not to tell my brothers. I felt such shame in that moment. The conversation wasn't anything special, really, just a lot of the usual—her going on about what she had planted in her garden, what was doing well and what wasn't, but it crushed me to know that such idle chatter which at one time would have annoyed me was now something precious. Something we had to keep secret. Before she hung up, she told me something I know I'll never forget, no matter how hard I try.

"I love you, sissy. Even if I can't say it, I hope you know it in your heart."

There came two short raps on the bedroom door and she gasped. Her eyes opened just a little and I could see her pupils scanning from side to side. I stood to my feet and crossed the room to the door. I opened it and saw the Gentleman standing there. He craned his head around the door frame, trying to look into the room.

"Is she still with us?"

"Jesus, you fucking vulture. Yes, she's still alive," I said, closing my eyes as hard as I could to block out his face. I couldn't believe I was letting this happen. "Make it quick, okay? She's completely out of her fucking gourd, so I don't know how much good it's gonna do you but knock yourself out."

I let the door swing into the room and the Gentleman stepped through. He stood over my ma, looking up and down the length of her. I closed the door and leaned against it, watching him as he bent at the waist, lowering himself gently onto the bed. A pain stabbed my heart when she opened her eyes as wide as she could and looked at me.

"Why, sissy?" she asked, twisting beneath all her layers of blankets. "Why did you bring him here?" She squirmed, trying to move away from the Gentleman's approach, but her attempts were pitifully weak and soon he was staring directly into her eyes. He held her gaze for a long moment and dropped his head onto the pillow next to hers. His mouth lingered near her ear and a harsh rasp rose up out of his throat, more insect than human. Her chest began to heave, and she sobbed with all she had in her, clapping her hands over her ears and whimpering. "Sissy, no . . ."

I had become Judas to my mother's Christ—a snake loosed upon the garden. A chill crawled over my skin.

I pushed myself off the door and shot out one hand, grabbing hold of the Gentleman's arm. I knew then that I had somehow grasped something I would never quite comprehend. I hadn't seized the flesh of a man at all, but the horrible nature of a man. He wasn't warm, and he wasn't cold, and he wasn't like anything I could ever hope to describe. He was void. A voice no longer heard by God. He turned and looked at me with a sadness in his eyes as honest as I'd ever seen. He knew what I had felt in him. His gaze fell to the floor and he stepped out of the room. "Thank you," he said and closed the door.

Stage Five—Acceptance
I never saw the Gentleman after that. He left through the back door, walked across the property, and disappeared into the woods out past the pond. Ma couldn't sleep for more than twenty minutes at a time without terrible screams ripping her from an already fitful rest. She passed just a few days later. Karen arrived in time to say goodbye and she hugged me through the night when I finally let myself feel everything that had been building inside me. She wiped at the tears that fell down my cheeks and smiled at me through her own.

"I'm so sorry, darlin'," she whispered as she rocked me in her arms. I could feel the urgency in the way she held onto me and I knew she needed me as much as I needed her. "Let's go home."

ROOM 4 AT THE HAYMAKER

JOSH MALERMAN

THE U-HAUL WAS two hours gone, Evelyn was behind the wheel of her Buick Skylark, a single suitcase on the back seat, fooling herself into considering it light travel when actually she was leaving an entire sullied life behind. Sherry and Mark were driving the U-Haul, younger lovers, excited, it seemed, to be given a road trip, tailor made; moving Sherry's mother cross country. At last. It wasn't that they were eager to get rid of her, Evelyn knew better than that; the pair appeared genuinely thrilled at the prospect of hundreds of miles and a radio, no partition between them on the U-Haul front bench.

"Twenty-five year olds," Evelyn said, her hands on the wheel of the parked Skylark. "They don't know yet."

She'd been sitting that way, parked, hands at ten and two, her glasses wiped spotless, for the full one hundred and twenty minutes since her daughter and son-in-law pulled away from the curb and disappeared around the first turn on Belcrest. She'd told them not to wait for her, claiming a desire to travel at her own pace, unrushed, giving her time, of course, to process the move. And they surely understood: Evelyn Davies was leaving the house she'd lived in for thirty-one years, since the day she and Bob bought it in 1987, a week after returning from their honeymoon in Hawaii. They'd been twenty-five themselves then and probably looked no different than Sherry and Mark, but boy did it *feel* like her and Bob were wise while it was happening. Hell, Sherry still liked getting candy at the movie theater and Mark sometimes drank like he was in college. They looked the parts, too. But herself and Bob? Why, they'd been young professionals then, adults on the cusp of a full life together, *day one*, Bob had called it, a title that came off as romantic at the time but, in hindsight, sounded more like the words of a man making note of the beginning of his prison sentence.

Day one.

How many days had he made it? How long exactly did Evelyn share the house with Bob before he ... before he ...

Still with her hands on the wheel, Evelyn looked right, through the passenger window, to the front door of the ranch house she was already moved out of. The window to the right of the front door was where she'd stood for the first two weeks following Bob's fleeing, right at the very glass, thinking *now* must be the time he'd come back. *Now* must be it. It had to be any minute *now*.

Or any day now. Or week. Or month. Until friends, good friends, finally got Evelyn to accept the fact that her husband had left her. Not even a hundred day sentence of being forced to live with the woman he'd married, the woman he'd vowed to be there for, through sickness and health, thick and thin. Three months of petty arguments that had developed into seemingly mortal wounds, things Bob either couldn't or refused to get over; the man hardly resembled the one she'd spent five days with in Hawaii, the carefree and shirtless fellow who seemed primed to climb volcanoes and swim with the jellyfish. Why, on that trip they'd made love twice the number of nights they'd paid for. They'd eaten better than either had in their lives. They'd had fun.

"Weak," Evelyn said, thirty-one years later, turning to face the road through the windshield, the road she'd lived on all this time, in the house she'd been left in.

She started the car.

She knew why Sherry and Mark were so enthusiastic about this trip from Detroit to Denver. And she knew why they'd agreed when she insisted she drive alone. It wasn't that they were excited at the prospect of having somewhere to visit. It wasn't even that they were young and ungrounded enough to want to be in motion, on the road, across America.

It was because they were ecstatic to see Evelyn was *moving on.*

"Move on," she said.

She shifted the car into drive.

She tried not to look back at the house, tried not to think of how it looked in 1987, when the now yellowing bricks were browner. She succeeded, but not without looking to the neighbor's house, where, thirty-one years ago, a very confident Arthur Morrison stood on his front porch and, work shirt unbuttoned to his chest hair, hands on his hips, thinning hair flapping in the wind, waved to them for the first time.

Evelyn ended up living next to Arthur and Linda for ten years. They helped her out in the early days, immediately following Bob's departure. Helped her out a lot.

"He fled," Evelyn said. Then she wished she hadn't. If Sherry and Mark heard her say that, would they think she wasn't moving on, after all? Would they say she was only . . . moving?

She pressed on the gas, made it a couple feet, and stopped. It wasn't easy, no, leaving a place you'd spent more than half your life. A place you'd moved into with hope and were leaving with damage control. A home in which you had gotten married a second time to Larry, had a baby girl named Sherry, and lived with that second husband for four years before he died in an accident at the plant. No, it wasn't easy saying goodbye to a thing that haunted you for so long, even when another man was living under the same roof, the fact that someone had once left this place without saying goodbye.

"Fuck you, Bob," Evelyn said, looking once more to her (not hers anymore) front door.

Then she drove. Away from the house and the bitter life she'd led within it. But not from the gnawing nagging voice that still, thirty-one years later, would not stop asking . . .

. . . *why?*

***

Up Belcrest and a left on Donner and Evelyn wondered if this wasn't the same exact series of directions Bob had taken so long ago. It was the only way to leave town and there was no question he'd done that much. In a neighborhood the size of Maris Oak, Evelyn would've known if he was anywhere near the strip malls and chain stores she'd passed almost every day on her own. Christ, if he'd been living in downtown Detroit she would've known. It was easier to find someone these days. Back in '87? Hell, Bob Davies up and vanished like a coin in a good magician's hand. She'd looked for him, when the internet came along, when social media came along, a search that was allegedly accidentally discovered by Sherry, a thing that prompted her daughter to begin talking to her about leaving Maris Oak for a change.

For a while.

For good.

You're obviously not over it, Mother. And you need to be.

It was a scary thing, searching for him online. Typing his name into search bars and watching the spinning icons that told her the computer was thinking. She'd checked different spellings, the names of his parents, any place he'd ever expressed interest in seeing, wedding announcements, obituaries. She checked Hawaii because it was the last time they'd had a *good* time and, often, she imagined him flying back, starting something over again that she hadn't been aware needed redoing.

A mile to the highway and Evelyn wished she had a cigarette. She hadn't smoked since Sherry was born but it seemed like the right time to have one now. She rolled down the window, then rolled down the window on the passenger side, and let the cool Spring air give her the relief she was looking for. But the colder air acted more as an instigator, made her feel tremendously alive, too alive, too awake, as if, for the first time since deciding to leave Detroit, she realized she was doing it.

Ahead, a hitchhiker on the shoulder of the entrance ramp.

A dim distant figure but a hitcher, no doubt. Had her thinking back to the late 70s, when something like that was safe, both to do and to assist with. She'd been too young then to offer rides to the people her mother and father passed as they drove from Detroit down to Florida, but she'd wanted to stop, to pick up a stranger, to hear that stranger's story. To a much younger Evelyn, there was something especially mysterious about inviting an entirely foreign life into the car, sliding over on the bench, making room for a world she knew nothing about. But Mom and Dad didn't like the idea and Evelyn watched the many figures pass by her window like she might the many doors to so many secrets.

If she was honest with herself, she'd admit she didn't feel that way anymore. She had no desire to ask a strange man, young as this one looked, into her car. Yet, wasn't that exactly why she'd arranged to drive alone? To leave her practical life behind? To become someone *new*, here, at fifty-six? If she didn't do something just like this, what was she doing at all? Was she planning on driving the eleven hundred miles with her heart and head wrapped in foam just so she could unpack it exactly as it'd been for thirty-one years?

The hitcher looked younger the closer she got. Had his thumb out the way people used to do. Had a worried look on his face, a thing she could spot from the distance she was at.

The car ahead of her slammed on its brakes and Evelyn came to a sudden stop, too. Ahead, the young man in a brown leather coat, short dark hair, eyebrows that nearly met in the middle, looked familiar. As if her parents had passed him without giving him a ride, many years ago.

The car behind her honked as she squinted, trying to make out the man's features. Familiar, to be sure, but in a way that she didn't feel comfortable with. As if the man was the son of a friend, in trouble, and here Evelyn had caught him doing something he shouldn't have been doing.

Did the man have a sign? Was he homeless? Maybe that was it. Maybe she'd seen him before, panhandling.

The car behind her honked again and Evelyn saw the traffic was clear, a clean shot to the entrance ramp, no reason for her to be idling in the middle of the road. So she drove, closing in on the young man, the hitcher, as he wagged his thumb out, his face neither hardened by drugs or hard living, after all; a fresh faced youth looking for a ride.

"Oh!" Evelyn suddenly said. The one syllable was like an inverse hit, as if she'd suddenly hit back at all and everything in the negative space surrounding her body; the inside of the car, the outside of the car, the city of Detroit, her home, her history, her abandonment.

Because she was close enough now to see that the man wasn't only familiar.

The man was Bob.

"Oh!" she said again, feeling suddenly dizzy, like the car was nothing she could control. For what seemed like the duration of a single photo taken, the Skylark was aimed directly at the young man, thumbing, until his eyes got wide and he leaped back, out of the way. But Evelyn had the car on the road before it got close to him, had it under control as she came level with him, as she stared, as she passed, as he looked to her pleadingly, needing a ride, no baggage with him, just his dark jeans and leather coat and a strange sense of urgency that bothered her more than the fact that he was still only twenty-five years old.

Bob.

Young Bob.

Then he was in the rearview mirror, still watching her, no doubt because she was a passing driver who had expressed interest in his predicament.

Or maybe he recognized her, too?

Evelyn slammed on the brakes, then pulled off to the shoulder. She was at least a hundred yards past him and didn't think she should be driving. She wished she had Sherry or Mark, wished she was sitting between them or even sitting in a chair secured to the wall in the back of the U-Haul. What she really wanted was to be back home, sitting in the recliner she'd sat in countless lonely nights, her back to the window she once stared out of, waiting for a man who looked just like the hitcher to come home, to explain himself, to say anything that would make sense of the sudden inexplicable way he'd left.

Without a word.

The hitcher had given her a real scare. And now the hitcher was trotting toward the Skylark. She watched him grow bigger, a look of insane confusion on her face, mouth open, her lower jaw drawn back, her eyes neither wide nor wet but laser locked on the rearview mirror.

He was coming fast now. He had something of a grateful smile, but he seemed to sense she wasn't fully decided. Maybe it was because she hadn't gotten out of the car and officially invited him. Maybe it was the way she'd stopped. Or maybe it was because everyone in the entire world outside her car could sense the truth that, while the car itself wasn't experiencing a breakdown, the driver inside it was.

"Bob?"

Oh, God. To say his name, as the man came up along the shoulder. The man didn't only look the spitting image of Bob on the day Bob left, but he moved like him, too.

"Bob," she said again, as cars passed on her left, getting on the highway, on the way to their jobs, their travels, with what looked like no anxiety and no loss. The man was now level with the trunk, then the back door on the passenger side, then the passenger door itself, then the open window.

"Thanks," he said, bending at the waist, looking her directly in the eye. There was a flash of what could've been recognition, a slight tilt of his head. Then it was gone. "Were you stopping for me? I couldn't tell."

Evelyn hadn't realized how hard she was gripping the wheel. As if she were in a perpetual near-wreck. As if for the last minute or so she'd experienced something that should have been a mere fraction of a second, if only for the sanity of the person living it.

"For you?" she heard herself say. It wasn't any good, her voice. Sounded like a dog, perhaps, or a cat. Something not as sophisticated in speech as a woman.

The man inched back from the car.

"I'm sorry," he said. "I'm just looking to get a ride out of town. If you're–"

"Is that it?" Evelyn said. Again, a flash of recognition. But Evelyn could only imagine how crazed she looked, how meek, and how interesting, too, to a man who thought, subconsciously, she might look familiar. "Just a ride out of town?"

He made it sound so . . . simple.

"Yeah," he said. "I'm heading–"

"Get in."

He stared a moment. Looked up the road. Like there might be a better option than Evelyn in this life for him.

But he opened the door and got in. And Evelyn, trembling, pulled from the shoulder at last and joined the flow of every day traffic heading west.

***

She had a hard time looking at him and also a hard time *not.* He was on edge; a child would've been able to tell that much. The way he fidgeted and adjusted himself in the seat, the way he looked out the window then the windshield, the window then the windshield. She caught him checking the passenger side mirror many times, as if making sure the life he was leaving wasn't trailing him out of town.

"So," Bob said. "Where are you going?"

"What's your name?" Evelyn asked. She already knew it. But she had to hear it. Driving in the slow lane, cars whizzing past her on the left, she had to hear him say it.

"I'm Bob."

"Oh."

That one syllable again. As if she'd just been told she had an incurable disorder. As if she'd been physically hurt.

"Are you okay?" Bob asked.

Now Evelyn did look at him. And the expression she flashed him caused him to look to see if the car door was locked. If there was even a handle on the inside.

"You, Bob, are wondering if *I'm* okay?"

A car merged closely ahead of them. Too close for Bob's comfort.

"I didn't mean to ask something personal," he said. "I was just making small talk."

"You mean you *don't* really wanna know if I'm okay?"

"Hey, I didn't mean that, either. Look, if you wanna–"

"I'm driving because my husband left me thirty-one years ago and I'm attempting, today, to start a new life."

Silence. Heavy. Deep and dark.

"Oh," Bob said. And his one syllable had none of the horror or surprise of hers. Rather, he sounded concerned, the way people do when a coincidence feels a little too big. Then, anxiously, "So where are you going to start this new life?"

"Ha!" Evelyn couldn't resist. Had to release a bark of frustrated laughter. What she really wanted to do was go off like a hyena, turn to face him and open her mouth as wide as it would go and laugh until her throat was hoarse and her eyes popped out of her head. What she *really* wanted to do was bite him, hit him, kick him against the passenger door until it swung open and he went tumbling into traffic. But she managed to say, "Denver," instead.

After considering her response, he said, "Really? That's great. I'm heading west, too."

"You are?" Evelyn felt as if a single shovelful of dirt had fallen into one of the many holes that had long marred the lawn of her life. "Is that your entire plan?"

"Yeah," Bob said, moving so that he was leaning forward now, elbows on his knees. When he spoke again, he sounded eager. "I've always wanted to see the west."

But you have, Evelyn wanted to say. *You've seen farther than the west. You've seen Hawaii.*

"And what's out west?" she asked, holding back emotions she couldn't fathom the size of.

He's going to say a woman is out there. A true love. The one. *He's going to say something that's going to make you crazy, that's going to make you slam on the brakes hard enough for his head to crack against the windshield..*

292

"Nothing really," he said. "Just . . . something new."
Then, after a pause, "Like you're doing, I suppose."

"I see."

Oh how Evelyn wanted to strangle him. How dare he equate his abandoning her to her dealing, finally, with his abandonment?

"And are you leaving anybody . . . behind?" she asked. Outside, the sun had gotten visibly higher and the Detroit skyline was firmly in the rearview. She was on the road now. With Bob. And she'd just asked him if he'd left her.

"Anybody?" He seemed to sink deep into thought, unselfconsciously, as if he assumed anybody who would pick up a hitchhiker would also understand ponderous silence. "Yes. A wife."

Evelyn couldn't *not* look at him. Did she see shame there?

"A wife."

"Yes."

"And does she know you're heading . . . west?"

They were far enough outside Detroit now that the traffic had mostly cleared. The sun was higher, but the spring air hadn't gone warm yet. Evelyn touched the chest pocket of her puffy jacket, as if she might find a cigarette there.

"Need one?"

Bob was holding one out to her. She reached for it and stopped. Really? Was she going to accept anything at all from this man? On the day he left her?

In his eyes she saw he was oblivious. A man with no real plan and no explanation.

She took the smoke. He lit it.

"Thank you."

Thank you. Oh how black those two words felt coming out of her, sent his way.

"She asked a lot of questions," Bob said, lighting one of his own.

"Oh?"

"Like . . . I couldn't do anything without her asking questions."

"About what?"

"About . . . everything really. When are we gonna have dinner. When are we gonna go to bed. When are we gonna wake up? She's just . . . full of questions. And I didn't have answers all the time. Felt like I was being interrogated."

"Are you kidding me?"

"Well, no. I'm not."

"You couldn't answer simple questions like what time you'd like to eat? You're leaving your wife because of *that?*"

Bob took a drag, blew it out the window.

"Did I say I was leaving my wife?"

"Well, you're talking about her like she's in the past."

"Am I?" Then, "I guess I am."

Evelyn felt a flare of unmanageable rage.

"That's what you're doing. I know."

"Well . . . *I* don't know exactly."

"But your wife is back home. Probably just waking up. Wondering *where you went?*"

"Hey, if I've hit a sore spot, I'm sorry. I didn't say I was *leaving* . . . Christ, that sounds so . . . mean."

"It is mean! It's about the meanest thing a man can do! Why not *tell* her?"

She was yelling now.

"Jeez! I did. In . . . so many words."

"Not enough words, Bob." The Skylark was roaring now. "No matter how many words you told her, you needed to say a few more."

Silence then. Smoking. Bob reached for the radio and stopped. Evelyn watched his hand come near the dial and she imagined snapping his fingers straight off. Imagined smoking them, ashing them out the window. This piece of shit was acting like nobody was going to get hurt.

They drove without speaking for some time. Hours, it seemed, though Evelyn couldn't be bothered with checking the clock. The way she felt, it was as if she'd driven into a pool of amber. As if the car and herself and her shit one-time husband were stuck the way mosquitoes get stuck.

In time.

"Coming up on Chicago sooner than later," Bob said. "You could drop me off there."

"Why there? You got a girlfriend there?"

"What? No. I just . . . "

"Why there?"

"It just seems like you're angry with me, ma'am."

Ma'am.

"Do I look familiar to you, Bob?"

This after so much silence. Right back into it again.

"No. I'm sorry. Should you?"

"Ha!"

"Look. You can drop me off here."

"*No.*" Evelyn refused to say the word *sorry*, but there were other ways to keep him in the car. "I worked with you is all."

"We worked together?"

"Yep. At Miller's on Grand."

"You . . . you worked at Miller's?"

No, she hadn't. But she knew Bob had. She also knew he paid about as much attention to his coworkers at that trashy themed restaurant as he did his wife the day he left her.

"I worked in accounting. In the back offices."

"Holy cow," Bob said. There was relief in his voice. As if, by affirming this link, Evelyn had both made sense of her (to him) odd behavior and reduced the sense (for him) of being driven into oblivion by a stranger. "I had no idea. Well . . . that's great."

"Yes. It is." She smiled coldly his way. "Small world, isn't it? Coincidences at every entrance ramp."

Bob smiled. She wondered what she ever saw in that smile. So young. So . . . dumb.

"Well I'm glad to hear that," he said.

"Why?"

"Well, I don't know. It's just . . . for a minute there it seemed like you . . . "

"I what?"

"Like you were asking a lot of questions."

Evelyn looked steadfast to the road ahead. She gripped the wheel hard and the Skylark continued, closing in on the middle of southern Michigan, the sun not quite yet directly above them, but not yet ready to sink below the horizon either. No closure on this day. Not yet.

✻✻✻

They got gas just before leaving Michigan. Evelyn was surprised when Bob said he'd pump it. Didn't think he had it in him. She also wouldn't let him, told him to go on and get a coffee or whatever he wanted to do inside. She would pump her own gas, thank you. Had done so for the better part of three decades.

She watched him walk into the station, that same silly gait he'd always had. Only, when they were twenty-five years old (when *she* was twenty-five; Bob still was or was again), that walk made her laugh. Made her smile. She recalled thinking it was sexy even, or, at the very least, his own. But now, with the smell of gasoline on her fingers (she'd spilled some, watching him), and a cool northern wind against her jacket, she realized the man looked small. Incredibly small. In gait, in body, in mind. Everything about him. Was she sure he was even twenty-five? He didn't look old enough to carry a driver's license. Did he know how to drive? Did he know how to do anything at all?

She watched as he didn't hold the door open for the older woman who entered the station behind him.

"Just a jerk in love with himself."

This felt true. So true. As if she needed any more proof that Bob was a selfish man, watching him interact with others, or not interact, was enough to make her fume. She saw him behind the glass, walking a food aisle. How much money did he have on him? Could he have much? She couldn't remember the specific details from that day. What time they'd gone to bed the night before. The weather. How much money he'd taken. She remembered it was some. But enough to cross the country and to expect to start a new life?

"Well," she said. "He must've."

Yes. He must've started anew. Unless, of course, something had happened to him on the way.

She didn't think something had. She'd searched everywhere online for that obituary. And the note he'd left her that morning (this morning, for him) made it so the police looked at her with the same sympathetic faces her friends did, and left them with no reason to file a missing persons report.

Evelyn,
What can I say? I gotta go.
Bob.

"Hey," Bob said. Evelyn was torn from her revelry. The gas tank had long been full, the pump no longer pumping. He had a bottle of soda in one hand, bread in the other. "I haven't asked your name yet."

"You haven't?" she said. "I hadn't noticed." But of course, she had. "It's Eve . . . it's *Eve.*"

"Like Adam and . . . ?"

"No," Evelyn said, pulling the pump from the Skylark. "Like Eve all by herself. No Adam in sight."

✳✳✳

Night came quick as Evelyn drove in deep silence, attempting to make sense of the man beside her. Surely her mind was breaking apart at the seams. Surely Bob wasn't asleep beside her in the passenger seat. And surely the last thing he'd said before snoring was not, *Let me know when we're west.*

Even now he was taking her entirely for granted. Even now, thirty-one years later, he was assuming she could handle whatever work there was to do on her own. Like driving across the country. Like starting his new life for him.

They were deep into Iowa when she realized that, despite years of unanswered questions, she really didn't have that many to ask him. She'd already asked where to and why. What more was there to wonder at? The good thing about having three decades on the piece of shit was that she now knew what mattered to her and what didn't. The dense cruelty beside her didn't have a clue. She understood now, by just being near him, that he didn't know why or where any more than she did.

"Fuckin A," she said, reaching across the car and pulling the cigarettes from his coat pocket. He didn't seem to notice. Not even when she took the lighter from the palm of one of his hands.

She rolled down the window and lit up and thought about the life Bob had led, no, the life he was *about to lead.* Would he get a job at another themed restaurant? Move up to management? Meet an equally dull woman? Have a baby? Prior to today it was real easy to imagine him in a large, warm, comfortable home, taking holiday photos with a real smile on his face, surrounded by an unfathomably happy wife and kids. It had been too easy to imagine him eating warm meals, sleeping in a warm bed, constantly laughing, always good. But now, able to look at him and hear his voice again, why . . . he just looked . . .

"Ordinary," Evelyn said.

But a question lurked, one she hadn't asked him yet. She looked right, thought about tapping his shoulder, thought about shoving him out of the car, but saw her opportunity to wake him in the middle of the road.

A half a rubber tire, the kind of thing any decent driver knew to avoid. But Evelyn aimed the Skylark just shy of straight at it, with a mind to run it over.

It worked better than she'd expected, as Bob was lifted up out of his seat and smacked his head against the roof. He opened his eyes quick, brought his hands in front of his face, and squealed.

"What's going on?!" he yelled.

Evelyn laughed. Oh, to have Bob in the car with her, to be able to *do* things to him.

"Bump in the road," she said.

Bob looked out the back window, out the side, then to Evelyn.

"Wow. Woke me straight up." Then, "How goes it?"

Evelyn didn't answer this because she didn't want to tell Bob how she was doing. Now or ever again.

"I was having the craziest dream." He said, rubbing his head where he'd hit it.

"Oh?"

"I dreamt I was late for something . . . or really early. Either way . . . it had to do with time. Either squandering it or having too much of it."

"Do you feel bad?"

"Not really. I mean, it was weird but–"

"About leaving your wife. Today. Do you feel bad for doing it?"

Bob slid deeper into the seat. He opened the window a crack, watched dark Iowa blur past.

"No," he said.

"Why not?"

"Because we only live once, I guess. I don't know." Then, "Because it wasn't the right life for me."

Evelyn didn't respond. The weird thing was, the closure she'd longed for hadn't come, but she wasn't so sure she needed it now.

"Well I hope you find the life you're looking for out west," she said.

"Hey, you know where my smokes are? I didn't leave them somewhere, did I?"

"I took them."

"Oh, good. Can I have them back?"

Evelyn turned to him, her face lit up by the dashboard, the teeth in her smile blue from the odometer.

"Sure. Just give me those thirty-one years back and they're all yours."

Bob's stare back was almost blank. There was a single speck of fear in it.

She tossed him the pack and got off at the next exit. She slowed to the pump and Bob got out. As he shut his door, Evelyn's phone rang.

It was Sherry.

Evelyn watched Bob cross the lot, didn't answer. Instead, she texted her daughter.

Near Nebraska. Good thing I drove alone. Getting answers after all.

***

Past Omaha, just shy of Lincoln, they fought.

Bob had got to talking about how eager he was to get out west. Said he would never work at a place like Miller's again. Evelyn asked him what else he had in mind. Bob said he didn't know. Evelyn told him he might want to have planned that part out first, rather than leaving his wife and life because of a few questions and a vague feeling that there was something more out there. Bob told her she didn't understand. Evelyn told him she did.

"Look," Bob said. "I get it. I'm sorry that your husband left you. It's an insane coincidence that's gotta be driving you nuts. Here you've been left and here I'm leaving someone. I understand." Twelve hours in a car together, it was the most philosophical thing he'd said so far. "But don't take your anger out on me. Whatever happened with you is different than what's happening with me. We're not the same people."

"We most definitely are not."

"You're . . . what? Sixty?"

"Fifty-six."

"Oh. Well, I'm twenty-five. It's a different world now. In your day people stuck together no matter what, through thick and thin, like they were all arranged marriages. As if you weren't allowed to leave. But it isn't like that anymore. Things are freer now. People understand. You know? And my wife? She'll understand. She'll be upset for a few days, but she'll get it and she'll be happier for it."

"She will, huh."

"Yes. Because we're progressive people, her and I."

"Sounds like someone you could've talked to then."

"Yeah, I know. But I didn't. And she'll realize two weeks from now that I wasn't worth piss to her."

"Maybe she'll realize that today."

"Yes. She might. I hope she does. I hope she wakes up and feels relief. I know I do."

"You're a cruel man, Bob."

"Cruel? You don't even know me."

Evelyn turned to face him. She had no way of knowing but, because of the darkness and the blue light from the dash, her features were made younger again, just enough so that Bob actually leaned back in his seat, as if he'd suddenly realized he was riding shotgun with an impossibility behind the wheel.

"I do too know you. I know you all too well. You think your life matters more than the life of the people around you. You think you can take a vow, go on a honeymoon, move into a new house, and then leave your wife with a nine word note of goodbye. You think you can justify that by imagining a wide-open west, a world of plenty. But the truth is, out west isn't going to be any different than it was in Detroit. You'll meet a woman there, you'll marry, you'll honeymoon in Hawaii, and one morning you'll leave her, too. You'll head east and the whole way there you'll tell yourself it's your *roots* that you really need."

Silence then as they passed Lincoln.

Eventually, Bob pulled a smoke from his pack.

"Wow," he said, staring through the glass. "Did I tell you all that at Miller's?"

"All what?"

"I don't know. Hawaii?"

"No. You did not."

"Well shit. What can I say. It sounds like you do kinda know me."

***

"It's three in the morning," Evelyn said, acknowledging one of the blue signs on the shoulder, the kind that announced the services and restaurants in a town. "Let's get a hotel."

"Okay. That's a good idea. Sleep. Then start all over again."

He'd been talking this way for the last few hours; brief clipped sentences that suggested deeper sentiments. *Start all over again. Big world out here. There's a lot of living in life, huh.*

The blue sign told Evelyn there was a Roadway Inn in Cozad, Nebraska. Good enough. She needed to get out of the car. Book a room. Walk to it.

"Ah shoot," Bob said. "They're full."

They were. The sign told them so.

Evelyn drove on through the small town, saw the red single word they were looking for a half-mile from the Roadway.

Vacancy at the Haymaker Hotel.

She pulled the Skylark into the gravel lot. It was the ranch sort, a long row of rooms, no second floor. The room doors all faced the lot. The office was lit up.

Evelyn parked. They got out.

"Two rooms?" he asked. The way he asked it, so completely uninterested in her, even now, even here in the middle of the trip, the country, the dark. She knew some part of her must have been his type. He'd married her younger self, after all. But it wasn't that. That didn't bother her. It was the fact that he'd consider getting his own room and not contribute to the cost of the room for the person who just drove him fifteen hours from his wife.

"Absolutely," Evelyn said.

She entered the office first and he followed. Behind the desk, a woman much older than Evelyn sat reading a paperback.

"Latecomers," the woman said. Her sweater was of a fishing scene. A man catching a fish bigger than himself. "One or two?"

"Need two," Evelyn said. "Gonna work?"

She nodded. "Full price, though. Late night or not."

"That's fine."

It took the woman a long time to write up their bill, to take the money from them, to give them their keys. When Bob handed his money over, Evelyn saw it as her own, money she'd had a claim to thirty-one years ago. She wanted to ask him how much he had on him. And did he think maybe his abandoned wife back home might be able to use some of that?

They exited the office and walked the planked boardwalk to their rooms. Room 3 for Evelyn. 4 for Bob. Bob unlocked his and walked right in. Evelyn watched him disappear into the small room then opened her own. She walked in, too, left the door open, turned on a lamp, and sat on the edge of the bed. She stared at the yellow carpet beneath her shoes, shoes that had pressed the gas pedal for fifteen hours, driving her away from home.

Her phone rang. Sherry. This time she answered.

"Hello."

"Mom! You good?"

"Yes. I'm good."

"Where are you?"

Evelyn looked to the nightstand. Stationary there? What town was this?

"Cozad, I think it's called."

"Nebraska?"

"Yes. Well into it."

"Hang on. Let me check my phone."

Evelyn waited as Sherry looked for Cozad on the map.

"Ah! You're ahead of us!"

"Is that so?"

She felt behind. In the half darkness of the Haymaker Hotel, with the door still partially open, she felt very far behind. In the room next to hers, Bob was most likely already asleep, able to despite the incredibly cruel thing he'd done this day.

"Yeah. We're an hour behind you," Sherry said. Evelyn heard Mark call her a lead-foot in the background.

A fist appeared in the open door frame. Bob. Knocking. He peered around the corner.

"Can I come in?"

"I'll talk to you in the morning, Sherry," Evelyn said. "Good night to you both. And thank you, again."

She hung up.

"Come on in," she told Bob.

Bob entered, still wearing the leather coat, still looking like a man who had something on his mind after all.

"Look," he said, "I've been thinking." Evelyn tilted her head the way a dog does when it hears something curious but can't make complete sense of the sound. "I'd like to go back."

She felt her lips part. Knew her jaw was hanging partially open. Bob was saying he wanted to go back. Back home?

"Why?"

He shoved his hands in his pockets, then brought them out again.

"I don't know. All that stuff you said. All those questions. Just . . . got me thinking I wanna turn back. Go home. Talk to my wife."

"Really."

But the rush of golden relief she imagined would follow words like these did not come. There was no sense of vindication. No feeling that she was in the right or had been righted. She still sat on the edge of a mattress in a hotel room in the middle of Nebraska. She still wore her jacket because it was a cold night outside.

"Well," she finally said. "I'm heading west. But you're welcome to hitch a ride home."

Bob smiled uneasily.

"Oh, I wasn't thinking you'd take me back. That'd be crazy." Then, "I just wanted you to know . . . I might not be here in the morning."

Evelyn smiled, and it felt like her face was made of taffy. Candy so close, but none she could eat.

"Alright, Bob."

"Yeah? You think it's a good idea?"

Evelyn held his gaze. "I'm tired. I'm going to sleep. If you're here in the morning, I'll take you west. If you're already gone . . . you're already gone."

"But do you think–"

Evelyn got up and removed her coat. She stepped to the sink outside the bathroom door and set her glasses on the counter. She ran the water and started washing her face. Behind her, she heard Bob mumble thanks, then exit the room.

She did not dry off. Rather, she gripped the edge of the counter like she'd been gripping the wheel all day and stared into her own wet face, as if finally she was able to see all the tears she'd shed for thirty-one years, all in one frozen moment at once.

***

Despite the long hours behind the wheel, she did not sleep. She didn't even pull back the blankets on the bed. Rather, she sat on the edge of the mattress and stared at the ugly carpet before she finally rose and stepped to her door. She believed he was asleep. Bob had always been the sort to fall right to sleep the second he laid himself down. She wondered if he'd found peace in that room next door or if peace really mattered to him at all.

Outside, the air was warmer than it'd been all day. Spring was rising, winter lowering, and it felt good against her face and hands. At the door marked 4, she paused.

She knew Bob. Knew him well. Knew he childishly slid all the greens from any meal to the side of the plate. Knew he didn't hold doors open for people. Knew he didn't lock doors either.

It was something she'd noticed before Hawaii, in Hawaii, and of course when they found their home and moved in together. She'd asked him, *Why don't you ever lock the door?* To which he'd answered, in character, *I don't?*

Maybe she shouldn't have asked him. Maybe she should've just told him to lock it next time.

She reached for the handle now, found it turned easy, and entered his room.

Silence. Only silence. She imagined him sitting up in bed, staring at her by the closed door, knowing she was there but waiting for her to do something before asking what she was planning. She waited for her eyes to adjust. Listened for any sign of him sleeping. Bob usually snored. But there was no snoring. Had he already found a ride back? Back to his wife? Was he already an hour closer to Detroit again? An hour closer to erasing thirty-one years of confusion, grief, and a confounding eternal hollow?

When she could see the shape of the bed and blankets in a bunch upon it, she stepped to the nightstand. She crouched till her knees touched the carpet and she reached behind the nightstand until she found the plug for the lamp. She unplugged it. When she got up again, she eyed the bed. Where was he in all that tangle? Hard to know. But she thought she knew.

She lifted the lamp from the nightstand and brought

it down upon his head. The crack it made sounded like a toilet exploding from pressure, sounded like a porcelain egg dropped to the driveway from the roof of a house. A hushed grunt accompanied the cracking and Evelyn brought the lamp up, then back down again. Sounded more like footsteps in rubble now; shoes upon broken hope. She stood above him for some time, bringing the lamp down over and over, on repeat, like revolutions around the sun, like years passing, piling up.

Finally, exhausted, she set the lamp on the nightstand, got to her knees, and plugged it in again.

She turned it on.

Kneeling there on the carpet, still wearing her jacket, she saw him on the bed. A red smear at the top of a naked chest.

She turned the light off. She got up, left the room, and closed the door quietly behind her.

Back in her own room, she sat on the edge of the bed until the sun came up. She called Sherry.

"Meet me in an hour? I'll buy you two breakfast."

"In Cozad?"

"Sure."

"Is there a diner?"

"We'll find one."

"Okay. Yeah. Then we'll . . . "

"Then we'll caravan the last four or five hours to Denver if you'd like."

"Awesome. Leaving soon. Love you, Mom."

"Love you, too."

She hung up. She stared at the carpet and watched the sun climbing, by way of shadow and reach, until she'd guessed something like an hour had passed.

∗∗∗

They ate at the diner, the three of them, all so far from home. Mark said how cool it was that they were still in America but in a completely new setting. Sherry said it felt good, like she was recharging her mind. Evelyn agreed with it all. There was something extraordinary about moving on, even if only for a week, a month, the rest of your life. Just to wake up under a different sky, to look out a different window, was really something and *did* something for you. They feasted on omelets and toast and drank juice and coffee and they talked with the energy of people on the road. When they were done, Mark and Sherry hopped into the U-Haul and Evelyn got behind the wheel of the Skylark. She thought of how she'd signed in at the hotel with the name "Eve" and how close that name was to her own and how, when they found Bob, they'd probably contact her or call her because her name was Evelyn and he was married to her after all. But as she pulled out of the diner lot, as she watched the U-Haul start up and follow her in the rearview mirror, she knew this wouldn't happen. Because thirty-one years ago she never received a phone call telling her Bob was dead. She'd never received any information at all. Why would she now?

She rolled down both windows and took a cigarette from the pack Bob left in the car. She smoked it and turned on the radio and listened to modern music, music that hadn't been made in the 1980s, hadn't been dreamt of thirty-one years ago, new stuff, new moods, new points of view.

And she drove.

Toward Denver. Toward who knew what in a city she'd never been. She thought of new homes there, new windows. She even thought of new men. She imagined one who held doors open and didn't mind answering the questions of the person he'd agreed to share his life with. She imagined the kind of man who, when struggling, didn't only talk to her about it, but was excited to do so, believing he might find some solution to his problems in the form of the union he'd vowed.

She drove.

To Denver.

Only moving on.

THE WIDOW

RIO YOUERS

"WHAT ARE YOU DOING?"

"I'm stopping you."

The man drew whistling breaths and his chest flexed against the rope that bound him. Blood trickled from his nose and mouth. Naked light washed him, emphasizing every bruise and abrasion. Had she thought him immortal . . . supernatural? Here he was now, weak and bleeding all over her floor. His ancient skin could break, after all.

"Stopping me?" He blinked and shook his head. A tear gathered in the corner of one eye. "From what, exactly?"

She stepped towards him, throwing her shadow like a blanket. A large woman. Not fat, but solid. Her thick arms were packed with toil and angst. She had a prominent brow and square shoulders. Very little could be described as feminine. Not her military surplus jacket, nor her scuffed leather boots. Only her fingernails, perhaps, painted—incongruously—bubblegum pink.

"By my count, you have killed a total of fifty-three people." Cloud-coloured eyes peered through unkempt hair. "Fourteen of them were children. I can only go back to when records began, of course, so the actual number may well be greater."

"Are you out of your mind?"

"And now it ends."

"This is madness." He fought the rope again, twisting his upper body. It chewed into his arms and chest. No give. He pushed against the wooden post he'd been bound to. It creaked but didn't budge. More blood leaked from his nose.

There was a workbench against the back wall, strewn with tools. Various wrenches and screwdrivers. A handsaw. A nail gun. A claw hammer. She turned and walked towards it, her heavy boots kicking up dust.

"Timothy Peel," she said.

"What? *What?*"

"One of the men you killed . . . Timothy Peel." Her hand moved from the handsaw to the nail gun. Back to the handsaw. "He was my husband."

"I don't know what you're talking about. I swear I don't."

"We'd only been married eleven months." She selected the nail gun. Cordless, 15-gauge, loaded with two-inch finish nails. Her fingers curled around the handle. "I loved him very much. He was my . . . my *balance.*"

No one would hear him scream. Not here, in the basement of her house, fifty yards from the road, and a quarter of a mile from her nearest neighbour. And scream he did, looking at the nail gun in her hand. A shrill and desperate effort. Eyes wide. Body jerking. His throat turned dark with the strain, like a bruise.

She let him expend both voice and energy, until he was left rasping and drooling. Tears soaked his shirt. His upper body sagged against the rope. He'd been tied in a sitting position. His legs were splayed. She kicked them closer together, then straddled them and lowered her weight onto his ankles. The muscles in his calves tensed but he couldn't move. Another weak sound and he looked at her with shattered eyes.

"You're making a terrible mistake," he said.

"Seventh of April, 2009. Almost four years ago. To the day." She pressed the nail gun's nose piece against his left kneecap and he squirmed and struggled but was held tight. "Timothy wasn't just an accomplished driver, he was a *careful* driver. Yet, mysteriously, he flipped his car one morning on his way to work. Conditions were perfect. No wind. No rain. Good visibility. He died while emergency services worked to cut him from the wreckage."

"A car accident." The man's voice was cracked. His eyes pleading. Blue and large and wet. "He died on the road."

The widow smiled. She looped her index finger around the trigger and fired three nails into the cartilage below his kneecap.

He found the energy to scream again.

"But, mister," she said. "You *are* the road."

✲✲✲

There had long been concerns about Faye Peel *née* Lester's mental stability, but when she decided to build a house on Thornbury Road—less than one hundred yards from where Timothy was killed, in fact—her friends and family deduced that she had finally come unhinged. Not irrevocably so, but sufficient to warrant professional intervention.

Her father was a worrisome rabbit of a man with fleet gestures and small eyes. He rarely finished a sentence.

"Your mother and I feel that . . . " He proffered a sheet of paper, upon which had been printed the particulars of a one Dr. Matthew Claridge, MA, MBBS, MRCPsych. His logo was a smiling flower.

"A psychiatrist?"

"We're worried about you, Faye."

"Indeed." She placed the sheet of paper facedown on the kitchen table. Her mother busied herself cooking, humming something, as if she didn't have one ear—or both—on the conversation.

"It's just that, since Timothy . . . " Her father made half a move to take her hand but drew back. His mouth twitched. "And all that nonsense about . . . and now this, with the house . . . "

"Thank you for your concern." Faye smiled, and it was she who reached across to take his hand. It felt small, somehow, and she noted how it trembled. "I'm fine, though. I feel stronger and more focused than I have in years."

"But the house . . . do you really . . . ? Oh, Faye, it's just so *close*."

She squeezed his fingers gently. Her smile was sure. Her voice confident.

"I have my reasons."

And she did; the "nonsense" to which her father referred was her erstwhile assertion that Timothy's death had not been an accident, and her subsequent vow to find the man responsible. These claims were met with sympathy, a great deal of love, but very little understanding. Faye eventually let it slide—even professed a misjudgement, for her parents' sake—although she secretly, passionately, pursued her suspicion.

It began shortly after Timothy's death. The first two months had been an emotional blur. She recalled only damp and grey patches, like fragments of cloud snatched from the sky. The funeral was dreamlike. Red flowers. So many red flowers. Timothy's brother playing "Let It Be" on a guitar the same colour as his coffin. As many hands as there were flowers, all offered in support. The world revolved too slowly, and with a grinding sound that kept her awake at night. She imagined its ancient machinery full of pain, coughing black smoke, and God crippled by the weight of His dead.

This lassitude fractured, finally, when Faye opened the bathroom cabinet one morning and saw Timothy's aftershave on the shelf. She'd been with him when he bought it, neither of them knowing that he wouldn't live long enough to finish the bottle. It occurred to her—and it was like a hand gently leading her through the rain—that she would never again smell that aftershave on his throat, or the vague trace of it on his shirt collar when doing the laundry. She took the bottle off the shelf, unscrewed the cap, and lifted it to her nose. Her tears were copious, but not without healing. As she wiped the last of them from her face, she felt something give way inside her—an internal landslide that left her partly hollow, but with enough space to exist. She poured the aftershave down the sink and disposed of the bottle. She whirled, then, through the house, not removing Timothy, but clearing those possessions too replete with memories. His reading glasses. His favourite cardigan, threadbare and wonderful. The giant bar of Dairy Milk he'd been nibbling on since Christmas. In the end, a chestful of items that had no place in her half-formed life. And even though she still slept at night with her arm thrown across Timothy's side of the bed, it felt like a huge step in the right direction.

Another step was to visit the site of the accident. Thornbury Road was a seven-mile pencil-line on the countryside, linking the A4301 at Abbotsea to the Paisley Wood roundabout. It often provided a beautiful drive, with raised banks of daffodils in the spring, and clutches of woodland that flared with oranges and reds come autumn. Strings of mist clung to the farmland at dawn, made pink by the climbing sun, and wildlife revelled in the fields that rolled southward, where, on clear days, the English Channel could be seen skimming the horizon. Despite its charm, though, it had, understandably, become a sombre route for Faye. The shadows seemed suddenly denser. The dawn mists obscured secret things. Broken things. It was here—a stone's throw from where Timothy had died—that she first saw the sideways man.

He had a condition, she thought. Scoliosis, or perhaps spina bifida. His back was skewed and his head kinked to one side, always looking over his right shoulder. Uneven hips caused him to *drag* rather than walk, having to correct his direction every several steps. His face, too, sloped to the right, as if sympathizing with his body.

Faye had parked in a lay-by only a short distance away. She looked at the man through the windscreen. He had no purpose, apparently; he circled towards and then away from where Timothy died. Lank black hair covered his eyes.

She surmised his challenges went beyond physical. The poor man was lost, obviously, and confused. Thinking she could help, she stepped out of her car and onto the road. He looked up, alerted. A breeze blew back his hair and his eyes glimmered. They were notable not in their colour or shape, but in the way they regarded her. She felt suddenly naked, both body and soul laid bare. It was as if he touched—*probed*—her with those eyes and examined her history. Every smile. Every tear. Every hope and sadness exposed. Faye shivered. She crossed her arms over her bosom and took a step back.

She was about to get back into her car—return another day—when the man dragged himself sideways, onto the bank, and behind a cluster of evergreens. She saw his jacket sway between their narrow trunks, then he was gone. Faye staggered into the middle of the road and waited for him to emerge one way or the other, or to see him shuffling sideways across the field beyond the point where he had disappeared. She adjusted her position and peered through the branches.

Nothing.

"Hello."

Gone.

She shivered again, composed herself. Several deep breaths, focusing on Timothy and the reason she'd come here. She walked to the site of his death. Planted both feet firmly upon it. She thought she'd experience . . . something. A chill. A vision. A memory. There was nothing. The road felt the same here as anywhere else—as any other road. The broken glass had been swept away. The blood, too. As far as this unspectacular patch of Thornbury Road was concerned, it was as if Timothy Peel had never existed at all.

She cried again, deeply, and with a great pain in her

chest. She got into her car and drove away. Too fast. Moving forward, or so she hoped. What else was there to do?

The next six months were better. The pain never went away, but she could fold her hands around it. Contain it. She went out with her friends and smiled more often. She even regained the weight she'd lost after Timothy died. Her parents remarked on how well she was doing, and how proud they were. One morning in December, Faye awoke with her left arm curled beneath her pillow, rather than clutching Timothy's side of the bed. She gasped—feeling both delighted and guilty—and sat up quickly. Early sunlight seeped through a crack in the curtains.

That very day, a family of four was killed on Thornbury Road. Faye saw the wreckage of their Vauxhall Astra on the six o'clock news. Folded in the middle like paper. Roof pried away to get the bodies out. She saw the pulsing lights of the emergency services. She saw the POLICE ACCIDENT signs and solemn-faced officers at the scene. And she saw the sideways man, standing in the background like a large, stooped vulture.

From that moment, everything started to unravel.

✳✳✳

Something the reporter said picked at Faye's mind and wouldn't let go—that Thornbury Road had claimed eleven lives in the last ten years. An interesting choice of words that gave the seven-mile stretch of asphalt a certain character. She imagined it breathing, elongated lungs pounding beneath its surface, occasionally whipping snake-like to send some luckless vehicle spinning out of control.

Ridiculous, but it picked at her. Then it gnawed at her. Then it started to tear. She lay awake, night after night, grinding her teeth and imagining the road moving slickly beneath the stars. She often drove out there, stopping her car every two or three hundred yards, on hands and knees with her ear pressed to its gritty skin . . .

No heartbeat. No movement. No life.

She researched the road. More particularly, its nature. She was intrigued to find out just how many lives it had claimed over the years. She spent what amounted to months at the library and on her home computer, scrolling through links and news stories. Tracking deaths within the last forty years was easy enough. Most of them got front-page coverage in the Abbotsea *Echo*. Beyond 1965, though, it became more difficult. The library's files were incomplete and search engines provided only the more notable stories. She persevered, though, following every thread, however tenuous. Sometimes she worked through the night, with her eyes stinging and her worn body slouched across the desk. When she wasn't digging for information, she was cruising Thornbury Road, daring—almost *willing*—it to come to life.

She saw the sideways man twice. A different place each time. He scuttled along the edge of the road, and always disappeared before she reached him.

"Faye, what's happening? You haven't been . . . "

"You worry too much, Dad. You always have. Both of you."

"We love you."

"Then leave me alone."

Her parents tried to coax her from her mania, using increments of support that were dwarfed by their lack of understanding. They saw her desk buried beneath notes and old newspaper clippings, and files with headings like NON-FATAL and DRUNK DRIVERS stacked in teetering piles. They saw the magnified image of Thornbury Road taped to the wall, with coloured push-pins marking accident locations. They saw *her* too, of course, having derailed from whatever forward-moving track she'd been riding. Their concern was evident.

"What exactly," her mother sobbed, "are you hoping to find?"

"Connections. Evidence." Faye shrugged. "Maybe a motive."

"But it's a road."

"It kills people."

Her many hours of work were not without reward. She learned that the road claimed its first victim in 1877. Clyde Tummond, forty-three years of age, died of massive internal injuries after being first thrown, and then trampled by his horse. Before passing away, he recounted how Dolly, normally so stalwart, had been spooked by a man lurking at the edge of the road—one "of frightful countenance." Faye was willing to accept this a chilling coincidence . . . and then she uncovered a photograph from 1928. Its subject was a battered Austin Seven lying on its side, with its deceased driver sprawled nearby, covered by a sheet. The caption read, *WEEKEND TRAGEDY: Harold Leggatt, 32, was killed Saturday evening after his vehicle overturned on Thornbury Road.* The photograph was as grainy as one would expect of the era, but the crooked figure standing in a field to the left of the frame was unmistakable.

She searched, then—and with a frantically beating heart—every photo hitherto discovered, studying the periphery for anything she may have missed. She spent further weeks unearthing more photographs and found three instances of the sideways man. Two were, admittedly, inconclusive—faceless smudges that could be anyone, if not for that crippled stance. One was definite. From a May 1957 copy of the West Country *Voice* (she hadn't found it before because they'd misspelled "Thornbury"), the grim wreckage of a Ford Anglia wrapped around a tree, with the sideways man hovering in the foreground. He was staring at the camera, perhaps caught off-guard. Looking into his eyes, Faye again found herself laid bare to him, the strands of her life unravelled for him to paw among like a cat.

"Who are you?"

She arranged the photographs on the floor. From 1928 until the most recent: a screen grab of the mangled Astra news footage. She studied the sideways man in each. Never changing. Never aging.

"*What* are you?"

Faye sought reason—an explanation so obvious she would flush with embarrassment. Every lucid argument felt desperate, however . . . that it wasn't the same man, how *could* it be? Or maybe it was a hoax; photography as fake as that of the Loch Ness Monster. Having exhausted logic, she was left with hypotheses that could only be described as paranormal. She pondered them, and found they had substance. They took root in her mind and grew.

Countless nights were lost to nightmarish thoughts. She envisioned this man—this *creature*—scuttling along Thornbury Road in search of victims. A scourge that spanned generations. She wondered if every road in Britain had its own sideways man. The idea was ludicrous, but it felt *right.* She couldn't look at a map of the UK without imagining the motorways as arteries, the A- and B-roads as veins, all teeming with infection. A virus in the blood.

"Faye, sweetie, you've been under a lot of stress lately."

"Don't patronise me, Megan. Just tell me what you see."

Faye had, delicately, taken her findings to her parents, and received the response she expected: a concern so deep it drowned any vestige of open-mindedness. So, she called upon her friend, Megan, who deodorised with alum crystals and practised Reiki—an alternative disposition that would, Faye hoped, make her more accepting.

"Car crashes," Megan said, flipping through the photographs that Faye had handed her. "On Thornbury Road, no less. Oh, Faye, what *is* this all about?"

They were in Costa. A quiet Tuesday morning, with few of the tables and chairs occupied, and the occasional sound of the coffee machines grinding and steaming in the background. It was the first time Faye had been anywhere other than the library and Thornbury Road in so long, and she felt self-conscious, decidedly unattractive. She wore a too-big sweater and her hair was greasy. It didn't help that Megan was so pretty, with her swirl of chestnut hair and green eyes, and just a hint of patchouli on her skin.

"Not the crashes," Faye said. "The man. Look at the man."

"Which man?"

Faye pointed out the crooked figure in each photograph, from '28 to '09.

"And?"

"It's the same man," Faye replied.

There was a pause while Megan went through the photographs again, reading the captions, her brow furrowed as she counted the years. She shook her head, set the photos on the table between them, and sipped her rosehip tea.

"Impossible," she said.

"The camera never lies."

"It *can't* be the same person," Megan insisted. "Not with these dates. And honestly, Faye, the pictures are so grainy it's difficult to tell anything for certain. It may not be the same man at all."

"It is."

"Then they're fakes. It's the only explanation."

"I need you to be outside the box on this." Faye sipped her own tea. Twinings Earl Grey. Very normal. "Shouldn't be hard for you."

"I'm listening."

"I've heard you talk about auras and energy signatures. You once said that even inanimate objects have residual energy."

Megan nodded.

"So is it possible for a road to have energy?"

"Yes, of course. Drive down any road where a fatal accident has occurred, and it feels . . . different."

Faye took another sip of tea. Her hand trembled. "A person's energy manifests as an aura. A corona of colour around our bodies. But what if a road's energy—its *evil* energy—manifests as a physical presence? A demon." She tapped the photograph from 1957. The sideways man glared at the camera and his eyes were like probes. "Something cold and hateful. Something that kills."

"It doesn't work like that."

"Outside the box, Megan."

"There *is* no box." Her voice was sharp, touched with impatience. She sipped her tea and the expression in her eyes softened. She reached across the table and patted Faye's hand. "I'm sorry, sweetie, but I can't get behind this line of thinking. It's too negative. And damaging."

Faye tapped the photograph again. "What do you see?"

"It's eerie, yes, but I'm telling you it's not the same man."

"Megan, please."

"You want help from me?" Megan finished her tea, set her mug down too hard, and stood up. "I can recommend an excellent shiatsu practitioner. Failing that, a bottle of Jacob's Creek and a night of hot sex. But all of this . . . " She waved her hand dismissively over the photographs. "You're still hurting, Faye, and looking for a reason why Timothy died. You're looking for something that doesn't exist."

It did exist, though. Faye had seen it—seen *him*—with her own eyes. Megan had kissed her goodbye and left, and Faye sat for a long moment, feeling both alone and full of resolve. She flipped through the photographs for perhaps the thousandth time. So much twisted metal and spilled blood. But there were no accidents here. There had *never* been an accident on Thornbury Road. The sideways man was responsible for it all. He had killed so many people. He had killed Timothy. And one way or another, she was going to stop him.

***

There were three lay-bys on Thornbury Road and she started out parking in one of these and staying there all day, listening to the radio, eating junk food, only getting out if she needed to take a piss or a shit in the tall grass.

She waited.

Her rearview and side mirrors were positioned to give her optimum viewing without always having to crane her head. She had 10x42 binoculars with a dandy Mossy Oak camo and the seller on e-Bay said they were the kind used by the SAS. She had 1x26 night vision goggles and sometimes when it got dark she put them on, clambered into a tree where she couldn't be seen, and perched there like an owl. She had an elaborate digital camera that she didn't really know how to use, but she could zoom in on a bird's wing from one hundred yards away, and could push the button, which was all she cared about.

She had time.

She waited.

✸✸✸

It occurred to her after several weeks of being in one of three places that the sideways man knew her routine—such as it was—and was evading her. She thought she saw him on several occasions: a whisper of something dark in the binoculars, or in one of the mirrors, but by the time she positioned herself for a better look, he (or it) was gone. Maybe just dead leaves lifted by a breeze. Or a large crow taking wing from the hedgerow.

She needed to take him by surprise, which meant rethinking her strategy. Sitting in a car eating pizza wasn't going to get the job done, and she was getting fat, too. No way she could give chase on foot with her stomach bouncing ahead of her, even if he was a cripple. She stopped with the junk food. Switched to raw vegetables and water. She left her aging Mondeo in the Waitrose car park just off the Paisley Wood roundabout, packed a duffel bag with her equipment and supplies, and walked from there. After a few weeks she started to jog. Then run.

She lived in the trees and the long grass, moving stealthily along Thornbury Road, blending in by painting her face and the backs of her hands with green and brown paints. No one saw her. Not even the deer. She sometimes skulked to within feet of them and they carried on eating leaves, oblivious. During quieter moments she worked on her strength. Sit-ups and push-ups, mainly. At first, she could only do three or four of each. By the summer of 2011, eight months after committing to this new way of life, she could do three or four hundred.

She often sat beside the road where Timothy died and talked to him, feeling so desperately alone and with no one else to talk to. She couldn't go to her so-called friends and family. They had no idea what she was going through. And they didn't *want* to know. Not really. Better for them to live in ignorance. Timothy had always been her rock, though. He had always listened, and in doing so could make all the cracks in the world—and there were many—disappear.

"You once told me that I was fragile, like a book is fragile. That it can crumble with age, that its pages can tear and its cover fade. But even so, it remains a thing of beauty and depth. A limitless treasure that should be shared and remembered. Of all the wonderful things you said in our short time together, this was my favourite. It made me feel . . . alive."

She wished to hear his voice. Even on the wind. Never did.

"Every breath is a word, and every word has purpose."

She wished to see him again. Just a glimpse. Never did. But one time all the trees around her came to life, flaunting their leaves, and she looked at them with tears in her eyes and pretended it was him.

✷✷✷

The sign read LAND FOR SALE. Faye saw it within an hour of it being posted. By the end of the day someone had slapped a red sticker on top of it and this one read SOLD.

✷✷✷

There was a moment before building commenced on her new house that she really questioned what she was doing. It wasn't the money. Timothy had been paying into a corporate pension since he was sixteen years old, and coupled with a sizable life insurance payout, Faye was able to buy the land and pay for the house outright. Nor was it the fact that she'd be so close to where he died. According to the architect's design, she'd see that strip of Thornbury Road every time she looked out her bedroom window. It was her parents. Their unending concern. She had told them about the house, showing them the strength in her words and a spine that wasn't cracked at all, yet before she left her father had slipped that sheet of paper into her pocket and she'd found it when she returned home. Dr. Matthew Claridge, MA, MBBS, MRCPsych. That smiling flower. Tears welled in her eyes and she tried to fight them, and then she gave up. She cried deep into the night. Everything hurt.

She had her reasons, yes, but did she really want to live by herself in such a broken part of the world, chasing a shadow? Or did she want to be a smiling flower?

The next few days were spent in indecision. She kept that sheet of paper crumpled in her hand, and on several occasions reached for the phone—even dialled a few numbers before hanging up. She imagined Dr. Matthew Claridge to have a soft voice and a never-ending box of Kleenex that he'd keep on a table between them, and she ached for those comforts. They seemed enough to sway her, and then a cyclist was killed on Thornbury Road and that made fifty-three dead, assuming Clyde Tummond was the first and she hadn't missed any. Fifty-three, including Timothy, who'd told her she was fragile, yet deep, and could make all the cracks disappear.

Faye took a flame to that sheet of paper and watched it burn, and she never saw that smiling flower again.

***

Her house was built seven months later. Set back from the road, stylish and, though modern, designed to blend with the trees. Faye also had the builders construct a twenty-foot tower in her garden. For bird-watching, she said.

***

The crossbow she bought had 225lbs of draw weight and, despite her new muscle, she could only cock it with a rope cocking aid. She practised in her garden. To begin with, she couldn't hit a rain barrel from fifty feet away. Within weeks, she could nail an apple from one-eighty.

***

She caught him when the April showers were at their freshest and the evenings had that crisp reminder of the winter passed. She was in her tower, watching the east side of Thornbury Road through the trees. A rustling sound from the blackberry bushes where her land met the edge of Copp Farm. She swept the binoculars in that direction, expecting to see a badger or deer, and there he was, scuttling through the foliage at the side of the road.

She didn't panic. She lowered the binoculars, cocked the crossbow, and lifted it to her shoulder. One second later and his jerky, awkward body filled the sights. She targeted the middle of his forehead. Held her breath.

Pause.

The crossbow had an arrow speed of three hundred and fifty feet per second. The sideways man was a third of that distance away. He'd be dead in the blink of an eye. Too quick. Faye lowered the sights and targeted his crooked right leg. She curled her finger around the trigger.

"Suffer," she said.

He dropped quickly, as if someone had yanked the leafy verge out from under him. He tried to get back up but fell again, and then he started screaming. Faye was halfway to him by that point, sprinting between the trees. When she reached him, she saw that the arrow had passed through his leg. He clutched the hole it had left behind, blood flowing between his fingers. His endless eyes were filled with confusion. He pleaded for help and reached for her with one red hand.

She kicked him in the mouth and knocked out three of his teeth. He *still* reached for her, so confused. She kicked him again. Harder. The scream faded on his lips. He fell backwards into the leaves. His body resembled a gnarled branch hit by lightning.

Faye hoisted him onto her shoulder. An uneven weight. A bag of sticks.

She took him to her house.

✢✢✢

"You crazy bitch. Oh, you crazy fucking bitch."

Twelve hours later.

Faye had fired one hundred and sixty nails into his left leg. Into his kneecap, his shin, his thigh. Sometimes the nails didn't go all the way in and she had to drive them home with a hammer. After a while he stopped screaming. He fluttered in and out of consciousness. She recharged the gun and fired another one hundred-plus into his right leg. She thought he'd bleed more than he did.

Every now and then she read out the names of all the people who had lost their lives on Thornbury Road. In chronological order, except for Timothy. She saved his name until last. Vivaldi played in the background. Timothy's favourite. He also liked Status Quo, but she didn't think "Margarita Time" quite fit the mood.

"Crazy . . . fucking . . . "

Admittedly, Faye was a little surprised to find a wallet in the sideways man's jacket pocket. There was forty-five pounds in cash inside, some blank cheques, some credit and store cards. She didn't know what a demon would want with such things. They were props, she reasoned, allowing him to better blend with his current environment. The name on all cards and documentation was the same: Michael Cole. A very normal name. And while it all appeared genuine, it didn't faze her. It didn't stop her.

She selected the handsaw. He hissed and shook his head when he saw it in her hand. His ruined legs twitched, but of course he couldn't move them; they were nailed to the floor. Faye crouched and pressed the jagged blade to his right leg, three inches above the ankle. She started to saw. He passed out when she was halfway through the bone. When he came to—ash-pale and close to death—both severed feet were bundled into his lap.

"No more walking for you," Faye said, setting the saw aside. She was smeared with blood. It was even on her teeth. "Sideways or otherwise."

"Crazy bitch."

She picked up the nail gun, pressed the nose piece to his forehead, and fired two inches of galvanized steel into his brain. He didn't die. His eyes rolled crazily for a little while. Blood trickled from his nose.

Faye walked from the basement, leaving him still alive and with his feet—which had covered so many miles, over so many years—gathered in his lap. She walked from her house and into the pink grapefruit light of early morning. The grass was heavy with dew and the air smelled of new leaves and daffodils. She picked one, then pinched one of its petals between her thumb and forefinger, trying to turn it upwards in a smile. But it only bruised and drooped. A sad face.

✣ ✣ ✣

Megan's voice chimed in her mind: *You're still hurting, Faye, and looking for a reason why Timothy died. You're looking for something that doesn't exist.*

Faye saw the sideways man multiple times that day. On a bicycle. Driving a tractor. In nearly every vehicle that passed her on Thornbury Road. She sat in the spot she had come to think of as hers. The place where Timothy had died.

"Does exist," she said.

Her trained ear picked up the rumble of an approaching truck. She counted to ten. Stood up. Looked to her right. The truck—an eighteen-wheeled monster—rounded the bend. She would step in front of it at the optimum moment, giving the driver no chance to brake or steer around her. Not that he would, of course. Faye knew that, in the closing second of her life, she would see his buckled body propped behind the wheel, his timeless eyes reaching deep.

And like him, she would find what she was looking for.

ACKNOWLEDGEMENTS

I have to offer my gratitude to the following people who helped make this book possible: To all of the authors and artists who found inspiration in the theme and crafted such wonderfully dark things—thank you. To Joe Mynhardt and all the CLP staff who worked on and in the interest of the book and continue to do so. To Brian Keene and Mary SanGiovanni. To Doug Murano and the many folks who supported and encouraged me during the development of this anthology and the long road it took to get here. Thank you all a million times over.

ABOUT THE EDITOR

D. Alexander Ward is an author and editor of horror and dark fiction.

Both his Gothic thriller, *Beneath Ash & Bone*, and his Southern-flavored action-horror, *Blood Savages*, are available from Necro Publications and Bedlam Press wherever books are sold.

As an editor, he co-edited the acclaimed and Bram Stoker Award-nominated *GUTTED: Beautiful Horror Stories*. He also co-edited the Lovecraftian horror anthologies, *Shadows Over Main Street*, Volumes 1 and 2.

Along with his family and the haints in the woods, he lives outside of Richmond near the farm where he grew up in what used to be rural Virginia, where his love for the people, passions, and folklore of the South was nurtured. There, he spends his nights penning and collecting tales of the dark, strange and fantastic.

Follow him on Facebook (facebook.com/DAlexWard) and Twitter (@DAlexWard).

THE AUTHORS AND ARTISTS OF LOST HIGHWAYS

Michael Bailey is a freelance writer, editor and book designer, and the recipient of over two dozen literary accolades, such as the Bram Stoker Award and Benjamin Franklin Award. His novels include *Palindrome Hannah*, *Phoenix Rose*, and *Psychotropic Dragon*, and he has published two short story and poetry collections, *Scales and Petals, and Inkblots* and *Blood Spots*, as well as a children's book, *Enso*. Edited anthologies include *Pellucid Lunacy*, *Qualia Nous*, *The Library of the Dead*, *You Human*, *Adam's Ladder*, *Prisms*, and four volumes of *Chiral Mad*. His most recent publications are three standalone novelettes: *SAD Face*, *Darkroom*, and *Our Children, Our Teachers*.

Christopher Buehlman is a writer and comedian from St. Petersburg, Florida. He spends most of the year performing as a professional insultor, touring the renaissance festival circuit with his acrobat wife, his blind cat and his one-eyed dog. His first novel, *Those Across the River*, was a finalist for best novel in the 2012 World Fantasy Awards and has been optioned for film by Phoenix pictures. His fourth novel, *The Lesser Dead*, was the RUSA reading selection for horror in 2015, was nominated for a Shirley Jackson Award, and has been optioned for television development by Global Road. He is the winner of the 2007 Bridport Prize for poetry.

Cullen Bunn is the writer of creator-owned comic book series such as *Harrow County*, *The Sixth Gun*, *The Damned*, *Regression*, *Bone Parish*, and many others. He has also written numerous comics for Marvel and DC, including *Deadpool Kills the Marvel Universe*, *Deadpool: Assassin*, *Star Wars*, *X-Men Blue*, *Sinestro*, and *Suicide Squad*. He also writes prose, including a serialized action-horror novel, *Shadowcage*, on Patreon.

Rachel Autumn Deering is an Eisner and Harvey Award-nominated writer, editor, and book designer from the hills of Appalachia. Her debut prose novella, *HUSK*, was published in 2016 and drew praise from many critics and fellow writers. Her upcoming novel, *Wytchwood Hollow*, is set for publication in 2018.

She has also written, edited, lettered, designed, and published comics and short prose for DC/Vertigo Comics, Blizzard Entertainment, Dark Horse Comics, IDW, Cartoon Network, and more.

Deering is a rock 'n' roll witch with a heart of slime. She lives with a bunch of monster masks in rural Ohio.

Kristi DeMeester is the author of *Beneath*, a novel published by Word Horde, and the author of *Everything That's Underneath*, a short fiction collection published by Apex Publications. Her short fiction has appeared in publications such as Ellen Datlow's *The Best Horror of the Year Volume 9*, *Year's Best Weird Fiction* Volumes 1 and 3, Black Static, The Dark, Apex Magazine, and several others. She is currently at work on her fourth novel and seeking representation. Learn more at kristidemeester.com.

Robert Ford fills his days handling marketing and design projects and considering ripping the phone lines from the wall. He is author of the novel *The Compound*, the novellas *Samson and Denial*, *Ring of Fire*, and *The Last Firefly of Summer*, and has a collection of his short fiction *The God Beneath my Garden*. He can confirm the grass really is greener on the other side, but it's only because of the bodies buried there.

Wes Freed (b.1964) grew up on a cattle farm in Virginia's Shenandoah Valley, a place that still informs his work. He received a painting and printmaking degree from Virginia Commonwealth University in the eighties. In the late 20th century he met the Drive-By Truckers, and has been making art for the band ever since. He lives in Richmond Virginia's beautiful Fan district, where he can be seen scouring the alleys for paintable wood with his girlfriend Jackie, and a Schnauzer mix named Betsy whose moods run hot and cold.

doungjai gam's short fiction has appeared in LampLight, *Distant Dying Ember*, *Now I Lay Me Down to Sleep*, *Wicked Haunted*, and the Necon E-Books *Best of Flash Fiction Anthology* series since 2011. Her debut collection, *glass slipper dreams, shattered*, came out in July. She is a member of the New England Horror Writers. Born in Thailand, she currently resides in Connecticut.

Orrin Grey is a skeleton who likes monsters, as well as a writer, editor, and amateur film scholar who was born on the night before Halloween. His stories of monsters, ghosts, and sometimes the ghosts of monsters have appeared in dozens of anthologies and three collections, including *Painted Monsters & Other Strange Beasts* and *Guignol & Other Sardonic Tales*. He resides in the suburbs of Kansas City, and has driven along I-70 many, many times.

Matt Hayward is a Bram Stoker Award-nominated author and musician from Ireland. His books include *Brain Dead Blues*, *What Do Monsters Fear?*, *Practitoners* (with Patrick Lacey), and the upcoming *The Faithful*. He curated the anthology *Welcome To The Show*, and is currently writing a novel with Bryan Smith. Matt wrote the comic book *This Is How It Ends* with the band Walking Papers and received a nomination for Irish short story of the year from Penguin Books in 2017.

Jonathan Janz is the author of more than a dozen novels and numerous short stories. His work has been championed by authors like Joe R. Lansdale, Brian Keene, and Jack Ketchum; he has also been lauded by Publishers Weekly, the Library Journal, and the School Library Journal. His novel *Children of the Dark* was chosen by Booklist as a Top Ten Horror Book of the Year. Jonathan's main interests are his wonderful wife and his three amazing children. You can sign up for his newsletter, and you can follow him on Twitter, Instagram, Facebook, Amazon, and Goodreads.

Tyler Jenkins is an illustrator based in Calgary, Alberta, Canada.

Brian Keene writes novels, comic books, short fiction, and occasional journalism for money. He is the author of over forty books, mostly in the horror, crime, and dark fantasy genres and also hosts the popular podcast The Horror Show with Brian Keene.

Keene's work has been praised in such diverse places as The New York Times, The History Channel, The Howard Stern Show, CNN.com, Publisher's Weekly, Media Bistro, Fangoria Magazine, and Rue Morgue Magazine.

Keene serves on the Board of Directors for the Scares That Care 501c charity organization.

The father of two sons, Keene lives in rural Pennsylvania.

Nick Kolakowski is the author of the noir thrillers "Boise Longpig Hunting Club," "Slaughterhouse Blues," and "A Brutal Bunch of Heartbroken Saps." His fiction and poetry have appeared in the North American Review, McSweeney's Internet Tendency, Thuglit, Cleaver Magazine, and various anthologies. He lives and writes in New York City, and hates to drive.

Lisa Kröger is a writer and host of the Know Fear podcast. She has a Ph.D. in English; her interests include Gothic and horror literature, particularly women writers of the genre. She's edited two books: *Shirley Jackson: Influences and Confluences* (Routledge, 2016) and *Spectral Identities: Essays on Ghosting in Literature and Film* (Rowman and Littlefield, 2013). In addition, she's also contributed to *EcoGothic* (Manchester University Press, 2013), *The Encyclopedia of the Vampire* (Greenwood Press, 2010), and *Horror Literature through History* (ABC-CLIO, forthcoming). Her newest fiction is forthcoming in Cemetery Dance. You can find out more about her at www.lisakroger.com.

Ed Kurtz is the author of *The Rib from Which I Remake the World*, *Bleed*, *Nausea*, and other novels. Ed's short fiction has appeared in numerous magazines and anthologies and has been honored in both *Best American Mystery Stories* and *Best Gay Stories*. He lives in Connecticut.

Since picking up a pen a few years ago, **Jess Landry's** fiction has appeared in Crystal Lake Publishing's *Where Nightmares Come From* and *Fantastic Tales of Terror*, Unnerving's *Alligators in the Sewers*, Stitched Smile's *Primogen*, and DFP's *Killing It Softly*, among others.

She currently works as Managing Editor for JournalStone and its imprint, Trepidatio Publishing, where her goal is to publish diverse stories from diverse writers.

You can visit her on the interwebs at jesslandry.com, though your best bet at finding her is on Facebook and Twitter (@jesslandry28) where she posts cat gifs and references *Jurassic Park* way too much.

Joe R. Lansdale is the author of over forty novels and four hundred short pieces, including essays, stories, introductions, and articles. He has written for television and film, as well as comics, and has received numerous recognitions for his work. Among them, The Edgar, ten Bram Stokers, The Spur Award, The Grinzani Cavour Prize, and many others. *Bubba Hotep* and *Cold In July* were both made into films, and his series of novels about Hap and Leonard became a television series. Several novels, stories, films and comics, are in the works. He lives in Nacogdoches, Texas with his wife and Pitbull, Nicky.

Bracken MacLeod has survived car crashes, a near drowning, being shot at, a parachute malfunction, and the bar exam. So far, the only incident that has resulted in persistent nightmares is the bar exam. He is the author of the novels *Mountain Home*, *Come to Dust*, and *Stranded*, which was a finalist for the Bram Stoker Award, and a collection of short fiction, *13 Views of the Suicide Woods*. He lives outside of Boston with his wife and son, where he is at work on his next novel.

Josh Malerman is an American author and also one of two singer/songwriters for the rock band The High Strung, whose song "The Luck You Got" can be heard as the theme song to the Showtime show Shameless. His book *Bird Box* is also currently being filmed as a feature film starring Sandra Bullock, John Malkovich, and Sarah Paulson. *Bird Box* was also nominated for the Stoker Award, the Shirley Jackson Award, and the James Herbert Award. His books *Black Mad Wheel* and *Goblin* have also been nominated for Stoker Awards. His latest release is *Unbury Carol: A Novel*.

Born and raised in Wisconsin, **Kelli Owen** now lives in Pennsylvania. She's attended countless writing conventions, participated on dozens of panels, and has spoken at the CIA Headquarters in Langley, VA regarding both her writing and the field in general. Her works include *Six Days*, *Floaters*, *Waiting Out Winter* as well as other novels and novellas, and the collection *Black Bubbles*. Visit her website at kelliowen.com for more information.

Matthew Revert is a writer, musician and designer from Melbourne, Australia.

Luke Spooner is a freelance illustrator from the South of England. As 'Carrion House' he creates dark, melancholy and macabre illustrations and designs for a variety of projects and publishers.

Richard Thomas is the award-winning author of seven books—*Disintegration*, *Breaker*, *Transubstantiate*, *Herniated Roots*, *Staring into the Abyss*, *Tribulations*, and *The Soul Standard*. He has been nominated for the Bram Stoker, Shirley Jackson, and Thriller awards. His over 140 stories in print include Cemetery Dance (twice), *Behold!: Oddities, Curiosities and Undefinable Wonders* (Bram Stoker Winner), *Weird Fiction Review, Midwestern Gothic, Gutted: Beautiful Horror Stories, Qualia Nous, Chiral Mad* (numbers 2-4), and *Shivers VI*. He was also the editor of four anthologies: *The New Black, Exigencies, The Lineup: 20 Provocative Women Writers*, and *Burnt Tongues*. Visit www.whatdoesnotkillme.com for more information.

François Vaillancourt is a French-Canadian illustrator living in Montreal. He works with a variety of techniques, which he blends digitally. His illustrations are mostly of the horror and dark fantasy genre, with some science fiction thrown in for good measure. You can discover more of his work at francois-art.com

Damien Angelica Walters is the author of *Cry Your Way Home*, *Paper Tigers*, and *Sing Me Your Scars*, winner of This is Horror's Short Story Collection of the Year. Her short fiction has been nominated twice for a Bram Stoker Award, reprinted in *The Year's Best Dark Fantasy & Horror* and *The Year's Best Weird Fiction*, and published in various anthologies and magazines, including the Shirley Jackson Award Finalists *Autumn Cth*ulhu and *The Madness of Dr. Caligari*, World Fantasy Award Finalist Cassilda's Song, Nightmare Magazine, Black Static, and Apex Magazine. Until the magazine's closing in 2013, she was an Associate Editor of the Hugo Award-winning Electric Velocipede. She lives in Maryland with her husband and two rescued pit bulls and is represented by Heather Flaherty of The Bent Agency.

Rio Youers is the British Fantasy Award–nominated author of *Old Man Scratch* and *Point Hollow*. His short fiction has been published in many notable anthologies, and his novel, *Westlake Soul*, was nominated for Canada's prestigious Sunburst Award. He has been favorably reviewed in such venues as Publishers Weekly, Booklist, and The National Post. His recent novels include *The Forgotten Girl* and the upcoming *Halcyon*. Rio lives in southwestern Ontario with his wife, Emily, and their children, Lily and Charlie.

THE END?

Not quite . . .

Dive into more Tales from the Darkest Depths:

Novels:
House of Sighs (with sequel novella) by Aaron Dries
Beyond Night by Eric S. Brown and Steven L. Shrewsbury
The Third Twin: A Dark Psychological Thriller by Darren Speegle
Aletheia: A Supernatural Thriller by J.S. Breukelaar
Beatrice Beecham's Cryptic Crypt: A Supernatural Adventure/Mystery Novel by Dave Jeffery
Where the Dead Go to Die by Mark Allan Gunnells and Aaron Dries
Sarah Killian: Serial Killer (For Hire!) by Mark Sheldon
The Final Cut by Jasper Bark
Blackwater Val by William Gorman
Pretty Little Dead Girls: A Novel of Murder and Whimsy by Mercedes M. Yardley
Nameless: The Darkness Comes by Mercedes M. Yardley

Novellas:
Quiet Places: A Novella of Cosmic Folk Horror by Jasper Bark
The Final Reconciliation by Todd Keisling
Run to Ground by Jasper Bark
Devourer of Souls by Kevin Lucia
Apocalyptic Montessa and Nuclear Lulu: A Tale of Atomic Love by Mercedes M. Yardley
Wind Chill by Patrick Rutigliano

Little Dead Red by Mercedes M. Yardley
Sleeper(s) by Paul Kane
Stuck On You by Jasper Bark

Anthologies:
C.H.U.D. Lives!—A Tribute Anthology
Tales from The Lake Vol.4: The Horror Anthology, edited by Ben Eads
Behold! Oddities, Curiosities and Undefinable Wonders, edited by Doug Murano
Twice Upon an Apocalypse: Lovecraftian Fairy Tales, edited by Rachel Kenley and Scott T. Goudsward
Tales from The Lake Vol.3, edited by Monique Snyman
Gutted: Beautiful Horror Stories, edited by Doug Murano and D. Alexander Ward
Tales from The Lake Vol.2, edited by Joe Mynhardt, Emma Audsley, and RJ Cavender
Children of the Grave
The Outsiders
Tales from The Lake Vol.1, edited by Joe Mynhardt
Fear the Reaper, edited by Joe Mynhardt
For the Night is Dark, edited by Ross Warren

Short story collections:
Frozen Shadows and Other Chilling Stories by Gene O'Neill
Varying Distances by Darren Speegle
The Ghost Club: Newly Found Tales of Victorian Terror by William Meikle
Ugly Little Things: Collected Horrors by Todd Keisling
Whispered Echoes by Paul F. Olson
Embers: A Collection of Dark Fiction by Kenneth W. Cain
Visions of the Mutant Rain Forest, by Bruce Boston and Robert Frazier
Tribulations by Richard Thomas

Eidolon Avenue: The First Feast by Jonathan Winn
Flowers in a Dumpster by Mark Allan Gunnells
The Dark at the End of the Tunnel by Taylor Grant
Through a Mirror, Darkly by Kevin Lucia
Things Slip Through by Kevin Lucia
Where You Live by Gary McMahon
Tricks, Mischief and Mayhem by Daniel I. Russell
Samurai and Other Stories by William Meikle
Stuck On You and Other Prime Cuts by Jasper Bark

Poetry collections:
WAR by Alessandro Manzetti and Marge Simon
Brief Encounters with My Third Eye by Bruce Boston
No Mercy: Dark Poems by Alessandro Manzetti
Eden Underground: Poetry of Darkness by Alessandro
Manzetti

If you've ever thought of becoming an author, we'd also like to recommend these non-fiction titles:

*Where Nightmares Come From: The Art of Storytelling in
the Horror Genre*, edited by Joe Mynhardt and Eugene
Johnson
Horror 101: The Way Forward, edited by Joe Mynhardt
and Emma Audsley
Horror 201: The Silver Scream Vol.1 and *Vol.2*, edited by
Joe Mynhardt and Emma Audsley
*Modern Mythmakers: 35 interviews with Horror and
Science Fiction Writers and Filmmakers* by Michael
McCarty
Writers On Writing: An Author's Guide Volumes 1,2,3,
and 4, edited by Joe Mynhardt. Now also available in a
Kindle and paperback omnibus.

Or check out other Crystal Lake Publishing books for more Tales from the Darkest Depths. You can also subscribe to Crystal Lake Classics where you'll receive fortnightly info on all our books, starting all the way back at the beginning, with personal notes on every release. Or follow us on Patreon for behind the scenes access.

Hi, readers. It makes our day to know you reached the end of our book. Thank you so much. This is why we do what we do every single day.

Whether you found the book good or great, we'd love to hear what you thought. Please take a moment to leave a review on Amazon, Goodreads, or anywhere else readers visit. Reviews go a long way to helping a book sell, and will help us to continue publishing quality books. You can also share a photo of yourself holding this book with the hashtag #IGotMyCLPBook!

Thank you again for taking the time to journey with Crystal Lake Publishing.

We are also on . . .

Website:
www.crystallakepub.com

Be sure to sign up for our newsletter and receive two free eBooks: http://eepurl.com/xfuKP

Books:
http://www.crystallakepub.com/book-table/

Twitter:
https://twitter.com/crystallakepub

Facebook:
https://www.facebook.com/Crystallakepublishing/
https://www.facebook.com/Talesfromthelake/
https://www.facebook.com/WritersOnWritingSeries/

Pinterest:
https://za.pinterest.com/crystallakepub/

Instagram:
https://www.instagram.com/crystal_lake_publishing/

Patreon:
https://www.patreon.com/CLP

YouTube:
https://www.youtube.com/c/CrystalLakePublishing

We'd love to hear from you.

Or check out other Crystal Lake Publishing books for your Dark Fiction, Horror, Suspense, and Thriller needs.

With unmatched success since 2012, Crystal Lake Publishing has quickly become one of the world's leading indie publishers of Mystery, Thriller, and Suspense books with a Dark Fiction edge.

Crystal Lake Publishing puts integrity, honor and respect at the forefront of our operations.

We strive for each book and outreach program that's launched to not only entertain and touch or comment on issues that affect our readers, but also to strengthen and support the Dark Fiction field and its authors.

Not only do we publish authors who are legends in the field and as hardworking as us, but we look for men and women who care about their readers and fellow human beings. We only publish the very best Dark Fiction, and look forward to launching many new careers.

We strive to know each and every one of our readers,

while building personal relationships with our authors, reviewers, bloggers, pod-casters, bookstores and libraries.

Crystal Lake Publishing is and will always be a beacon of what passion and dedication, combined with overwhelming teamwork and respect, can accomplish: Unique fiction you can't find anywhere else.

We do not just publish books, we present you worlds within your world, doors within your mind, from talented authors who sacrifice so much for a moment of your time.

This is what we believe in. What we stand for. This will be our legacy.

Welcome to Crystal Lake Publishing—Tales from the Darkest Depths

CPSIA information can be obtained
at www.ICGtesting.com
Printed in the USA
LVHW03s1154180718
584144LV00004B/10/P

9 781643 704722